O LONGER PROPERTY OF
SEATTLE PUBLIC LIBRARY

tack

se

 use

cabin with roof construction

road to the freeway

warehouse

's house

clothing counter

Archer's graffiti

school

oss area

high stand

ise

night watch

main entrance

D1505957

GUNG-HO

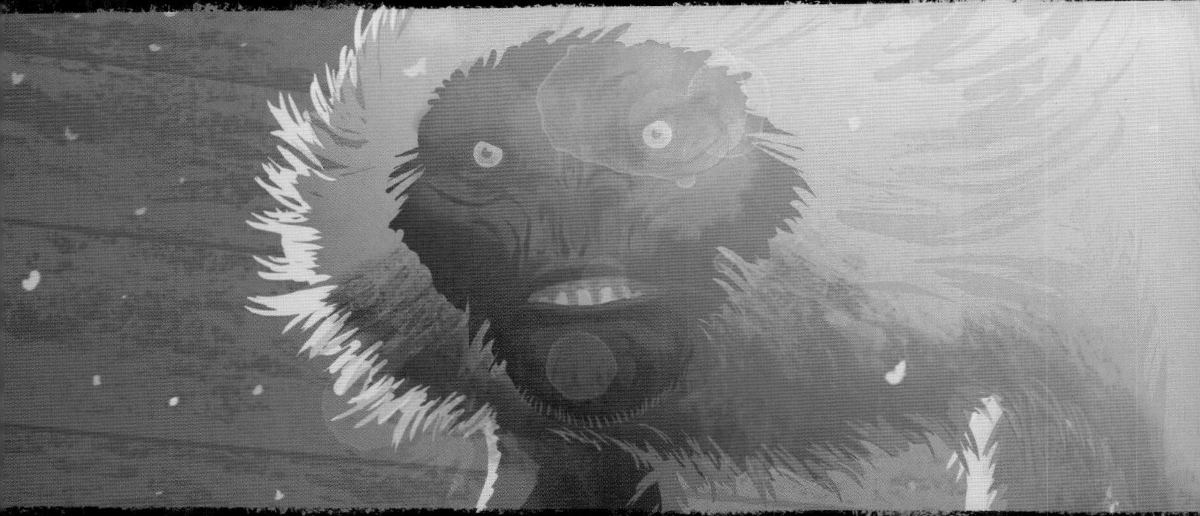

VOLUME 1

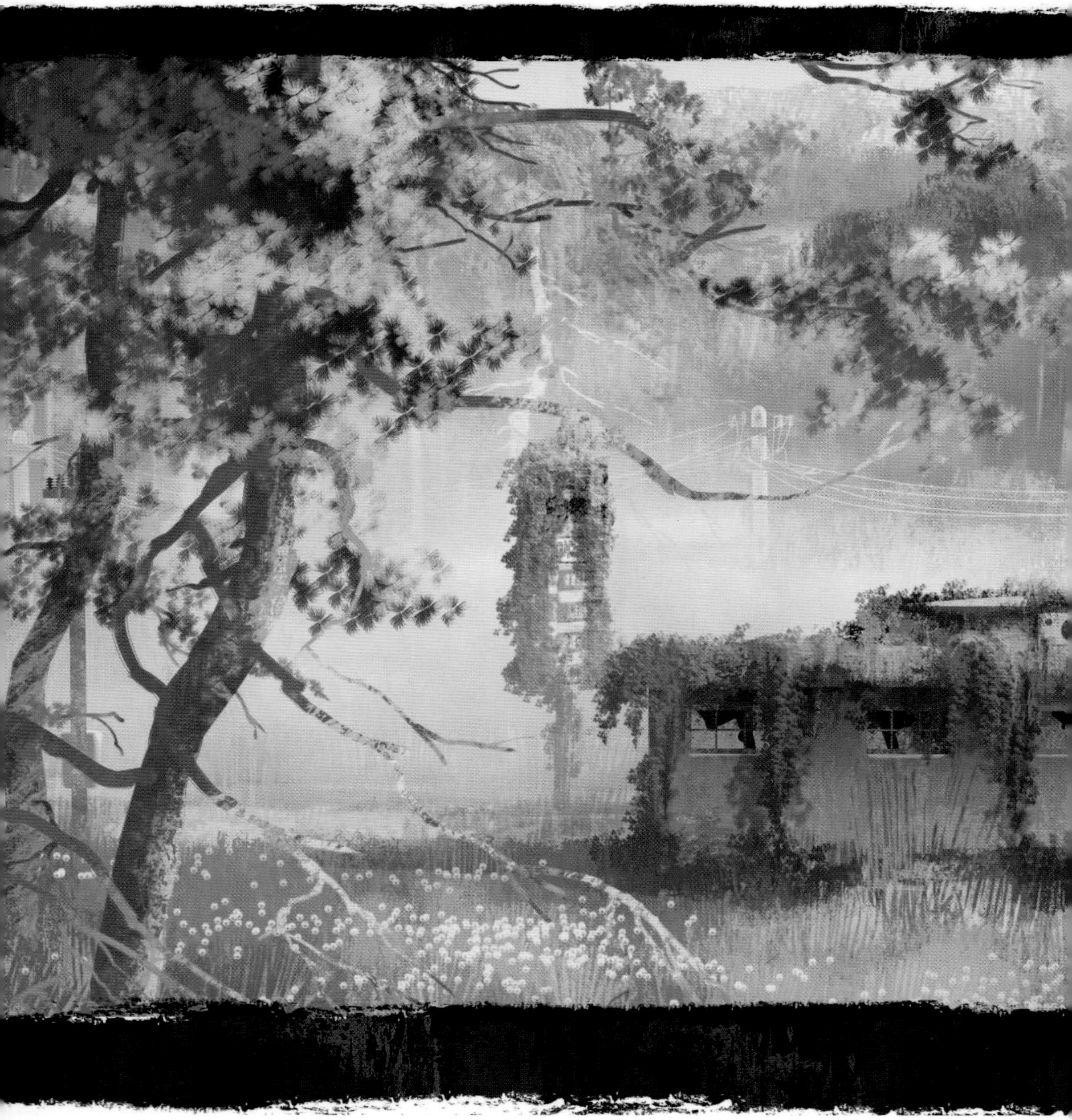

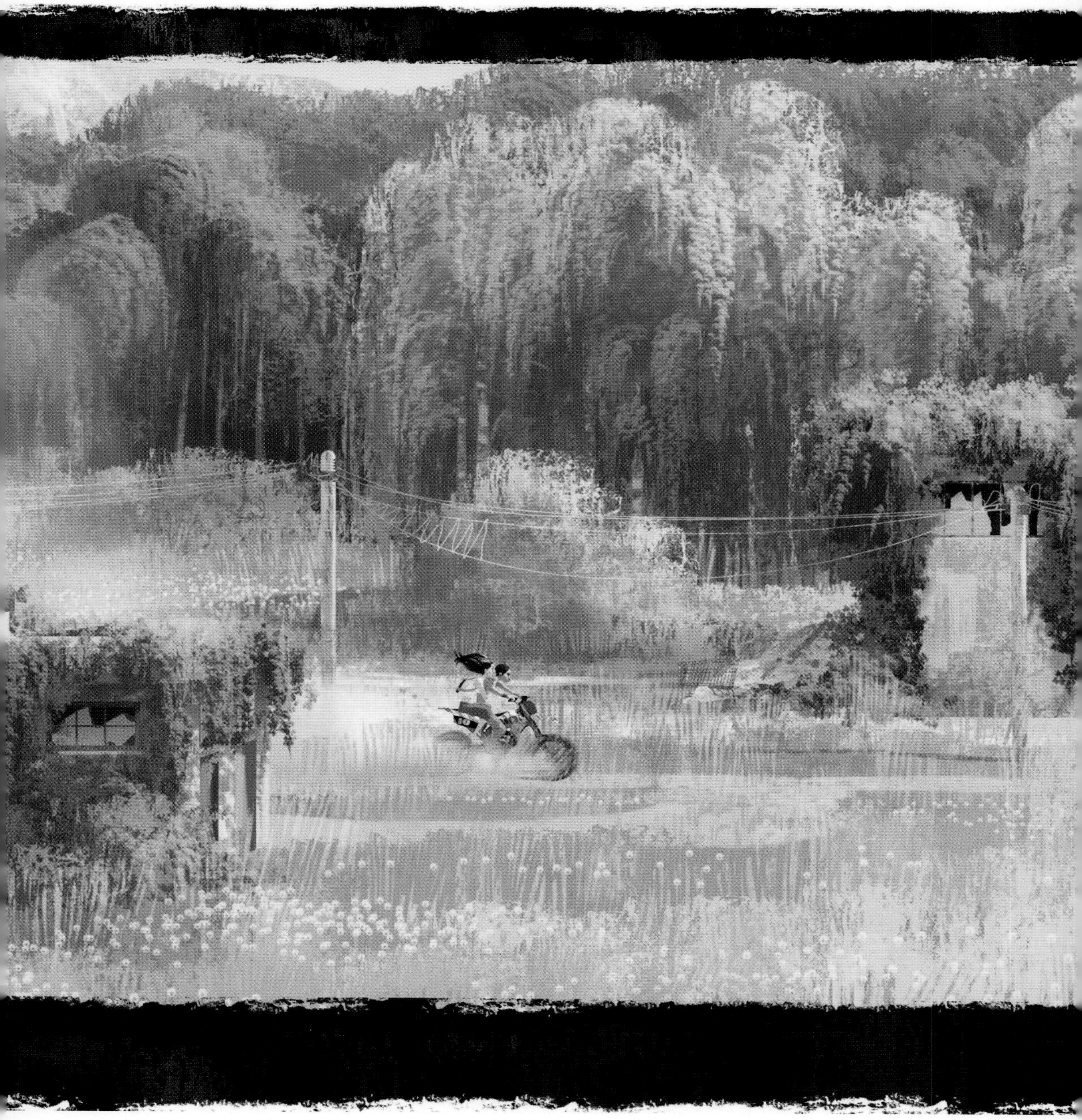

By
Benjamin von Eckartsberg
and
Thomas von Kummant

FOR ABLAZE

Managing Editor
Rich Young

Designer
Rodolfo Muraguchi

Publisher's Cataloging-in-Publication Data

Names: Eckartsberg, Benjamin von, author. I Kummant, Thomas von, illustrator.
Title: Gung ho, Volume 1 / Benjamin von Eckartsberg and Thomas von Kummant.
Description: Portland, OR: Ablaze Publishing, 2020.
Identifiers: ISBN: 978-1-950912-17-9
Subjects: LCSH Epidemics—Fiction. I Disasters--Fiction. I Survivalism—Comic books, strips, etc. I
Graphic novels. I Horror fiction. I Dystopian comics. I BISAC COMICS & GRAPHIC NOVELS / Horror
Classification: LCC PN6757 .E25 G86 2020 I DDC 741.5—dc23

GUNG-HO, VOLUME 1. First printing. Published by Ablaze Publishing, 11222 SE Main St. #22906 Portland, OR 97269.
GUNG HO © von Kummant / von Eckartsberg / Éditions Paquet 2013
Ablaze and its logo TM & © 2020 Ablaze, LLC. All Rights Reserved. All names, characters, events, and locales in this publication are entirely fictional. Any
resemblance to actual persons (living or dead), events or places, without satiric intent is coincidental. No portion of this book may be reproduced by any
means (digital or print) without the written permission of Ablaze Publishing except for review purposes. Printed in China.

For advertising and licensing email: info@ablazepublishing.com

Part 1: Black Sheep

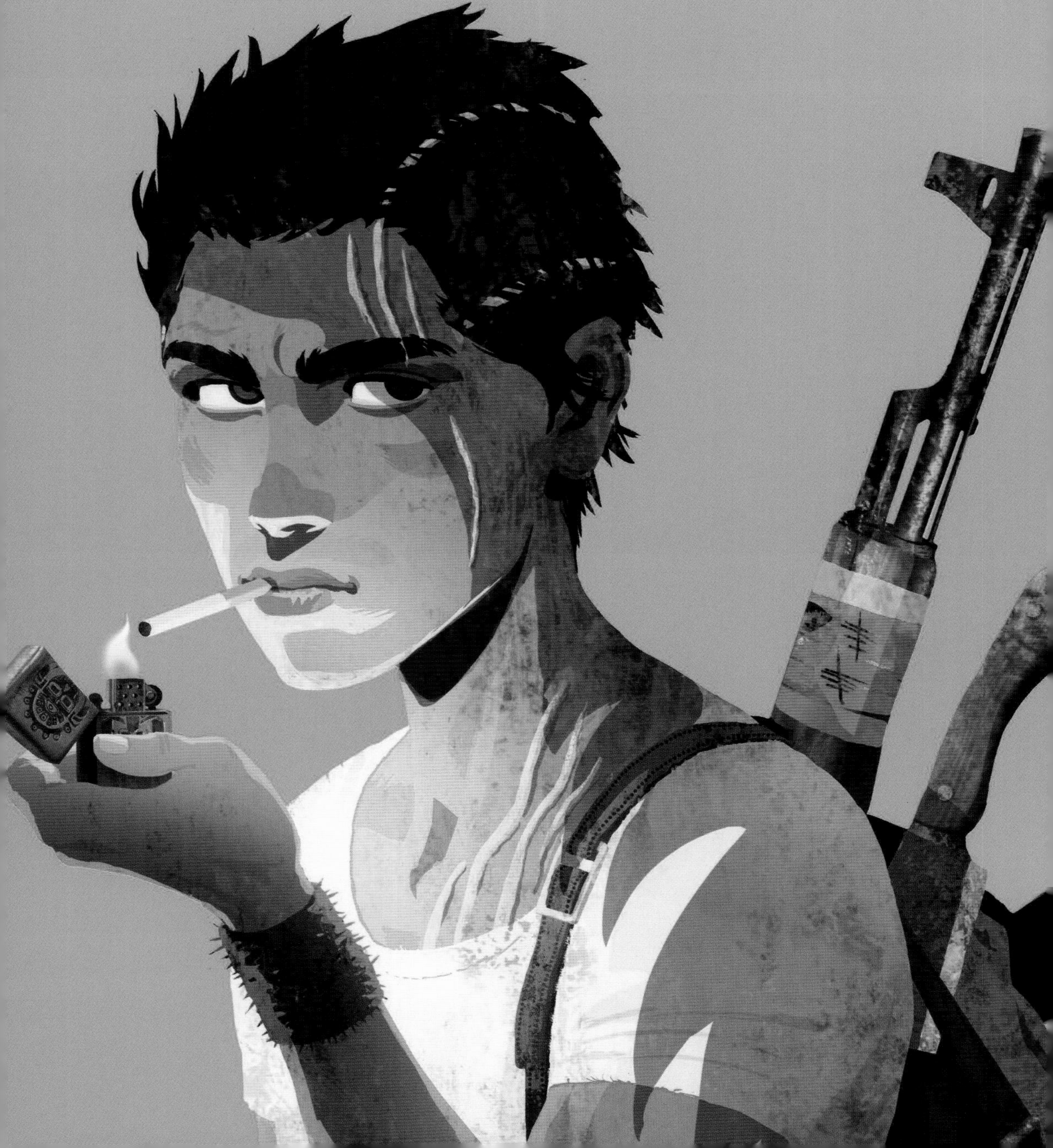

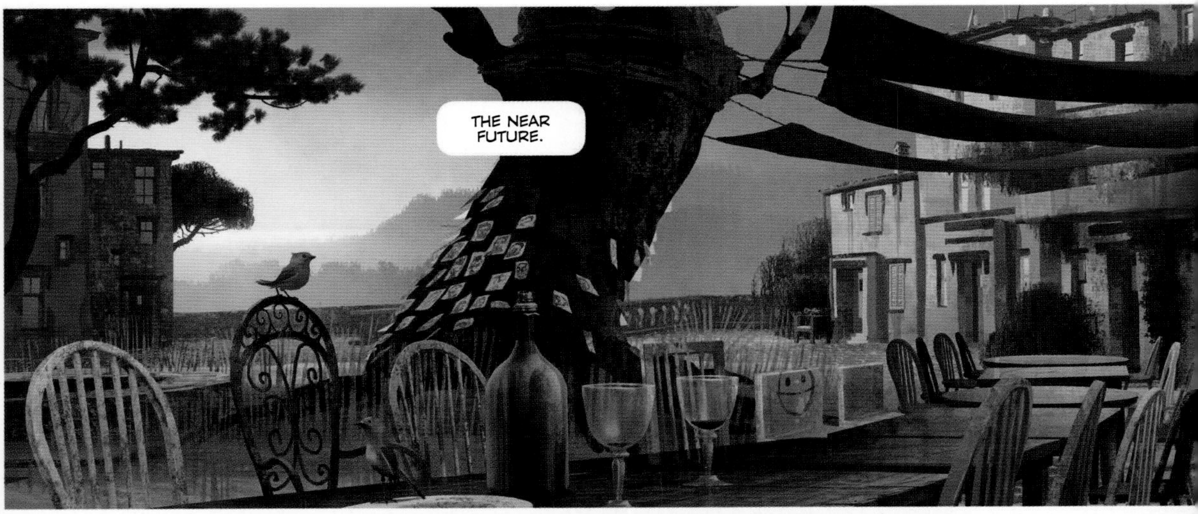
THE NEAR
FUTURE.

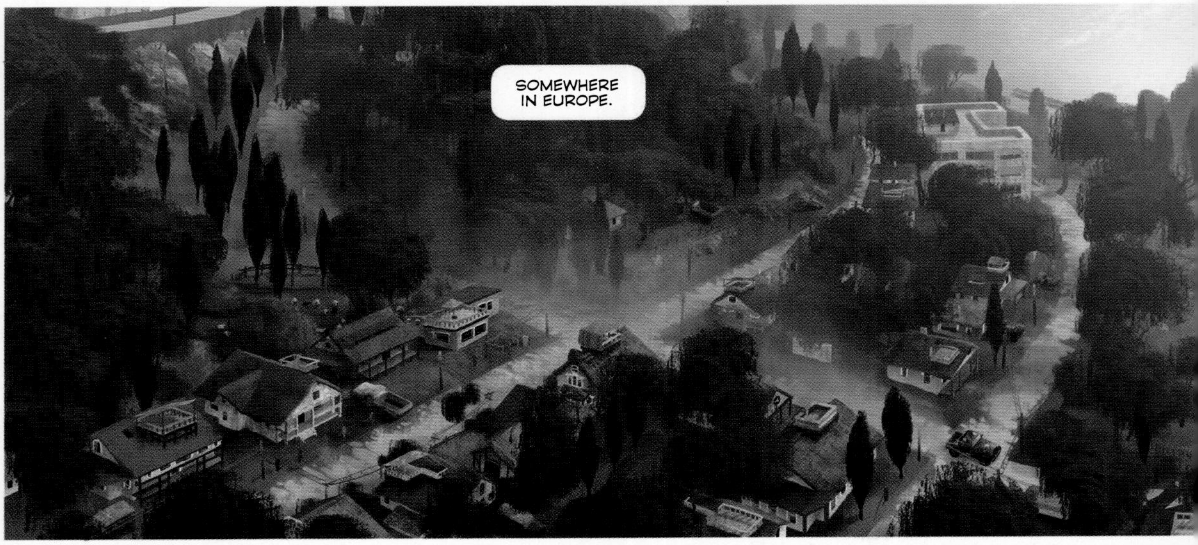
SOMEWHERE
IN EUROPE.

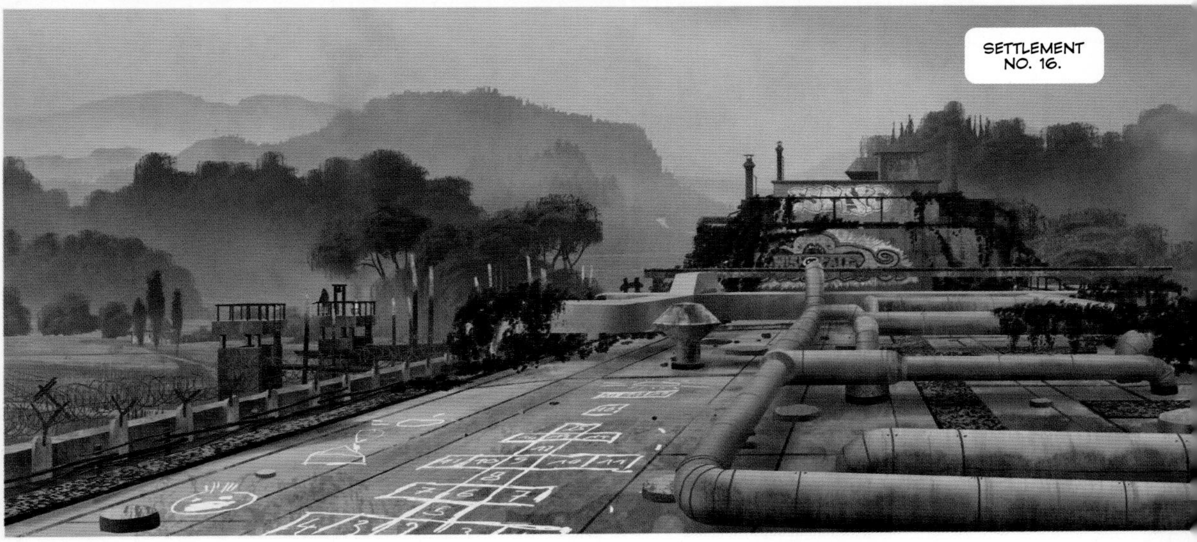
SETTLEMENT
NO. 16.

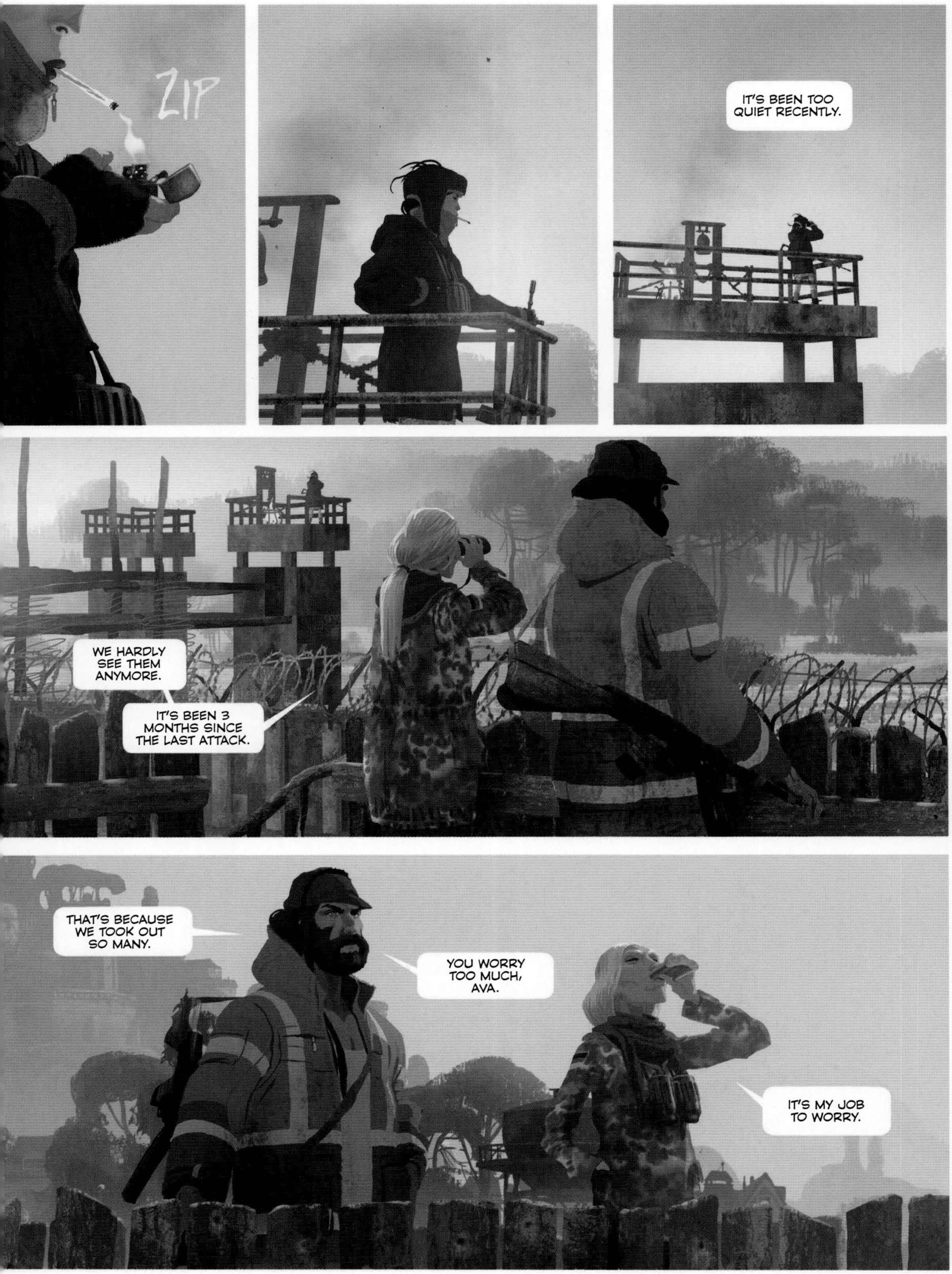
ZIP
IT'S BEEN TOO QUIET RECENTLY.
WE HARDLY SEE THEM ANYMORE.
IT'S BEEN 3 MONTHS SINCE THE LAST ATTACK.
THAT'S BECAUSE WE TOOK OUT SO MANY.
YOU WORRY TOO MUCH, AVA.
IT'S MY JOB TO WORRY.

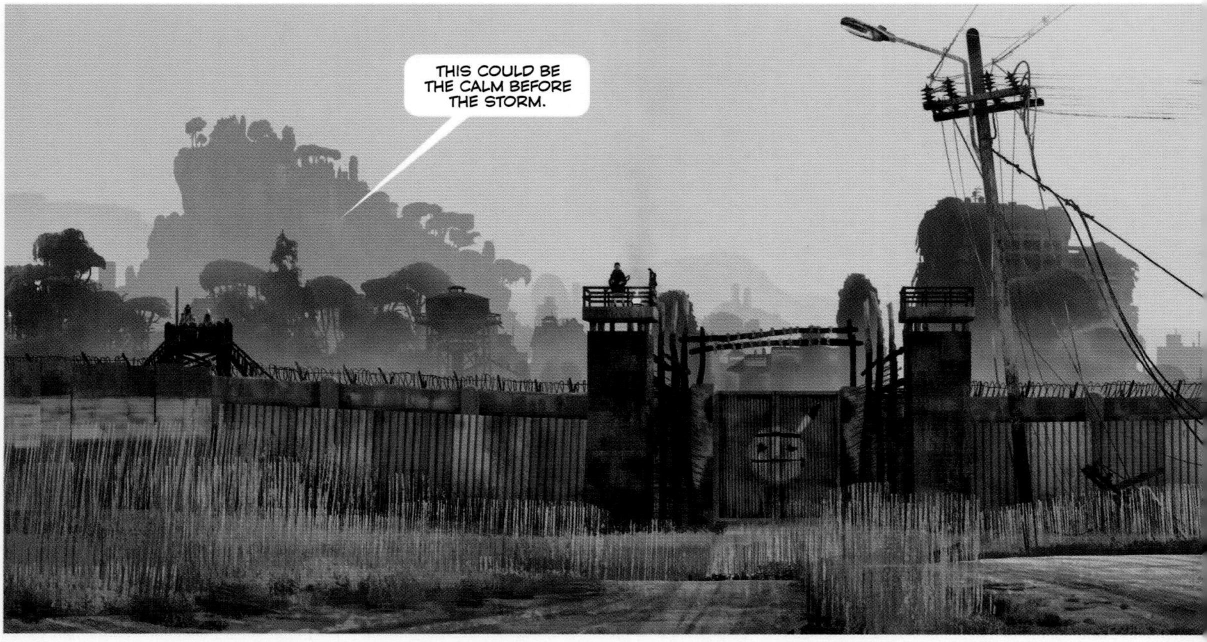
THIS COULD BE THE CALM BEFORE THE STORM.

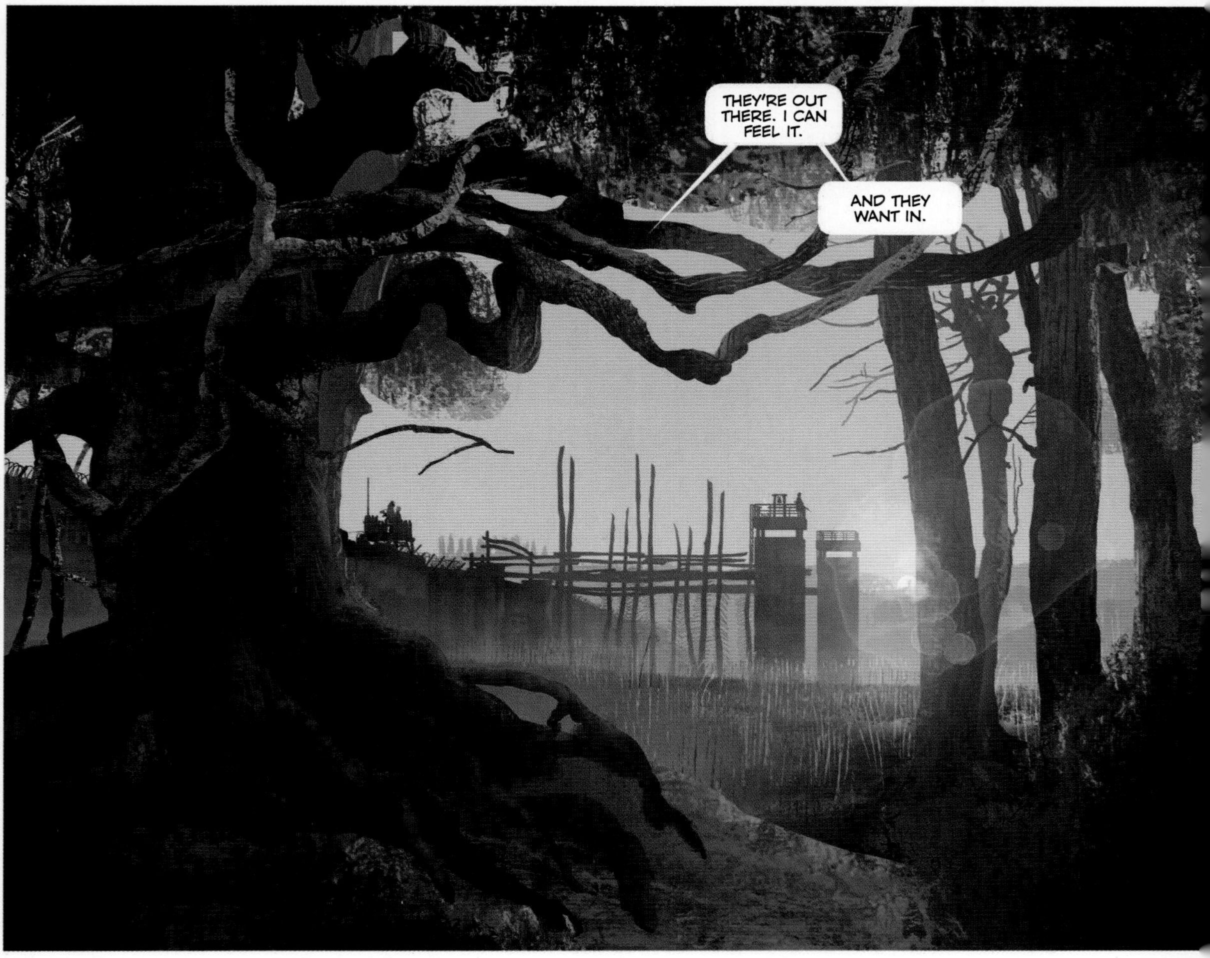
THEY'RE OUT THERE. I CAN FEEL IT.
AND THEY WANT IN.

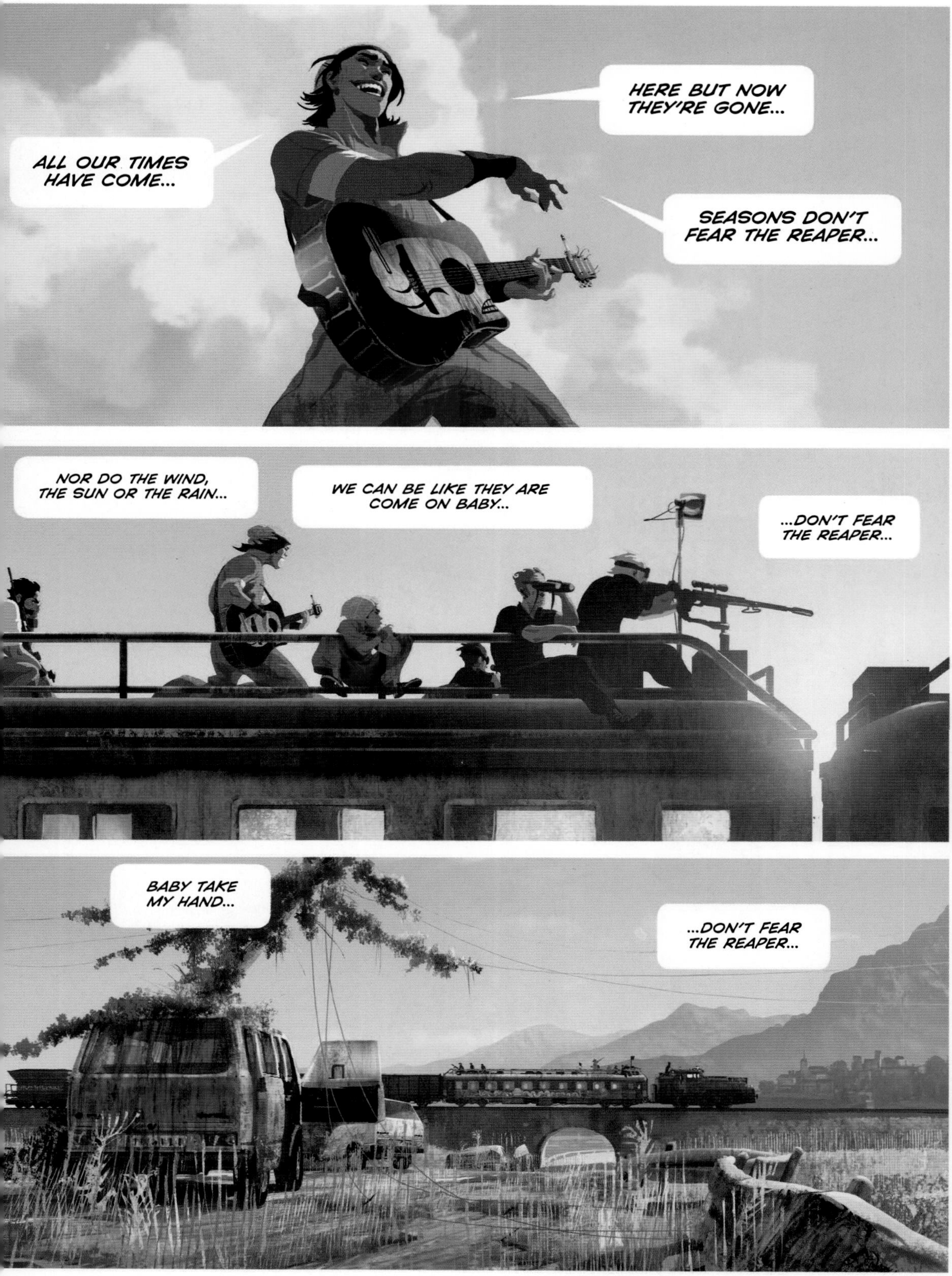
ALL OUR TIMES HAVE COME...
HERE BUT NOW THEY'RE GONE...
SEASONS DON'T FEAR THE REAPER...
NOR DO THE WIND, THE SUN OR THE RAIN...
WE CAN BE LIKE THEY ARE COME ON BABY...
...DON'T FEAR THE REAPER...
BABY TAKE MY HAND...
...DON'T FEAR THE REAPER...

LYRICS: *DON'T FEAR THE REAPER* BY BLUE OYSTER CULT

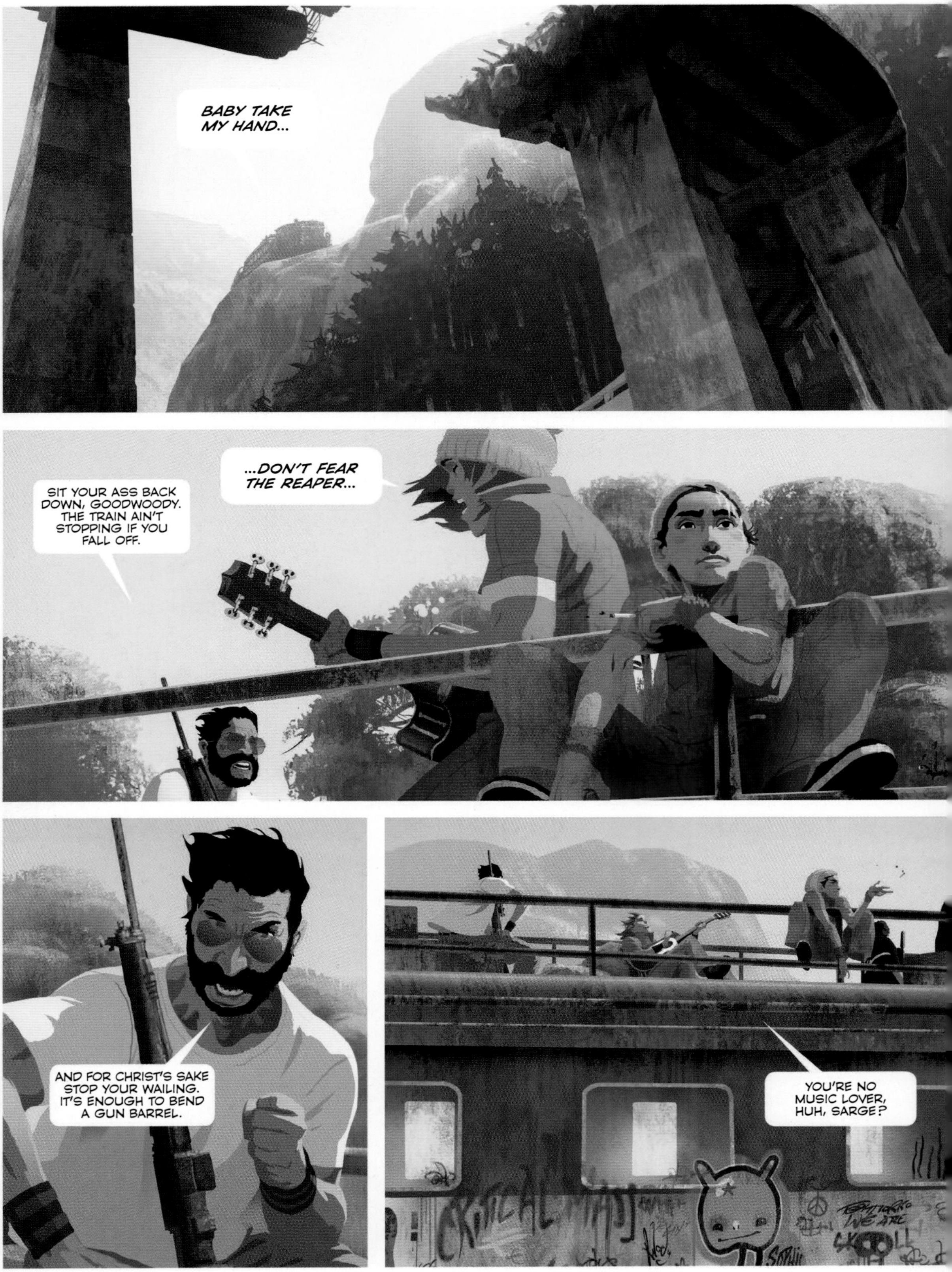
BABY TAKE MY HAND...
SIT YOUR ASS BACK DOWN, GOODWOODY. THE TRAIN AIN'T STOPPING IF YOU FALL OFF.
...DON'T FEAR THE REAPER...
AND FOR CHRIST'S SAKE STOP YOUR WAILING. IT'S ENOUGH TO BEND A GUN BARREL.
YOU'RE NO MUSIC LOVER, HUH, SARGE?

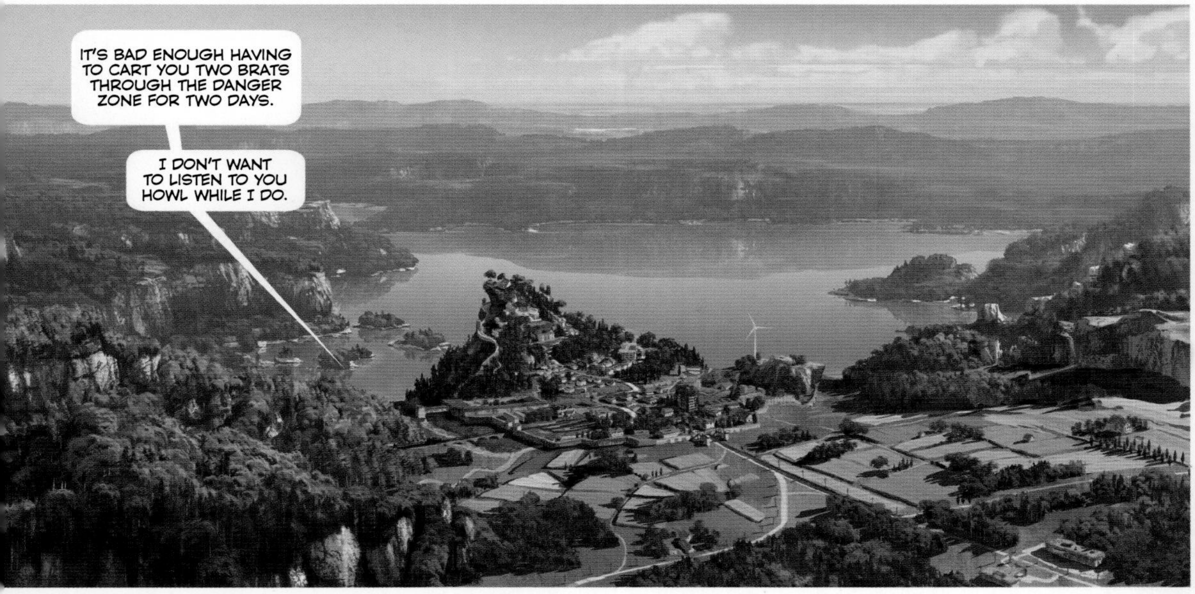
IT'S BAD ENOUGH HAVING TO CART YOU TWO BRATS THROUGH THE DANGER ZONE FOR TWO DAYS.
I DON'T WANT TO LISTEN TO YOU HOWL WHILE I DO.

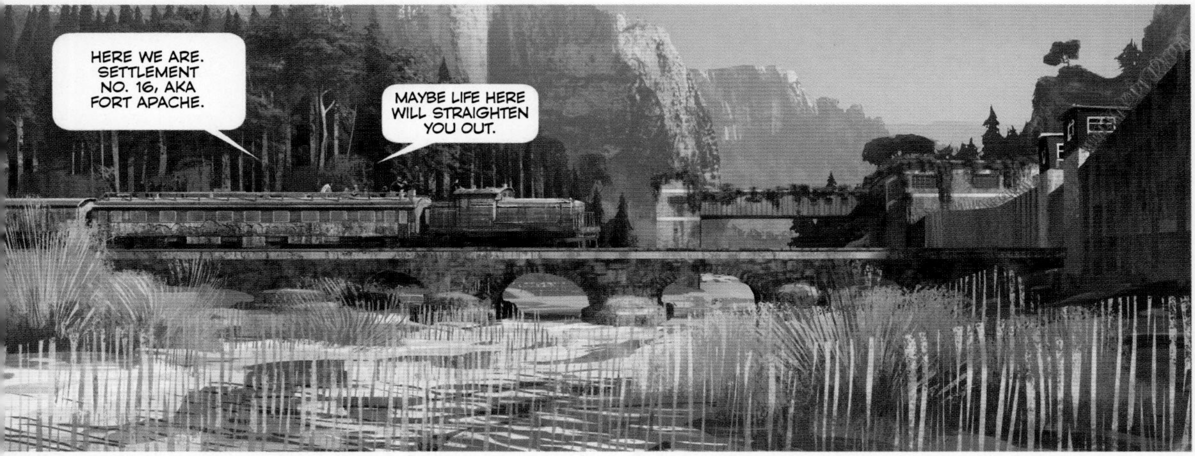
HERE WE ARE. SETTLEMENT NO. 16, AKA FORT APACHE.
MAYBE LIFE HERE WILL STRAIGHTEN YOU OUT.

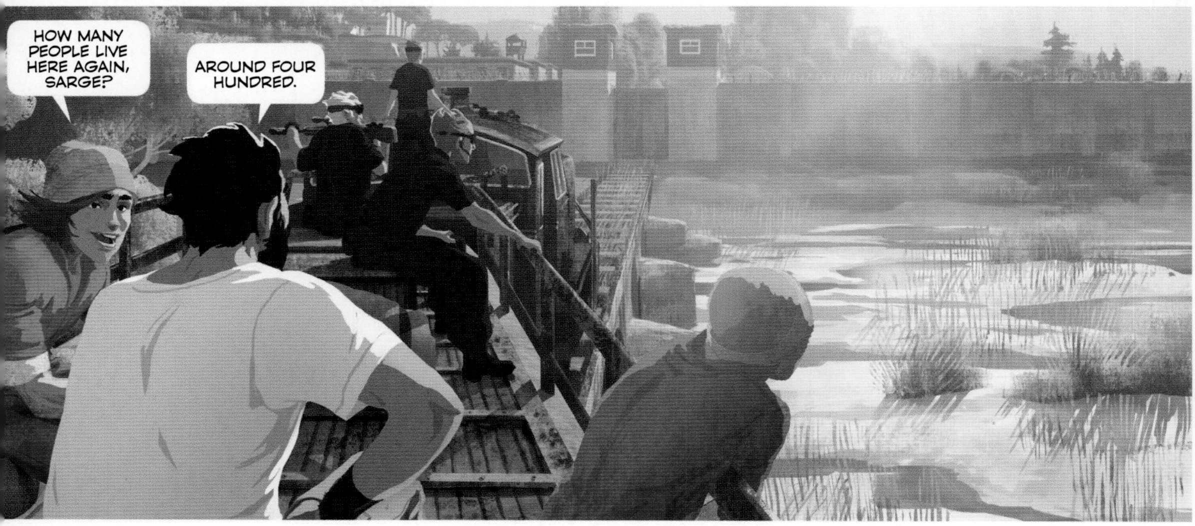
HOW MANY PEOPLE LIVE HERE AGAIN, SARGE?
AROUND FOUR HUNDRED.

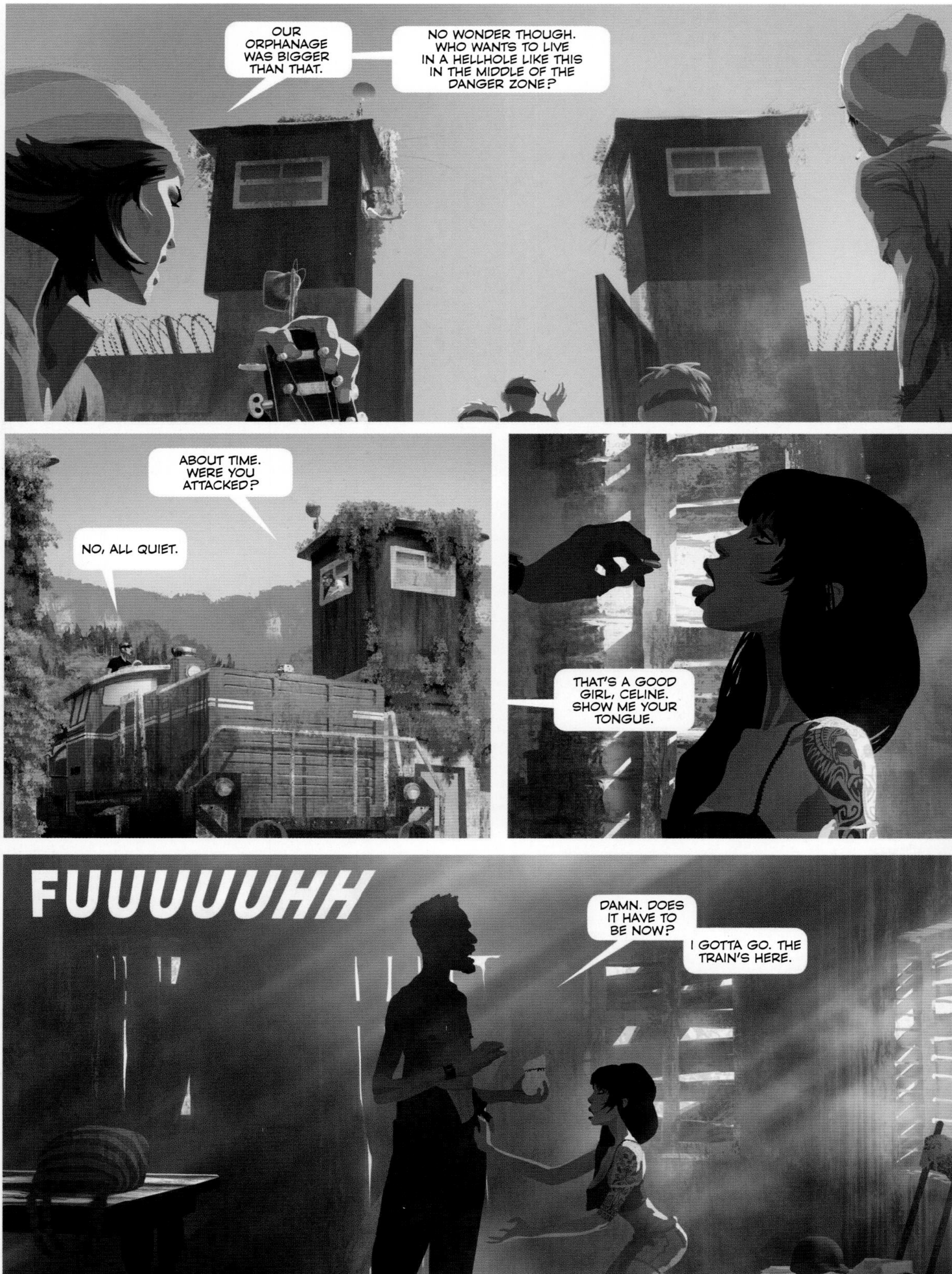
OUR ORPHANAGE WAS BIGGER THAN THAT.
NO WONDER THOUGH. WHO WANTS TO LIVE IN A HELLHOLE LIKE THIS IN THE MIDDLE OF THE DANGER ZONE?
ABOUT TIME. WERE YOU ATTACKED?
NO, ALL QUIET.
THAT'S A GOOD GIRL, CELINE. SHOW ME YOUR TONGUE.
FUUUUUHH
DAMN. DOES IT HAVE TO BE NOW?
I GOTTA GO. THE TRAIN'S HERE.

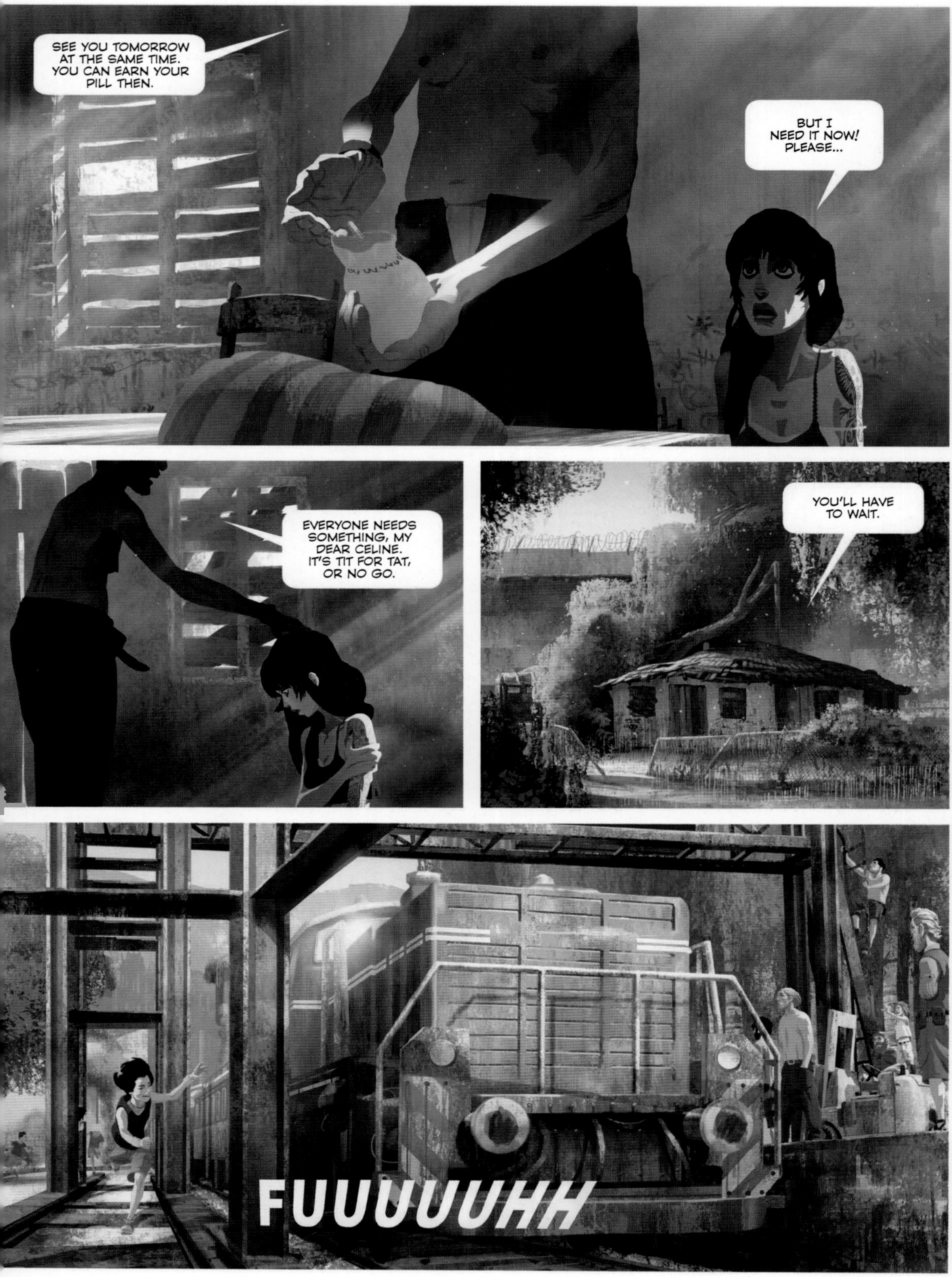
SEE YOU TOMORROW AT THE SAME TIME. YOU CAN EARN YOUR PILL THEN.
BUT I NEED IT NOW! PLEASE...
EVERYONE NEEDS SOMETHING, MY DEAR CELINE. IT'S TIT FOR TAT, OR NO GO.
YOU'LL HAVE TO WAIT.
FUUUUUHH

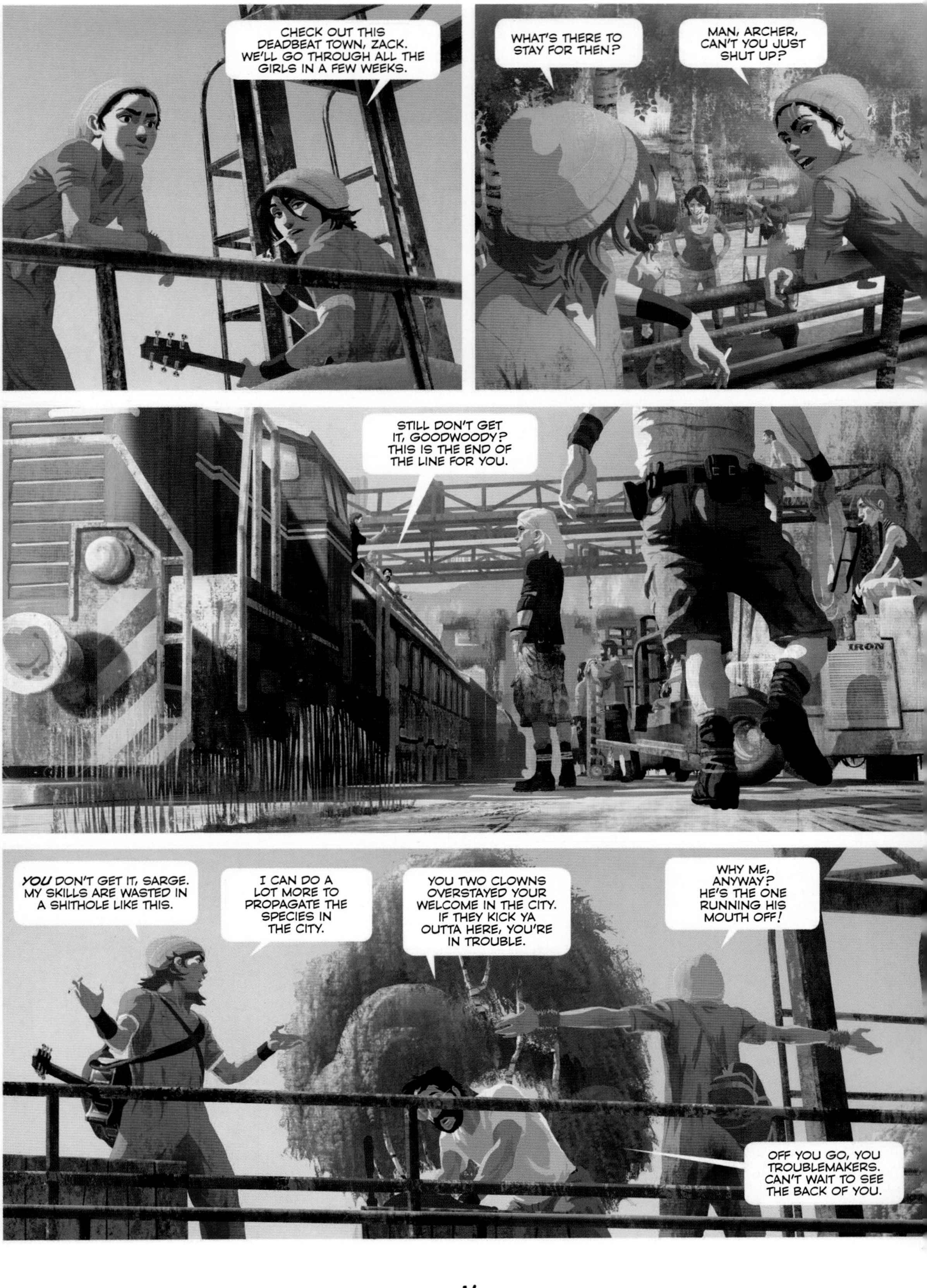
CHECK OUT THIS DEADBEAT TOWN, ZACK. WE'LL GO THROUGH ALL THE GIRLS IN A FEW WEEKS.
WHAT'S THERE TO STAY FOR THEN?
MAN, ARCHER, CAN'T YOU JUST SHUT UP?
STILL DON'T GET IT, GOODWOODY? THIS IS THE END OF THE LINE FOR YOU.
IRON
YOU DON'T GET IT, SARGE. MY SKILLS ARE WASTED IN A SHITHOLE LIKE THIS.
I CAN DO A LOT MORE TO PROPAGATE THE SPECIES IN THE CITY.
YOU TWO CLOWNS OVERSTAYED YOUR WELCOME IN THE CITY. IF THEY KICK YA OUTTA HERE, YOU'RE IN TROUBLE.
WHY ME, ANYWAY? HE'S THE ONE RUNNING HIS MOUTH OFF!
OFF YOU GO, YOU TROUBLEMAKERS. CAN'T WAIT TO SEE THE BACK OF YOU.

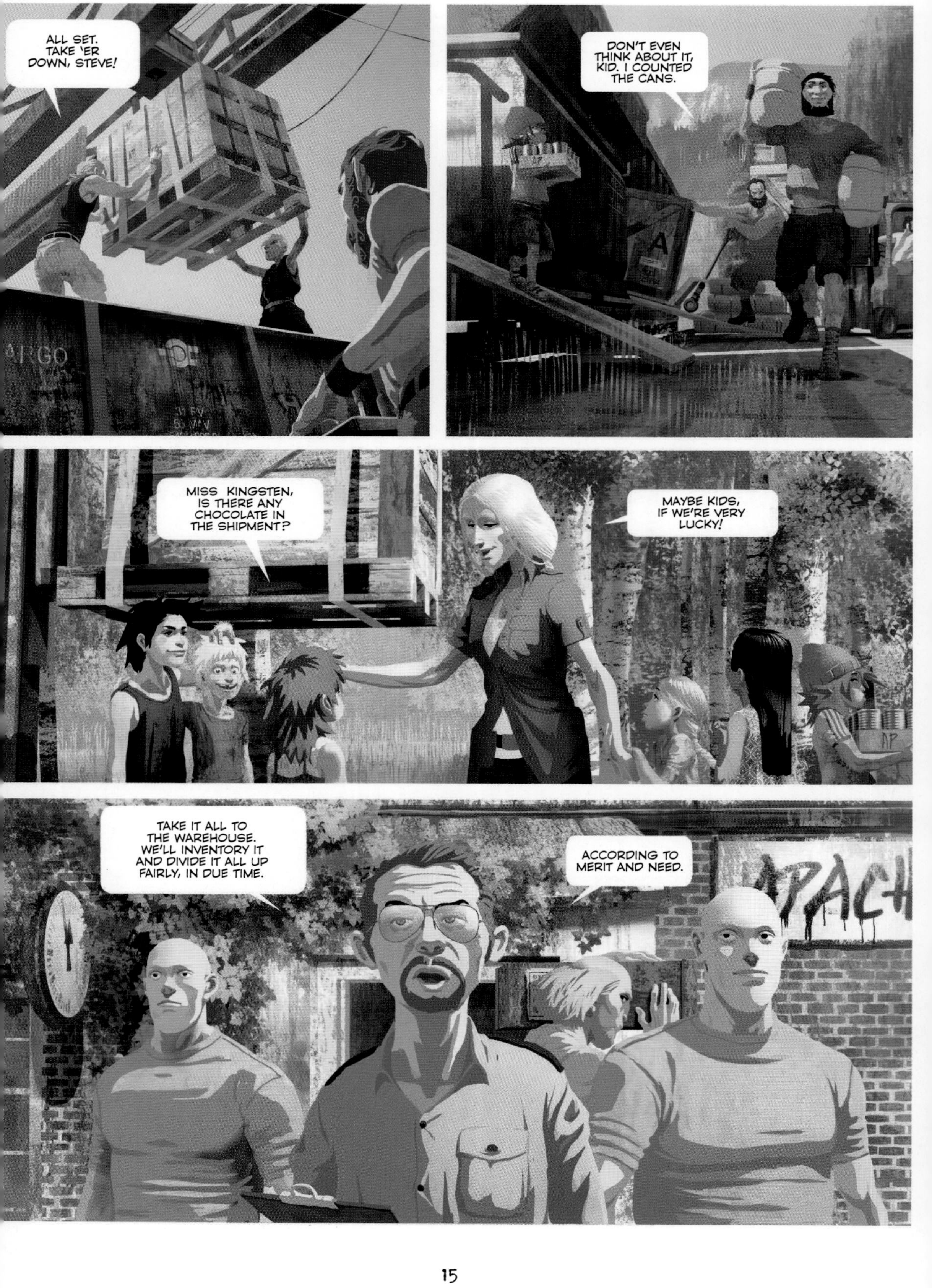
ALL SET. TAKE 'ER DOWN, STEVE!
DON'T EVEN THINK ABOUT IT, KID. I COUNTED THE CANS.
MISS KINGSTEN, IS THERE ANY CHOCOLATE IN THE SHIPMENT?
MAYBE KIDS, IF WE'RE VERY LUCKY!
TAKE IT ALL TO THE WAREHOUSE. WE'LL INVENTORY IT AND DIVIDE IT ALL UP FAIRLY, IN DUE TIME.
ACCORDING TO MERIT AND NEED.

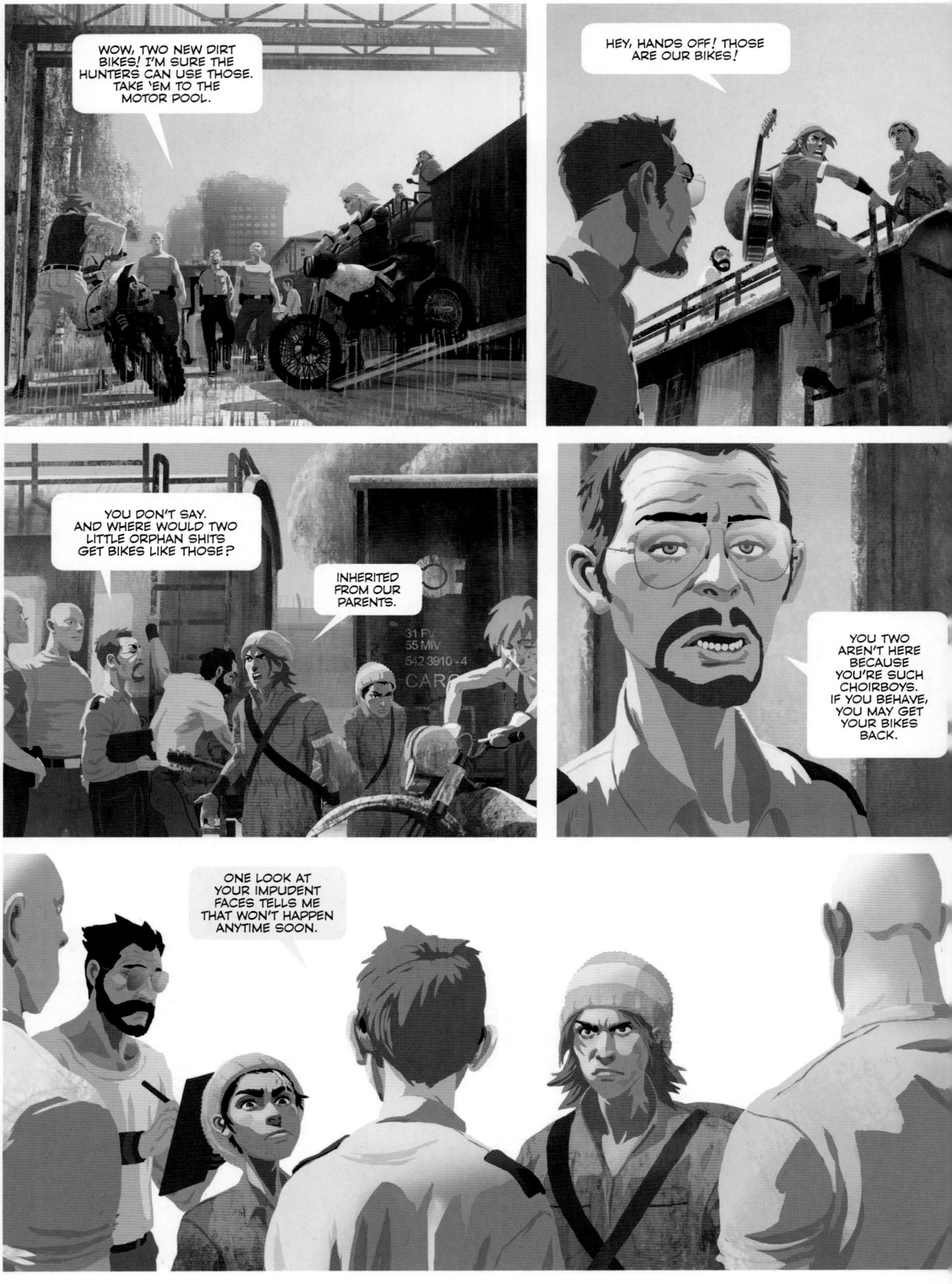
WOW, TWO NEW DIRT BIKES! I'M SURE THE HUNTERS CAN USE THOSE. TAKE 'EM TO THE MOTOR POOL.
HEY, HANDS OFF! THOSE ARE OUR BIKES!
YOU DON'T SAY. AND WHERE WOULD TWO LITTLE ORPHAN SHITS GET BIKES LIKE THOSE?
INHERITED FROM OUR PARENTS.
YOU TWO AREN'T HERE BECAUSE YOU'RE SUCH CHOIRBOYS. IF YOU BEHAVE, YOU MAY GET YOUR BIKES BACK.
ONE LOOK AT YOUR IMPUDENT FACES TELLS ME THAT WON'T HAPPEN ANYTIME SOON.

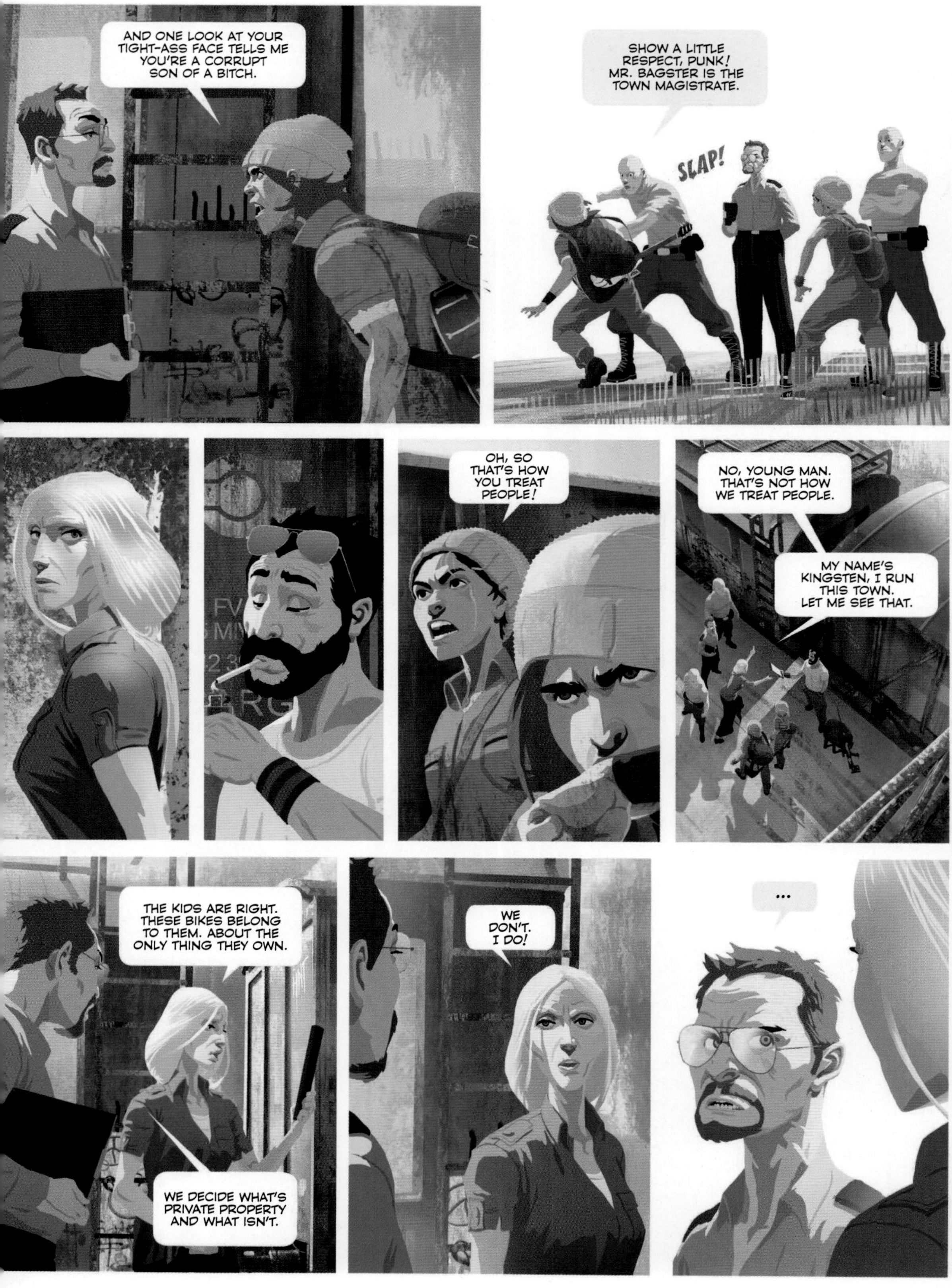

AND ONE LOOK AT YOUR TIGHT-ASS FACE TELLS ME YOU'RE A CORRUPT SON OF A BITCH.
SHOW A LITTLE RESPECT, PUNK! MR. BAGSTER IS THE TOWN MAGISTRATE.
SLAP!
OH, SO THAT'S HOW YOU TREAT PEOPLE!
NO, YOUNG MAN. THAT'S NOT HOW WE TREAT PEOPLE.
MY NAME'S KINGSTEN, I RUN THIS TOWN. LET ME SEE THAT.
THE KIDS ARE RIGHT. THESE BIKES BELONG TO THEM. ABOUT THE ONLY THING THEY OWN.
WE DECIDE WHAT'S PRIVATE PROPERTY AND WHAT ISN'T.
WE DON'T. I DO!
...

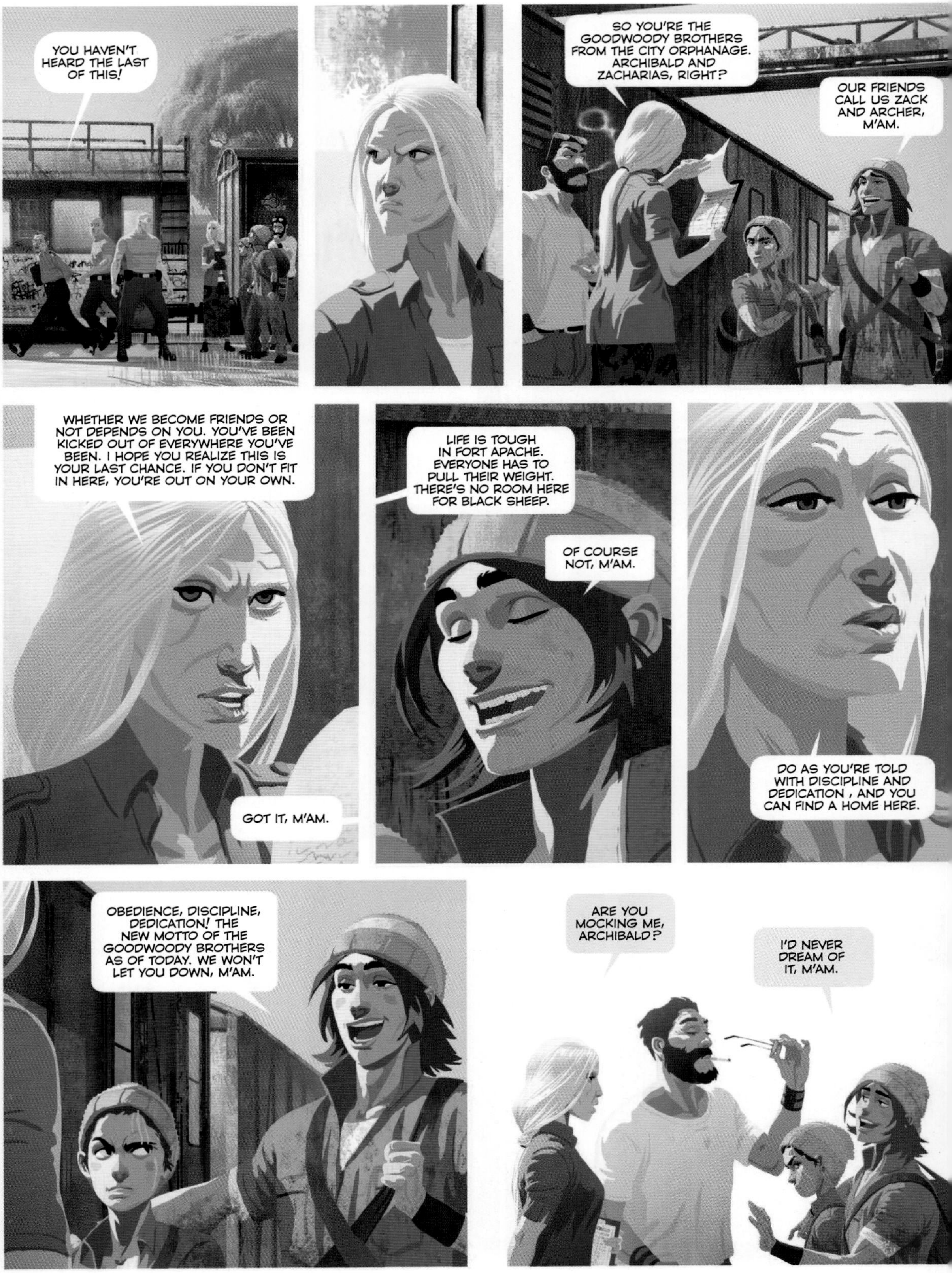
YOU HAVEN'T HEARD THE LAST OF THIS!
SO YOU'RE THE GOODWOODY BROTHERS FROM THE CITY ORPHANAGE. ARCHIBALD AND ZACHARIAS, RIGHT?
OUR FRIENDS CALL US ZACK AND ARCHER, M'AM.
WHETHER WE BECOME FRIENDS OR NOT DEPENDS ON YOU. YOU'VE BEEN KICKED OUT OF EVERYWHERE YOU'VE BEEN. I HOPE YOU REALIZE THIS IS YOUR LAST CHANCE. IF YOU DON'T FIT IN HERE, YOU'RE OUT ON YOUR OWN.
GOT IT, M'AM.
LIFE IS TOUGH IN FORT APACHE. EVERYONE HAS TO PULL THEIR WEIGHT. THERE'S NO ROOM HERE FOR BLACK SHEEP.
OF COURSE NOT, M'AM.
DO AS YOU'RE TOLD WITH DISCIPLINE AND DEDICATION , AND YOU CAN FIND A HOME HERE.
OBEDIENCE, DISCIPLINE, DEDICATION! THE NEW MOTTO OF THE GOODWOODY BROTHERS AS OF TODAY. WE WON'T LET YOU DOWN, M'AM.
ARE YOU MOCKING ME, ARCHIBALD?
I'D NEVER DREAM OF IT, M'AM.

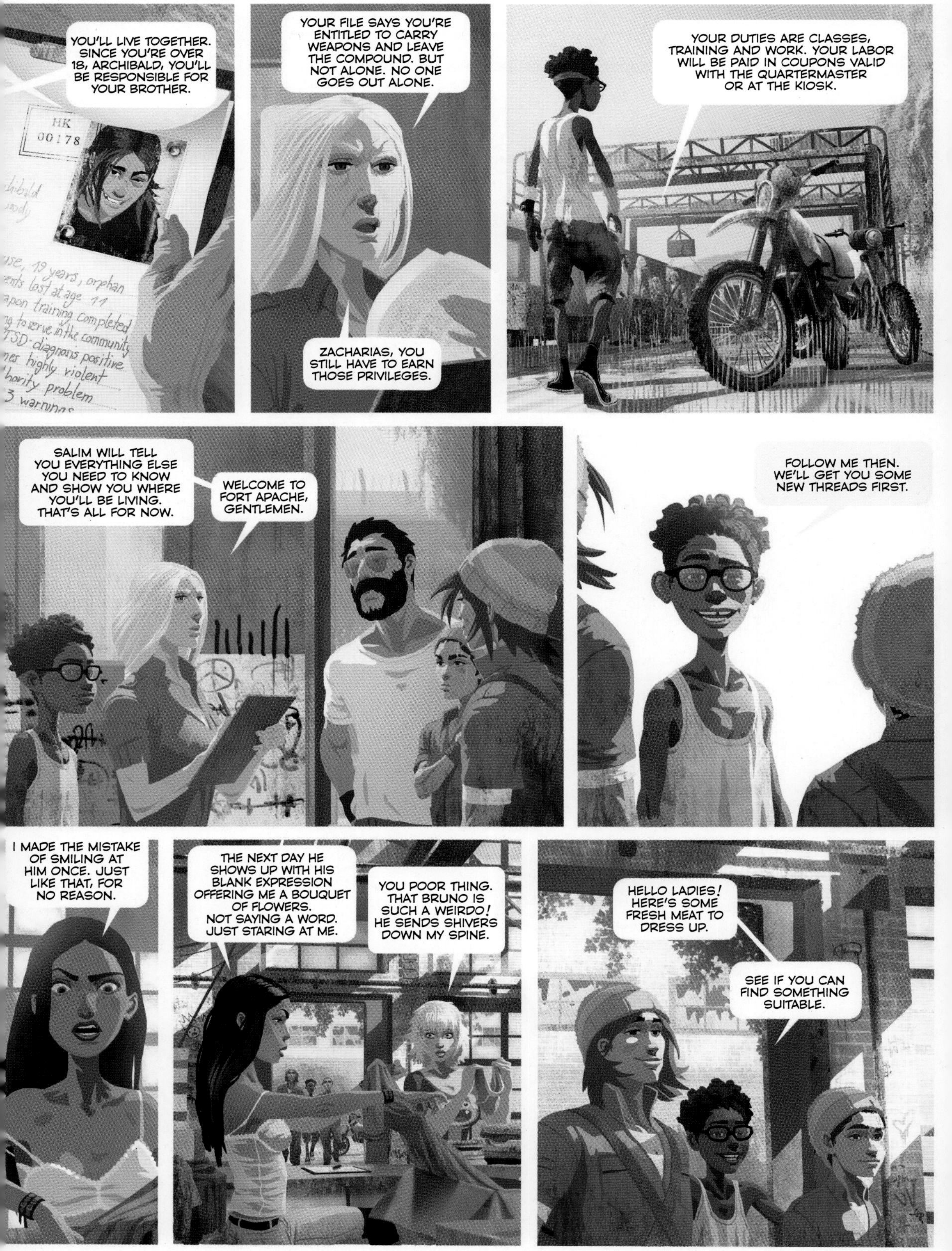
YOU'LL LIVE TOGETHER. SINCE YOU'RE OVER 18, ARCHIBALD, YOU'LL BE RESPONSIBLE FOR YOUR BROTHER.
HK
00178
YOUR FILE SAYS YOU'RE ENTITLED TO CARRY WEAPONS AND LEAVE THE COMPOUND. BUT NOT ALONE. NO ONE GOES OUT ALONE.
ZACHARIAS, YOU STILL HAVE TO EARN THOSE PRIVILEGES.
YOUR DUTIES ARE CLASSES, TRAINING AND WORK. YOUR LABOR WILL BE PAID IN COUPONS VALID WITH THE QUARTERMASTER OR AT THE KIOSK.
SALIM WILL TELL YOU EVERYTHING ELSE YOU NEED TO KNOW AND SHOW YOU WHERE YOU'LL BE LIVING. THAT'S ALL FOR NOW.
WELCOME TO FORT APACHE, GENTLEMEN.
FOLLOW ME THEN. WE'LL GET YOU SOME NEW THREADS FIRST.
I MADE THE MISTAKE OF SMILING AT HIM ONCE. JUST LIKE THAT, FOR NO REASON.
THE NEXT DAY HE SHOWS UP WITH HIS BLANK EXPRESSION OFFERING ME A BOUQUET OF FLOWERS. NOT SAYING A WORD. JUST STARING AT ME.
YOU POOR THING. THAT BRUNO IS SUCH A WEIRDO! HE SENDS SHIVERS DOWN MY SPINE.
HELLO LADIES! HERE'S SOME FRESH MEAT TO DRESS UP.
SEE IF YOU CAN FIND SOMETHING SUITABLE.

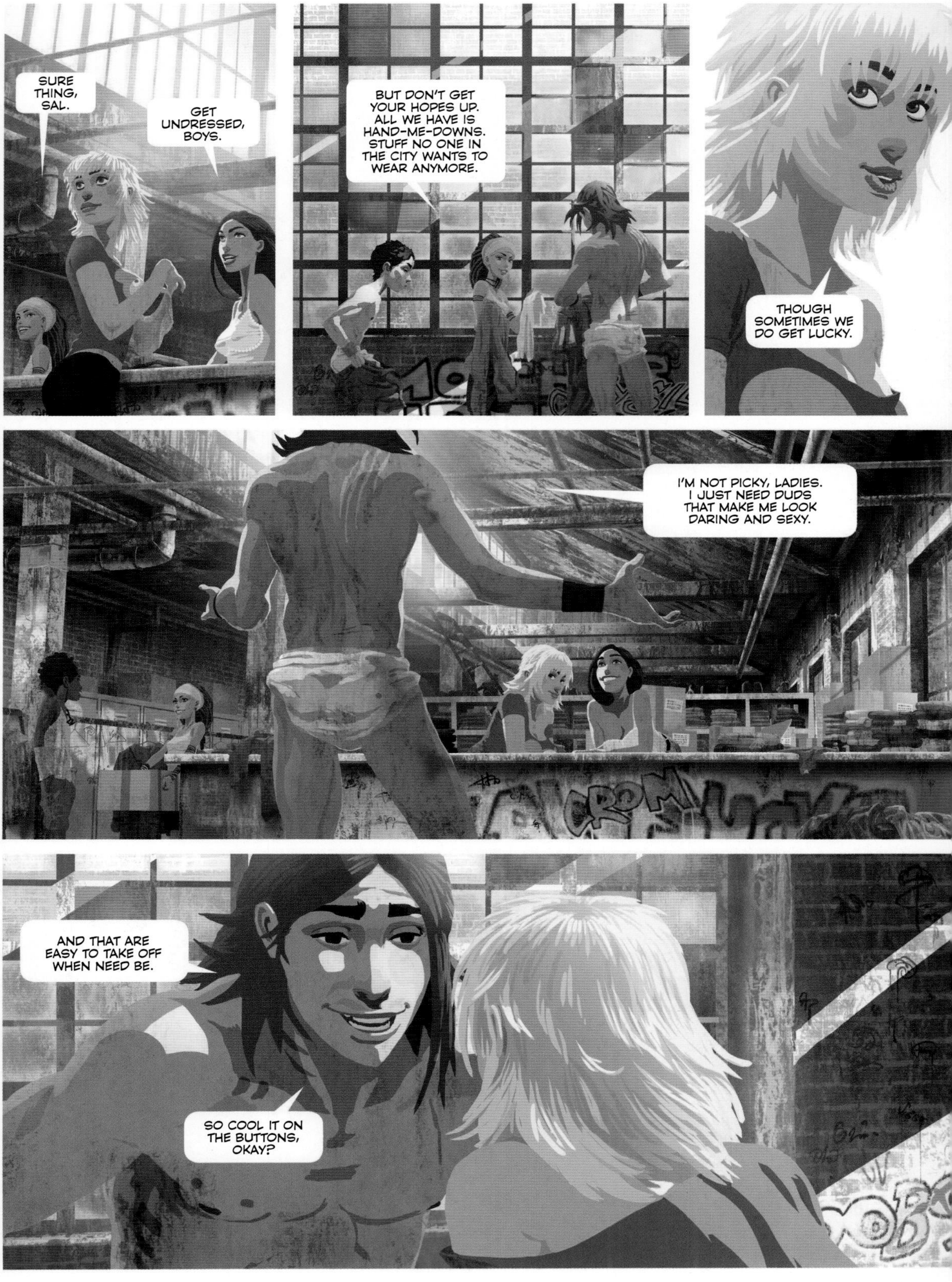

SURE THING, SAL.
GET UNDRESSED, BOYS.
BUT DON'T GET YOUR HOPES UP. ALL WE HAVE IS HAND-ME-DOWNS. STUFF NO ONE IN THE CITY WANTS TO WEAR ANYMORE.
THOUGH SOMETIMES WE DO GET LUCKY.
I'M NOT PICKY, LADIES. I JUST NEED DUDS THAT MAKE ME LOOK DARING AND SEXY.
AND THAT ARE EASY TO TAKE OFF WHEN NEED BE.
SO COOL IT ON THE BUTTONS, OKAY?

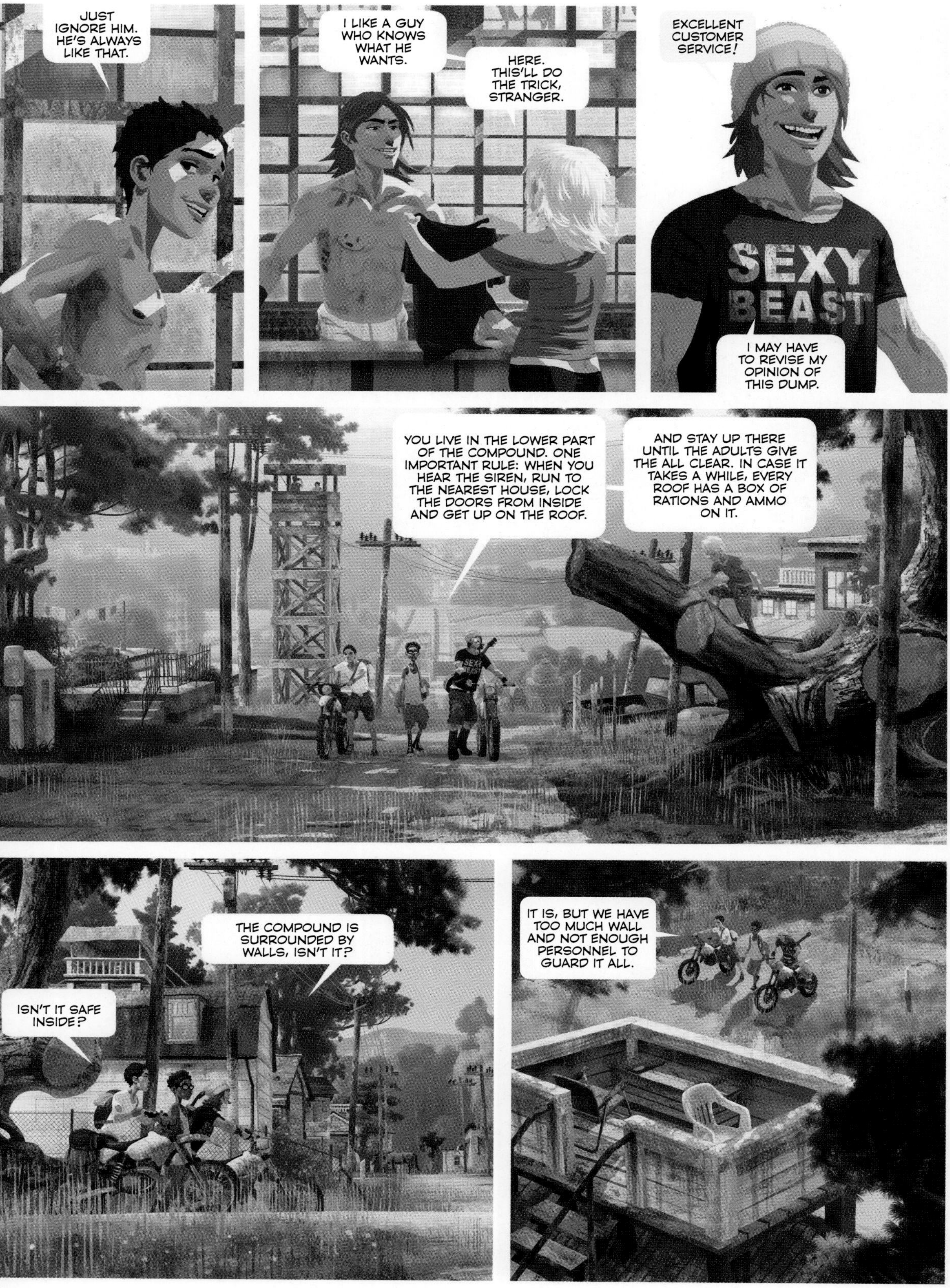
JUST IGNORE HIM. HE'S ALWAYS LIKE THAT.
I LIKE A GUY WHO KNOWS WHAT HE WANTS.
HERE. THIS'LL DO THE TRICK, STRANGER.
EXCELLENT CUSTOMER SERVICE!
SEXY BEAST
I MAY HAVE TO REVISE MY OPINION OF THIS DUMP.
YOU LIVE IN THE LOWER PART OF THE COMPOUND. ONE IMPORTANT RULE: WHEN YOU HEAR THE SIREN, RUN TO THE NEAREST HOUSE, LOCK THE DOORS FROM INSIDE AND GET UP ON THE ROOF.
AND STAY UP THERE UNTIL THE ADULTS GIVE THE ALL CLEAR. IN CASE IT TAKES A WHILE, EVERY ROOF HAS A BOX OF RATIONS AND AMMO ON IT.
THE COMPOUND IS SURROUNDED BY WALLS, ISN'T IT?
ISN'T IT SAFE INSIDE?
IT IS, BUT WE HAVE TOO MUCH WALL AND NOT ENOUGH PERSONNEL TO GUARD IT ALL.

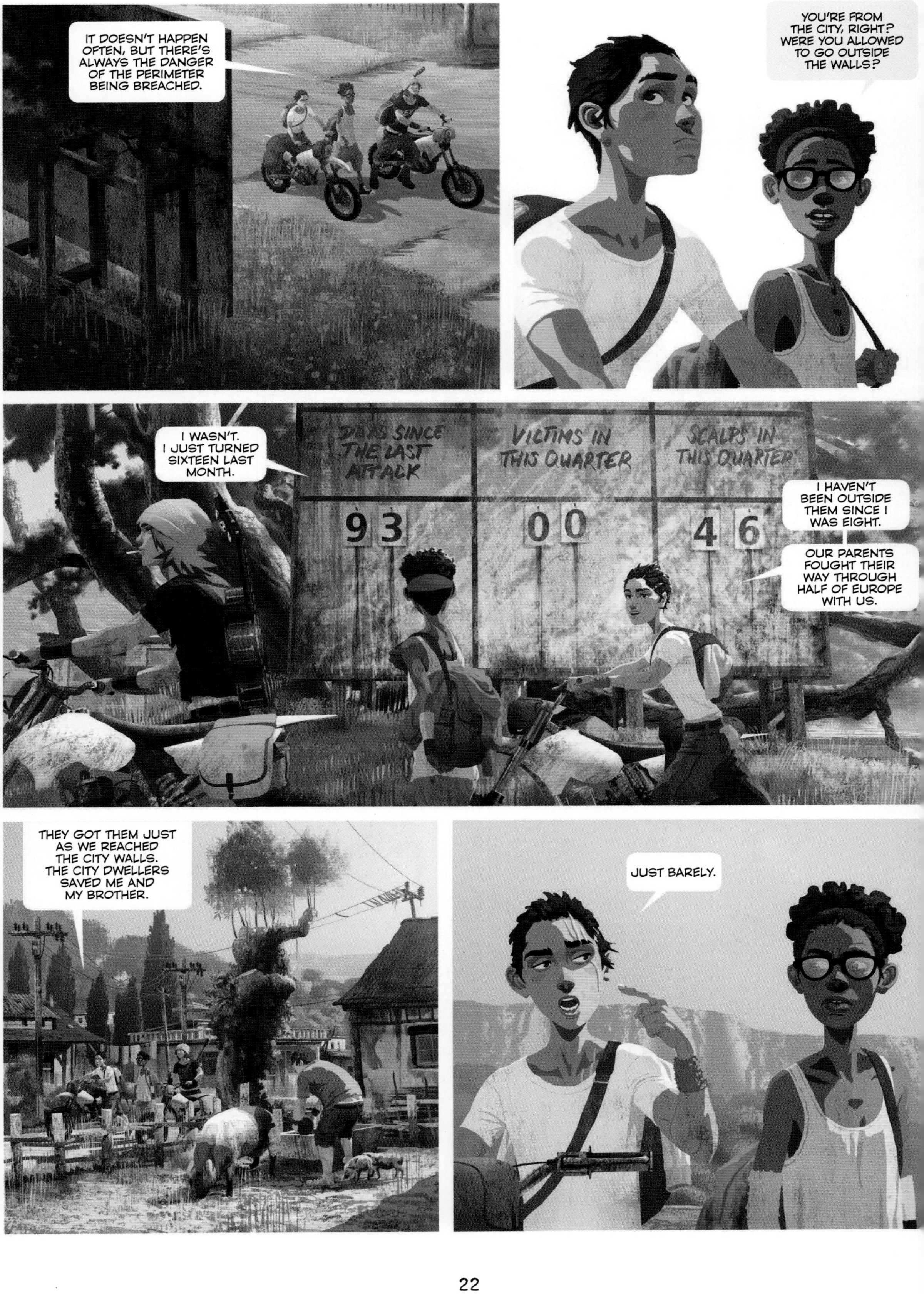
IT DOESN'T HAPPEN OFTEN, BUT THERE'S ALWAYS THE DANGER OF THE PERIMETER BEING BREACHED.
YOU'RE FROM THE CITY, RIGHT? WERE YOU ALLOWED TO GO OUTSIDE THE WALLS?
I WASN'T. I JUST TURNED SIXTEEN LAST MONTH.
DAYS SINCE THE LAST ATTACK
VICTIMS IN THIS QUARTER
SCALPS IN THIS QUARTER
93
00
46
I HAVEN'T BEEN OUTSIDE THEM SINCE I WAS EIGHT.
OUR PARENTS FOUGHT THEIR WAY THROUGH HALF OF EUROPE WITH US.
THEY GOT THEM JUST AS WE REACHED THE CITY WALLS. THE CITY DWELLERS SAVED ME AND MY BROTHER.
JUST BARELY.

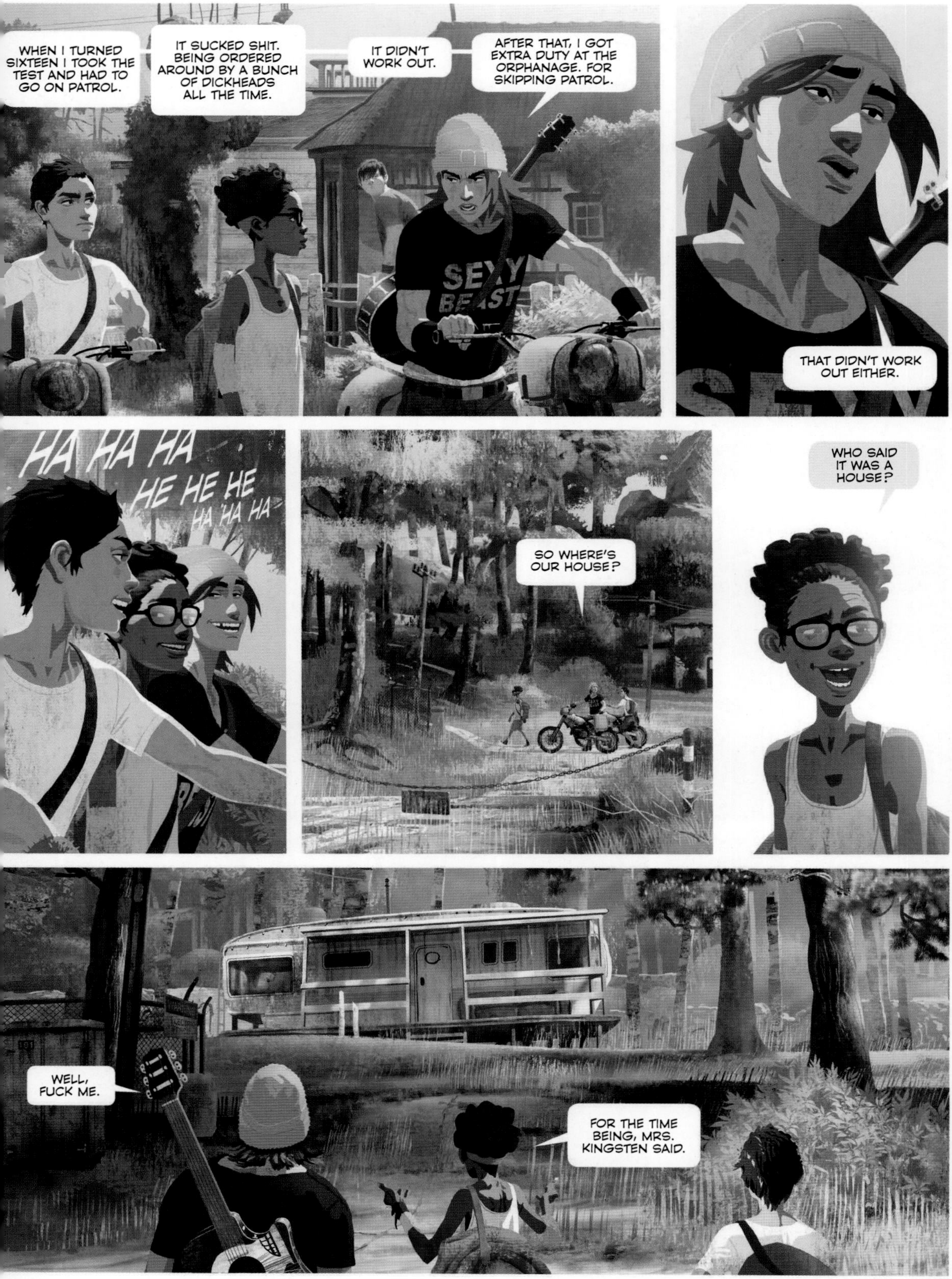
WHEN I TURNED SIXTEEN I TOOK THE TEST AND HAD TO GO ON PATROL.
IT SUCKED SHIT. BEING ORDERED AROUND BY A BUNCH OF DICKHEADS ALL THE TIME.
IT DIDN'T WORK OUT.
AFTER THAT, I GOT EXTRA DUTY AT THE ORPHANAGE. FOR SKIPPING PATROL.
SEXY BEAST
THAT DIDN'T WORK OUT EITHER.
HA HA HA
HE HE HE
HA HA HA
SO WHERE'S OUR HOUSE?
WHO SAID IT WAS A HOUSE?
WELL, FUCK ME.
FOR THE TIME BEING, MRS. KINGSTEN SAID.

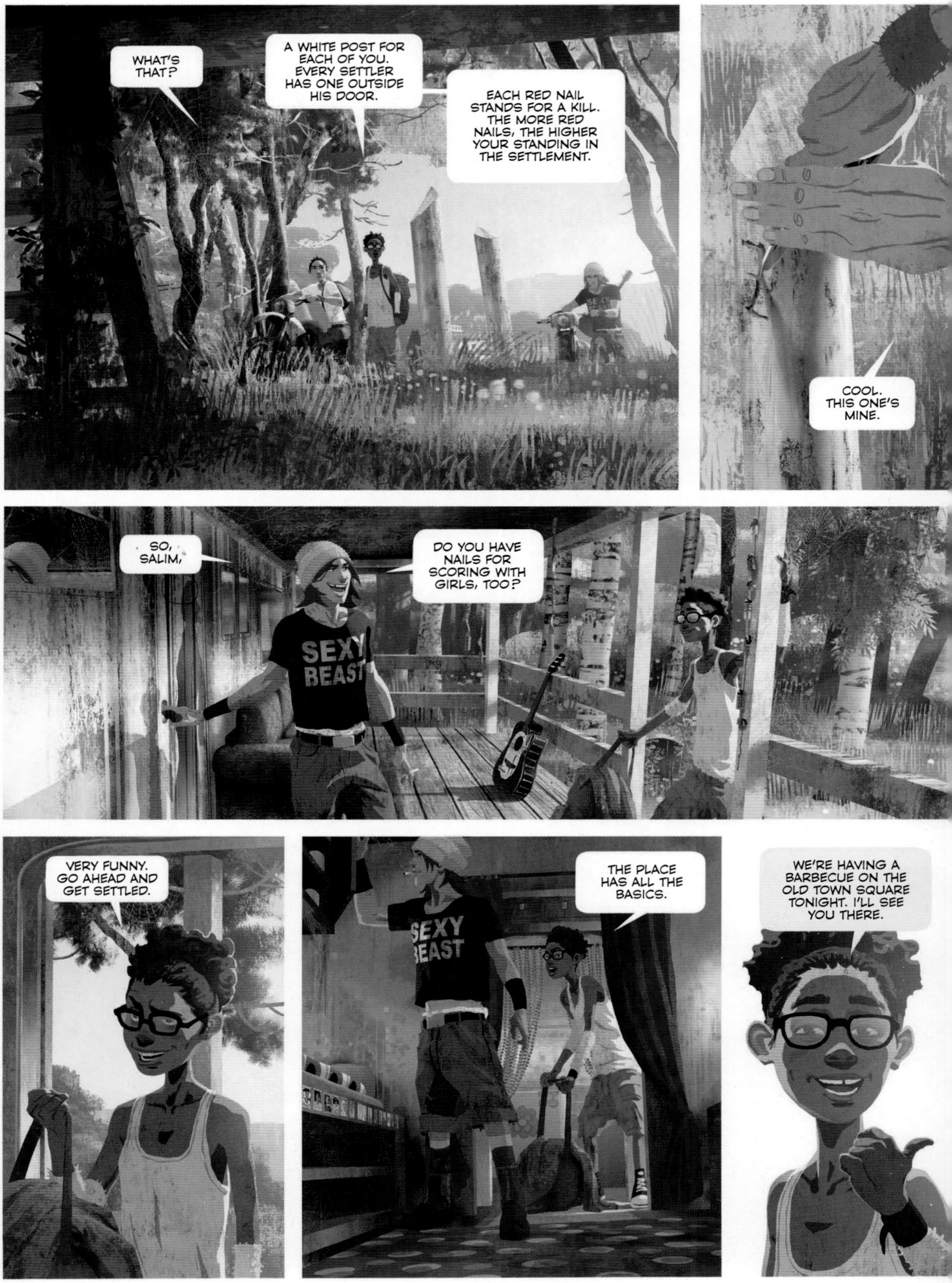
WHAT'S THAT?
A WHITE POST FOR EACH OF YOU. EVERY SETTLER HAS ONE OUTSIDE HIS DOOR.
EACH RED NAIL STANDS FOR A KILL. THE MORE RED NAILS, THE HIGHER YOUR STANDING IN THE SETTLEMENT.
COOL. THIS ONE'S MINE.
SO, SALIM,
DO YOU HAVE NAILS FOR SCORING WITH GIRLS, TOO?
SEXY BEAST
VERY FUNNY. GO AHEAD AND GET SETTLED.
SEXY BEAST
THE PLACE HAS ALL THE BASICS.
WE'RE HAVING A BARBECUE ON THE OLD TOWN SQUARE TONIGHT. I'LL SEE YOU THERE.

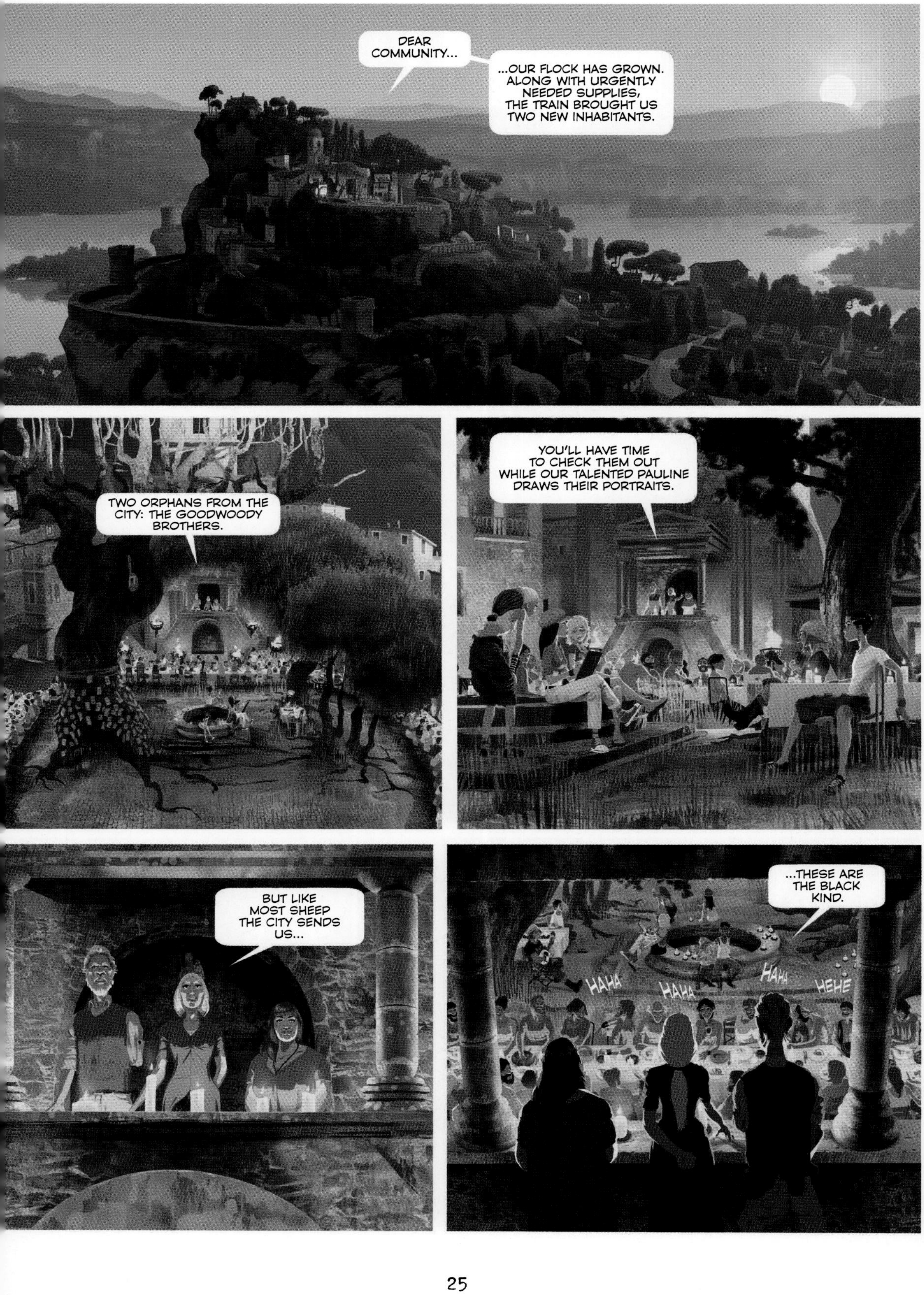
DEAR COMMUNITY...
...OUR FLOCK HAS GROWN. ALONG WITH URGENTLY NEEDED SUPPLIES, THE TRAIN BROUGHT US TWO NEW INHABITANTS.
TWO ORPHANS FROM THE CITY: THE GOODWOODY BROTHERS.
YOU'LL HAVE TIME TO CHECK THEM OUT WHILE OUR TALENTED PAULINE DRAWS THEIR PORTRAITS.
BUT LIKE MOST SHEEP THE CITY SENDS US...
...THESE ARE THE BLACK KIND.
HAHA
HAHA
HAHA
HEHE

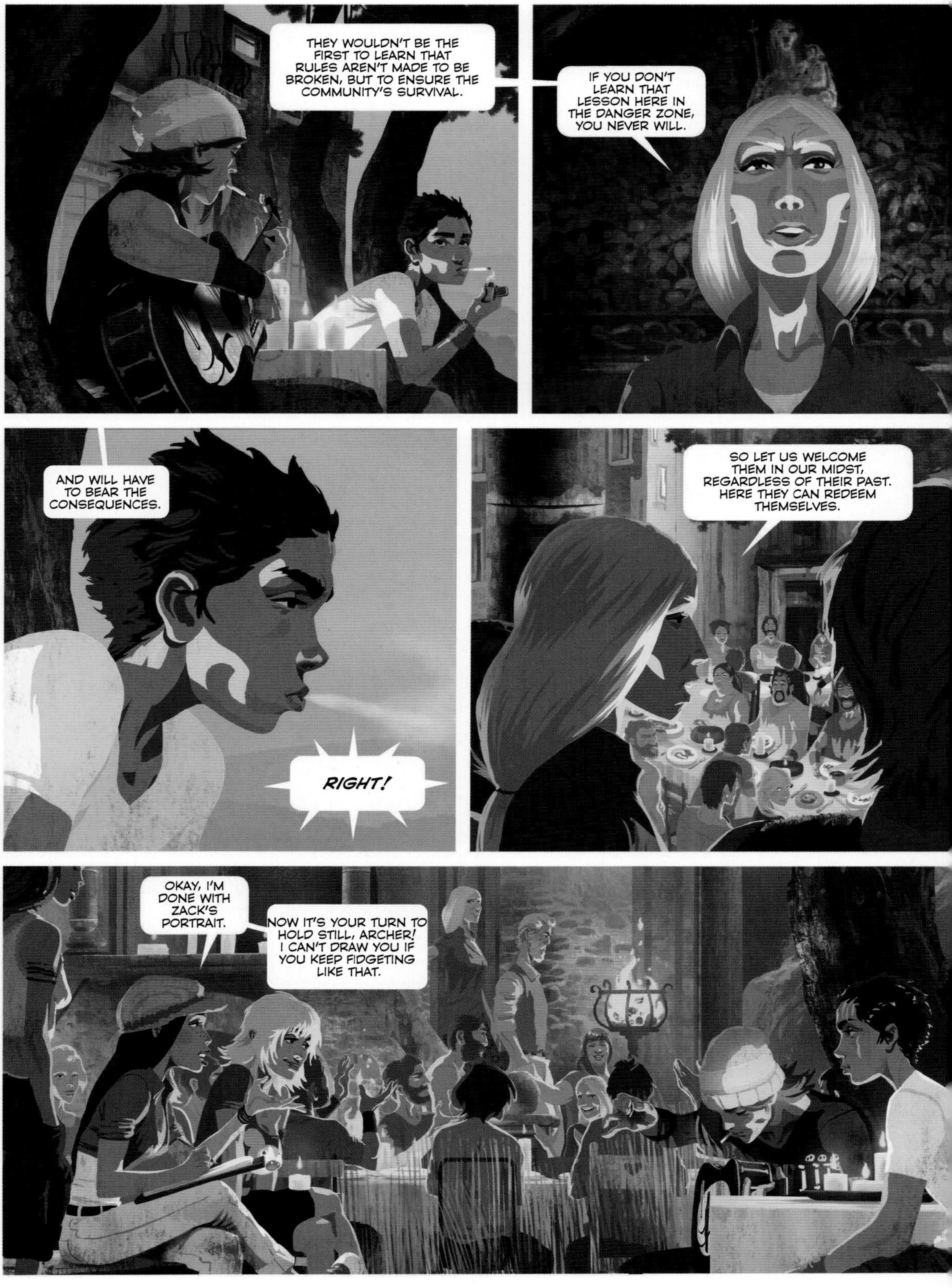
THEY WOULDN'T BE THE FIRST TO LEARN THAT RULES AREN'T MADE TO BE BROKEN, BUT TO ENSURE THE COMMUNITY'S SURVIVAL.
IF YOU DON'T LEARN THAT LESSON HERE IN THE DANGER ZONE, YOU NEVER WILL.
AND WILL HAVE TO BEAR THE CONSEQUENCES.
RIGHT!
SO LET US WELCOME THEM IN OUR MIDST, REGARDLESS OF THEIR PAST. HERE THEY CAN REDEEM THEMSELVES.
OKAY, I'M DONE WITH ZACK'S PORTRAIT.
NOW IT'S YOUR TURN TO HOLD STILL, ARCHER! I CAN'T DRAW YOU IF YOU KEEP FIDGETING LIKE THAT.

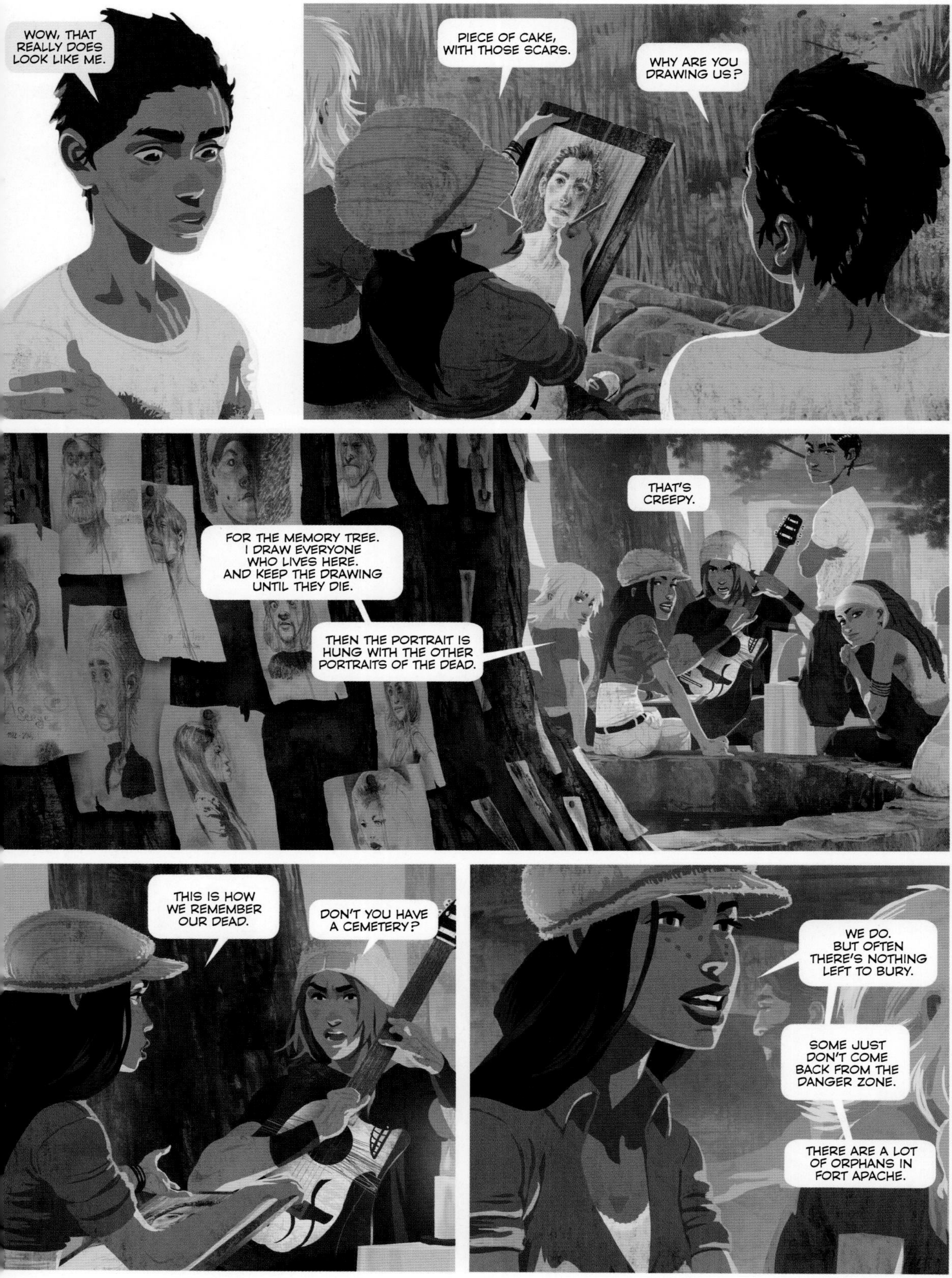
WOW, THAT REALLY DOES LOOK LIKE ME.
PIECE OF CAKE, WITH THOSE SCARS.
WHY ARE YOU DRAWING US?
FOR THE MEMORY TREE. I DRAW EVERYONE WHO LIVES HERE. AND KEEP THE DRAWING UNTIL THEY DIE.
THEN THE PORTRAIT IS HUNG WITH THE OTHER PORTRAITS OF THE DEAD.
THAT'S CREEPY.
THIS IS HOW WE REMEMBER OUR DEAD.
DON'T YOU HAVE A CEMETERY?
WE DO. BUT OFTEN THERE'S NOTHING LEFT TO BURY.
SOME JUST DON'T COME BACK FROM THE DANGER ZONE.
THERE ARE A LOT OF ORPHANS IN FORT APACHE.

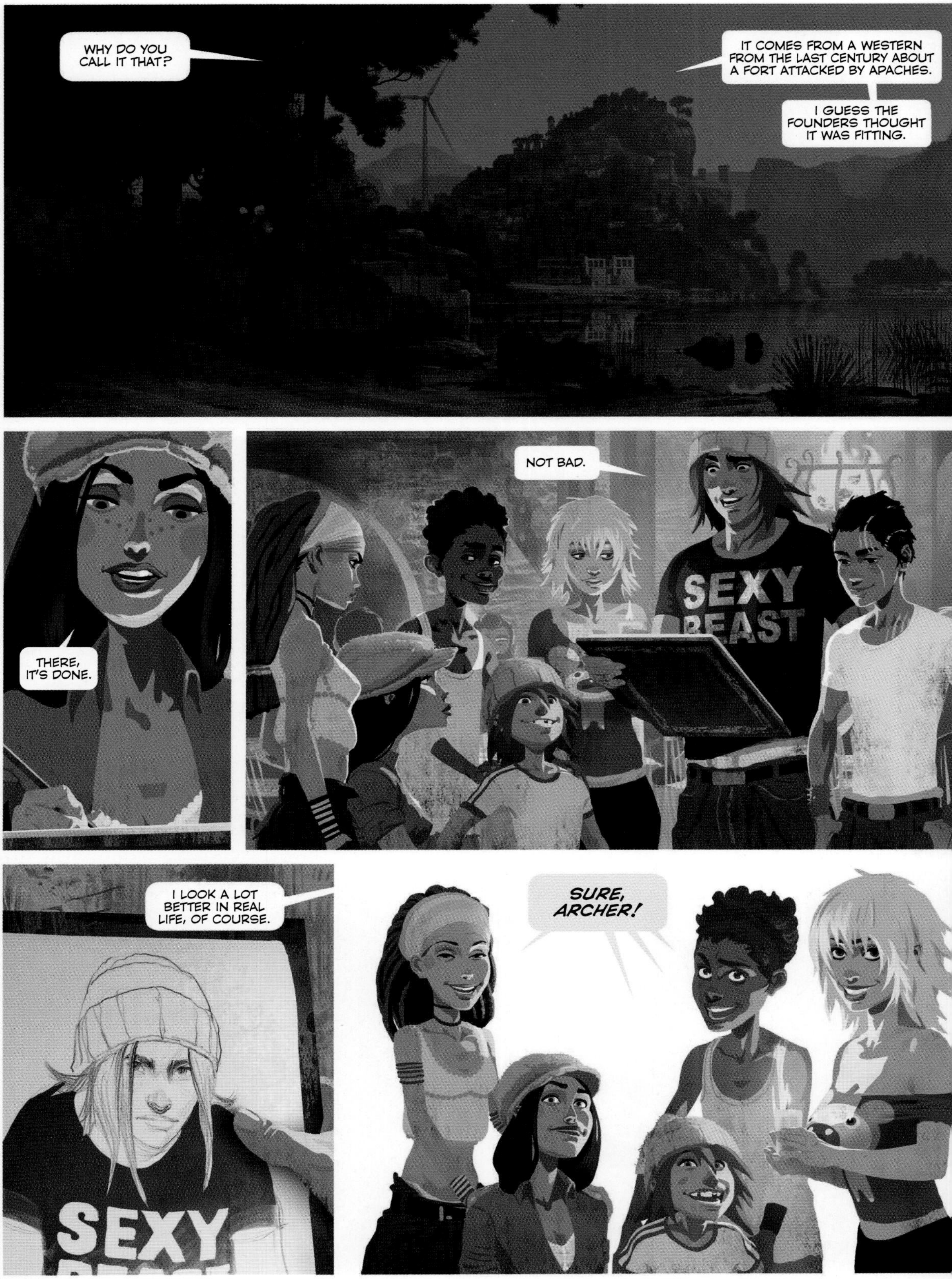
WHY DO YOU CALL IT THAT?
IT COMES FROM A WESTERN FROM THE LAST CENTURY ABOUT A FORT ATTACKED BY APACHES.
I GUESS THE FOUNDERS THOUGHT IT WAS FITTING.
THERE, IT'S DONE.
NOT BAD.
SEXY BEAST
I LOOK A LOT BETTER IN REAL LIFE, OF COURSE.
SEXY
SURE, ARCHER!

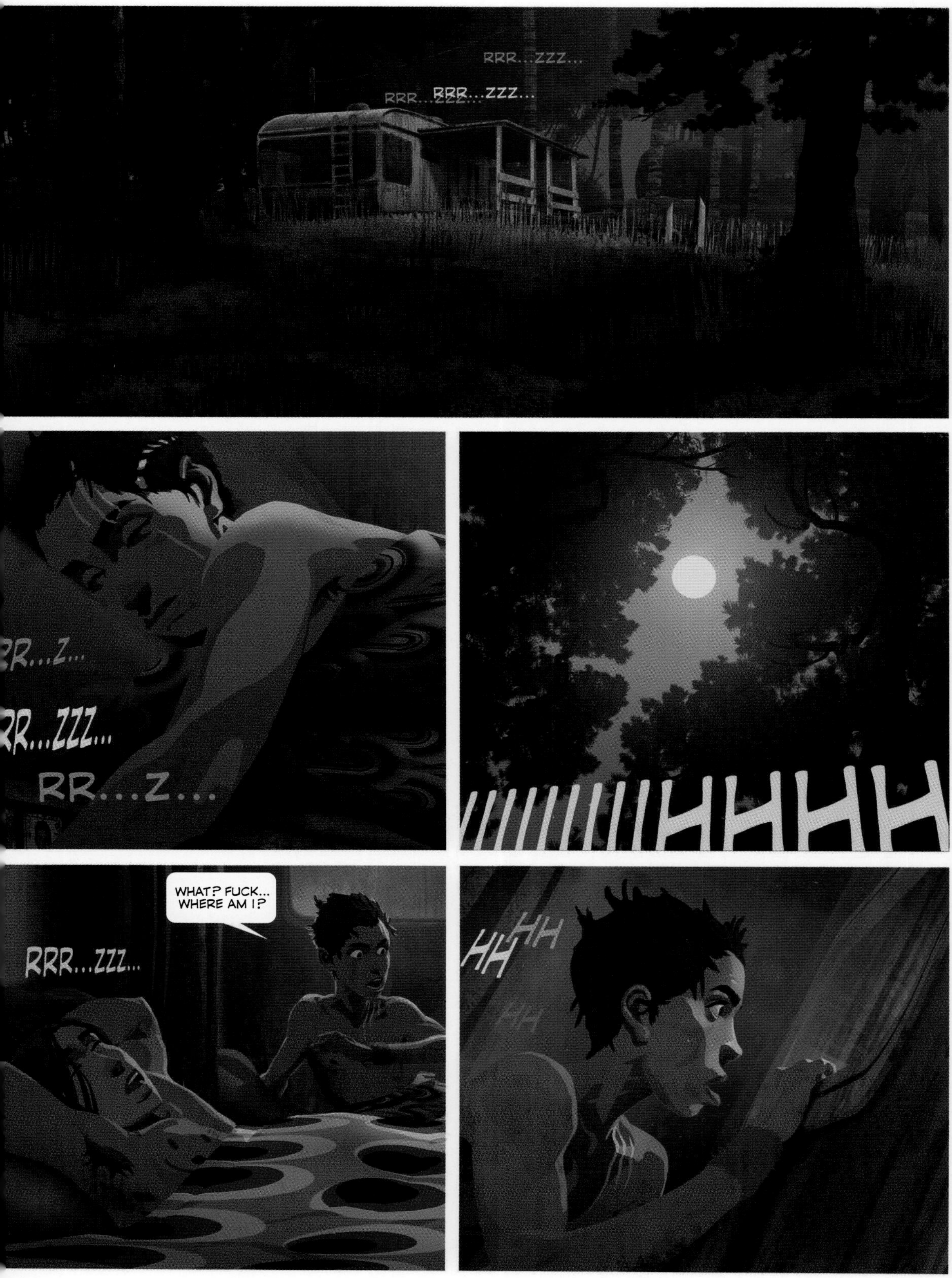
RRR...ZZZ...
RRR...ZZZ...
RRR...ZZZ...
R...Z...
R...ZZZ...
RR...Z...
IIIIIIIIIIIIHHHHH
RRR...ZZZ...
WHAT? FUCK... WHERE AM I?
HHHH
HH

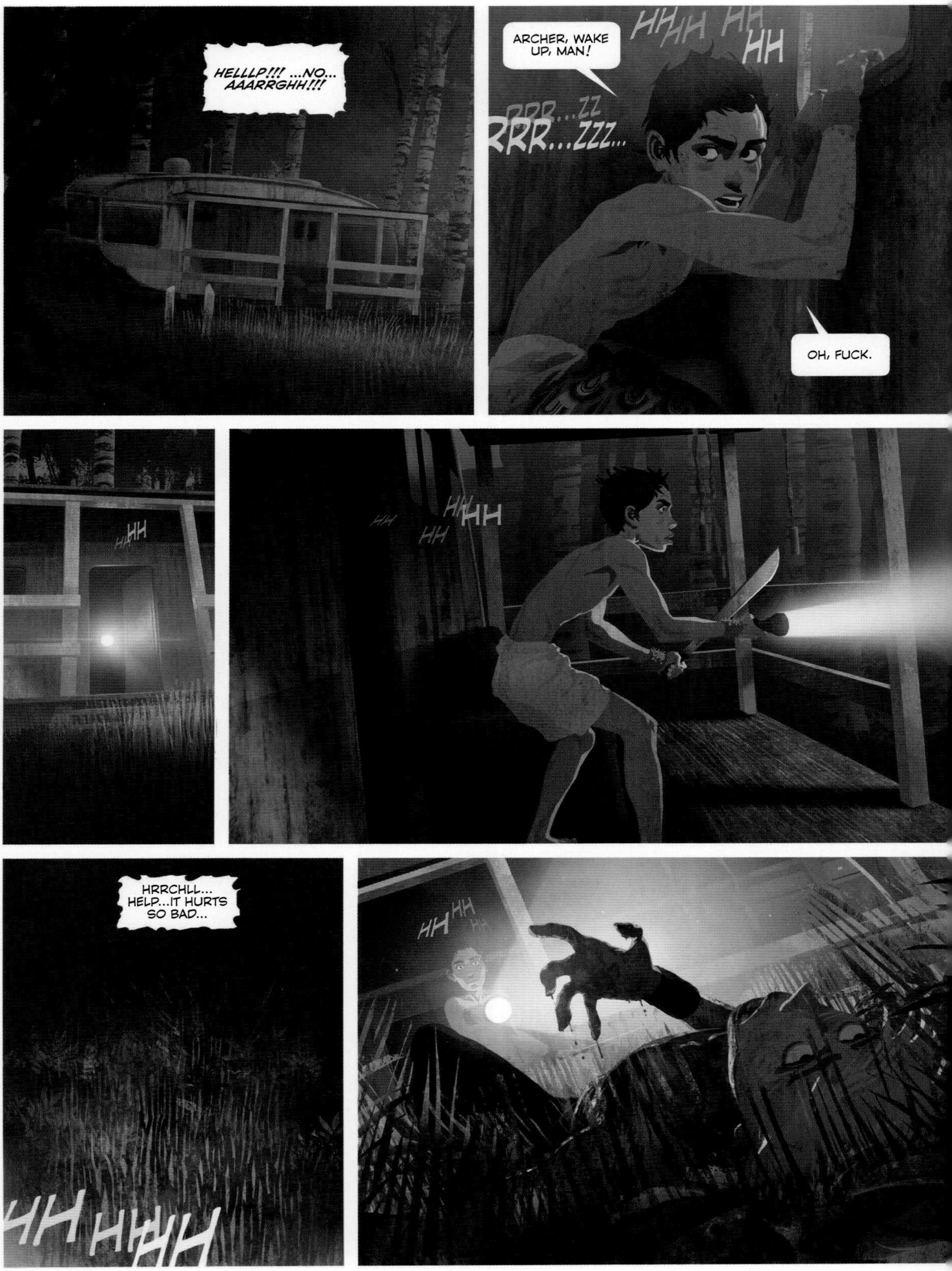
HELLLP!!! ...NO... AAARRGHH!!!
ARCHER, WAKE UP, MAN!
HH HH HH HH
RRR...ZZ
RRR...ZZZ...
OH, FUCK.
HH
HH HH HH HH
HRRCHLL... HELP...IT HURTS SO BAD...
HH HHHH
HH HH HH

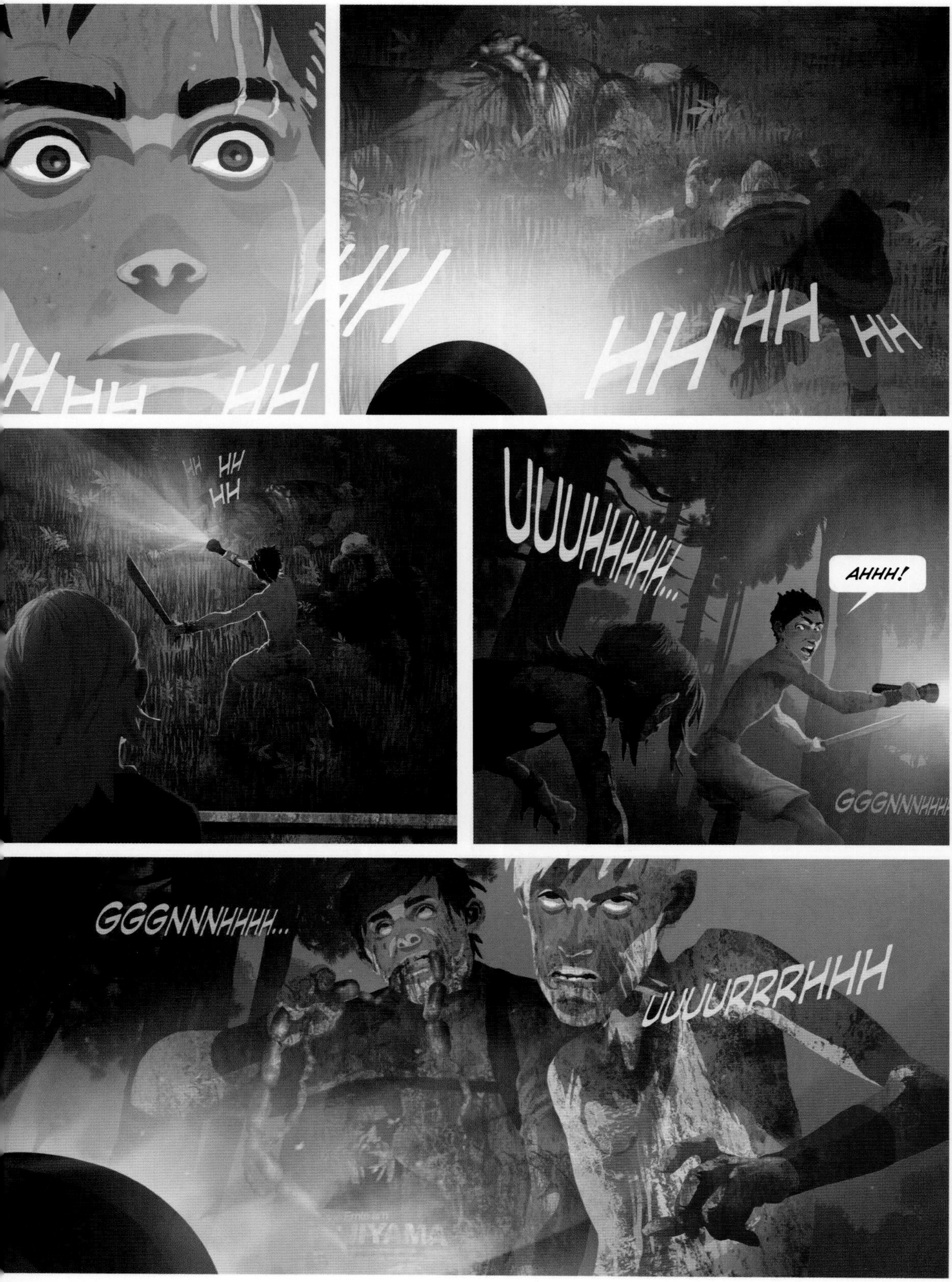
HHHHH HH
HHHHHH HH
HH HH
HH
UUUHHHHH...
AHHH!
GGGNNHHHH
GGGNNHHHH...
UUUURRRHHH

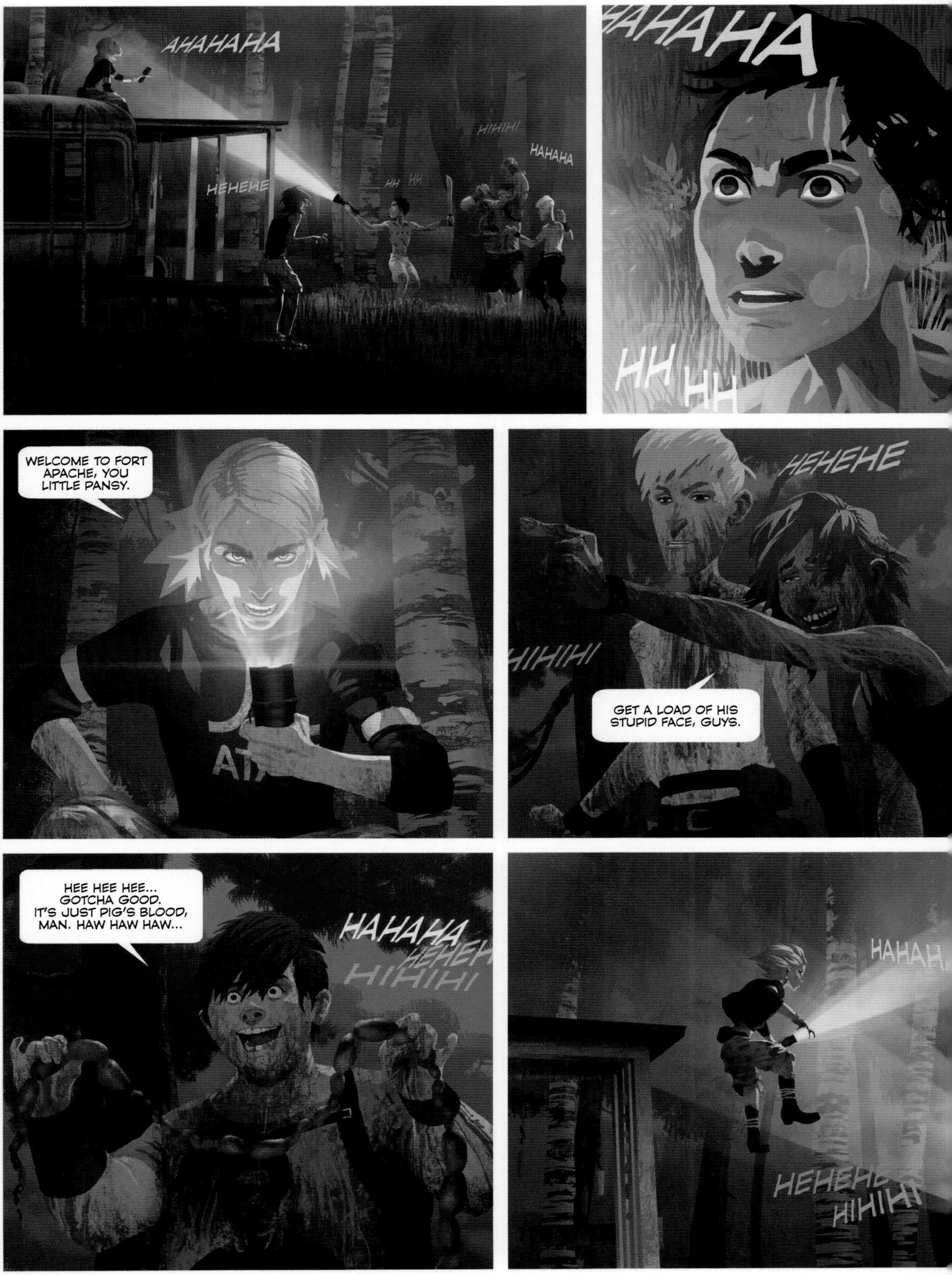
AHAHAHA
HIHIHI
HAHAHA
HEHEHE
HH HH
AHAHAHA
HH HH
WELCOME TO FORT APACHE, YOU LITTLE PANSY.
HEHEHE
HIHIHI
GET A LOAD OF HIS STUPID FACE, GUYS.
HEE HEE HEE... GOTCHA GOOD. IT'S JUST PIG'S BLOOD, MAN. HAW HAW HAW...
HAHAHA
HIHIHI
HAHAH
HIHIHI

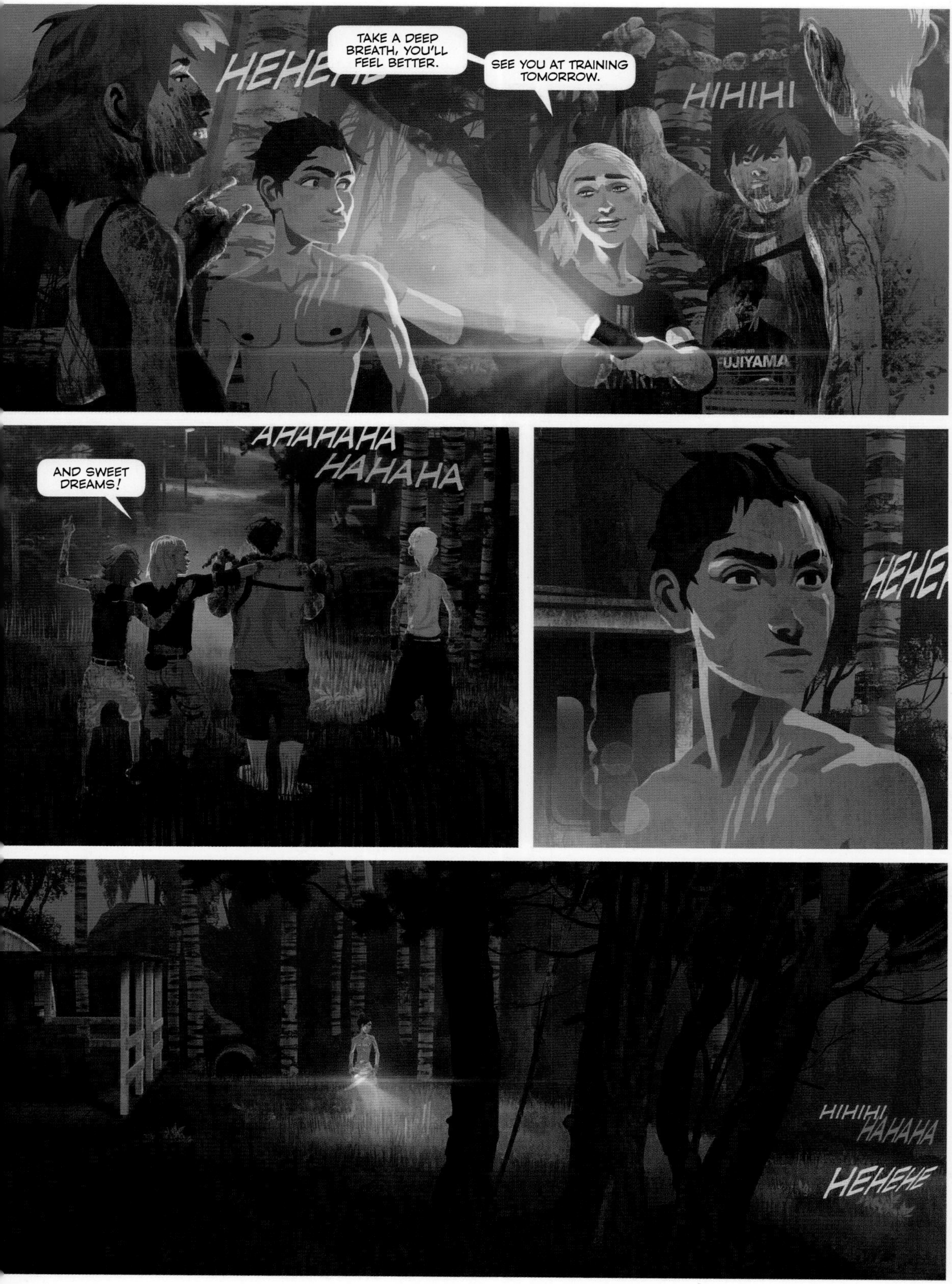
HEHEHE
TAKE A DEEP BREATH, YOU'LL FEEL BETTER.
SEE YOU AT TRAINING TOMORROW.
HIHIHI
FUJIYAMA
AND SWEET DREAMS!
AHAHAHA
HAHAHA
HEHEHE
HIHIHI
HAHAHA
HEHEHE

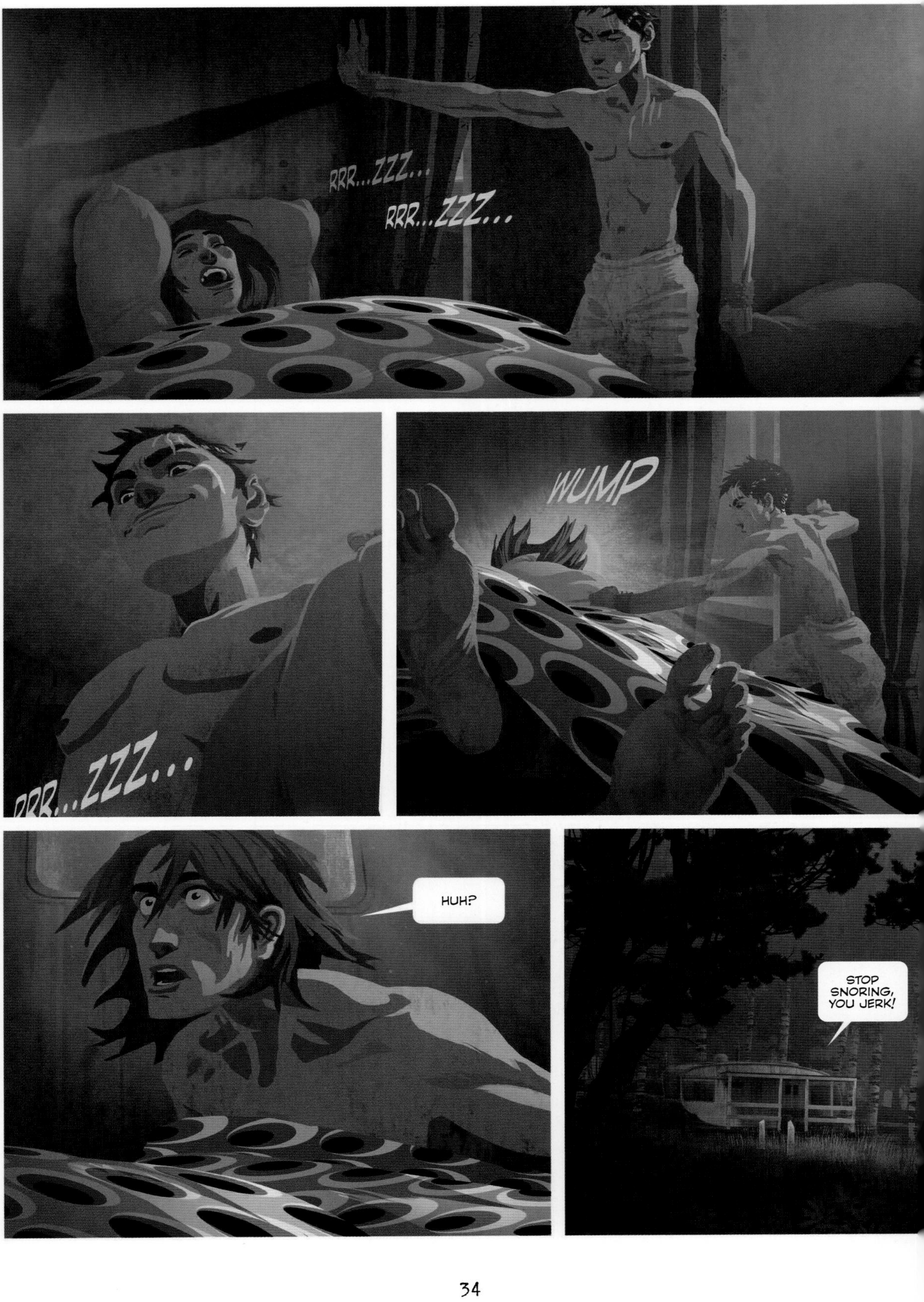
RRR...ZZZ...
RRR...ZZZ...
RRR...ZZZ...
WUMP
HUH?
STOP SNORING, YOU JERK!

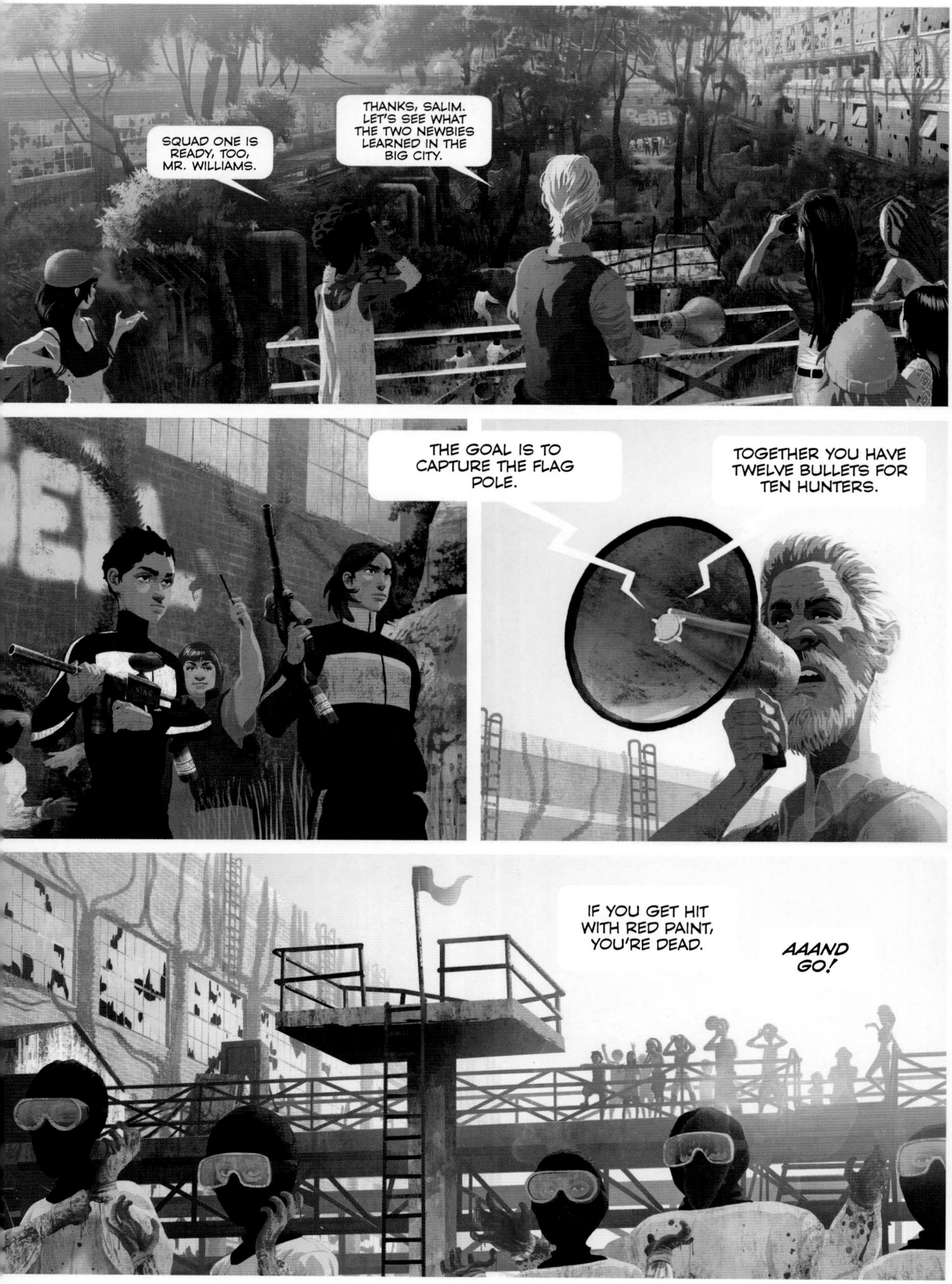
SQUAD ONE IS READY, TOO, MR. WILLIAMS.
THANKS, SALIM. LET'S SEE WHAT THE TWO NEWBIES LEARNED IN THE BIG CITY.
THE GOAL IS TO CAPTURE THE FLAG POLE.
TOGETHER YOU HAVE TWELVE BULLETS FOR TEN HUNTERS.
IF YOU GET HIT WITH RED PAINT, YOU'RE DEAD.
AAAND GO!

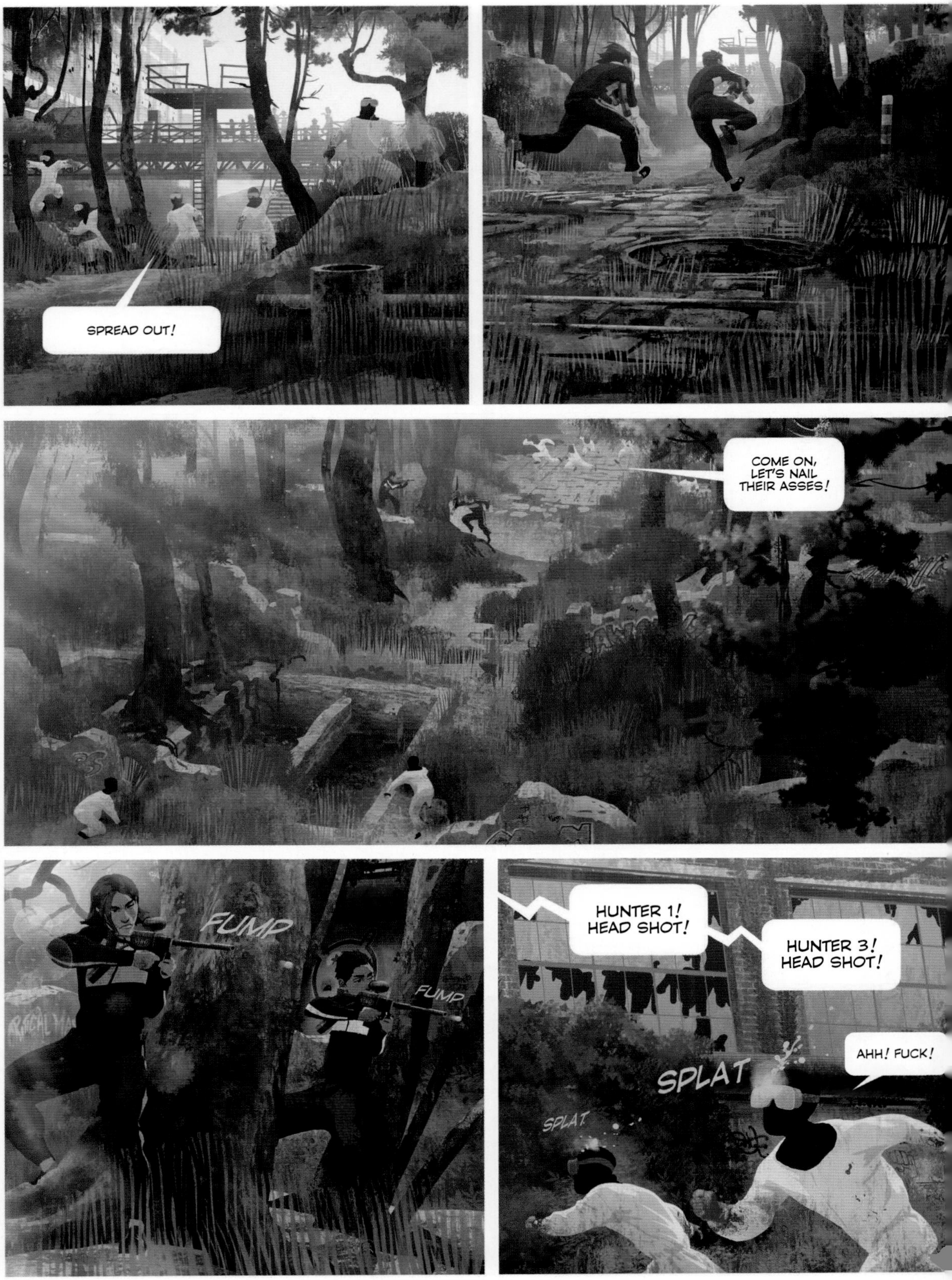
SPREAD OUT!
COME ON, LET'S NAIL THEIR ASSES!
FUMP
FUMP
HUNTER 1! HEAD SHOT!
HUNTER 3! HEAD SHOT!
SPLAT
SPLAT
AHH! FUCK!

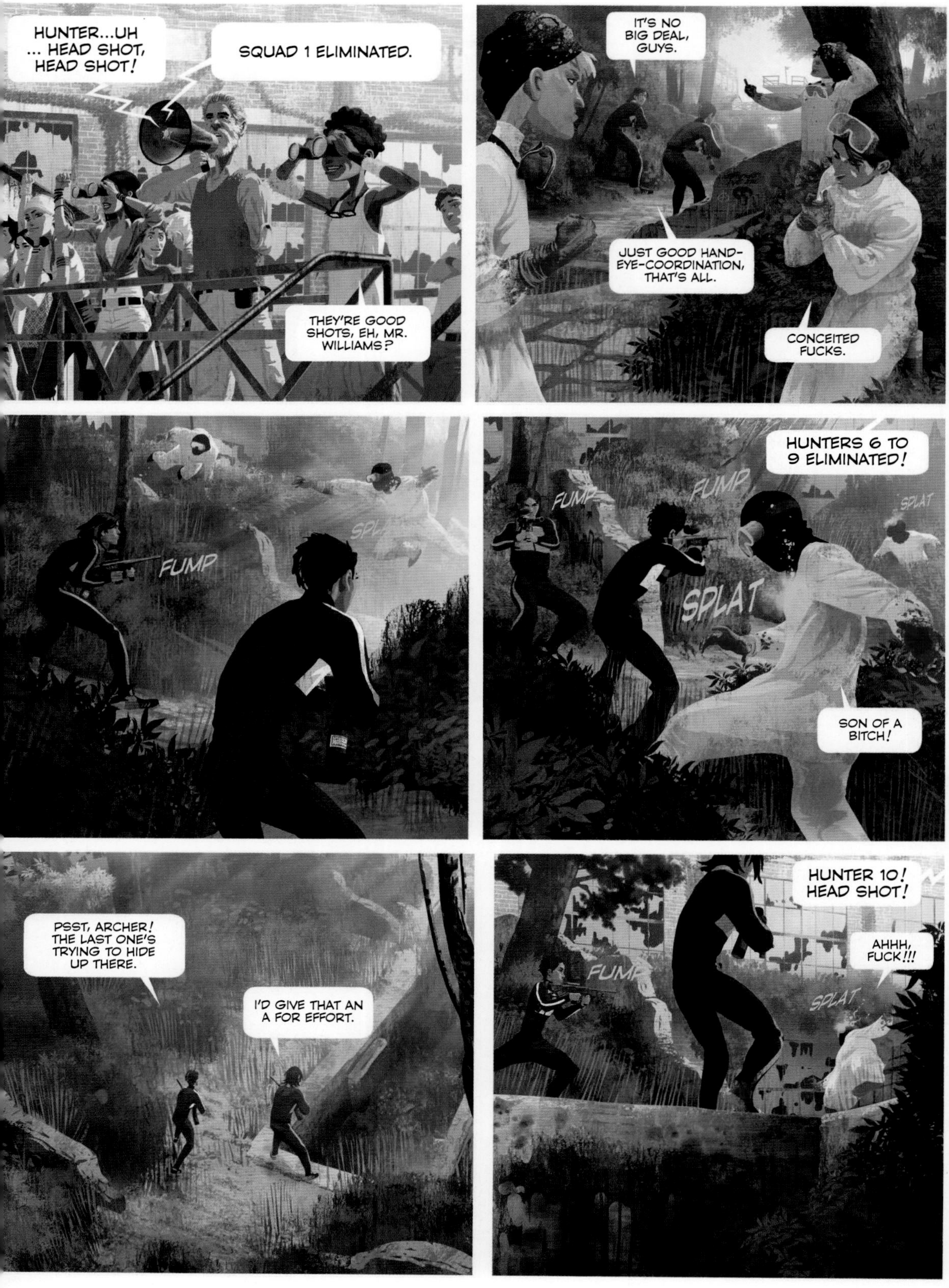

HUNTER...UH ... HEAD SHOT, HEAD SHOT!
SQUAD 1 ELIMINATED.
THEY'RE GOOD SHOTS, EH, MR. WILLIAMS?
IT'S NO BIG DEAL, GUYS.
JUST GOOD HAND-EYE-COORDINATION, THAT'S ALL.
CONCEITED FUCKS.
SPLAT
FUMP
HUNTERS 6 TO 9 ELIMINATED!
FUMP
FUMP
SPLAT
SPLAT
SON OF A BITCH!
PSST, ARCHER! THE LAST ONE'S TRYING TO HIDE UP THERE.
I'D GIVE THAT AN A FOR EFFORT.
HUNTER 10! HEAD SHOT!
AHHH, FUCK!!!
FUMP
SPLAT

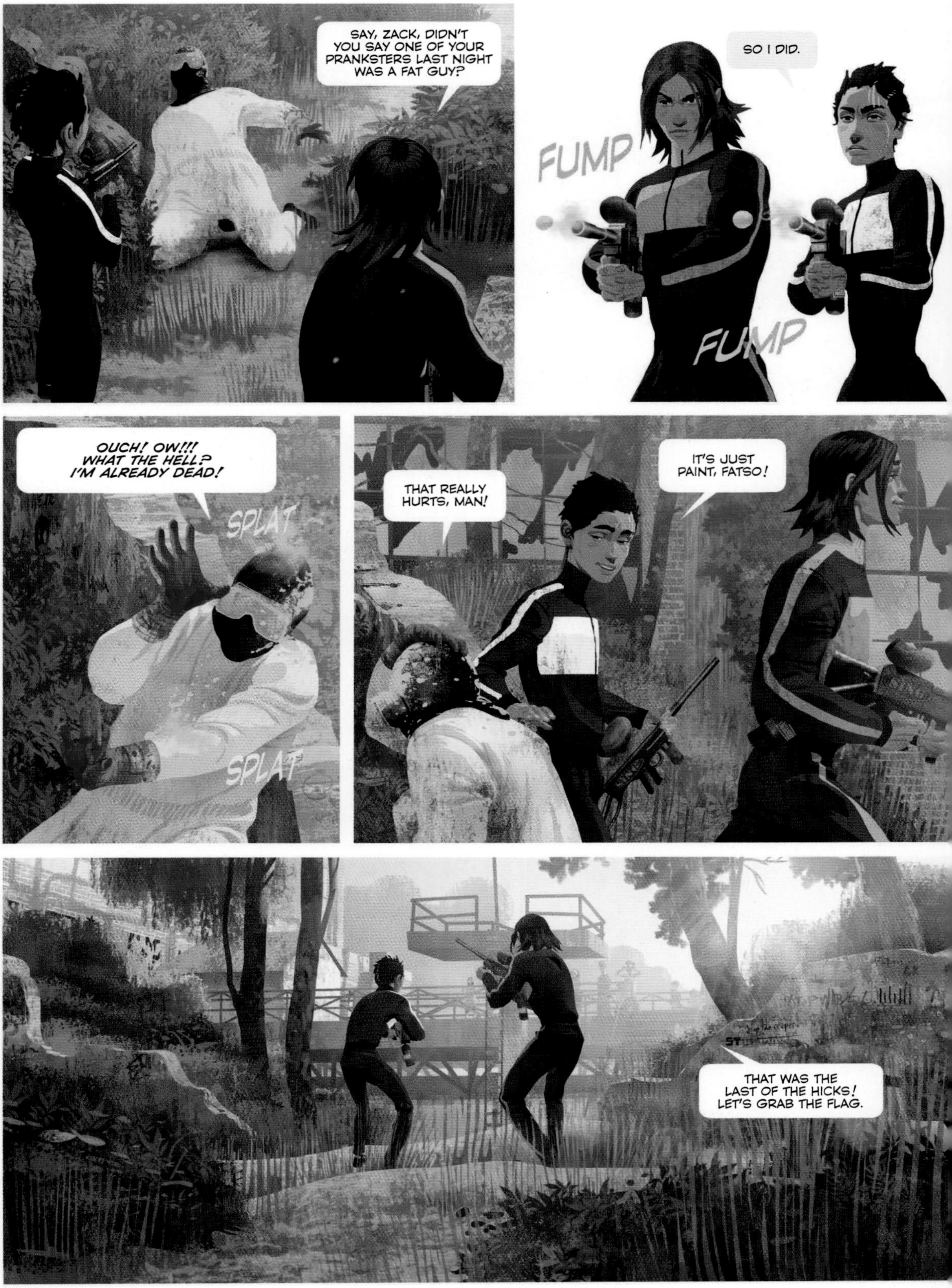
SAY, ZACK, DIDN'T YOU SAY ONE OF YOUR PRANKSTERS LAST NIGHT WAS A FAT GUY?
SO I DID.
FUMP
FUMP
OUCH! OW!!! WHAT THE HELL? I'M ALREADY DEAD!
SPLAT
SPLAT
THAT REALLY HURTS, MAN!
IT'S JUST PAINT, FATSO!
THAT WAS THE LAST OF THE HICKS! LET'S GRAB THE FLAG.

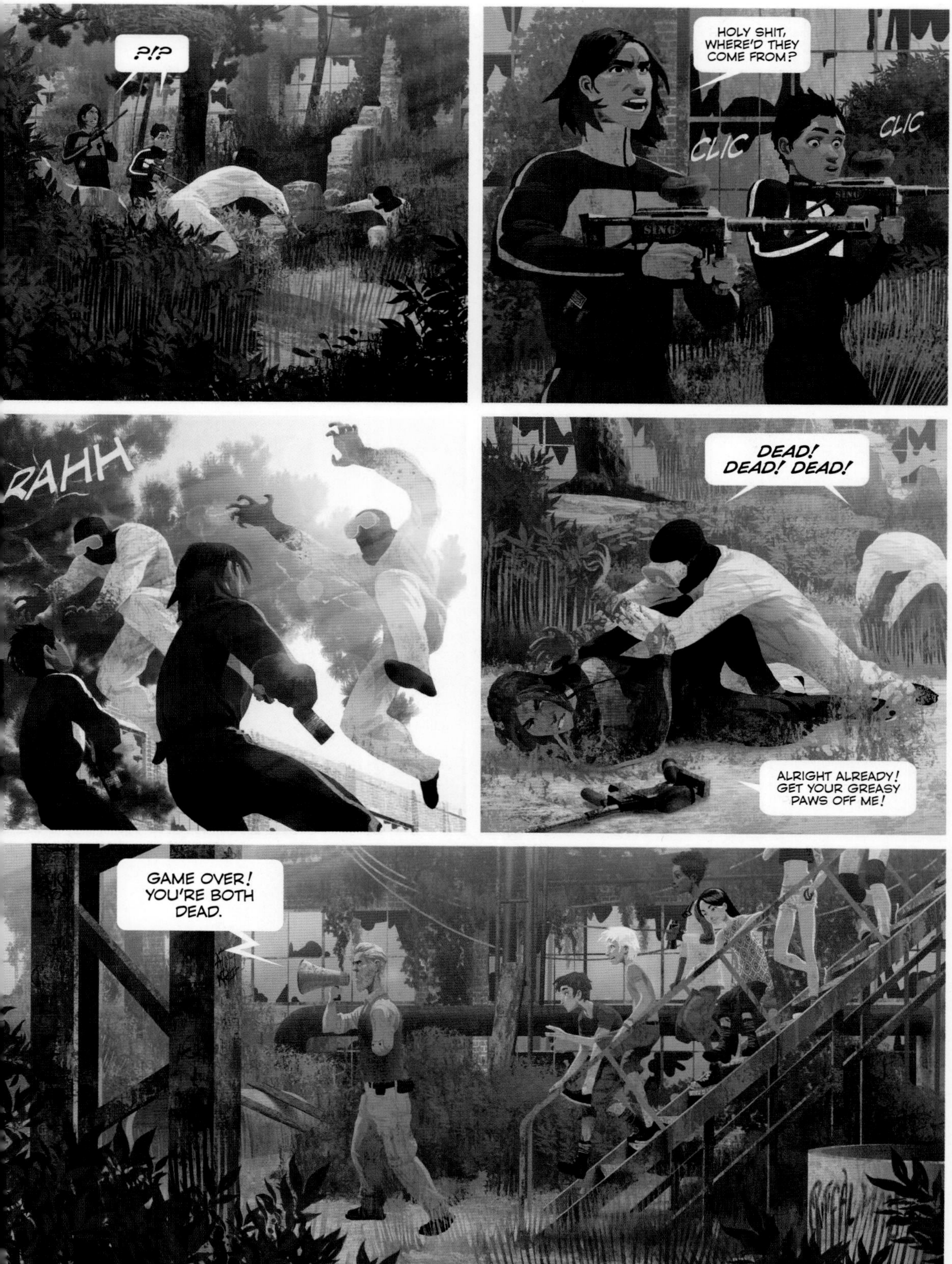
?!?
HOLY SHIT, WHERE'D THEY COME FROM?
CLIC
CLIC
RAHH
DEAD! DEAD! DEAD!
ALRIGHT ALREADY! GET YOUR GREASY PAWS OFF ME!
GAME OVER! YOU'RE BOTH DEAD.

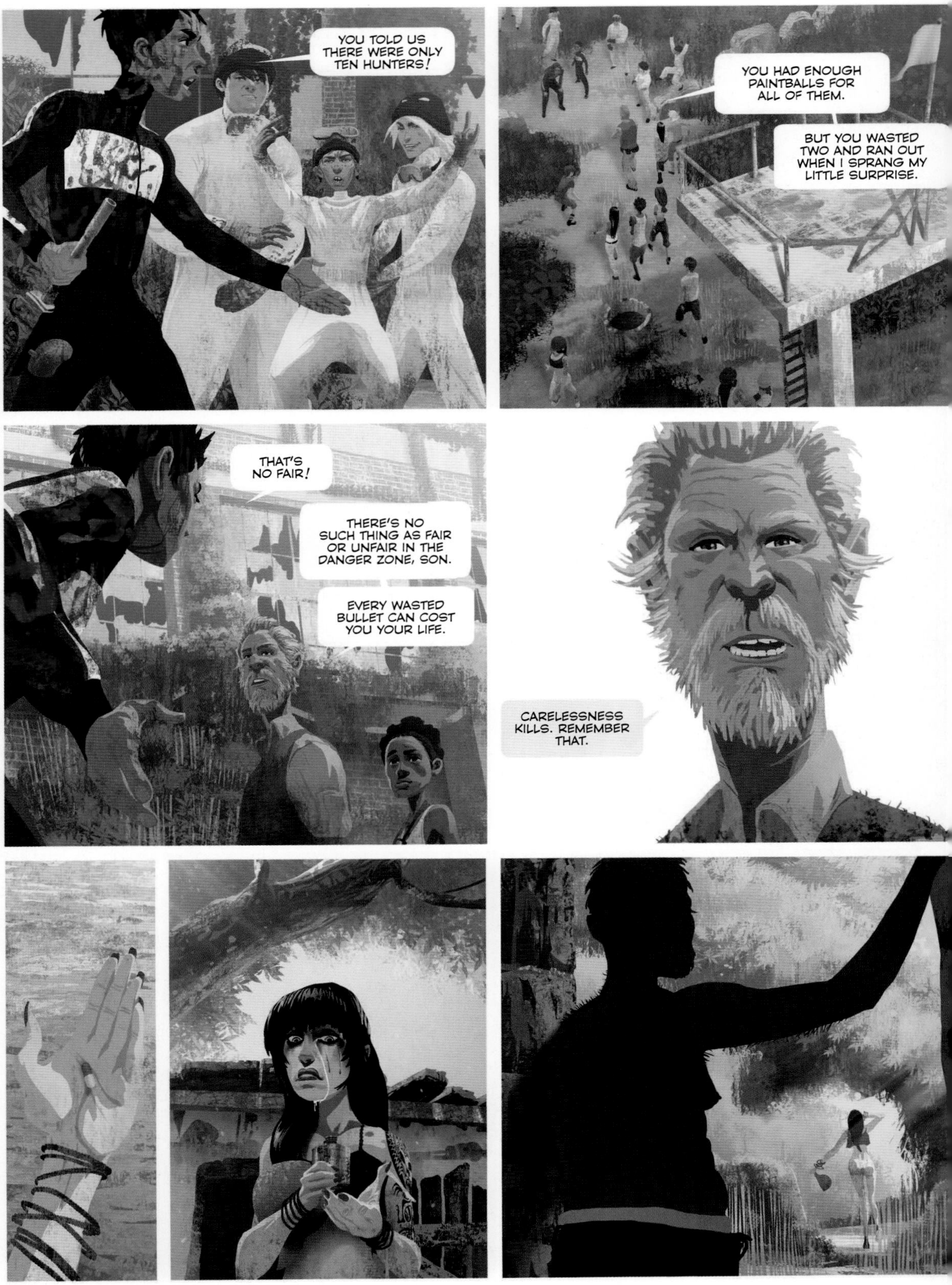
YOU TOLD US THERE WERE ONLY TEN HUNTERS!
YOU HAD ENOUGH PAINTBALLS FOR ALL OF THEM.
BUT YOU WASTED TWO AND RAN OUT WHEN I SPRANG MY LITTLE SURPRISE.
THAT'S NO FAIR!
THERE'S NO SUCH THING AS FAIR OR UNFAIR IN THE DANGER ZONE, SON.
EVERY WASTED BULLET CAN COST YOU YOUR LIFE.
CARELESSNESS KILLS. REMEMBER THAT.

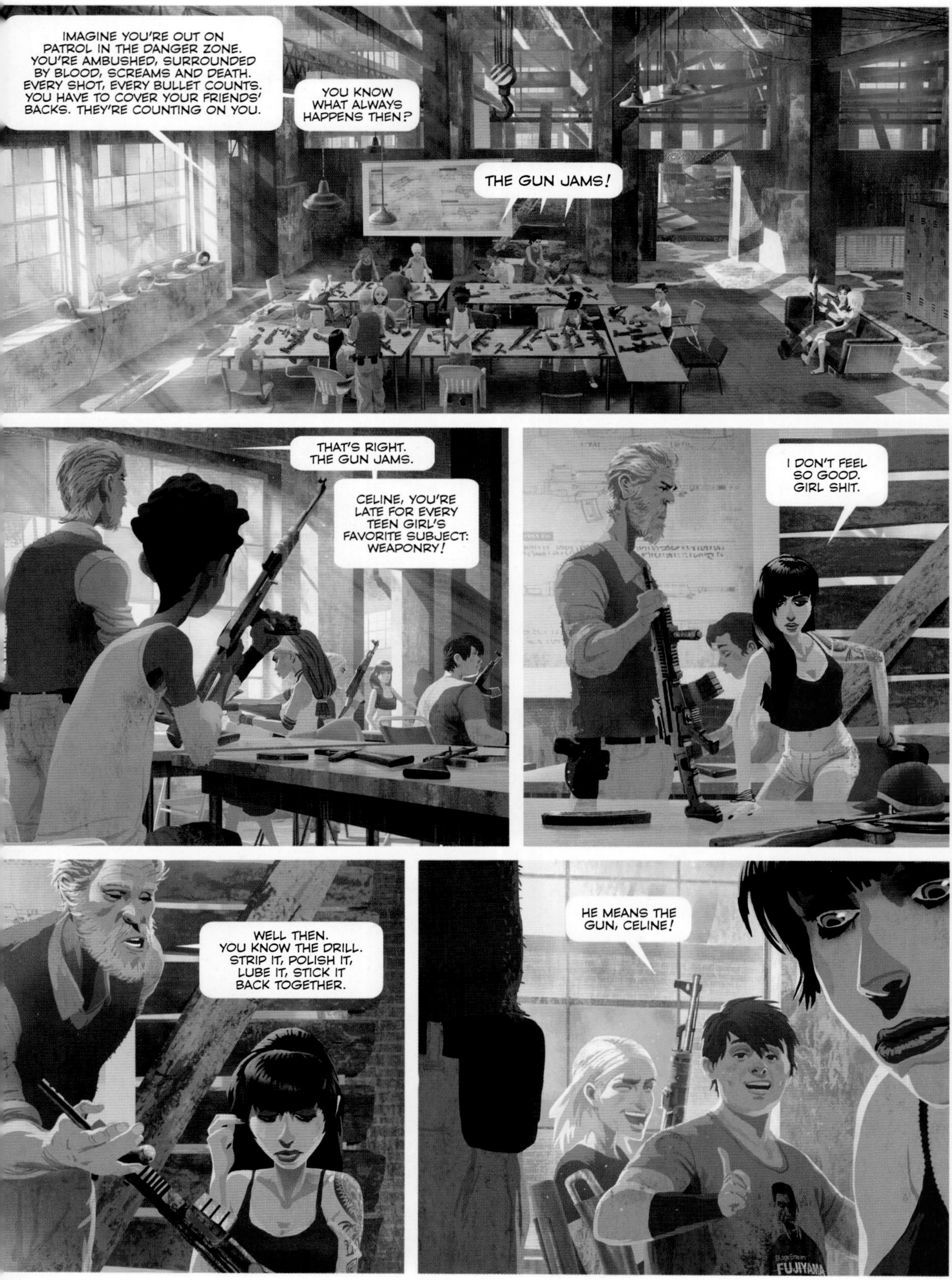
IMAGINE YOU'RE OUT ON PATROL IN THE DANGER ZONE. YOU'RE AMBUSHED, SURROUNDED BY BLOOD, SCREAMS AND DEATH. EVERY SHOT, EVERY BULLET COUNTS. YOU HAVE TO COVER YOUR FRIENDS' BACKS. THEY'RE COUNTING ON YOU.
YOU KNOW WHAT ALWAYS HAPPENS THEN?
THE GUN JAMS!
THAT'S RIGHT. THE GUN JAMS.
CELINE, YOU'RE LATE FOR EVERY TEEN GIRL'S FAVORITE SUBJECT: WEAPONRY!
I DON'T FEEL SO GOOD. GIRL SHIT.
WELL THEN. YOU KNOW THE DRILL. STRIP IT, POLISH IT, LUBE IT, STICK IT BACK TOGETHER.
HE MEANS THE GUN, CELINE!
FUJIYAMA

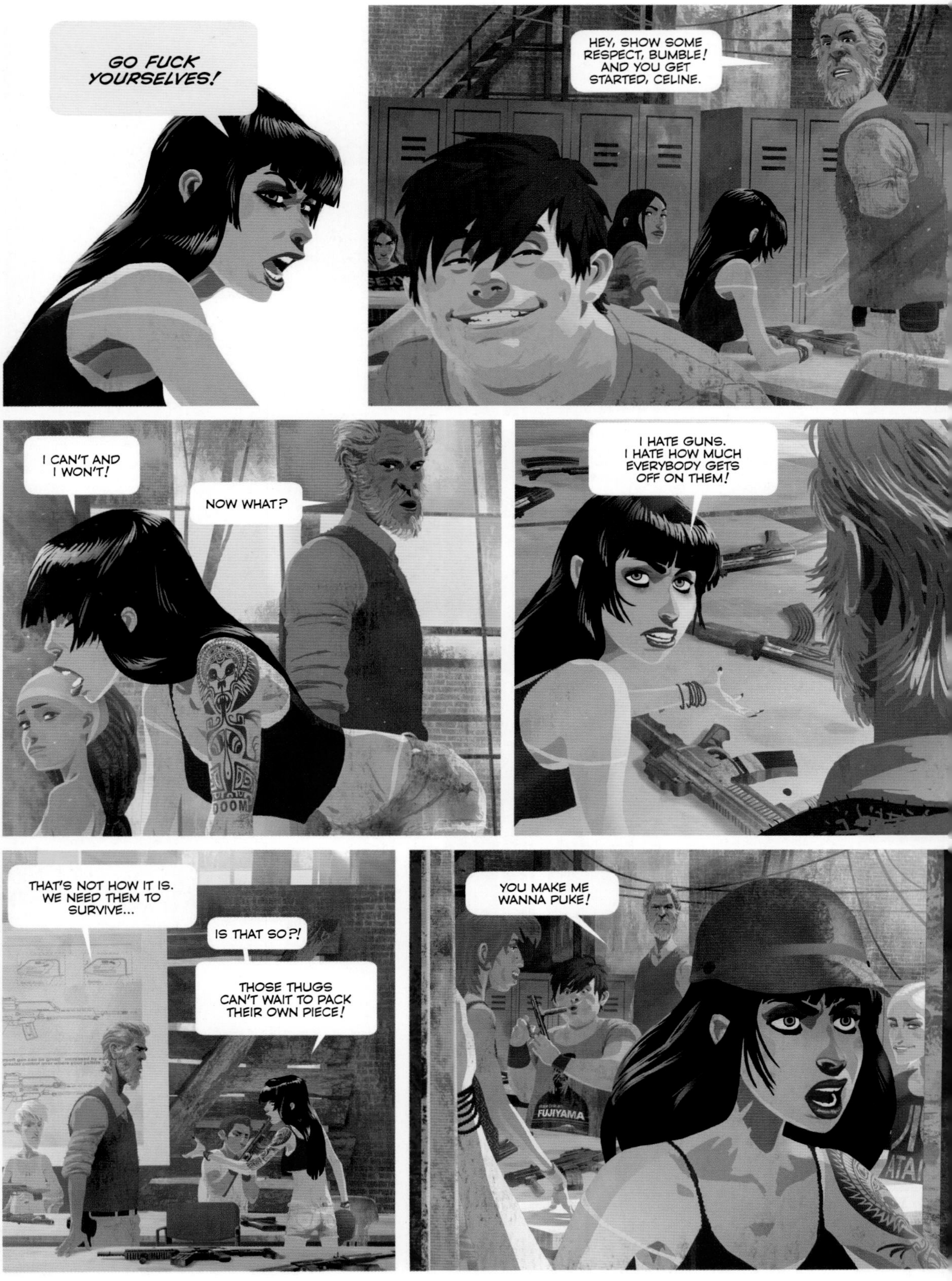
GO FUCK YOURSELVES!
HEY, SHOW SOME RESPECT, BUMBLE! AND YOU GET STARTED, CELINE.
I CAN'T AND I WON'T!
NOW WHAT?
I HATE GUNS. I HATE HOW MUCH EVERYBODY GETS OFF ON THEM!
THAT'S NOT HOW IT IS. WE NEED THEM TO SURVIVE...
IS THAT SO?!
THOSE THUGS CAN'T WAIT TO PACK THEIR OWN PIECE!
YOU MAKE ME WANNA PUKE!

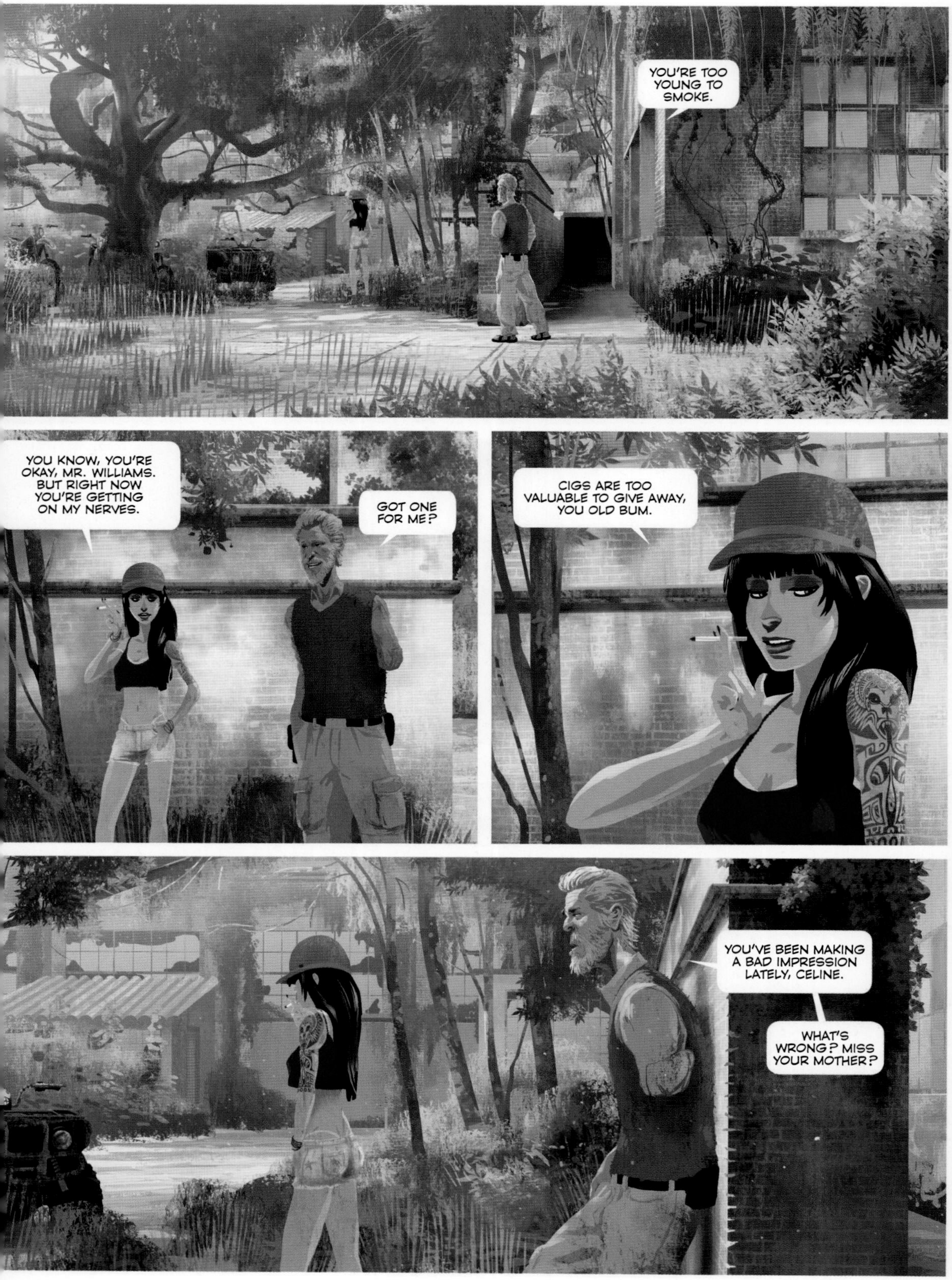
YOU'RE TOO YOUNG TO SMOKE.
YOU KNOW, YOU'RE OKAY, MR. WILLIAMS. BUT RIGHT NOW YOU'RE GETTING ON MY NERVES.
GOT ONE FOR ME?
CIGS ARE TOO VALUABLE TO GIVE AWAY, YOU OLD BUM.
YOU'VE BEEN MAKING A BAD IMPRESSION LATELY, CELINE.
WHAT'S WRONG? MISS YOUR MOTHER?

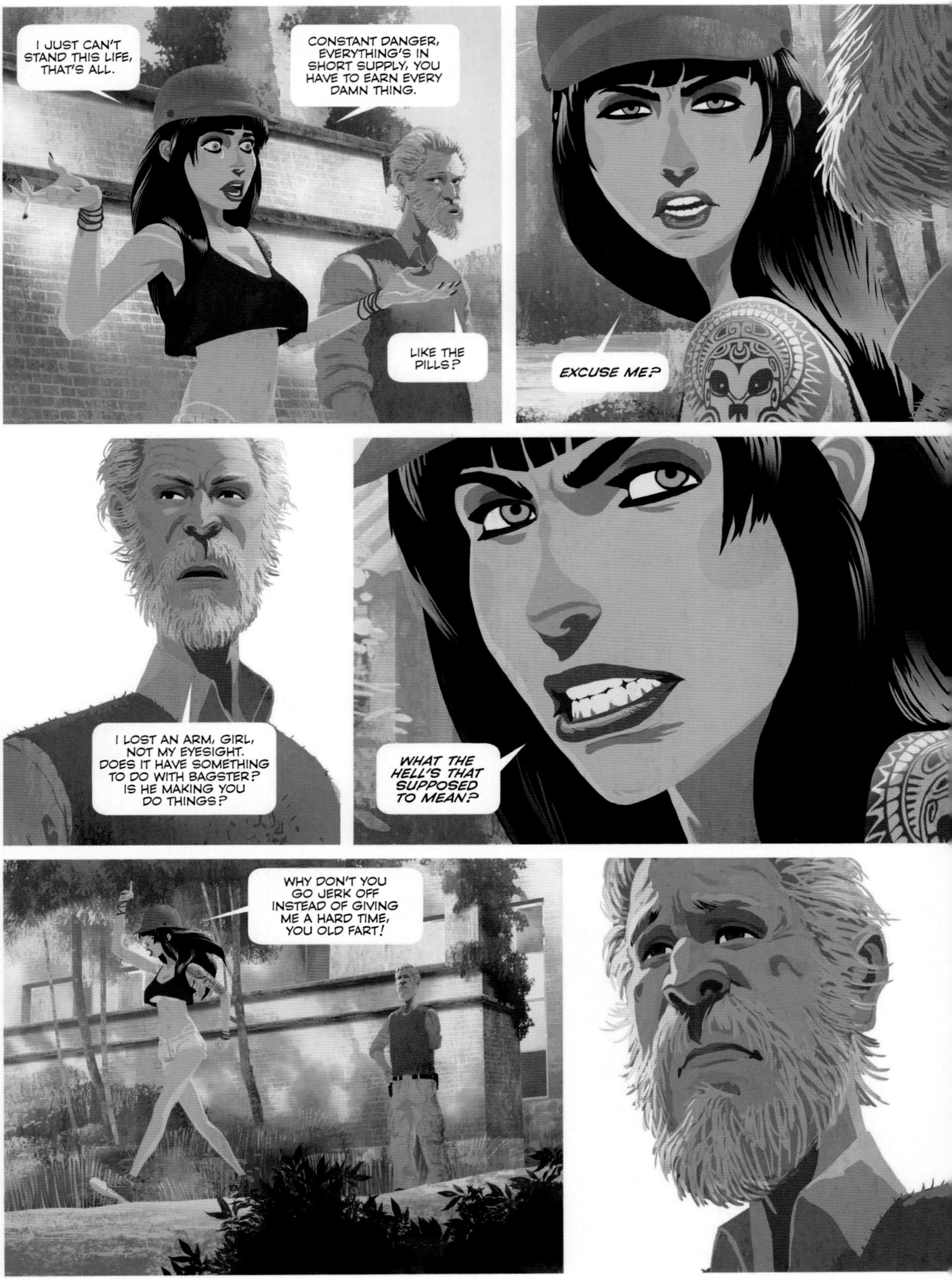
I JUST CAN'T STAND THIS LIFE, THAT'S ALL.
CONSTANT DANGER, EVERYTHING'S IN SHORT SUPPLY, YOU HAVE TO EARN EVERY DAMN THING.
LIKE THE PILLS?
EXCUSE ME?
I LOST AN ARM, GIRL, NOT MY EYESIGHT. DOES IT HAVE SOMETHING TO DO WITH BAGSTER? IS HE MAKING YOU DO THINGS?
WHAT THE HELL'S THAT SUPPOSED TO MEAN?
WHY DON'T YOU GO JERK OFF INSTEAD OF GIVING ME A HARD TIME, YOU OLD FART!

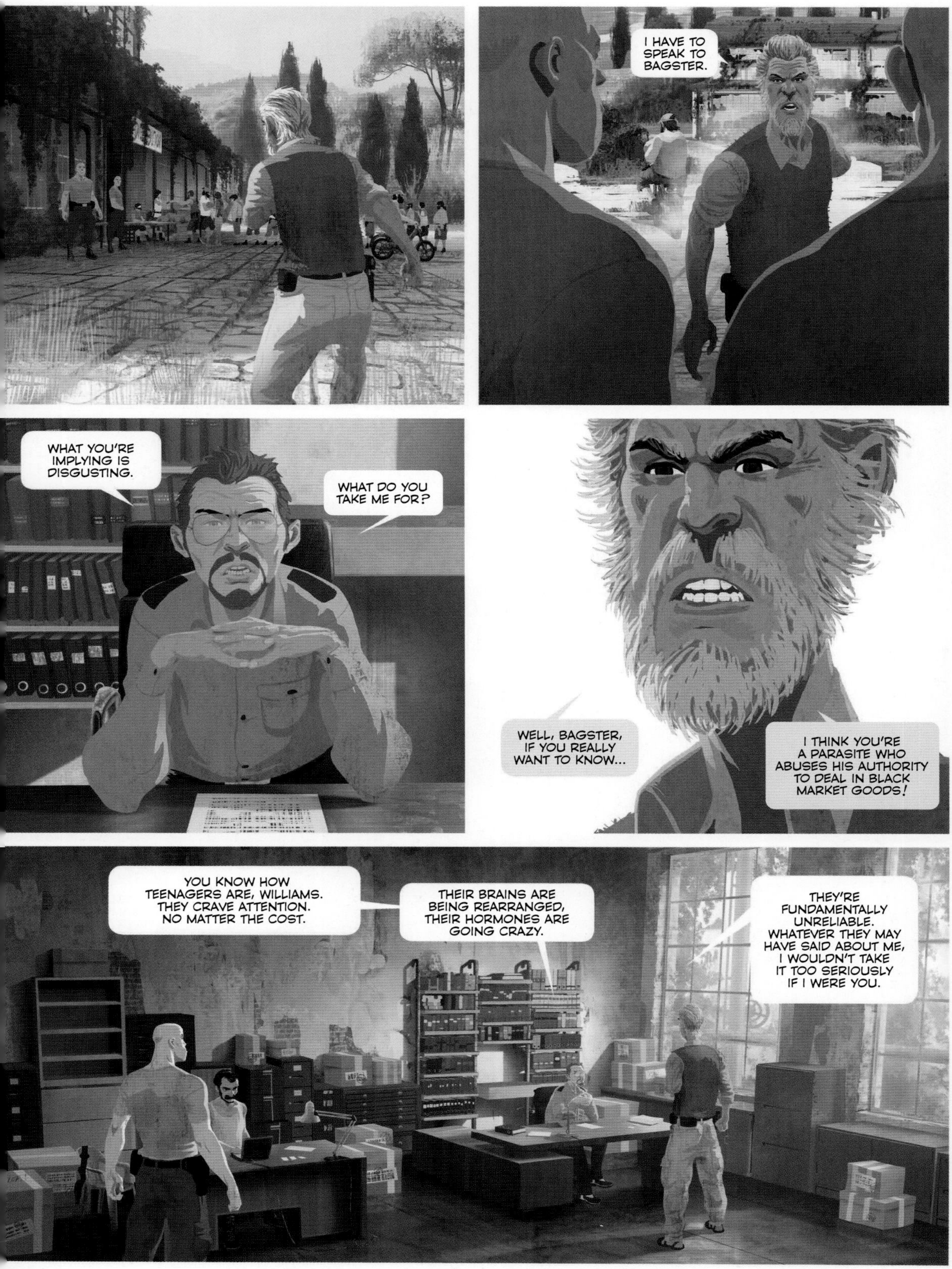
I HAVE TO SPEAK TO BAGSTER.
WHAT YOU'RE IMPLYING IS DISGUSTING.
WHAT DO YOU TAKE ME FOR?
WELL, BAGSTER, IF YOU REALLY WANT TO KNOW...
I THINK YOU'RE A PARASITE WHO ABUSES HIS AUTHORITY TO DEAL IN BLACK MARKET GOODS!
YOU KNOW HOW TEENAGERS ARE, WILLIAMS. THEY CRAVE ATTENTION. NO MATTER THE COST.
THEIR BRAINS ARE BEING REARRANGED, THEIR HORMONES ARE GOING CRAZY.
THEY'RE FUNDAMENTALLY UNRELIABLE. WHATEVER THEY MAY HAVE SAID ABOUT ME, I WOULDN'T TAKE IT TOO SERIOUSLY IF I WERE YOU.

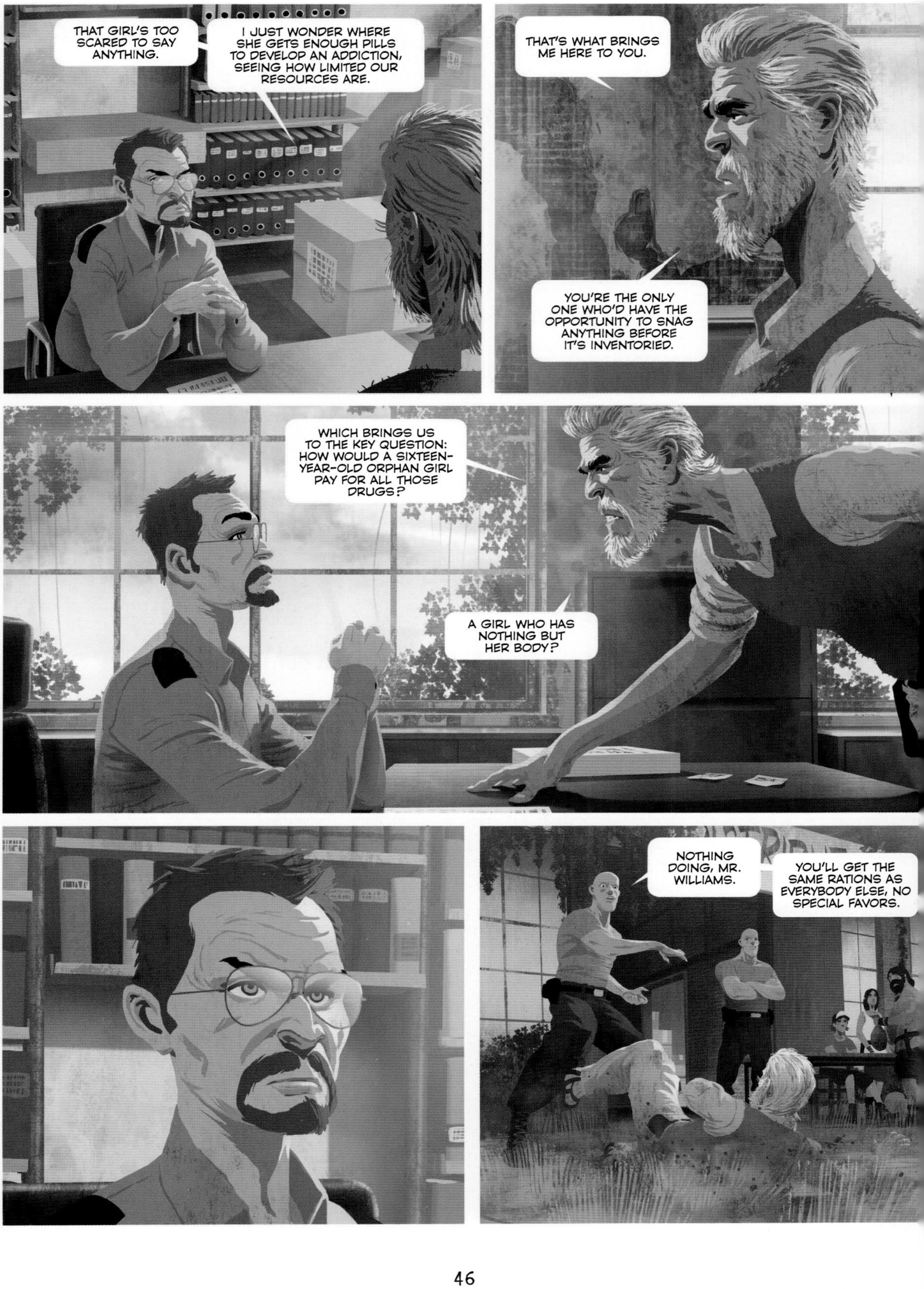
THAT GIRL'S TOO SCARED TO SAY ANYTHING.
I JUST WONDER WHERE SHE GETS ENOUGH PILLS TO DEVELOP AN ADDICTION, SEEING HOW LIMITED OUR RESOURCES ARE.
THAT'S WHAT BRINGS ME HERE TO YOU.
YOU'RE THE ONLY ONE WHO'D HAVE THE OPPORTUNITY TO SNAG ANYTHING BEFORE IT'S INVENTORIED.
WHICH BRINGS US TO THE KEY QUESTION: HOW WOULD A SIXTEEN-YEAR-OLD ORPHAN GIRL PAY FOR ALL THOSE DRUGS?
A GIRL WHO HAS NOTHING BUT HER BODY?
NOTHING DOING, MR. WILLIAMS.
YOU'LL GET THE SAME RATIONS AS EVERYBODY ELSE, NO SPECIAL FAVORS.

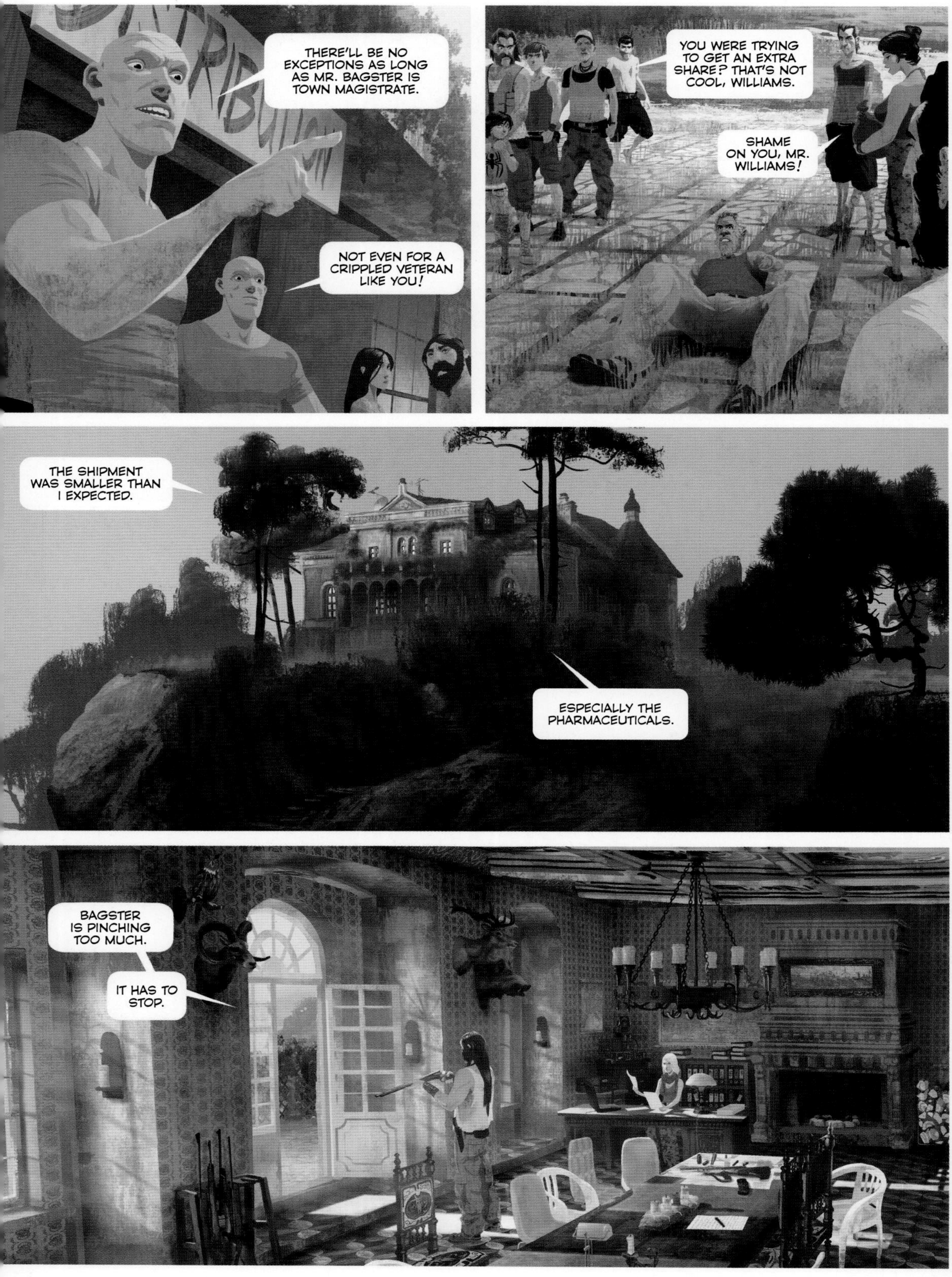
THERE'LL BE NO EXCEPTIONS AS LONG AS MR. BAGSTER IS TOWN MAGISTRATE.
NOT EVEN FOR A CRIPPLED VETERAN LIKE YOU!
YOU WERE TRYING TO GET AN EXTRA SHARE? THAT'S NOT COOL, WILLIAMS.
SHAME ON YOU, MR. WILLIAMS!
THE SHIPMENT WAS SMALLER THAN I EXPECTED.
ESPECIALLY THE PHARMACEUTICALS.
BAGSTER IS PINCHING TOO MUCH.
IT HAS TO STOP.

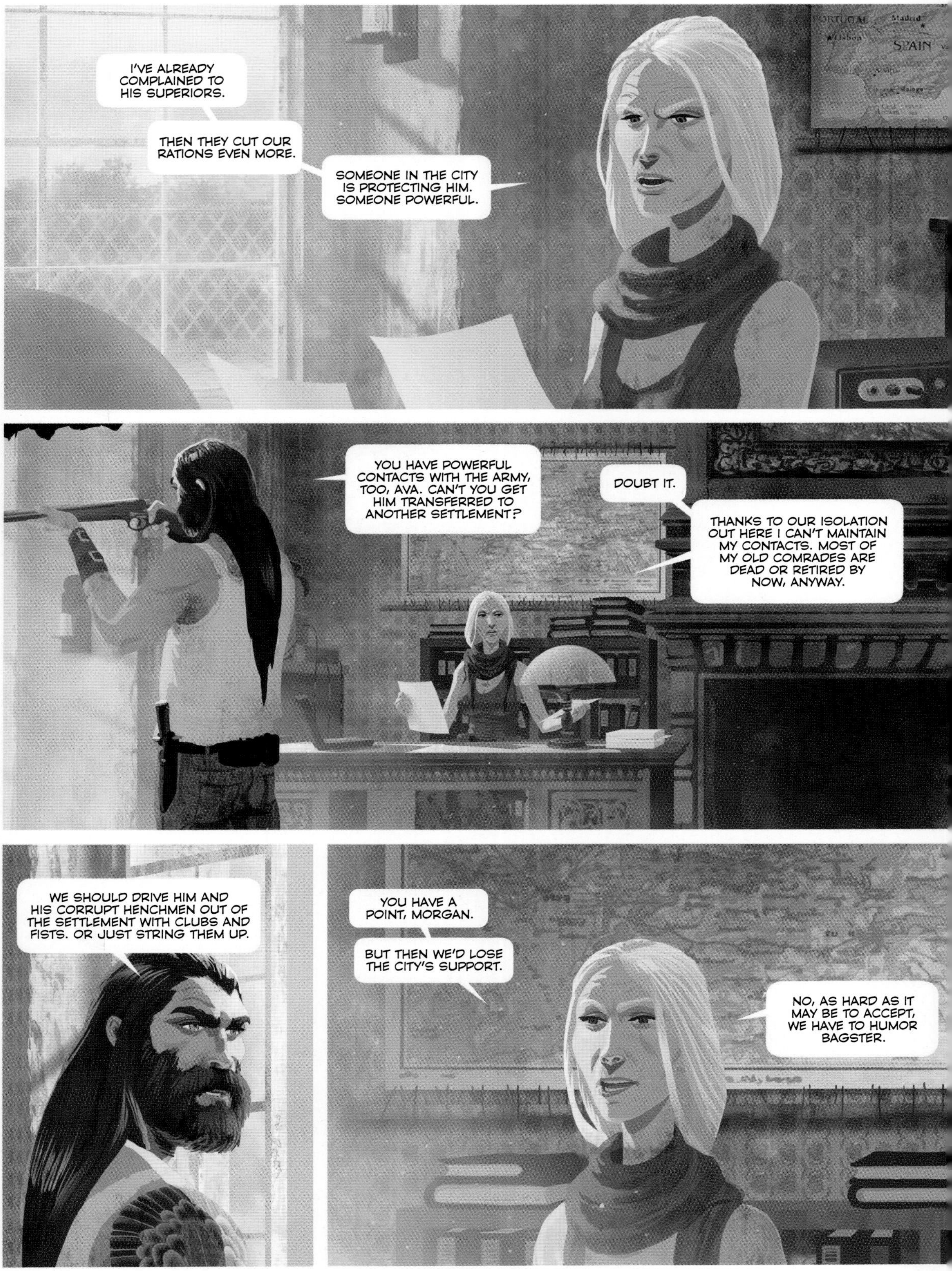
PORTUGAL
Madrid
Lisbon
SPAIN
I'VE ALREADY COMPLAINED TO HIS SUPERIORS.
THEN THEY CUT OUR RATIONS EVEN MORE.
SOMEONE IN THE CITY IS PROTECTING HIM. SOMEONE POWERFUL.
YOU HAVE POWERFUL CONTACTS WITH THE ARMY, TOO, AVA. CAN'T YOU GET HIM TRANSFERRED TO ANOTHER SETTLEMENT?
DOUBT IT.
THANKS TO OUR ISOLATION OUT HERE I CAN'T MAINTAIN MY CONTACTS. MOST OF MY OLD COMRADES ARE DEAD OR RETIRED BY NOW, ANYWAY.
WE SHOULD DRIVE HIM AND HIS CORRUPT HENCHMEN OUT OF THE SETTLEMENT WITH CLUBS AND FISTS. OR JUST STRING THEM UP.
YOU HAVE A POINT, MORGAN.
BUT THEN WE'D LOSE THE CITY'S SUPPORT.
NO, AS HARD AS IT MAY BE TO ACCEPT, WE HAVE TO HUMOR BAGSTER.

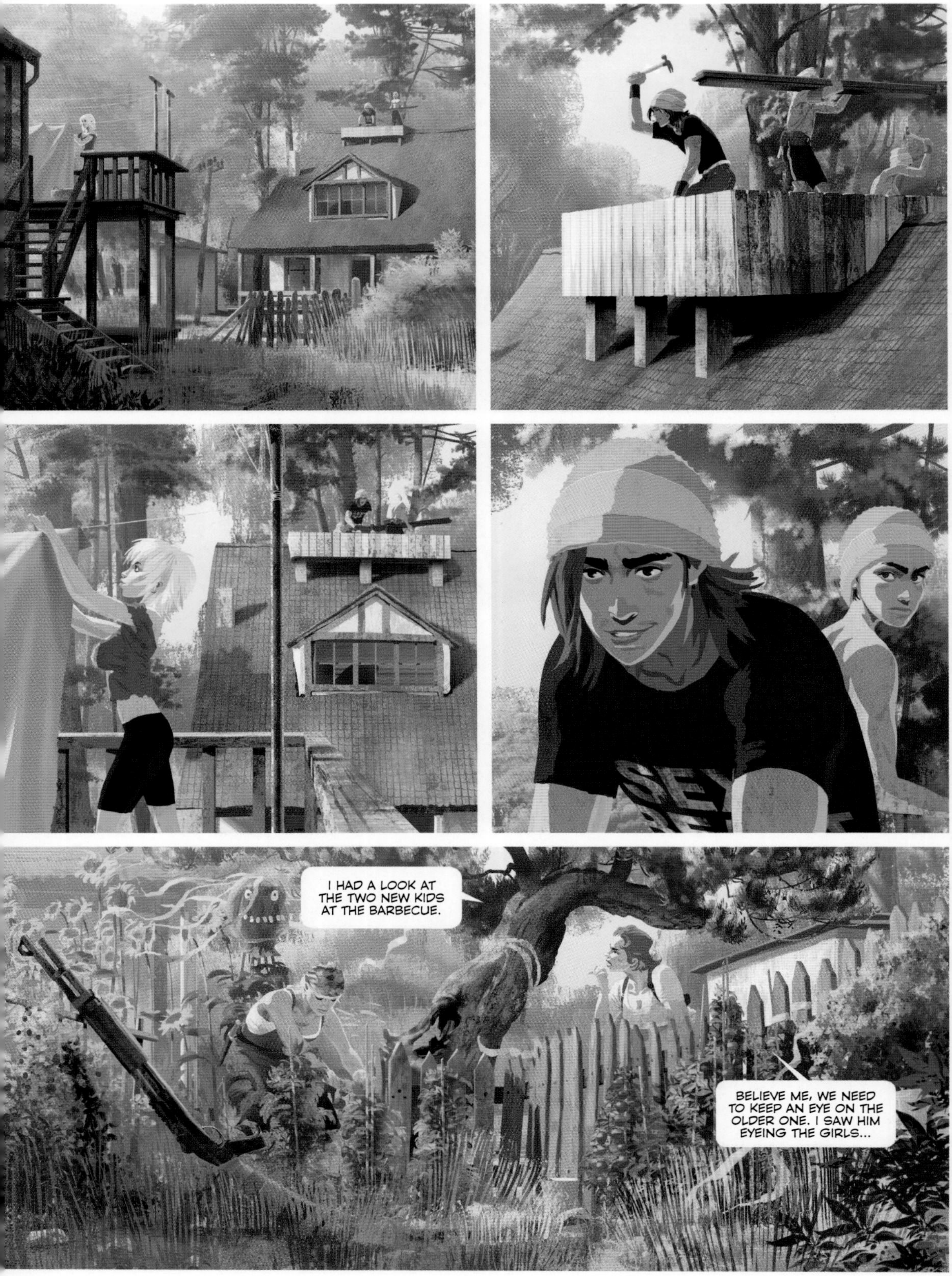
I HAD A LOOK AT THE TWO NEW KIDS AT THE BARBECUE.
BELIEVE ME, WE NEED TO KEEP AN EYE ON THE OLDER ONE. I SAW HIM EYEING THE GIRLS...

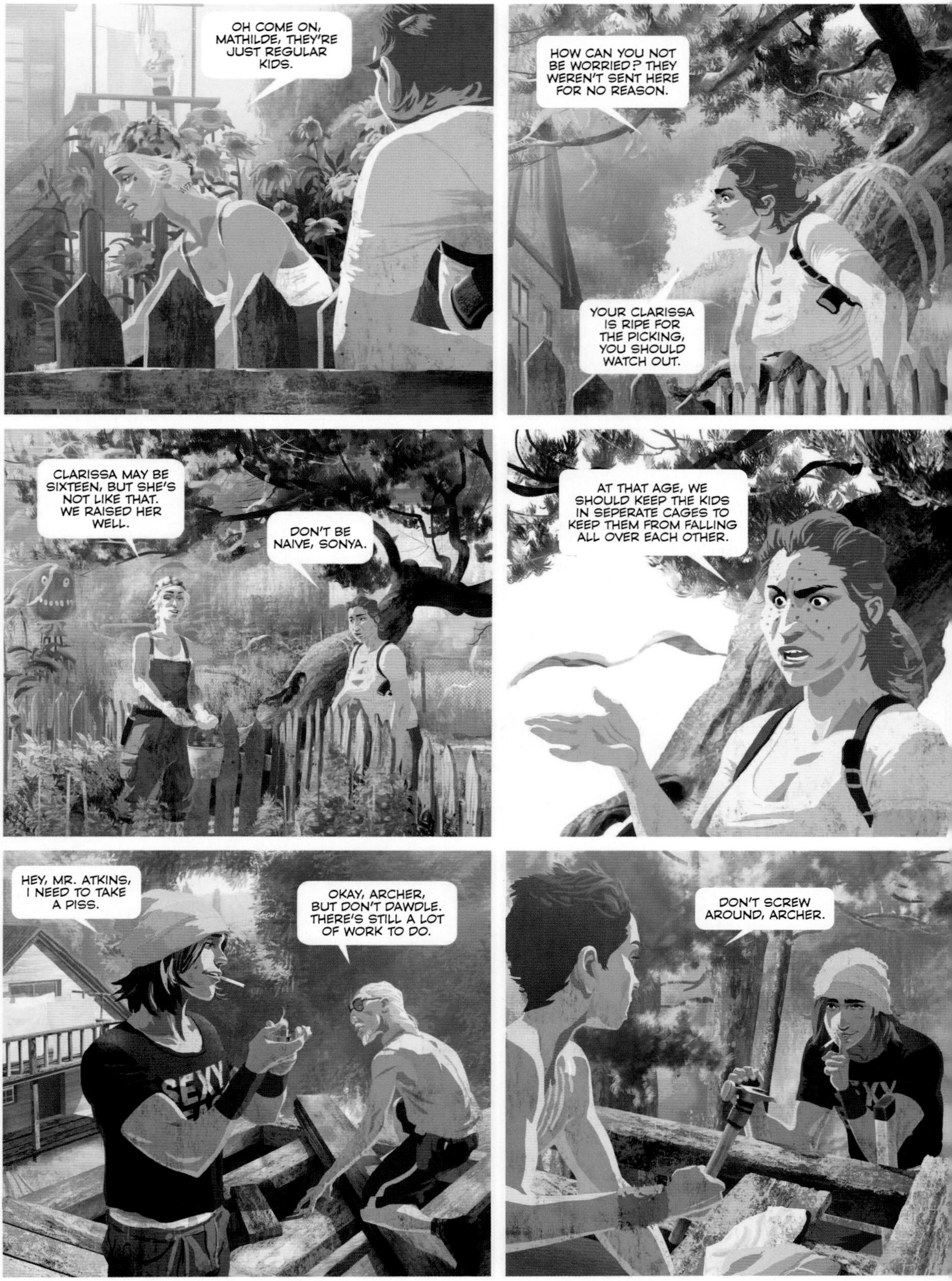
OH COME ON, MATHILDE, THEY'RE JUST REGULAR KIDS.
HOW CAN YOU NOT BE WORRIED? THEY WEREN'T SENT HERE FOR NO REASON.
YOUR CLARISSA IS RIPE FOR THE PICKING, YOU SHOULD WATCH OUT.
CLARISSA MAY BE SIXTEEN, BUT SHE'S NOT LIKE THAT. WE RAISED HER WELL.
DON'T BE NAIVE, SONYA.
AT THAT AGE, WE SHOULD KEEP THE KIDS IN SEPERATE CAGES TO KEEP THEM FROM FALLING ALL OVER EACH OTHER.
HEY, MR. ATKINS, I NEED TO TAKE A PISS.
OKAY, ARCHER, BUT DON'T DAWDLE. THERE'S STILL A LOT OF WORK TO DO.
DON'T SCREW AROUND, ARCHER.

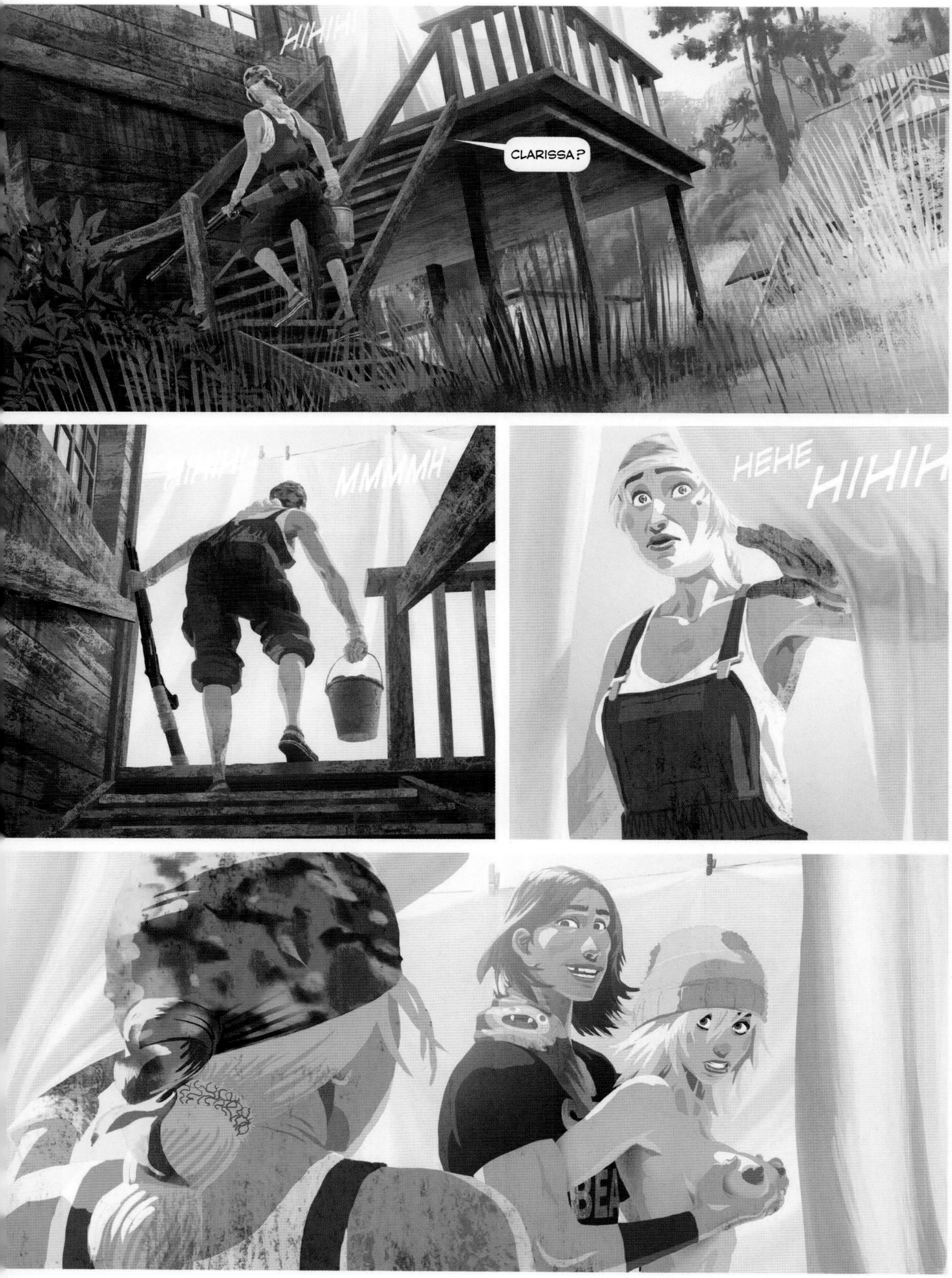
HIHIHI
CLARISSA?
HIHIHI
MMMMH
HEHE
HIHIH

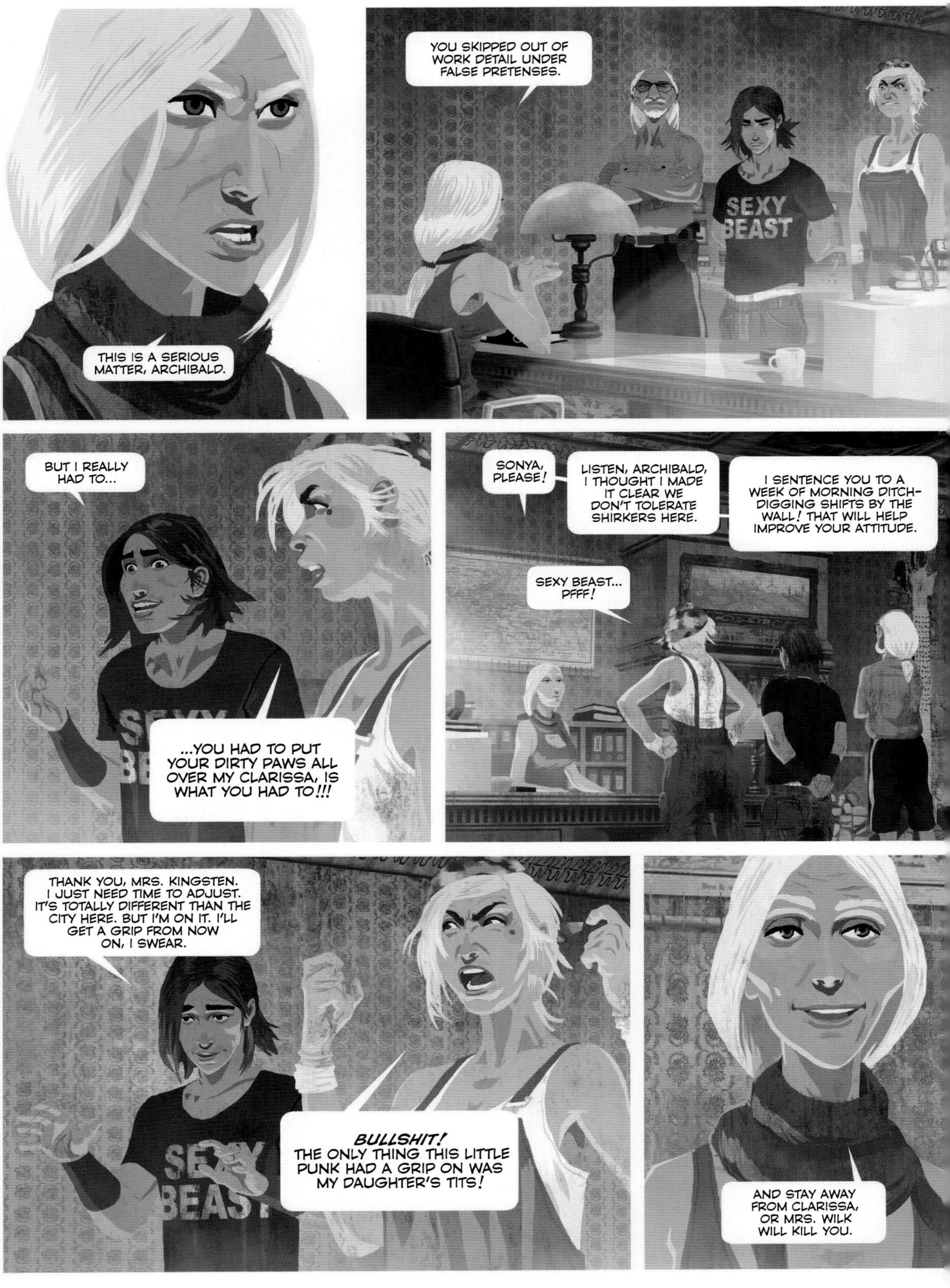

THIS IS A SERIOUS MATTER, ARCHIBALD.
YOU SKIPPED OUT OF WORK DETAIL UNDER FALSE PRETENSES.
SEXY BEAST
BUT I REALLY HAD TO...
...YOU HAD TO PUT YOUR DIRTY PAWS ALL OVER MY CLARISSA, IS WHAT YOU HAD TO!!!
SONYA, PLEASE!
LISTEN, ARCHIBALD, I THOUGHT I MADE IT CLEAR WE DON'T TOLERATE SHIRKERS HERE.
I SENTENCE YOU TO A WEEK OF MORNING DITCH-DIGGING SHIFTS BY THE WALL! THAT WILL HELP IMPROVE YOUR ATTITUDE.
SEXY BEAST... PFFF!
THANK YOU, MRS. KINGSTEN. I JUST NEED TIME TO ADJUST. IT'S TOTALLY DIFFERENT THAN THE CITY HERE. BUT I'M ON IT. I'LL GET A GRIP FROM NOW ON, I SWEAR.
BULLSHIT! THE ONLY THING THIS LITTLE PUNK HAD A GRIP ON WAS MY DAUGHTER'S TITS!
AND STAY AWAY FROM CLARISSA, OR MRS. WILK WILL KILL YOU.

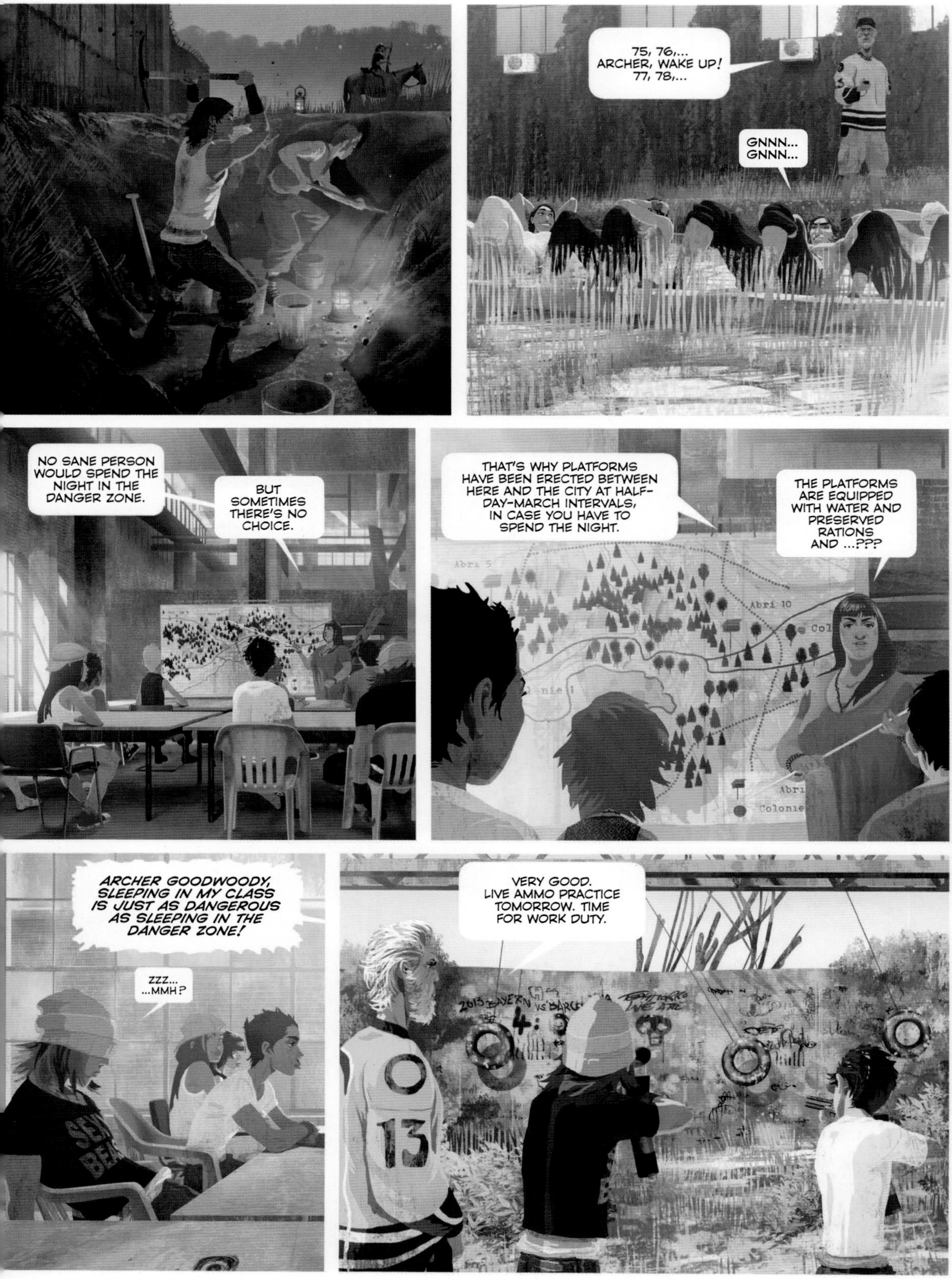
75, 76,...
ARCHER, WAKE UP!
77, 78,...
GNNN...
GNNN...
NO SANE PERSON WOULD SPEND THE NIGHT IN THE DANGER ZONE.
BUT SOMETIMES THERE'S NO CHOICE.
THAT'S WHY PLATFORMS HAVE BEEN ERECTED BETWEEN HERE AND THE CITY AT HALF-DAY-MARCH INTERVALS, IN CASE YOU HAVE TO SPEND THE NIGHT.
THE PLATFORMS ARE EQUIPPED WITH WATER AND PRESERVED RATIONS AND ...???
Abri 5
Abri 10
ARCHER GOODWOODY, SLEEPING IN MY CLASS IS JUST AS DANGEROUS AS SLEEPING IN THE DANGER ZONE!
ZZZ...
...MMH?
VERY GOOD. LIVE AMMO PRACTICE TOMORROW. TIME FOR WORK DUTY.
13

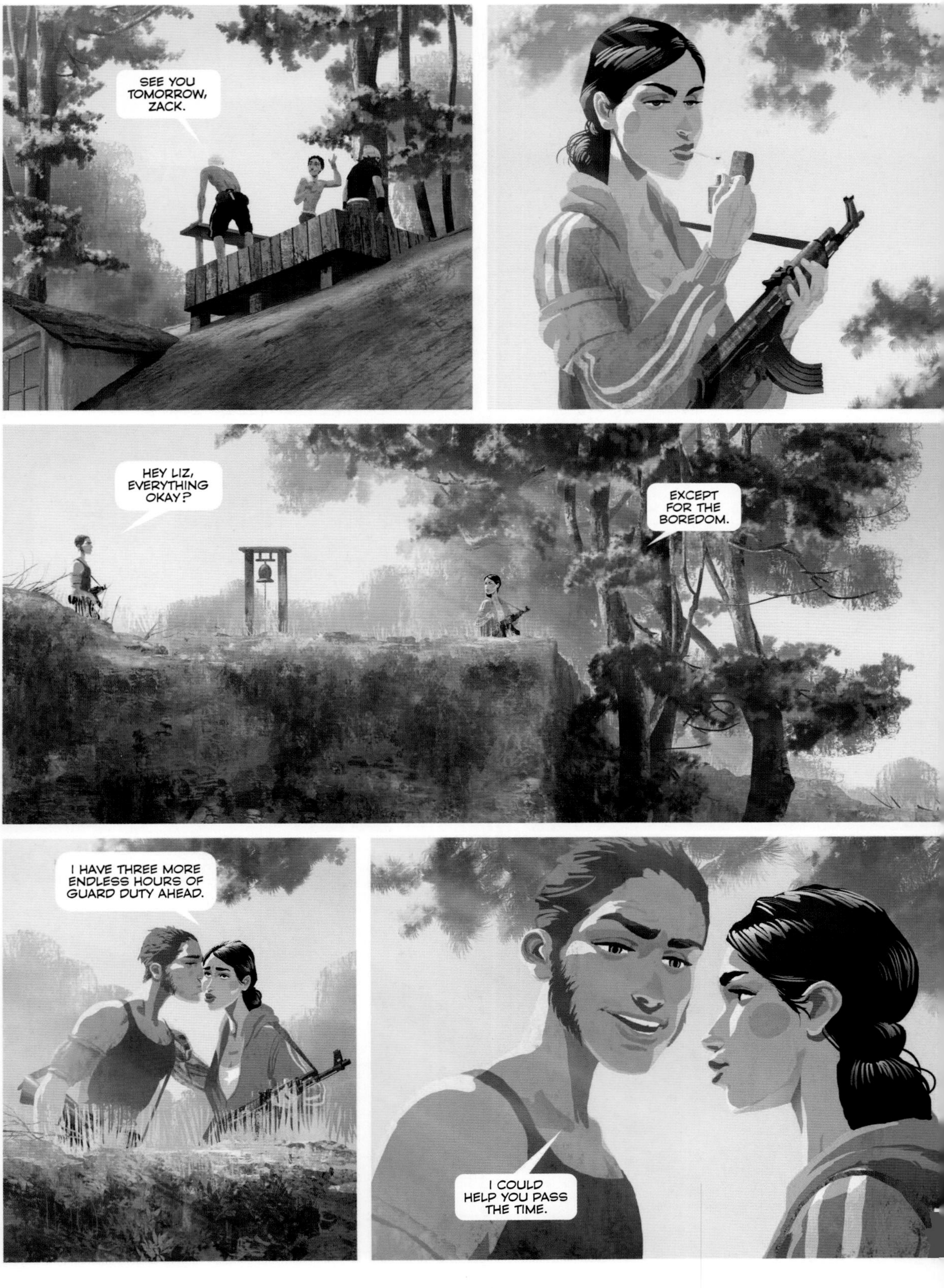
SEE YOU TOMORROW, ZACK.
HEY LIZ, EVERYTHING OKAY?
EXCEPT FOR THE BOREDOM.
I HAVE THREE MORE ENDLESS HOURS OF GUARD DUTY AHEAD.
I COULD HELP YOU PASS THE TIME.

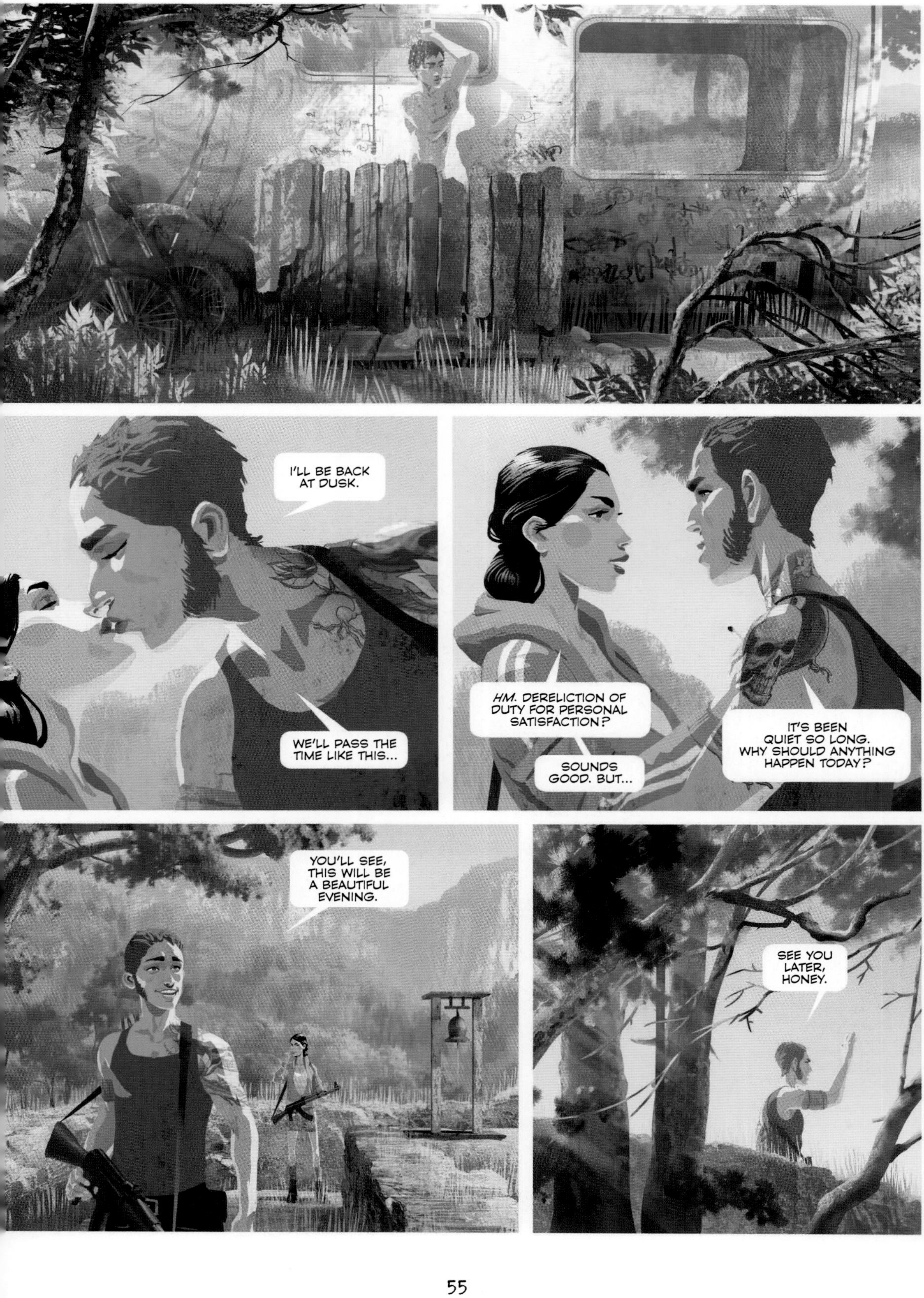

I'LL BE BACK AT DUSK.
WE'LL PASS THE TIME LIKE THIS...
HM. DERELICTION OF DUTY FOR PERSONAL SATISFACTION?
SOUNDS GOOD. BUT...
IT'S BEEN QUIET SO LONG. WHY SHOULD ANYTHING HAPPEN TODAY?
YOU'LL SEE, THIS WILL BE A BEAUTIFUL EVENING.
SEE YOU LATER, HONEY.

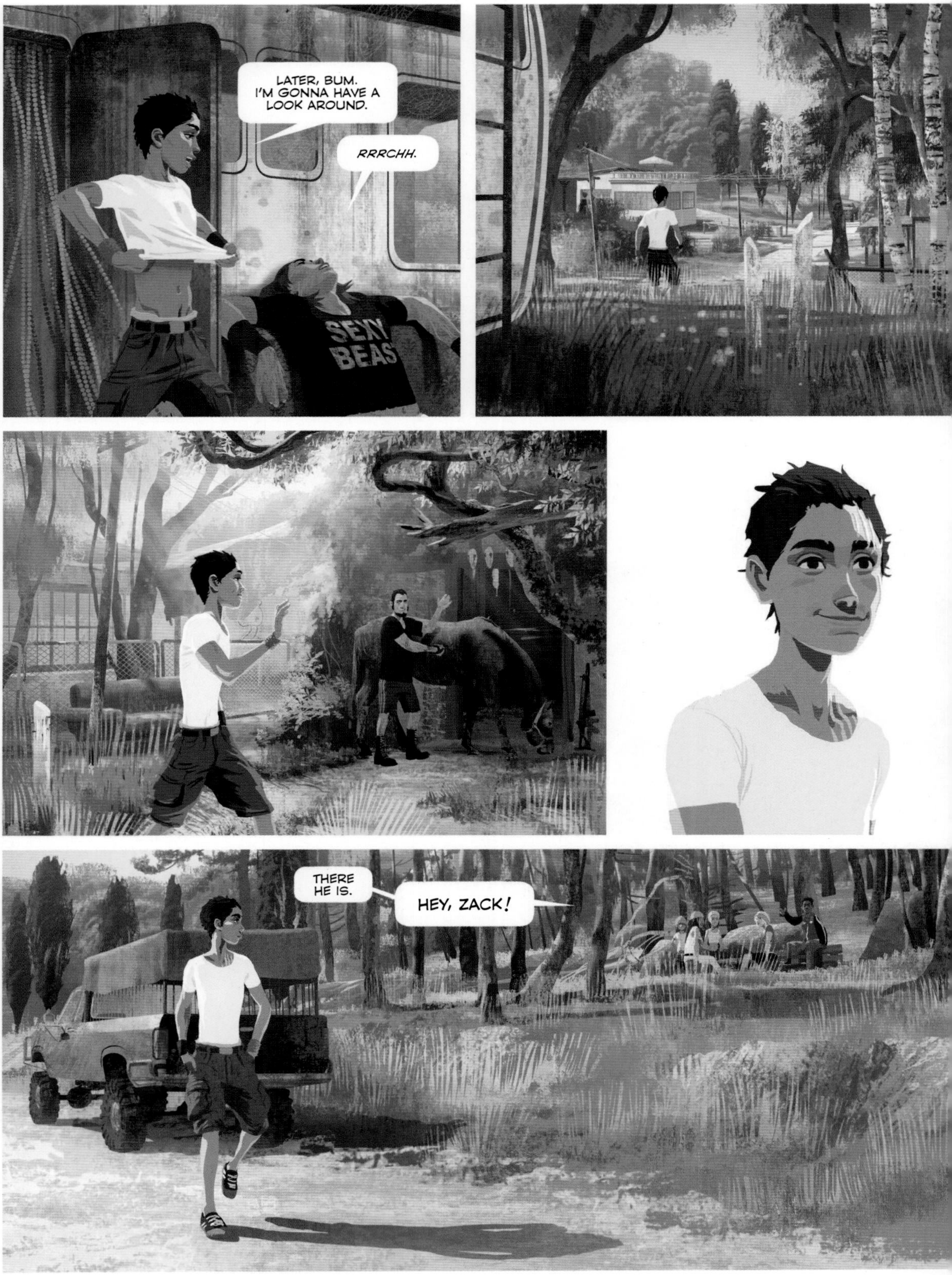
LATER, BUM.
I'M GONNA HAVE A
LOOK AROUND.
RRRCHH.
SEXY
BEAS
THERE
HE IS.
HEY, ZACK!

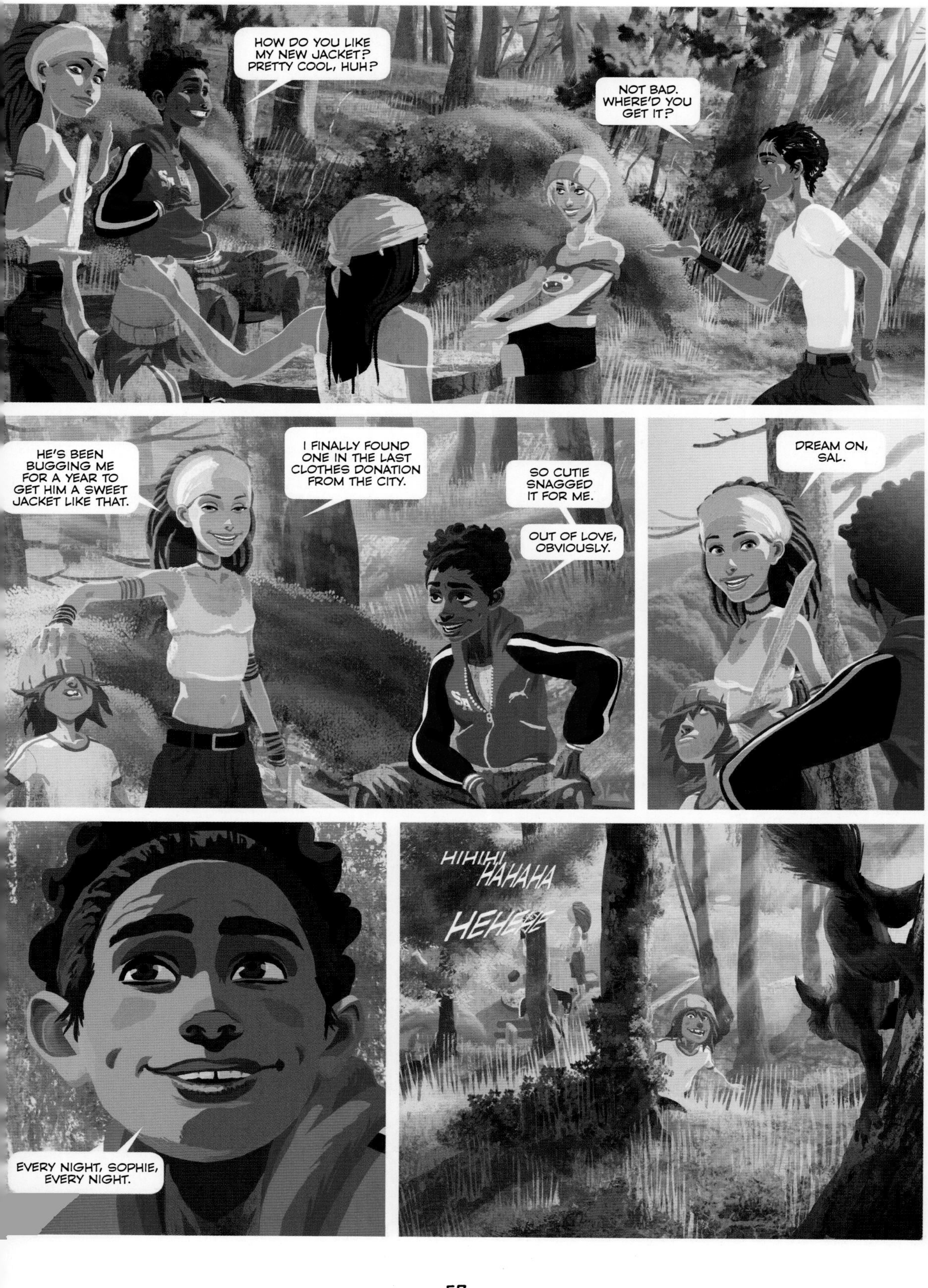
HOW DO YOU LIKE MY NEW JACKET? PRETTY COOL, HUH?
NOT BAD. WHERE'D YOU GET IT?
HE'S BEEN BUGGING ME FOR A YEAR TO GET HIM A SWEET JACKET LIKE THAT.
I FINALLY FOUND ONE IN THE LAST CLOTHES DONATION FROM THE CITY.
SO CUTIE SNAGGED IT FOR ME.
OUT OF LOVE, OBVIOUSLY.
DREAM ON, SAL.
EVERY NIGHT, SOPHIE, EVERY NIGHT.
HIHIHI
HAHAHA
HEHEHE

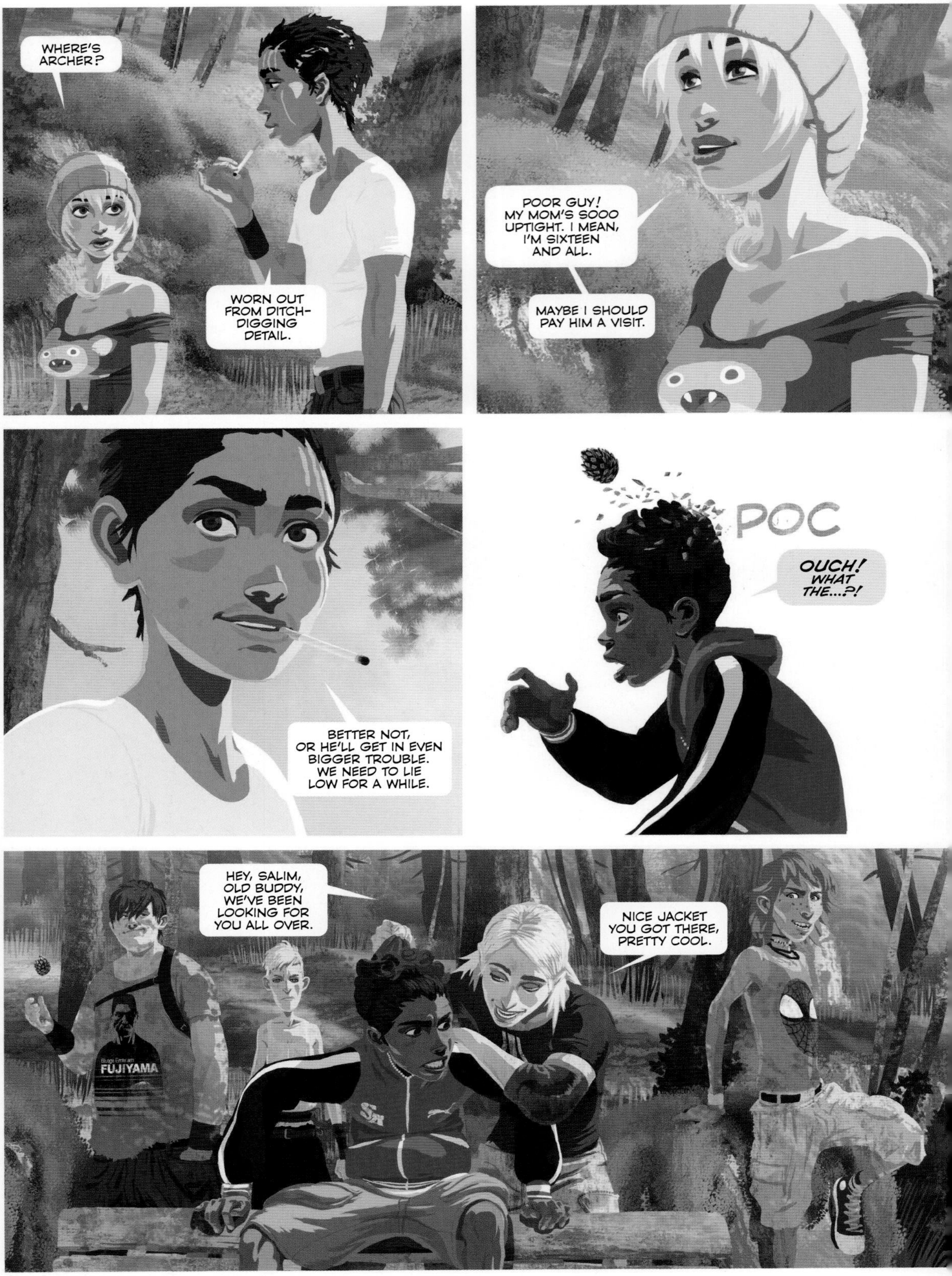
WHERE'S ARCHER?
WORN OUT FROM DITCH-DIGGING DETAIL.
POOR GUY! MY MOM'S SOOO UPTIGHT. I MEAN, I'M SIXTEEN AND ALL.
MAYBE I SHOULD PAY HIM A VISIT.
BETTER NOT, OR HE'LL GET IN EVEN BIGGER TROUBLE. WE NEED TO LIE LOW FOR A WHILE.
POC
OUCH! WHAT THE...?!
HEY, SALIM, OLD BUDDY, WE'VE BEEN LOOKING FOR YOU ALL OVER.
NICE JACKET YOU GOT THERE, PRETTY COOL.
FUJIYAMA

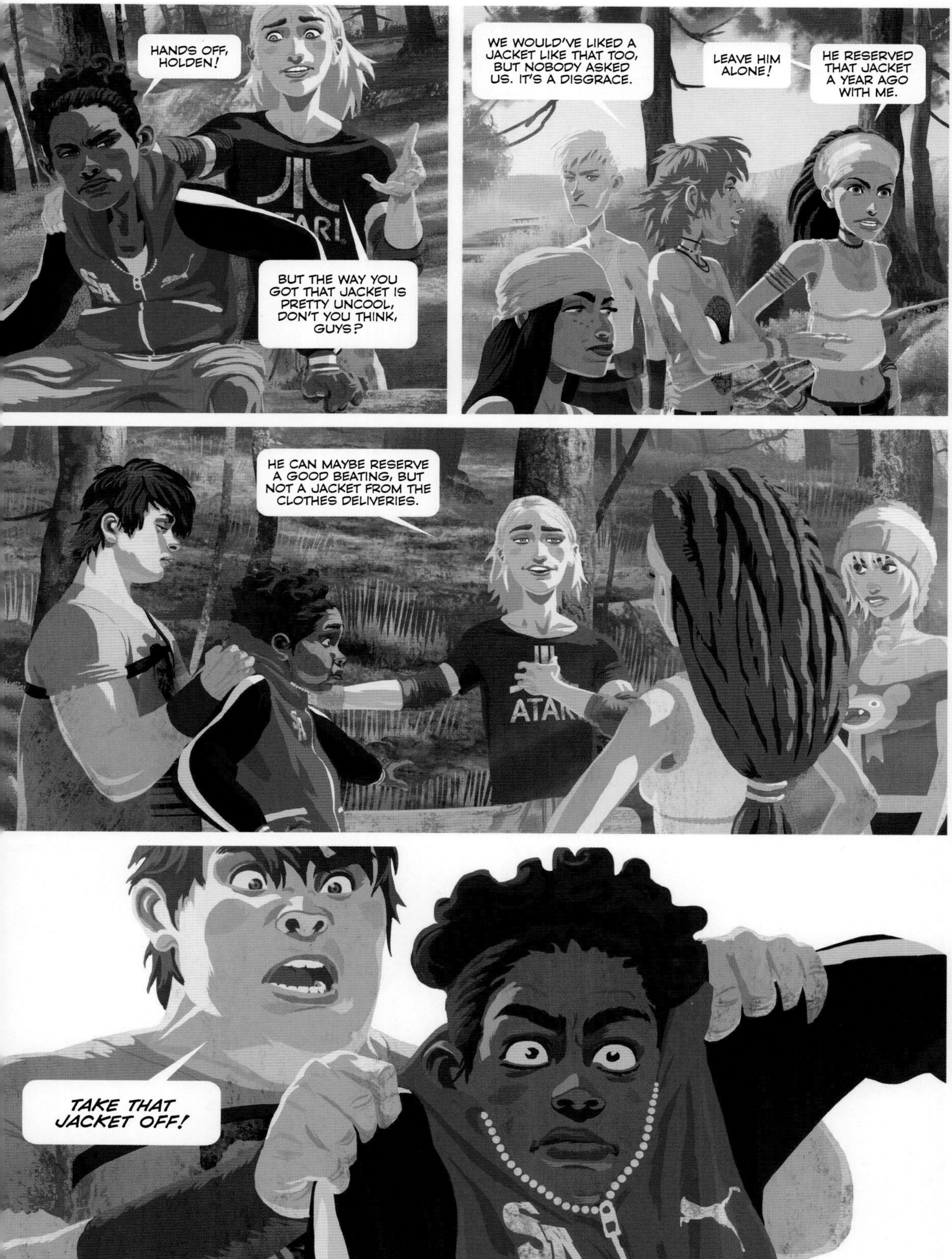
HANDS OFF, HOLDEN!
BUT THE WAY YOU GOT THAT JACKET IS PRETTY UNCOOL, DON'T YOU THINK, GUYS?
WE WOULD'VE LIKED A JACKET LIKE THAT TOO, BUT NOBODY ASKED US. IT'S A DISGRACE.
LEAVE HIM ALONE!
HE RESERVED THAT JACKET A YEAR AGO WITH ME.
HE CAN MAYBE RESERVE A GOOD BEATING, BUT NOT A JACKET FROM THE CLOTHES DELIVERIES.
TAKE THAT JACKET OFF!

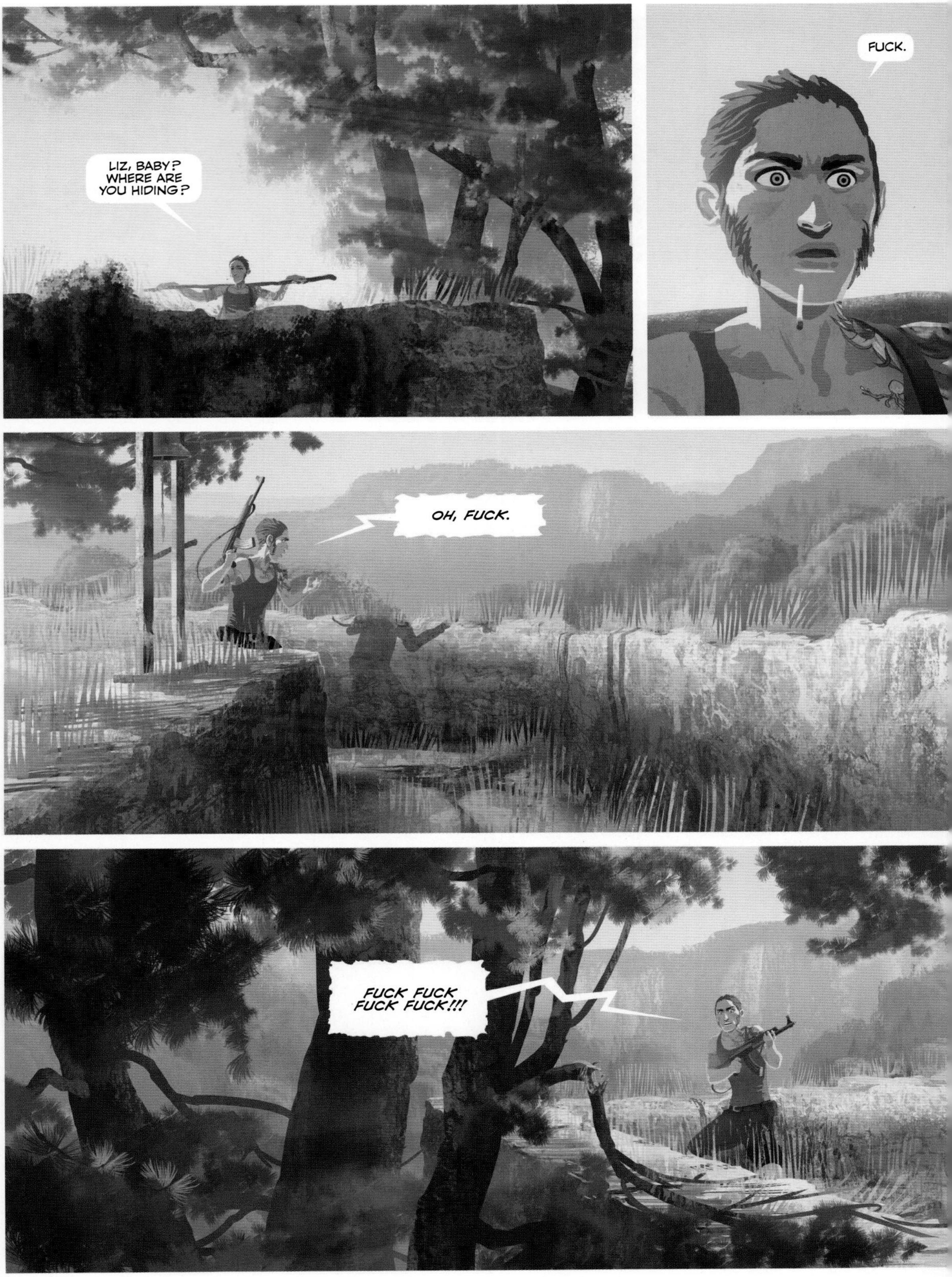
LIZ, BABY? WHERE ARE YOU HIDING?
FUCK.
OH, FUCK.
FUCK FUCK FUCK FUCK!!!

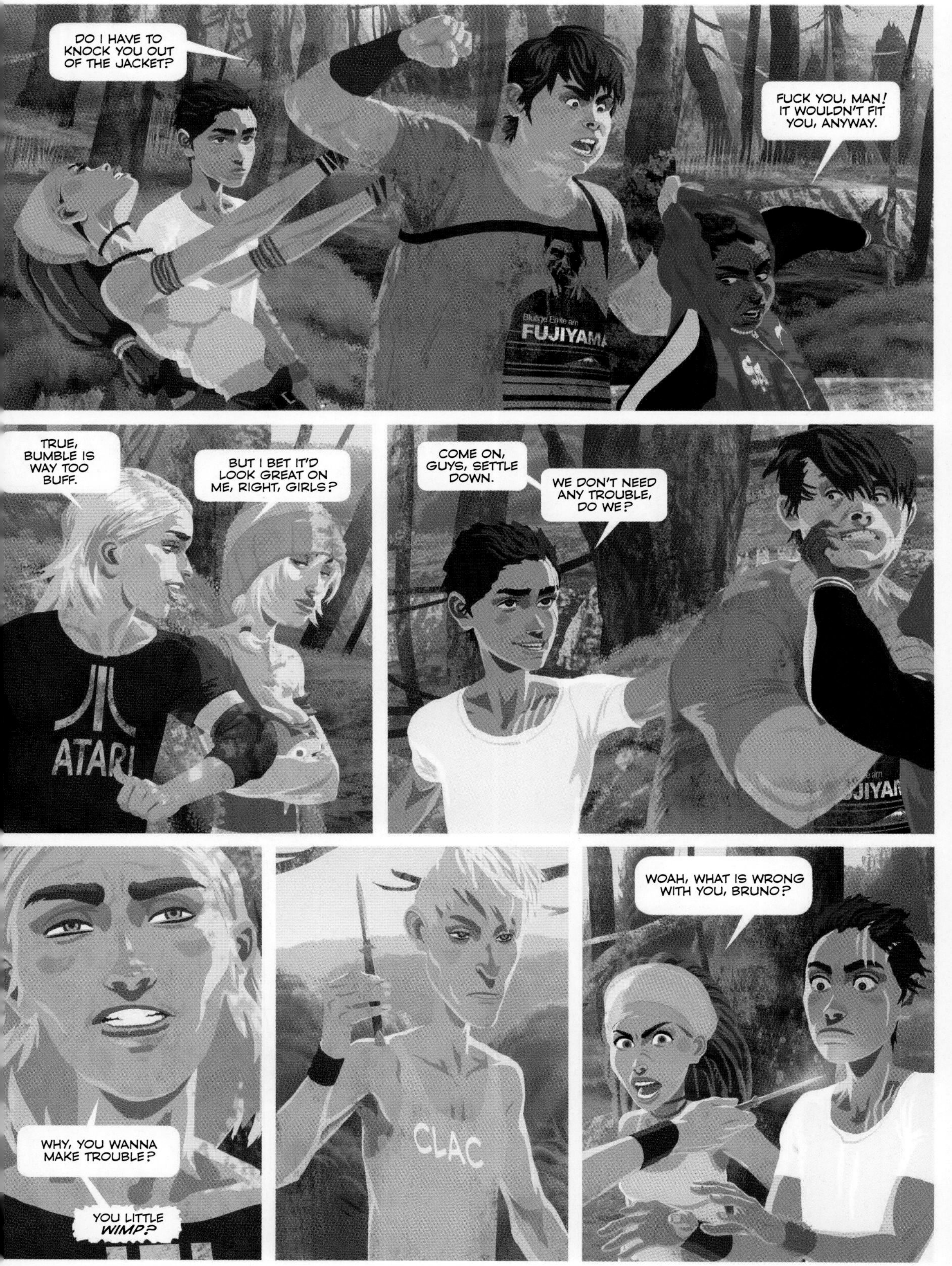

DO I HAVE TO KNOCK YOU OUT OF THE JACKET?
FUCK YOU, MAN! IT WOULDN'T FIT YOU, ANYWAY.
FUJIYAMA
TRUE, BUMBLE IS WAY TOO BUFF.
BUT I BET IT'D LOOK GREAT ON ME, RIGHT, GIRLS?
ATARI
COME ON, GUYS, SETTLE DOWN.
WE DON'T NEED ANY TROUBLE, DO WE?
WHY, YOU WANNA MAKE TROUBLE?
YOU LITTLE *WIMP?*
CLAC
WOAH, WHAT IS WRONG WITH YOU, BRUNO?

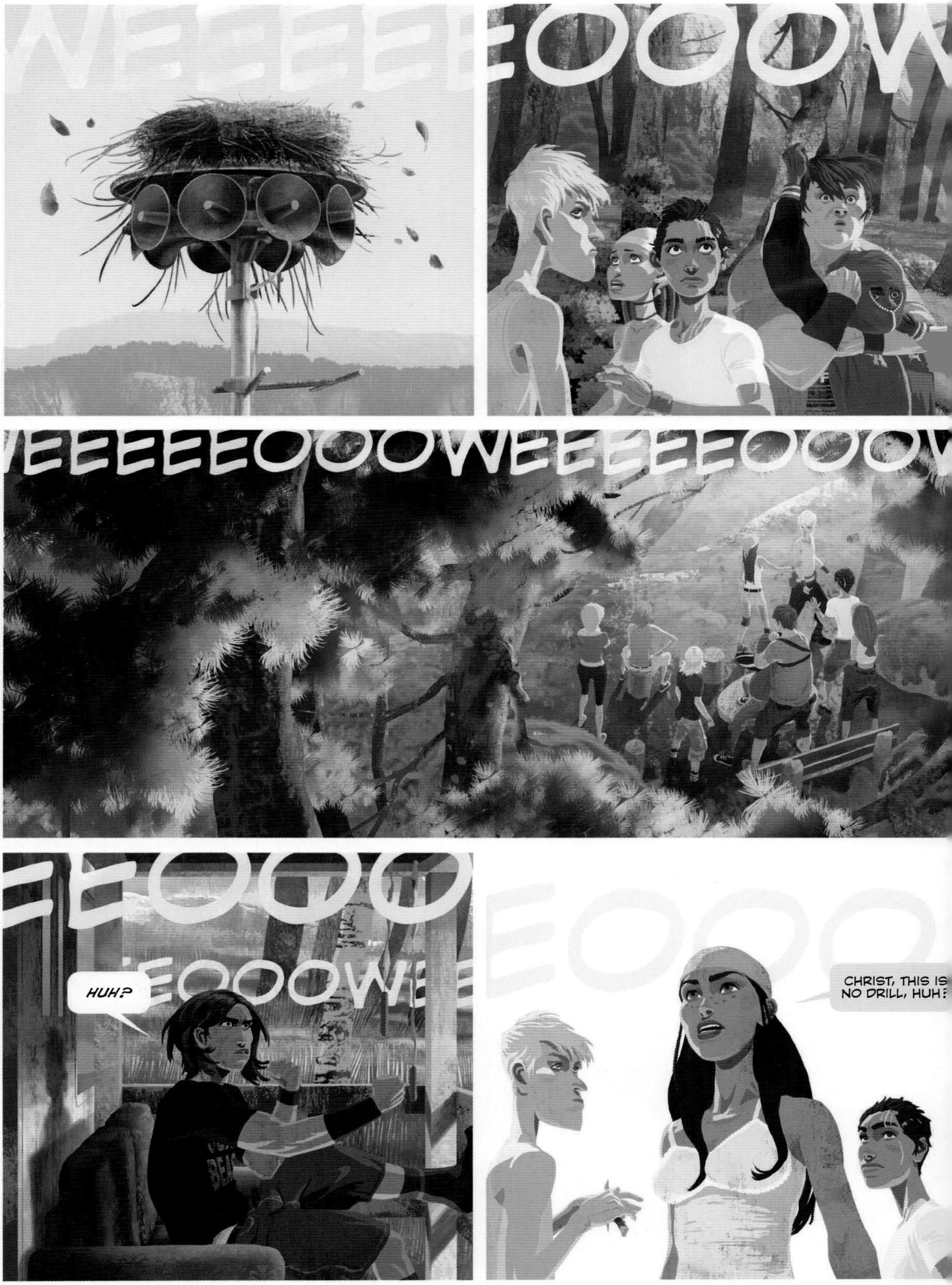
WEEEEEOOOW
WEEEEEOOOWEEEEEOOOW
EEOOO
EOOOWE
HUH?
EOOO
CHRIST, THIS IS NO DRILL, HUH?

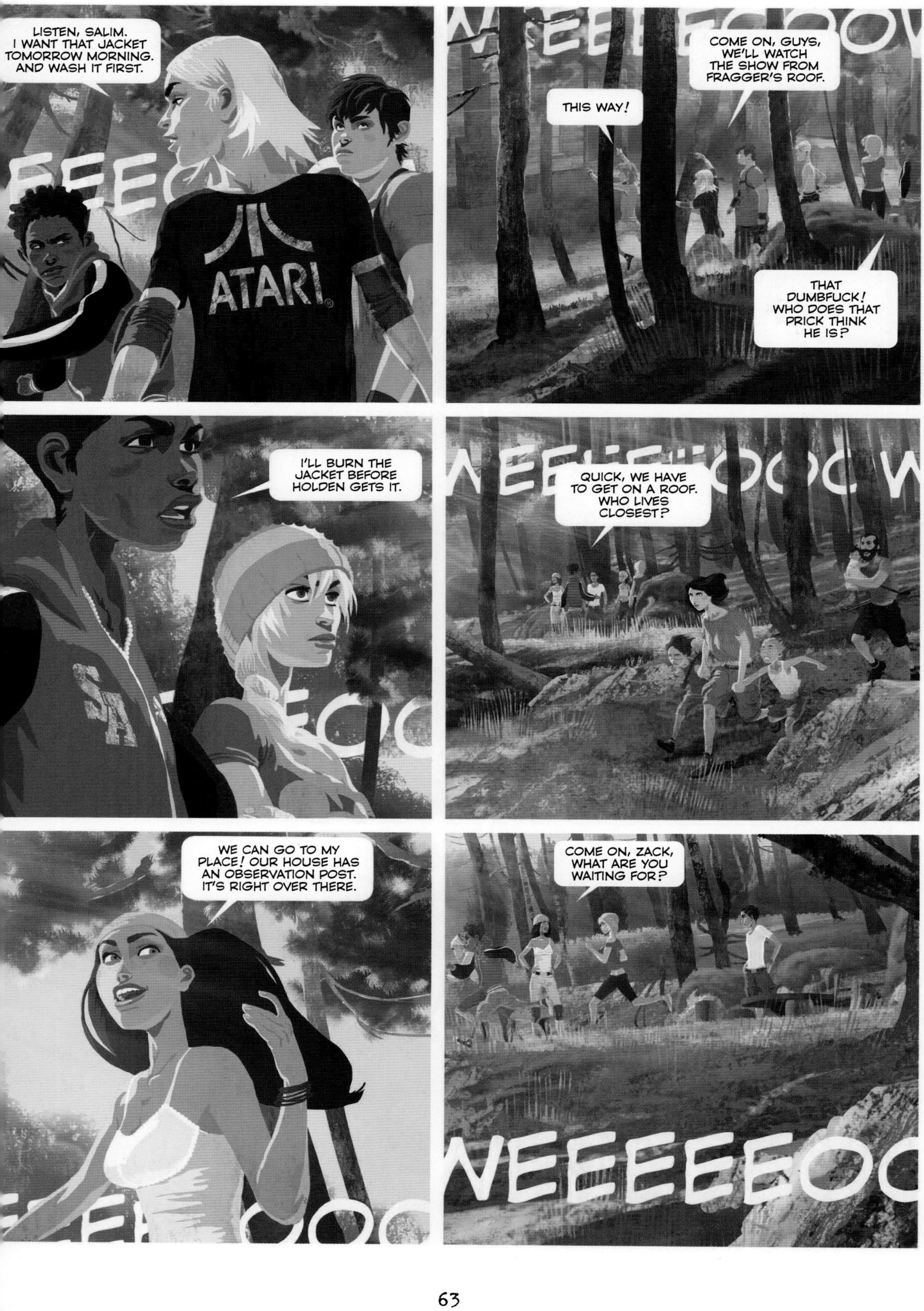
LISTEN, SALIM. I WANT THAT JACKET TOMORROW MORNING. AND WASH IT FIRST.
ATARI
WEEEEOOOW
COME ON, GUYS, WE'LL WATCH THE SHOW FROM FRAGGER'S ROOF.
THIS WAY!
THAT DUMBFUCK! WHO DOES THAT PRICK THINK HE IS?
I'LL BURN THE JACKET BEFORE HOLDEN GETS IT.
WEEEEOOOW
QUICK, WE HAVE TO GET ON A ROOF. WHO LIVES CLOSEST?
WE CAN GO TO MY PLACE! OUR HOUSE HAS AN OBSERVATION POST. IT'S RIGHT OVER THERE.
COME ON, ZACK, WHAT ARE YOU WAITING FOR?
WEEEEEEOO

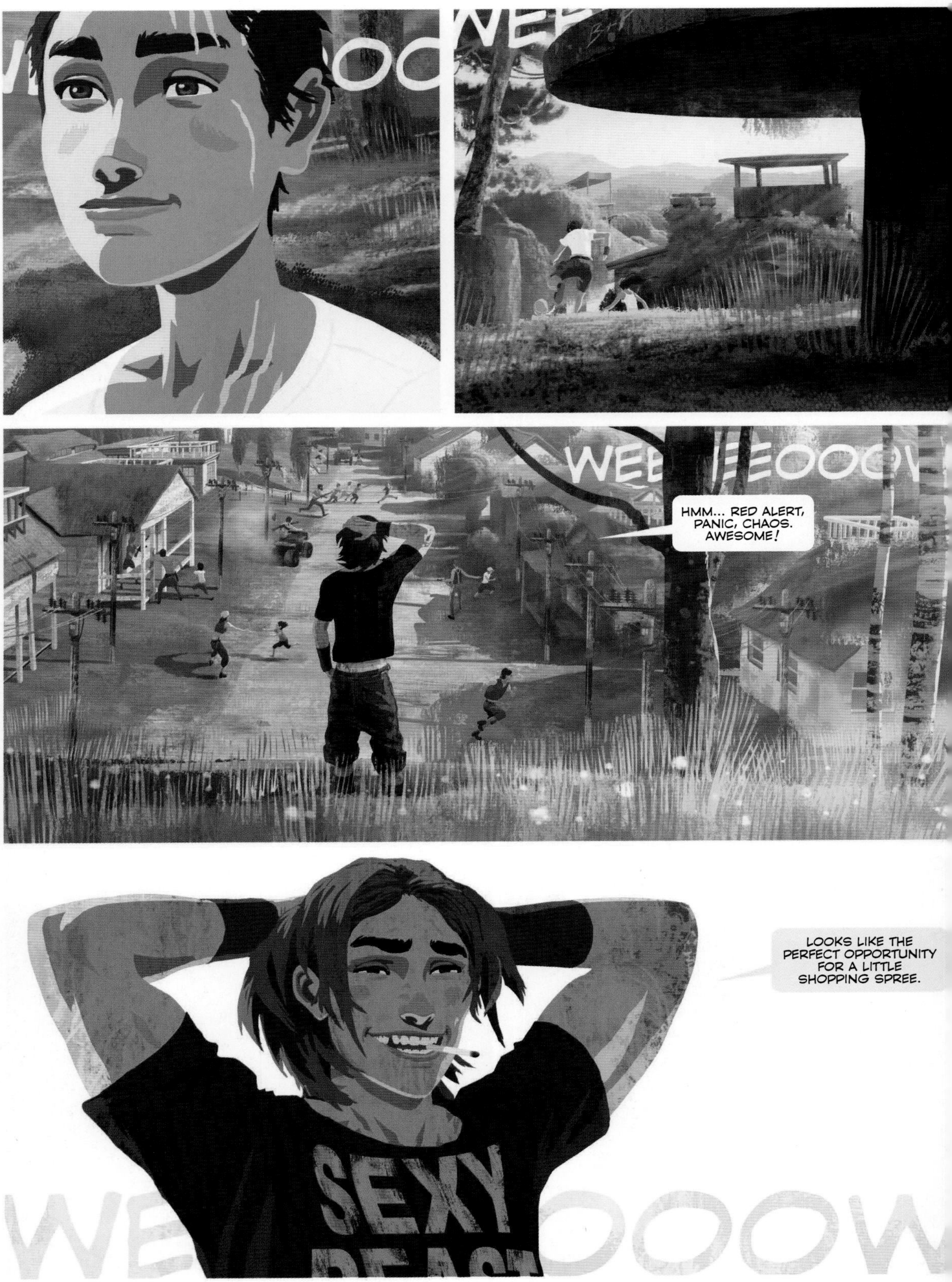
HMM... RED ALERT, PANIC, CHAOS. AWESOME!
LOOKS LIKE THE PERFECT OPPORTUNITY FOR A LITTLE SHOPPING SPREE.
SEXY

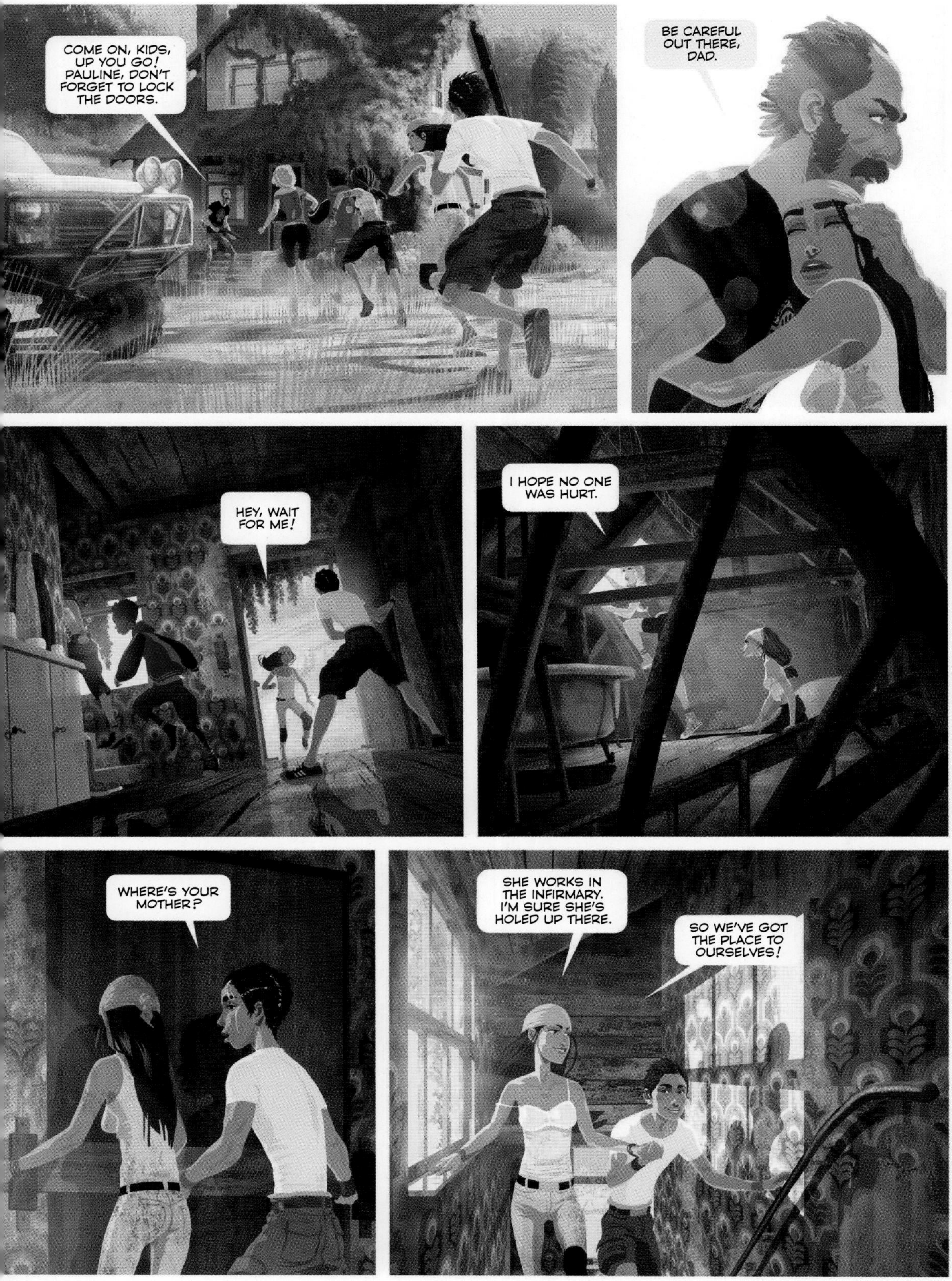
COME ON, KIDS, UP YOU GO! PAULINE, DON'T FORGET TO LOCK THE DOORS.
BE CAREFUL OUT THERE, DAD.
HEY, WAIT FOR ME!
I HOPE NO ONE WAS HURT.
WHERE'S YOUR MOTHER?
SHE WORKS IN THE INFIRMARY. I'M SURE SHE'S HOLED UP THERE.
SO WE'VE GOT THE PLACE TO OURSELVES!

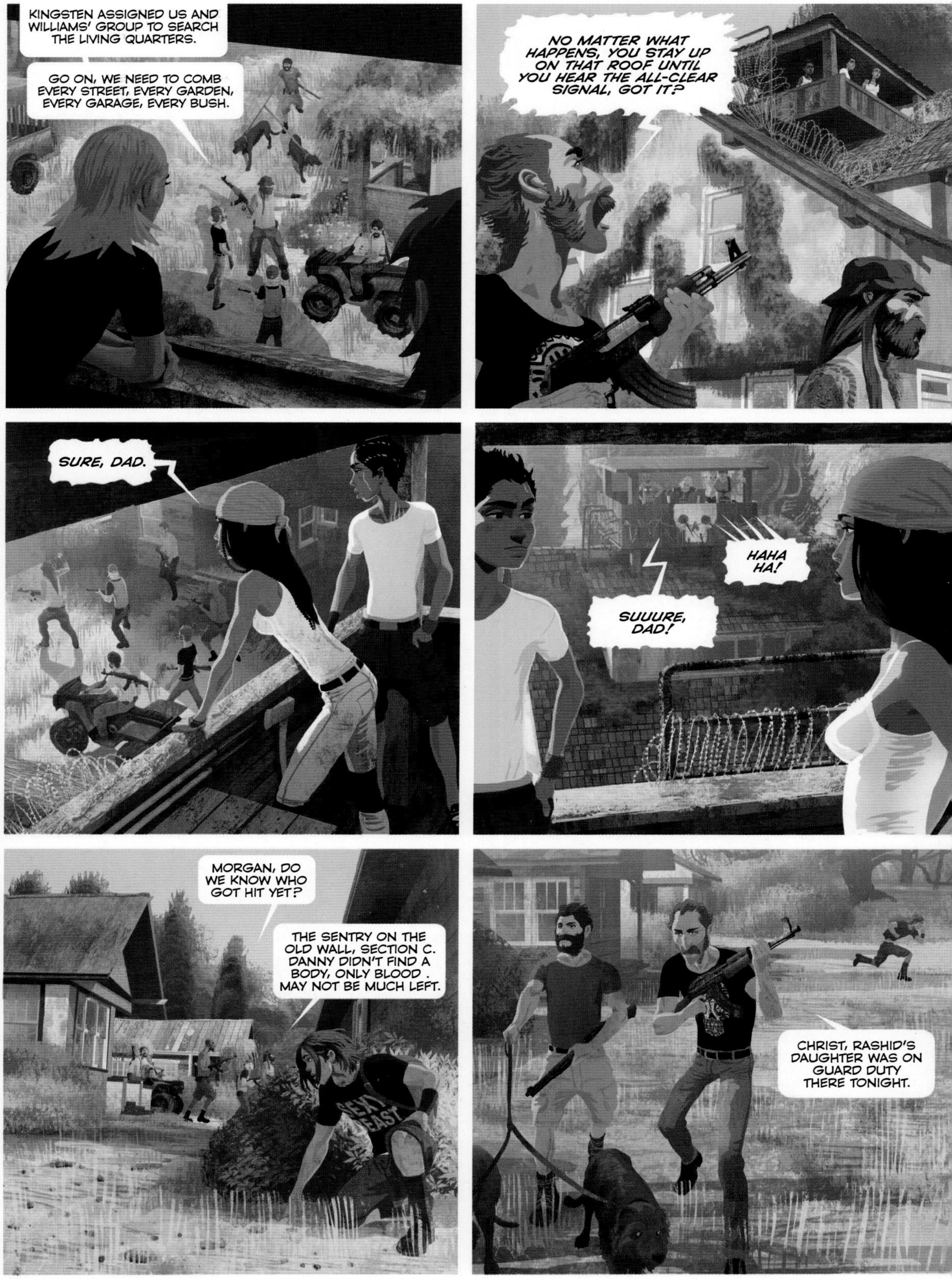
KINGSTEN ASSIGNED US AND WILLIAMS' GROUP TO SEARCH THE LIVING QUARTERS.
GO ON, WE NEED TO COMB EVERY STREET, EVERY GARDEN, EVERY GARAGE, EVERY BUSH.
NO MATTER WHAT HAPPENS, YOU STAY UP ON THAT ROOF UNTIL YOU HEAR THE ALL-CLEAR SIGNAL, GOT IT?
SURE, DAD.
SUUURE, DAD!
HAHA HA!
MORGAN, DO WE KNOW WHO GOT HIT YET?
THE SENTRY ON THE OLD WALL, SECTION C. DANNY DIDN'T FIND A BODY, ONLY BLOOD . MAY NOT BE MUCH LEFT.
CHRIST, RASHID'S DAUGHTER WAS ON GUARD DUTY THERE TONIGHT.

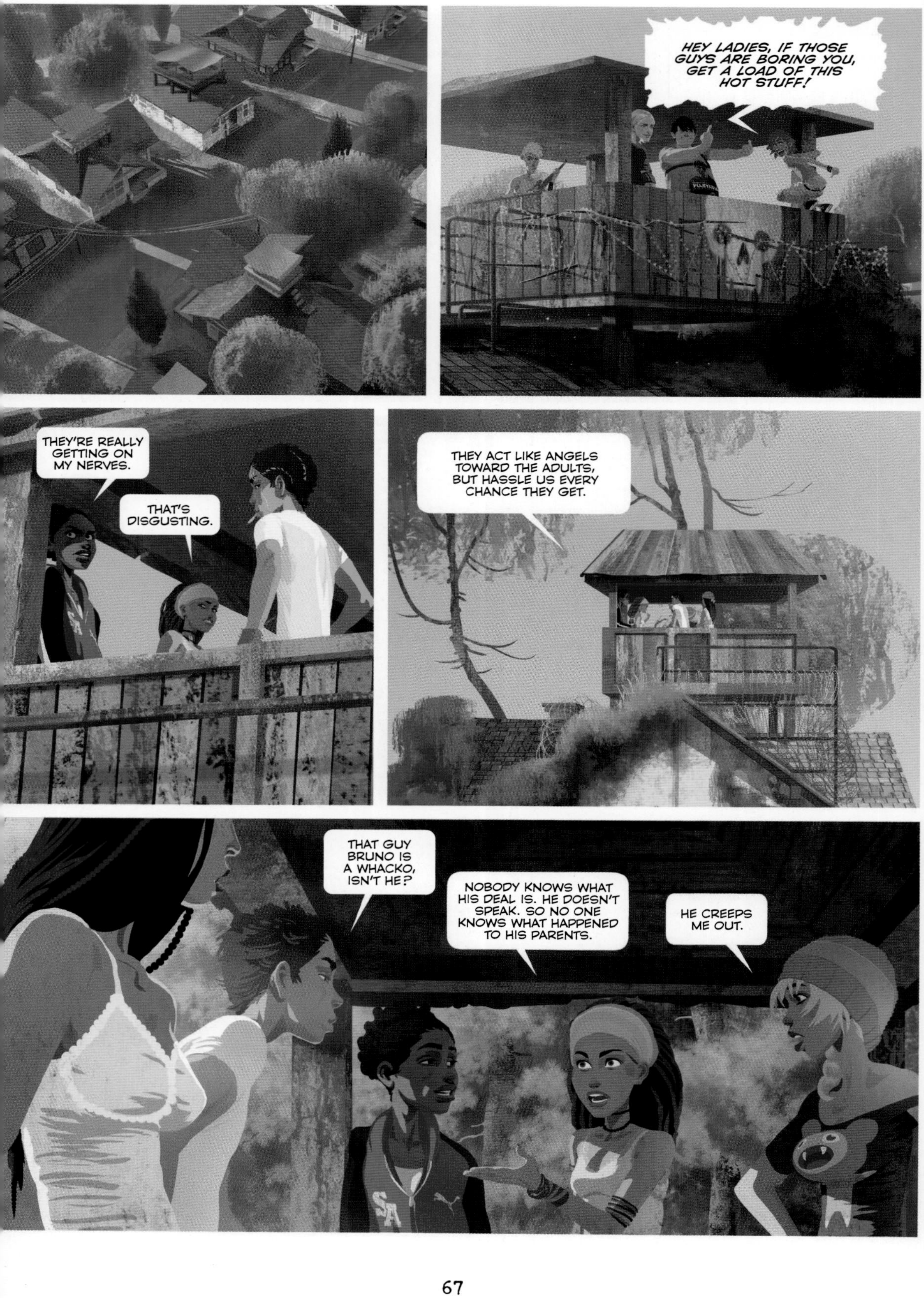
HEY LADIES, IF THOSE GUYS ARE BORING YOU, GET A LOAD OF THIS HOT STUFF!
THEY'RE REALLY GETTING ON MY NERVES.
THAT'S DISGUSTING.
THEY ACT LIKE ANGELS TOWARD THE ADULTS, BUT HASSLE US EVERY CHANCE THEY GET.
THAT GUY BRUNO IS A WHACKO, ISN'T HE?
NOBODY KNOWS WHAT HIS DEAL IS. HE DOESN'T SPEAK. SO NO ONE KNOWS WHAT HAPPENED TO HIS PARENTS.
HE CREEPS ME OUT.

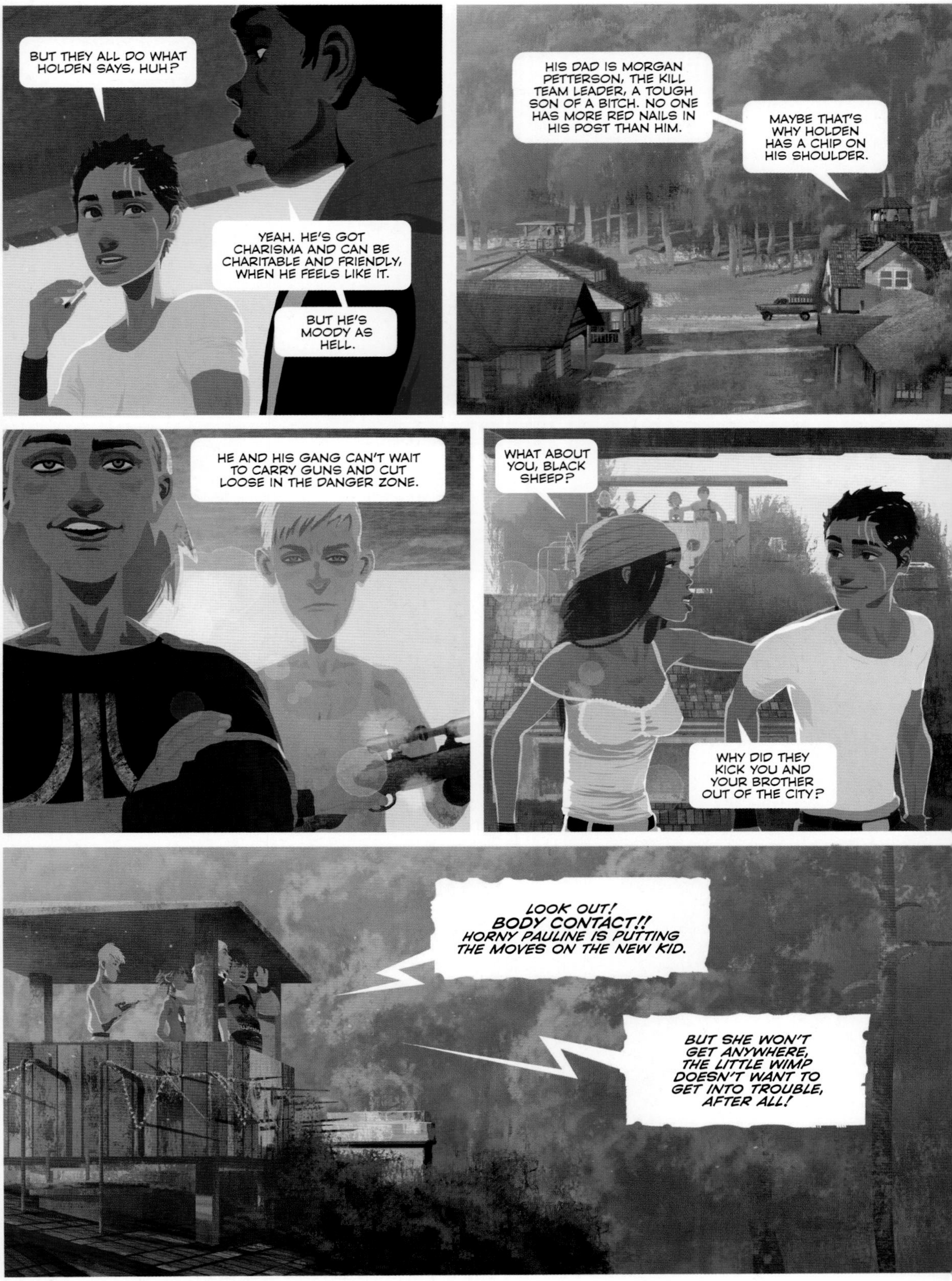
BUT THEY ALL DO WHAT HOLDEN SAYS, HUH?
YEAH. HE'S GOT CHARISMA AND CAN BE CHARITABLE AND FRIENDLY, WHEN HE FEELS LIKE IT.
BUT HE'S MOODY AS HELL.
HIS DAD IS MORGAN PETTERSON, THE KILL TEAM LEADER, A TOUGH SON OF A BITCH. NO ONE HAS MORE RED NAILS IN HIS POST THAN HIM.
MAYBE THAT'S WHY HOLDEN HAS A CHIP ON HIS SHOULDER.
HE AND HIS GANG CAN'T WAIT TO CARRY GUNS AND CUT LOOSE IN THE DANGER ZONE.
WHAT ABOUT YOU, BLACK SHEEP?
WHY DID THEY KICK YOU AND YOUR BROTHER OUT OF THE CITY?
LOOK OUT! BODY CONTACT!! HORNY PAULINE IS PUTTING THE MOVES ON THE NEW KID.
BUT SHE WON'T GET ANYWHERE, THE LITTLE WIMP DOESN'T WANT TO GET INTO TROUBLE, AFTER ALL!

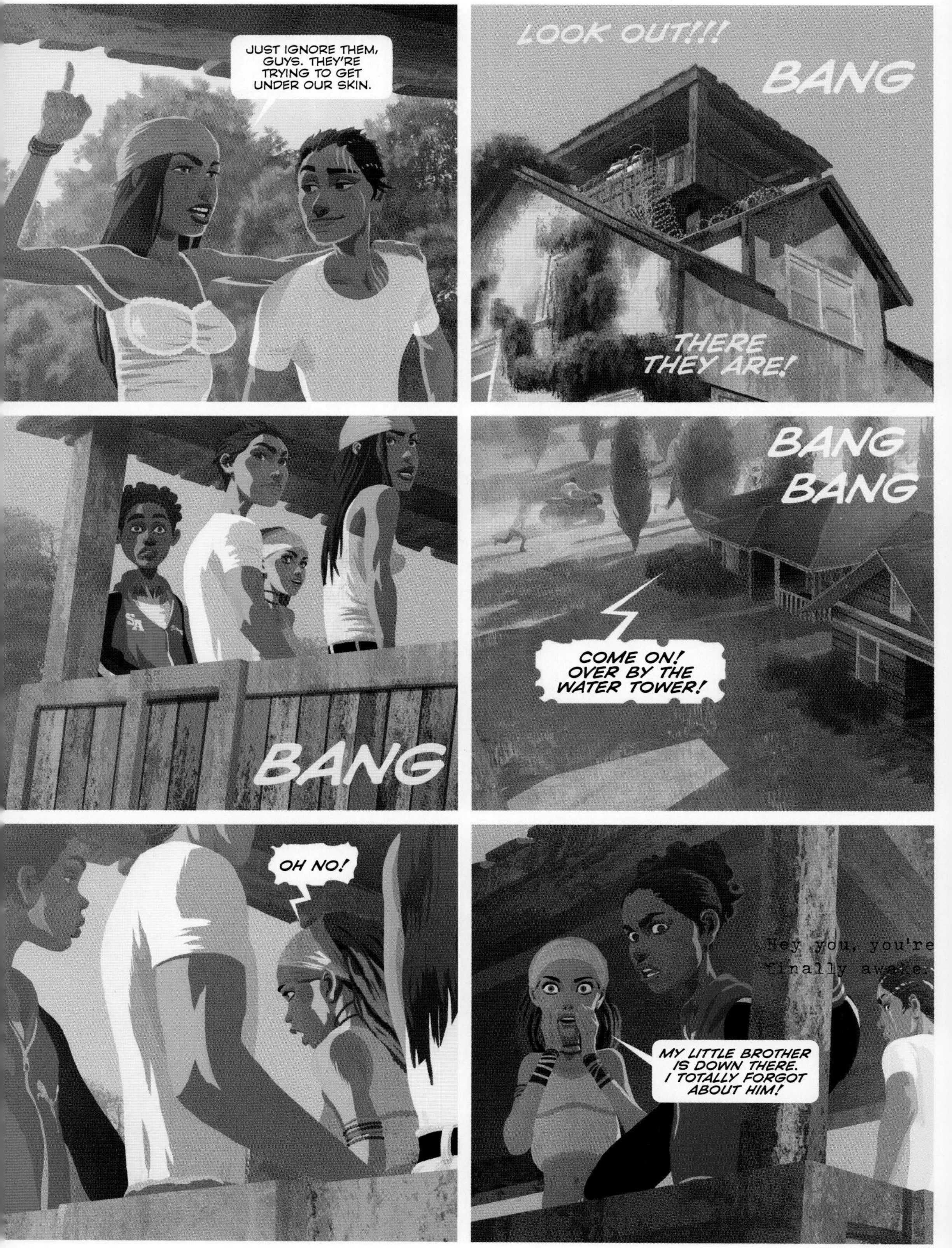
JUST IGNORE THEM, GUYS. THEY'RE TRYING TO GET UNDER OUR SKIN.
LOOK OUT!!!
BANG
THERE THEY ARE!
BANG
BANG BANG
COME ON! OVER BY THE WATER TOWER!
OH NO!
Hey you, you're finally awake.
MY LITTLE BROTHER IS DOWN THERE. I TOTALLY FORGOT ABOUT HIM!

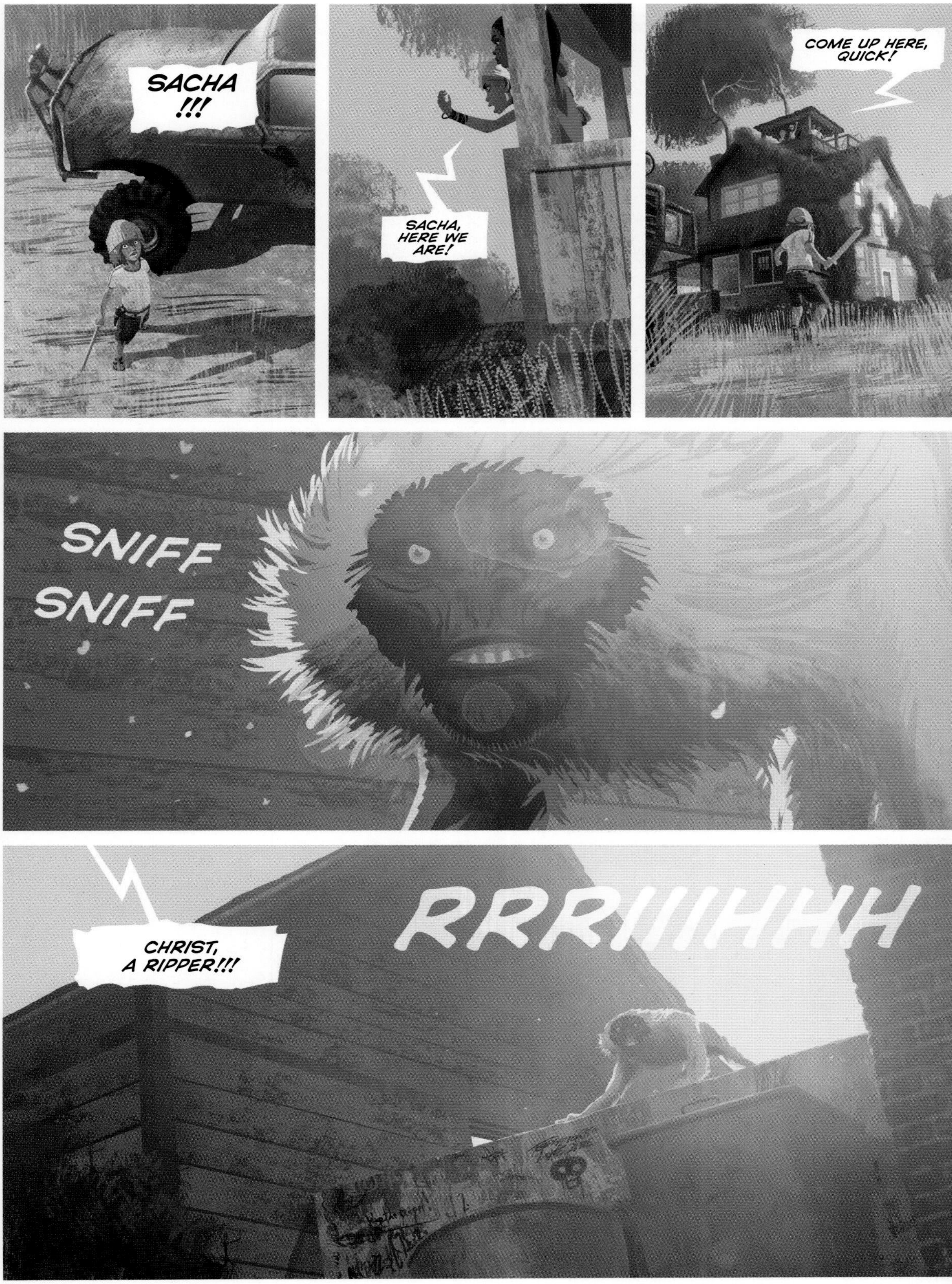
SACHA !!!
SACHA, HERE WE ARE!
COME UP HERE, QUICK!
SNIFF SNIFF
CHRIST, A RIPPER!!!
RRRIIIHHH

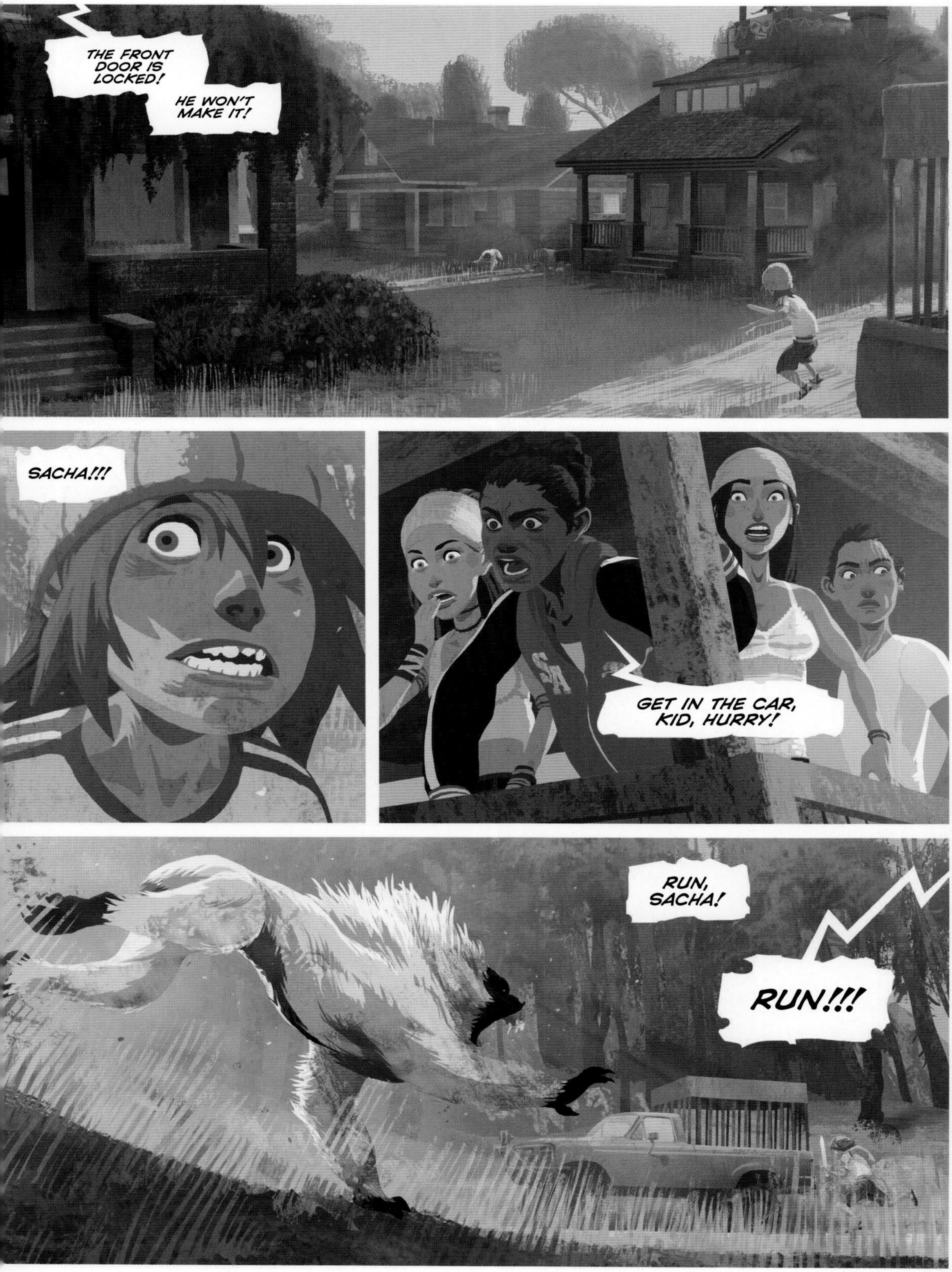
THE FRONT DOOR IS LOCKED!
HE WON'T MAKE IT!
SACHA!!!
GET IN THE CAR, KID, HURRY!
RUN, SACHA!
RUN!!!

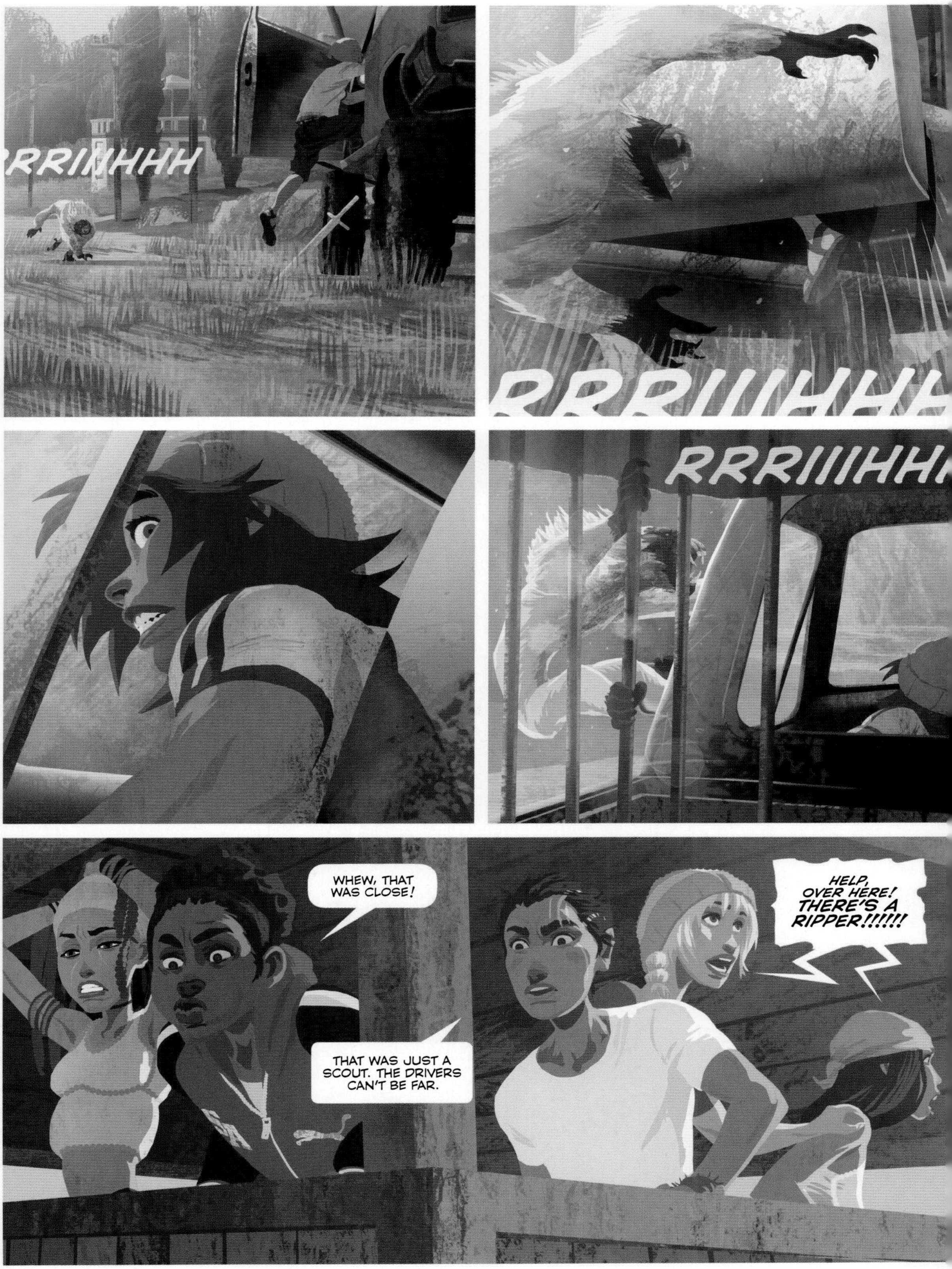
RRRINHHH
RRRIIIHHH
RRRIIIHHH
WHEW, THAT WAS CLOSE!
THAT WAS JUST A SCOUT. THE DRIVERS CAN'T BE FAR.
HELP, OVER HERE! THERE'S A RIPPER!!!!!!

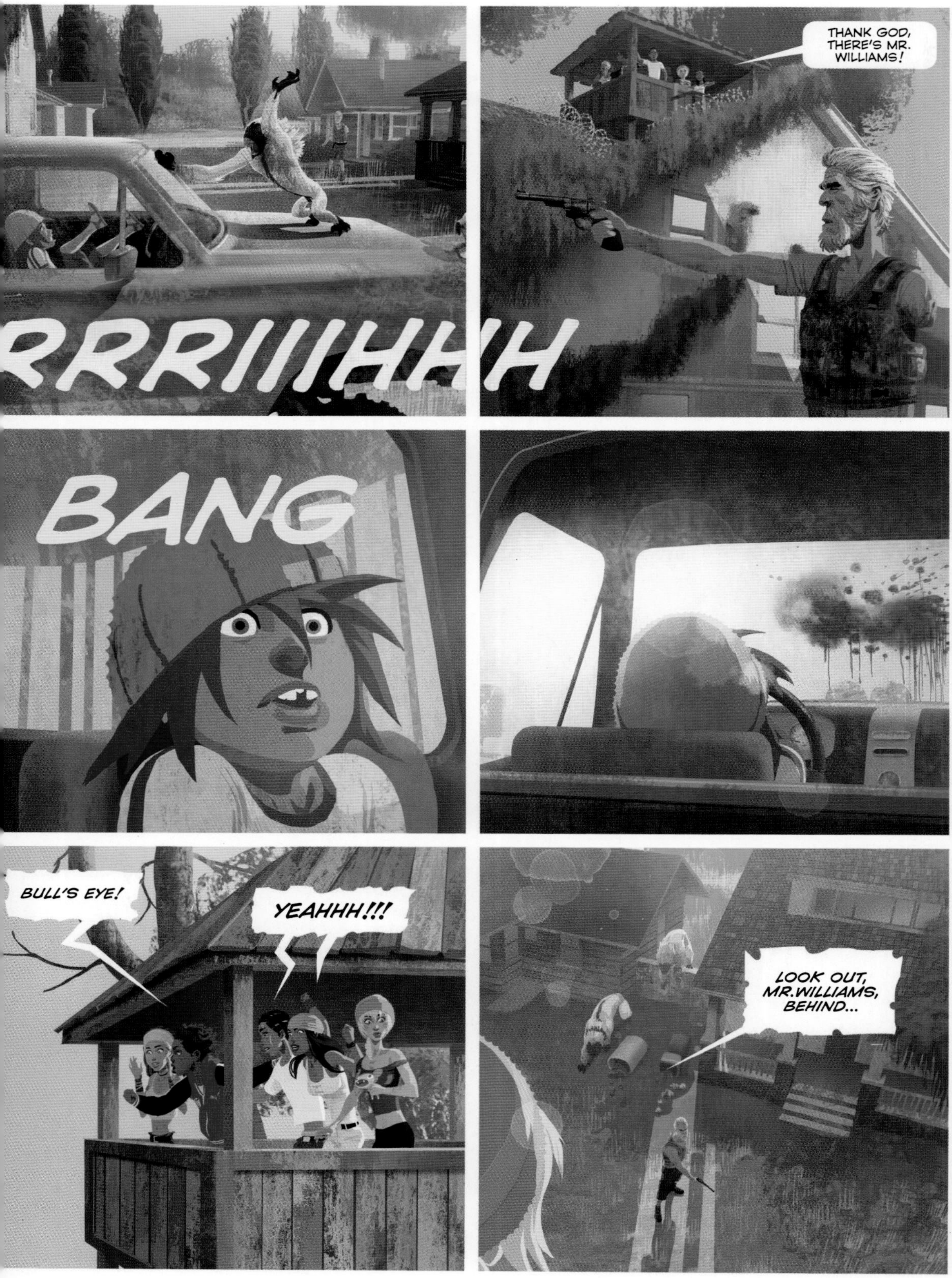
RRRIIIHHHH
THANK GOD, THERE'S MR. WILLIAMS!
BANG
BULL'S EYE!
YEAHHH!!!
LOOK OUT, MR.WILLIAMS, BEHIND...

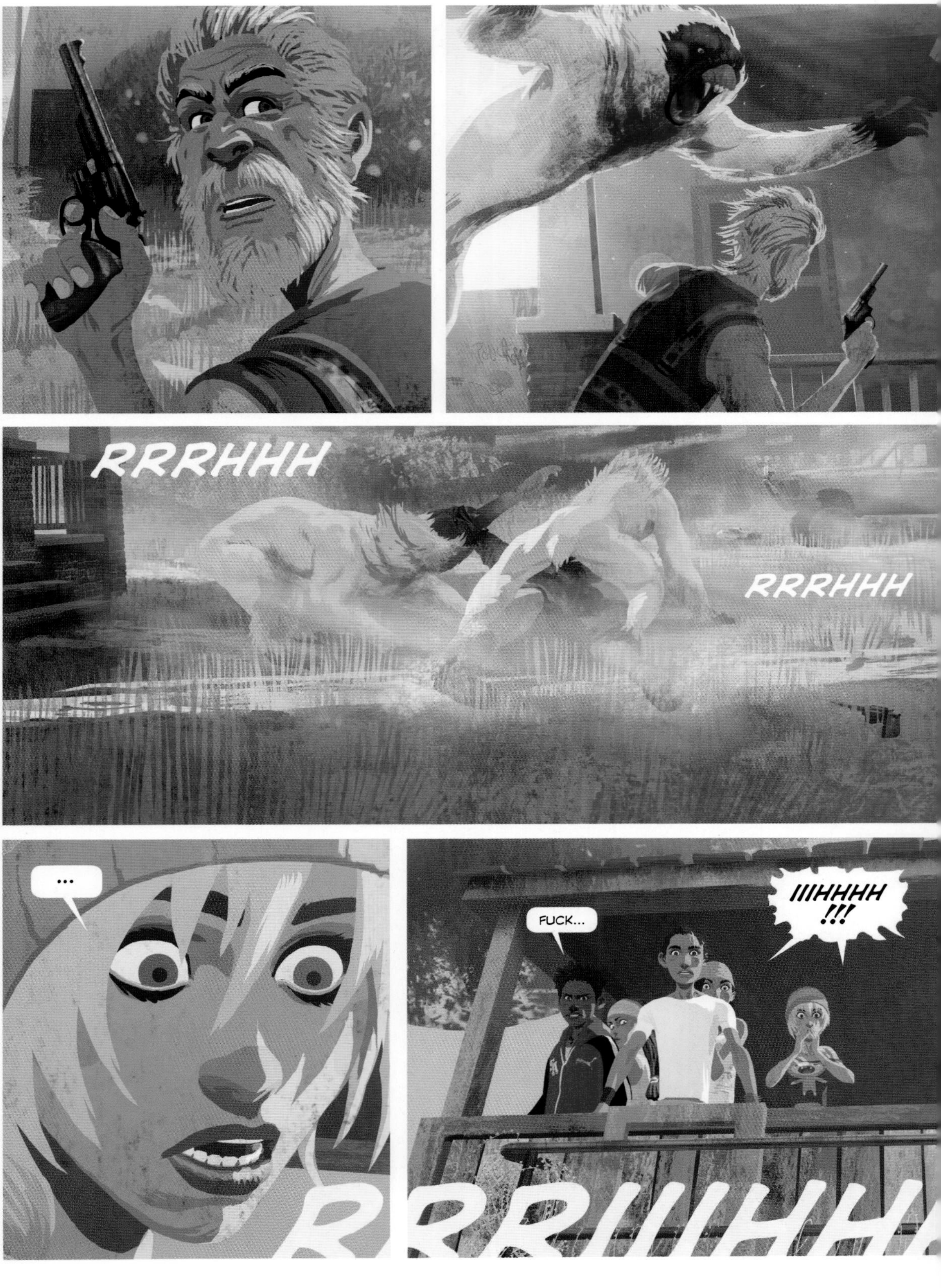
RRRHHH
RRRHHH
...
FUCK...
IIIHHHH
!!!
RRRIIIHHH

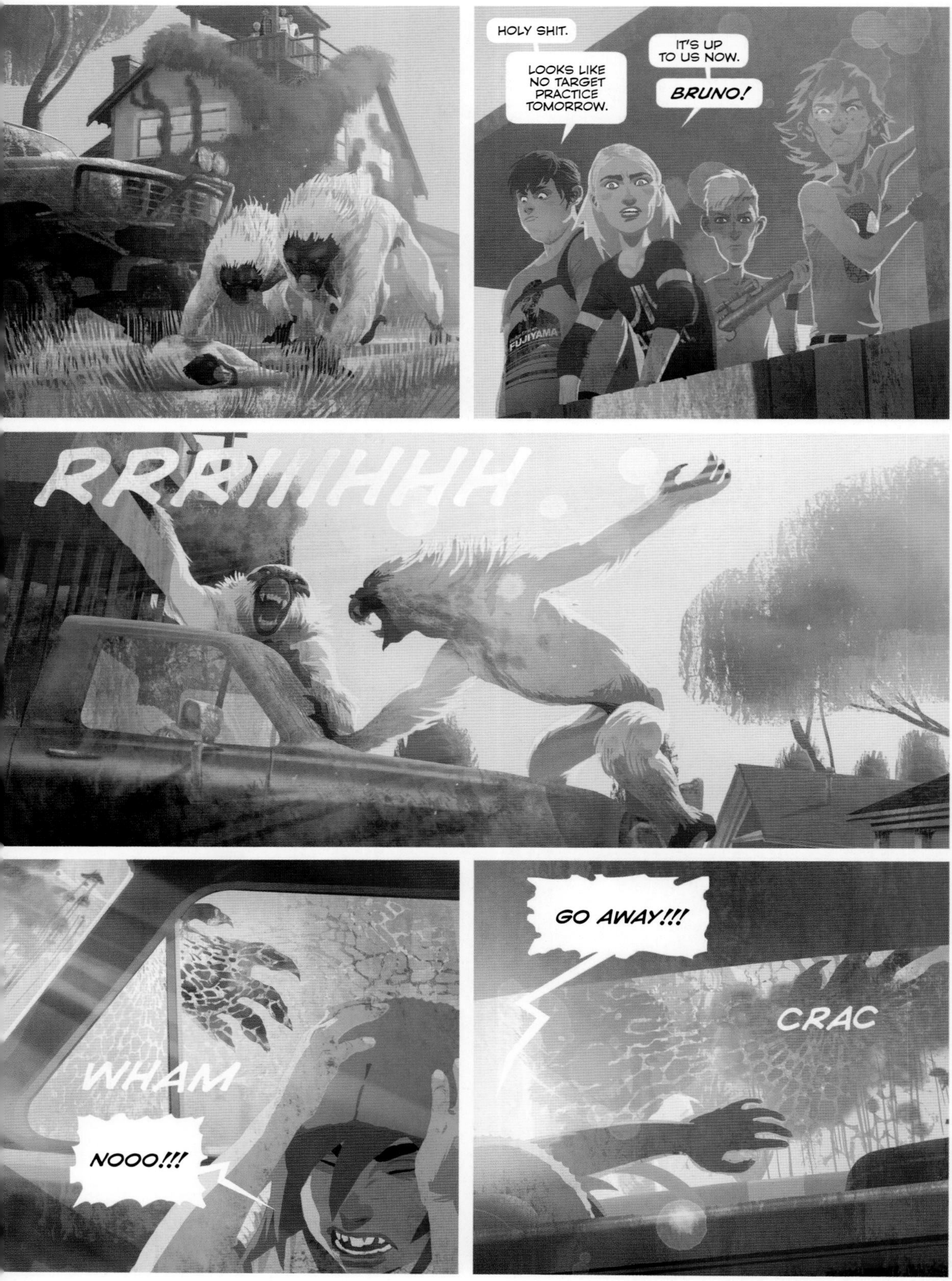
HOLY SHIT.
LOOKS LIKE NO TARGET PRACTICE TOMORROW.
IT'S UP TO US NOW.
BRUNO!
FUJIYAMA
RRRIIIHHH
WHAM
NOOO!!!
GO AWAY!!!
CRAC

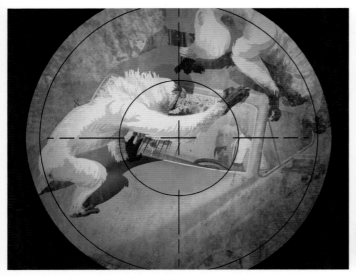

I WANT A SHOT, TOO!

BANG

FUCK, MISSED. FIRE AGAIN, BRUNO!

GO GET THOSE SCALPS!

THERE'S NO RED NAILS FOR KILLING CARS, MAN!

BRUNO!!! THE DRIVERS ARE THREE TIMES AS BIG AS THE SCOUTS. HOW CAN YOU MISS?

LET ME HAVE A SHOT, DAMN IT!!!

BANG BANG

BANG

BANG BANG

BANG

CRAC

CUT IT OUT, BRUNO!!! YOU COULD HIT SACHA!

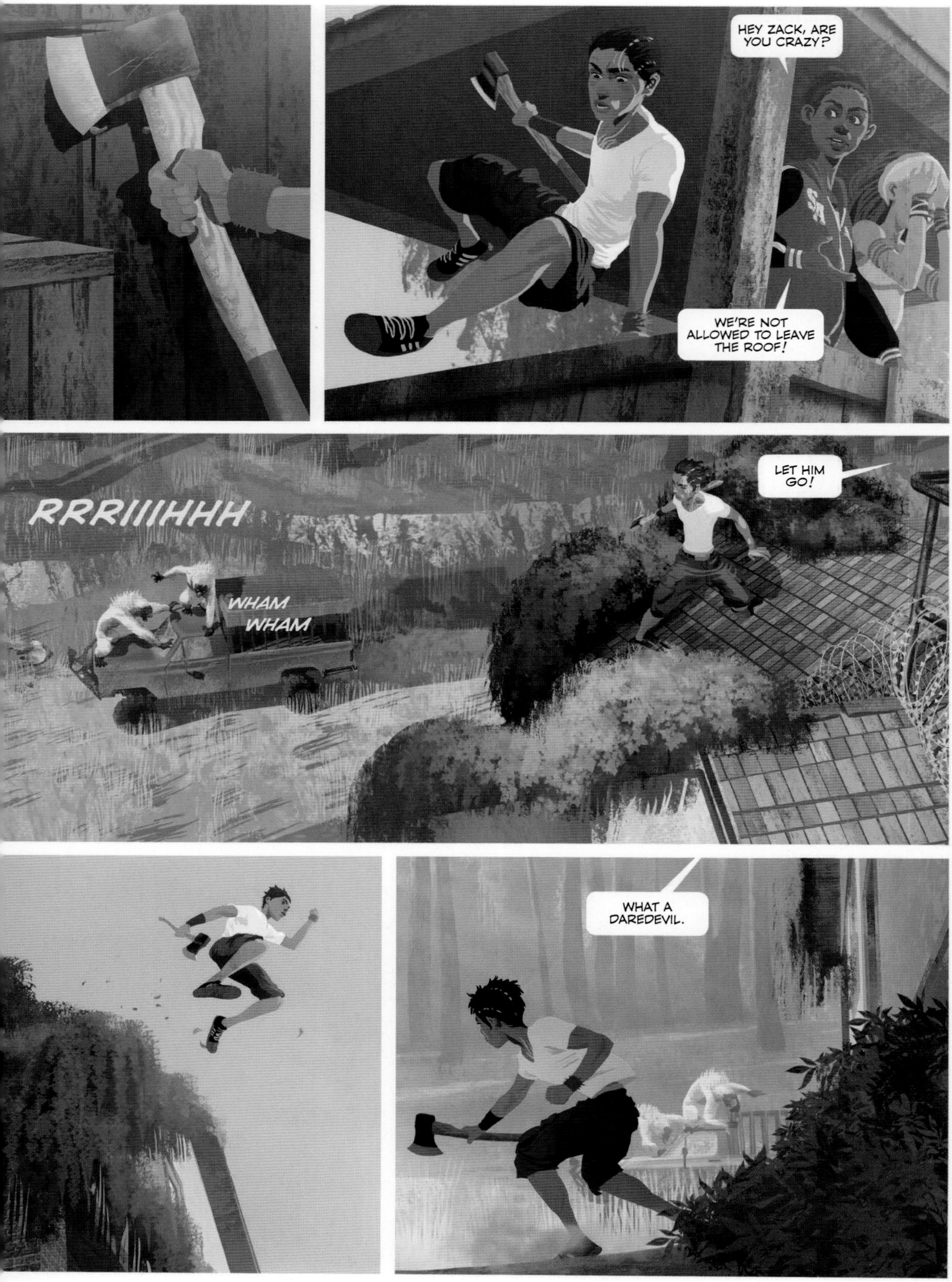
HEY ZACK, ARE YOU CRAZY?
WE'RE NOT ALLOWED TO LEAVE THE ROOF!
RRRIIIHHH
WHAM
WHAM
LET HIM GO!
WHAT A DAREDEVIL.

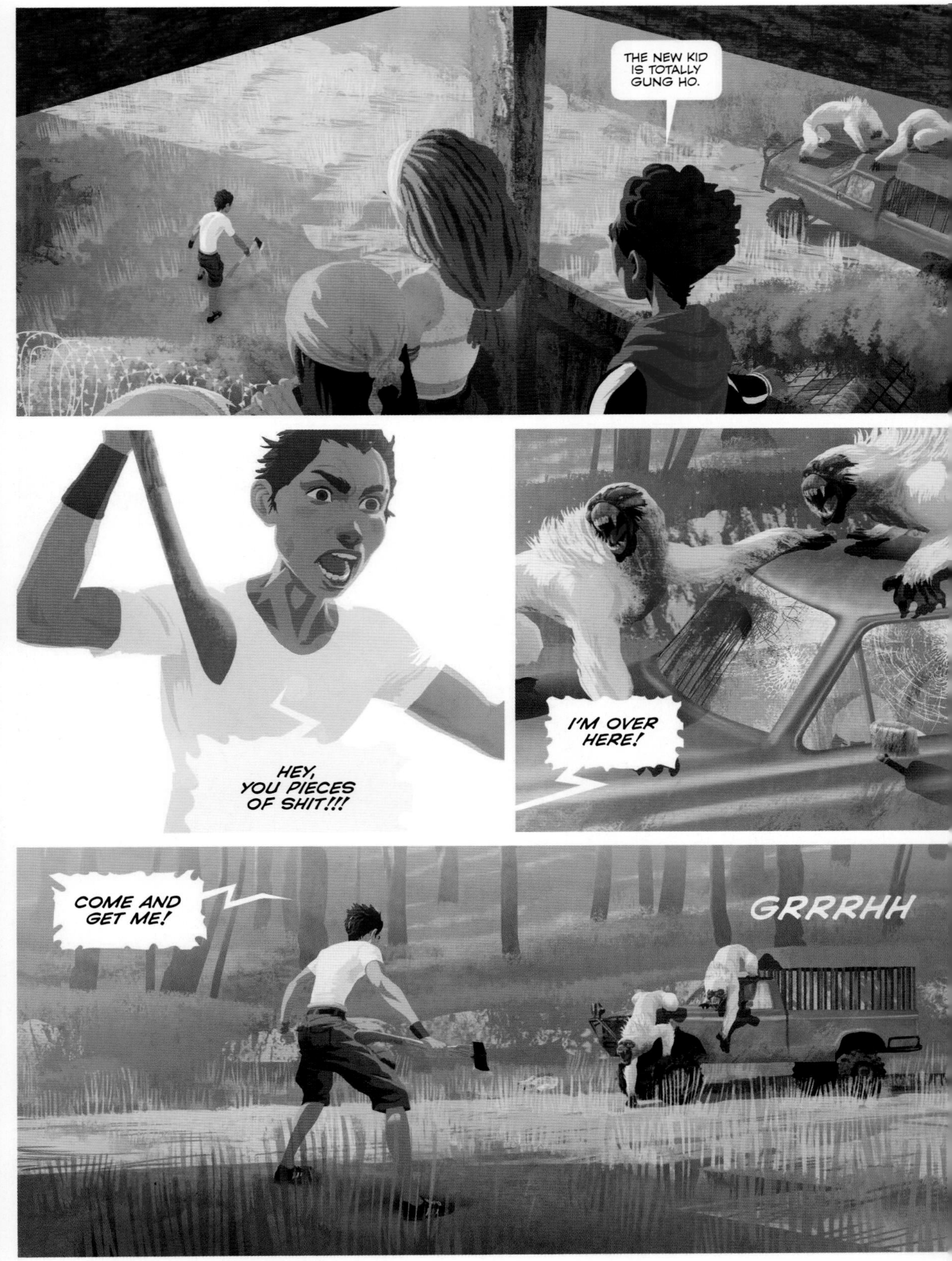
THE NEW KID IS TOTALLY GUNG HO.
HEY, YOU PIECES OF SHIT!!!
I'M OVER HERE!
COME AND GET ME!
GRRRHH

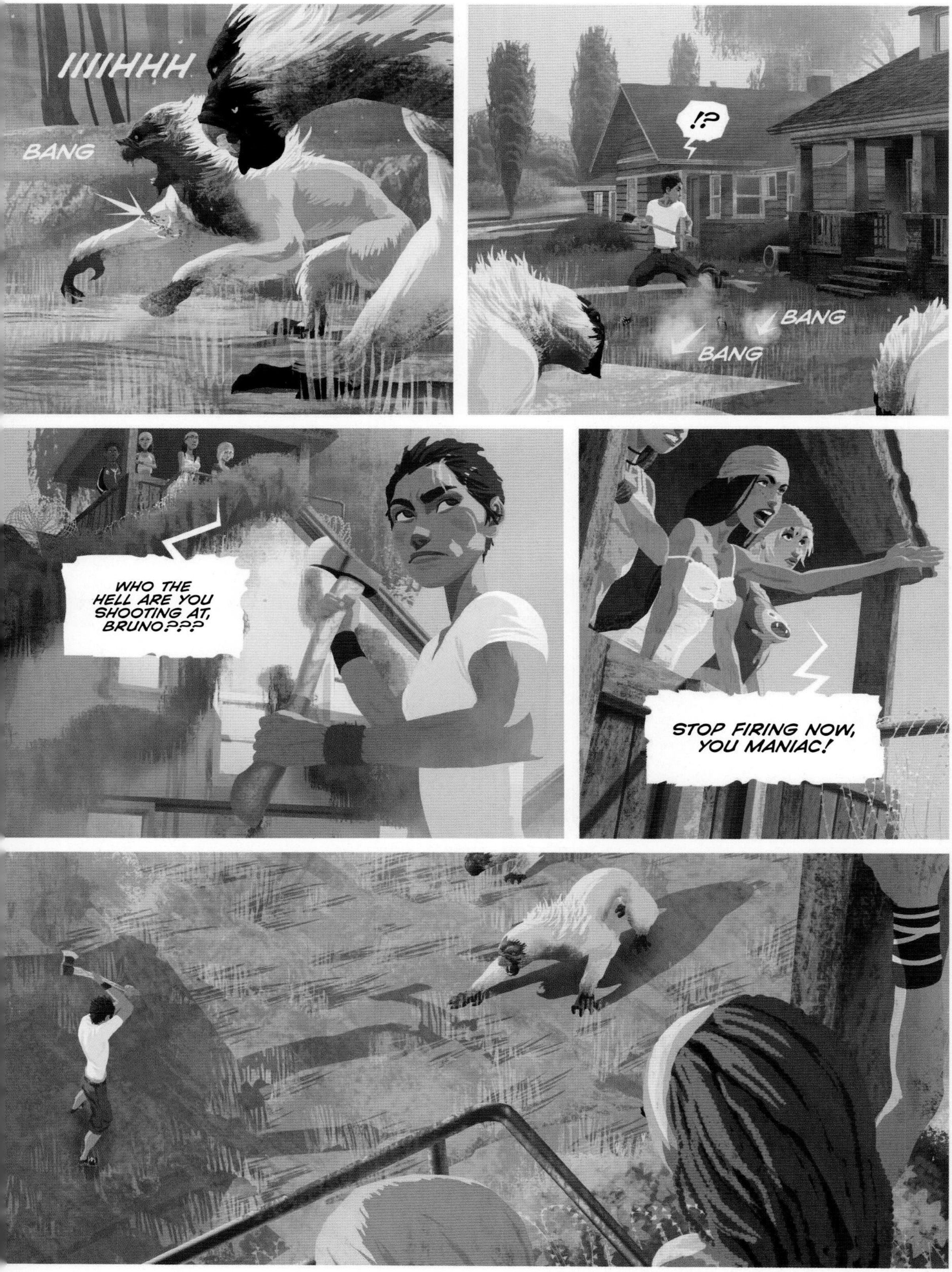
IIIIHHH
BANG
!?
BANG
BANG
WHO THE HELL ARE YOU SHOOTING AT, BRUNO???
STOP FIRING NOW, YOU MANIAC!

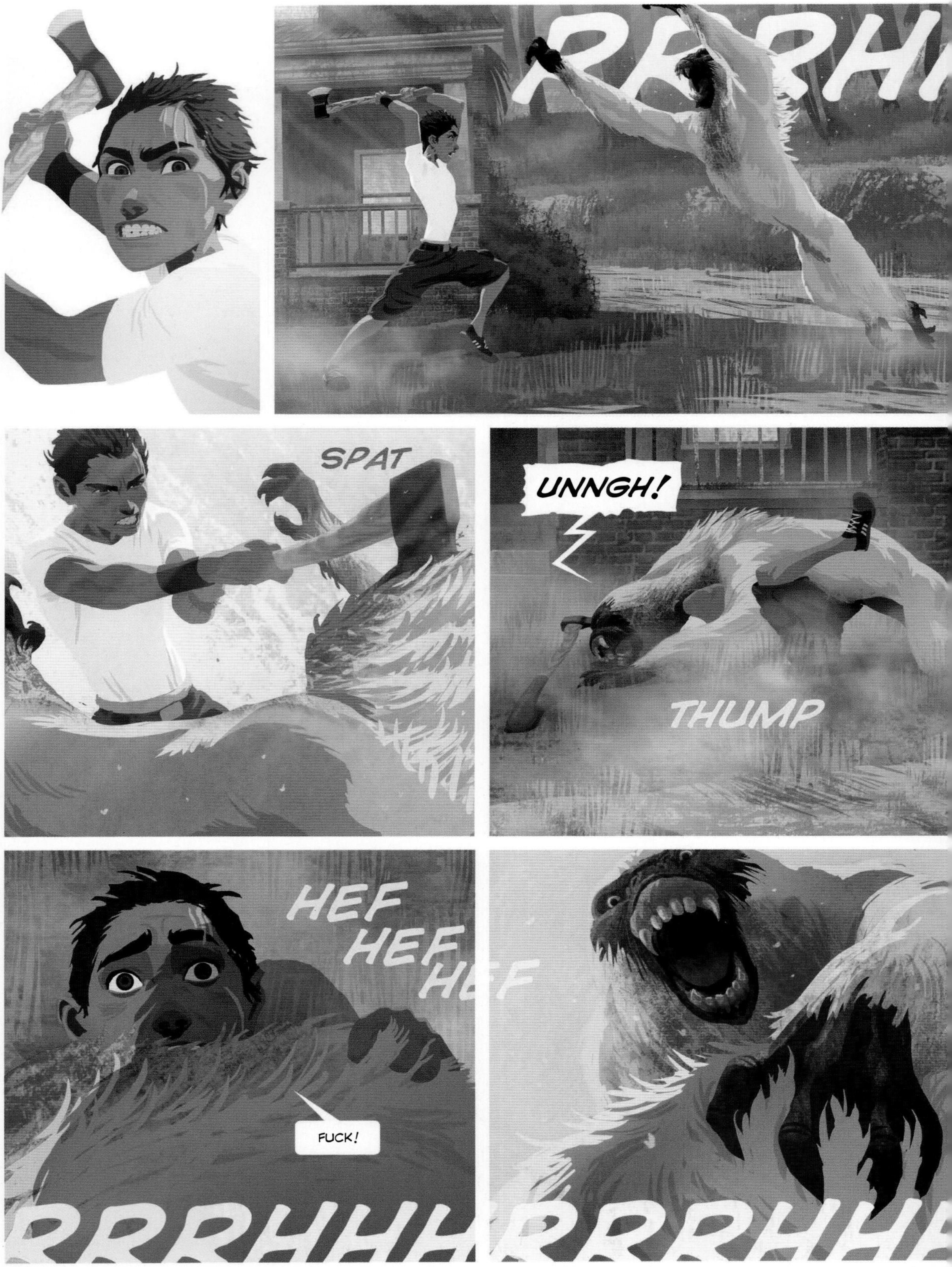
RRRHH
SPAT
UNNGH!
THUMP
HEF
HEF
HEF
FUCK!
RRRHHH
RRRHHH

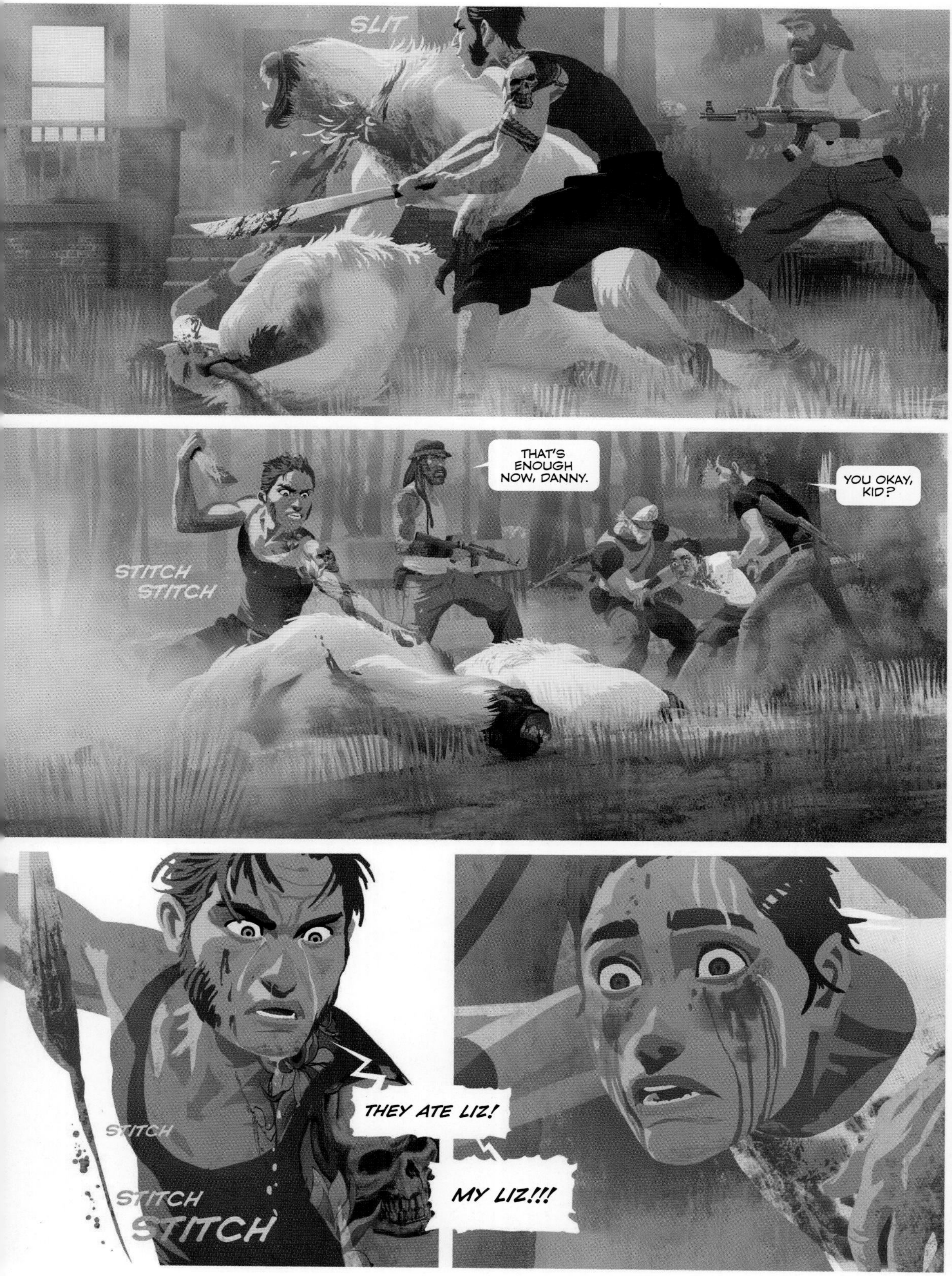
SLIT
THAT'S ENOUGH NOW, DANNY.
YOU OKAY, KID?
STITCH STITCH
STITCH
STITCH STITCH
THEY ATE LIZ!
MY LIZ!!!

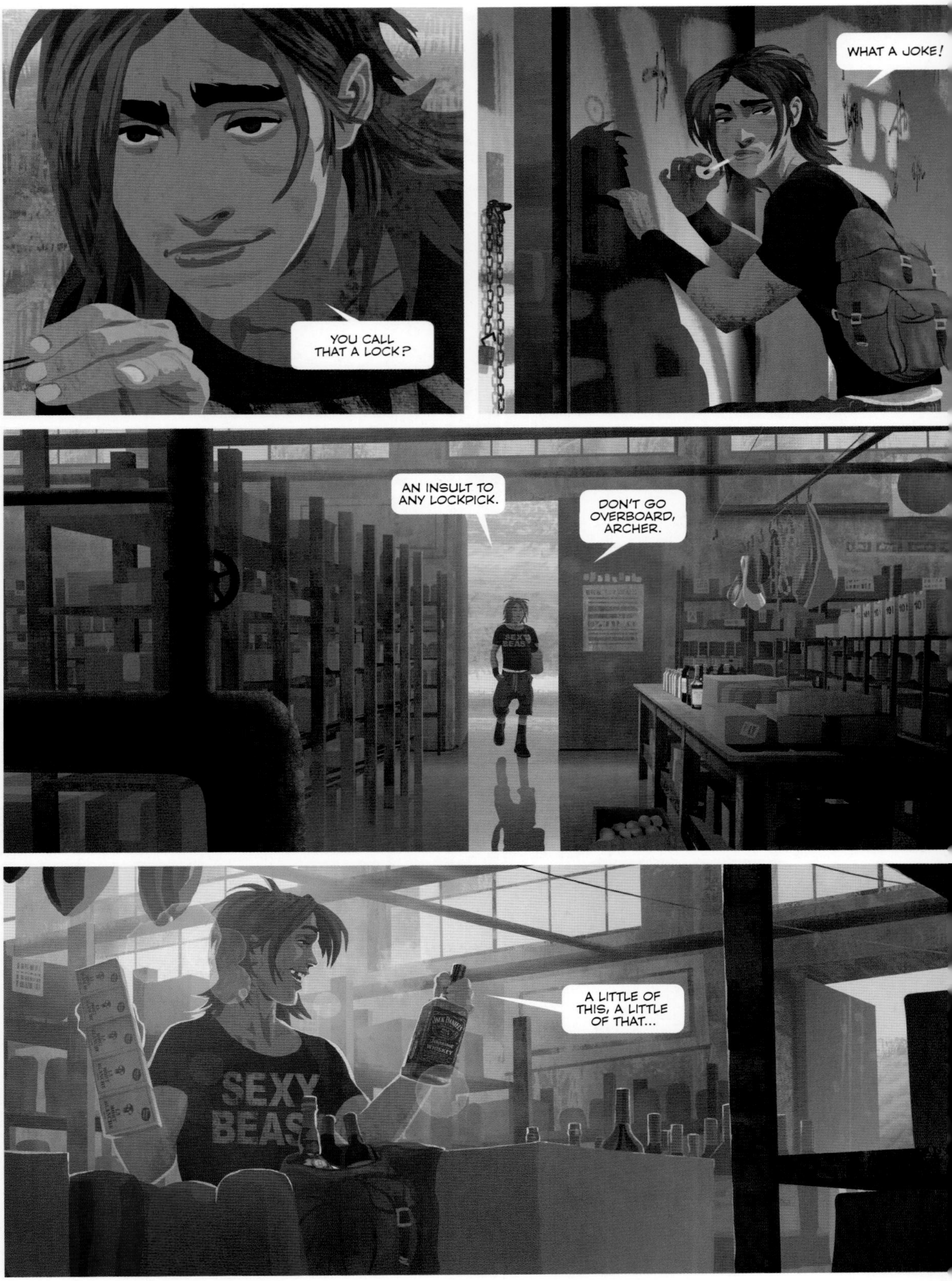
YOU CALL THAT A LOCK?
WHAT A JOKE!
AN INSULT TO ANY LOCKPICK.
DON'T GO OVERBOARD, ARCHER.
SEXY BEAST
A LITTLE OF THIS, A LITTLE OF THAT...
SEXY BEAS

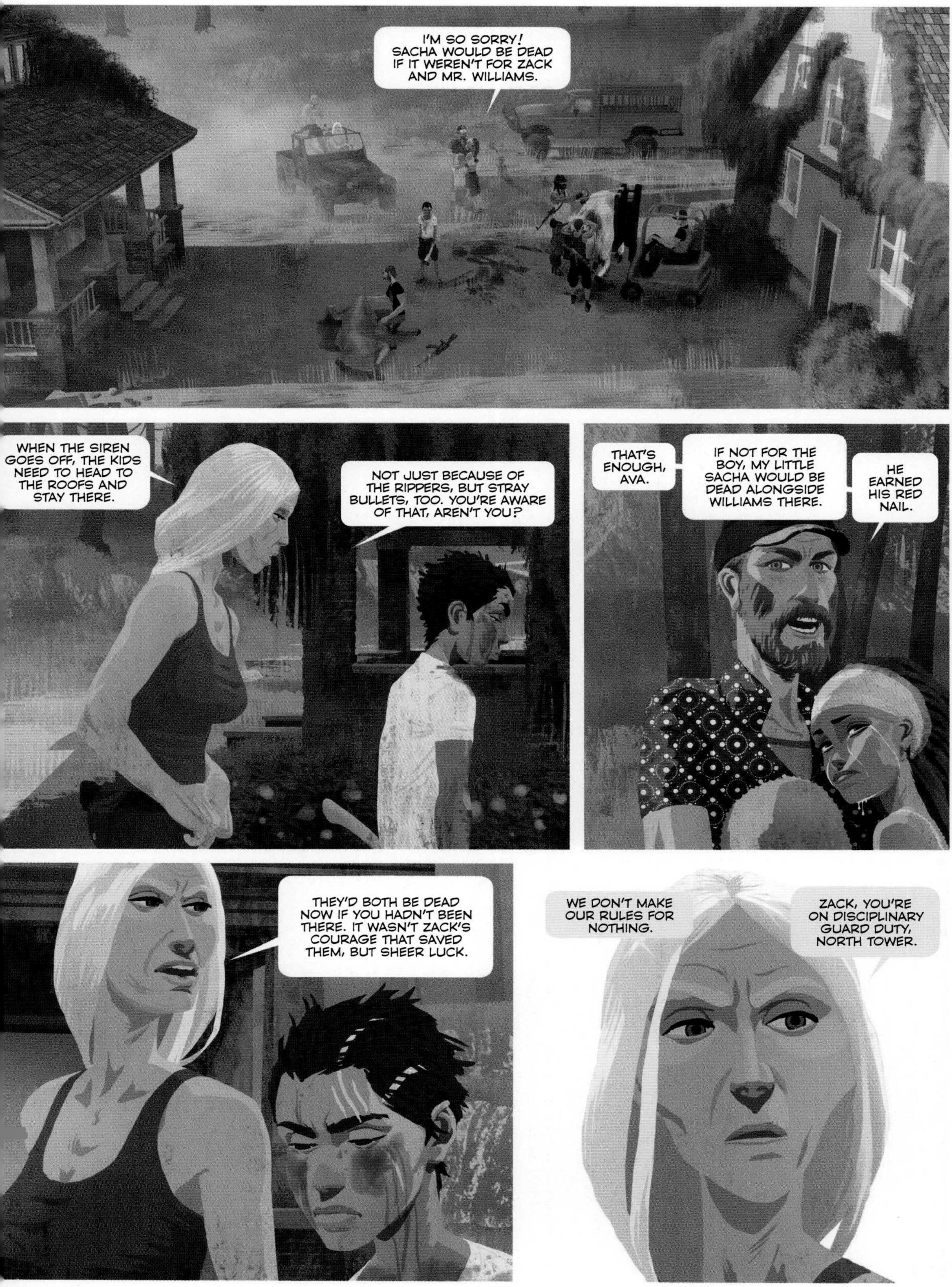
I'M SO SORRY! SACHA WOULD BE DEAD IF IT WEREN'T FOR ZACK AND MR. WILLIAMS.
WHEN THE SIREN GOES OFF, THE KIDS NEED TO HEAD TO THE ROOFS AND STAY THERE.
NOT JUST BECAUSE OF THE RIPPERS, BUT STRAY BULLETS, TOO. YOU'RE AWARE OF THAT, AREN'T YOU?
THAT'S ENOUGH, AVA.
IF NOT FOR THE BOY, MY LITTLE SACHA WOULD BE DEAD ALONGSIDE WILLIAMS THERE.
HE EARNED HIS RED NAIL.
THEY'D BOTH BE DEAD NOW IF YOU HADN'T BEEN THERE. IT WASN'T ZACK'S COURAGE THAT SAVED THEM, BUT SHEER LUCK.
WE DON'T MAKE OUR RULES FOR NOTHING.
ZACK, YOU'RE ON DISCIPLINARY GUARD DUTY, NORTH TOWER.

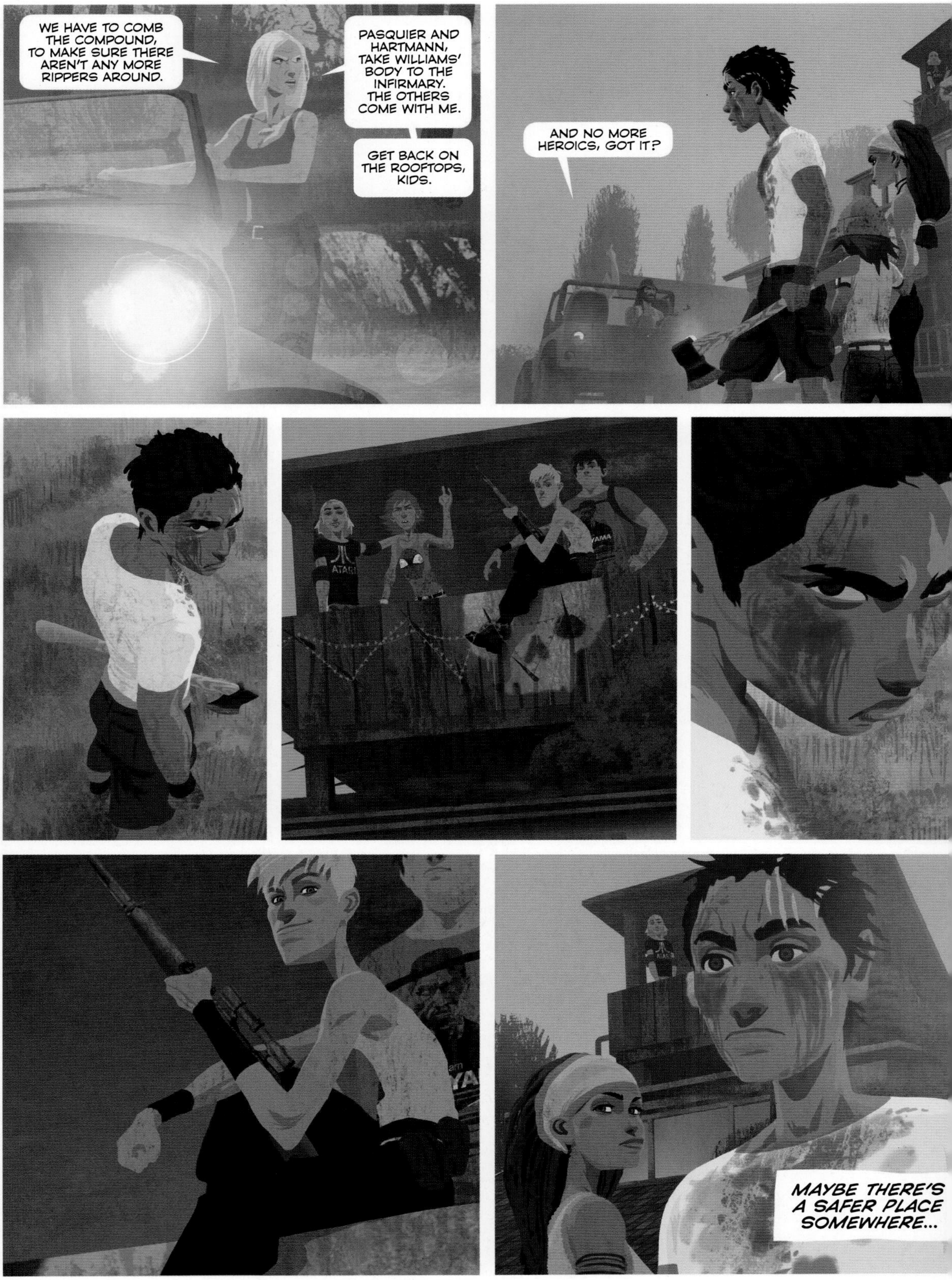
WE HAVE TO COMB THE COMPOUND, TO MAKE SURE THERE AREN'T ANY MORE RIPPERS AROUND.
PASQUIER AND HARTMANN, TAKE WILLIAMS' BODY TO THE INFIRMARY. THE OTHERS COME WITH ME.
GET BACK ON THE ROOFTOPS, KIDS.
AND NO MORE HEROICS, GOT IT?
MAYBE THERE'S A SAFER PLACE SOMEWHERE...

...BUT SURE AS HELL NOT DOWN HERE.

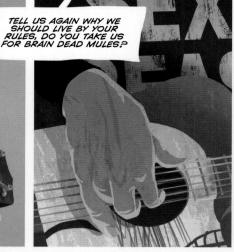

TELL US AGAIN WHY WE SHOULD LIVE BY YOUR RULES, DO YOU TAKE US FOR BRAIN DEAD MULES?

RIPPERS ON A KILLING SPREE, YOU SAY SAFETY TOPS BEING FREE.

WE'RE GUNG HO TO JUMP THE SHARK
GONNA EARN THE OUTCASTS' MARK

DON'T BOTHER TO USE YOUR HEAD
'CAUSE TOMORROW WE'LL BE DEAD

GONNA LIVE THE LIFE FOR ALL WE KNOW
THAT'S HOW THE WASTELANDS FLOW

THAT'S WHAT WE CALL GUNG HO!

85

Part 2: Short Circuit

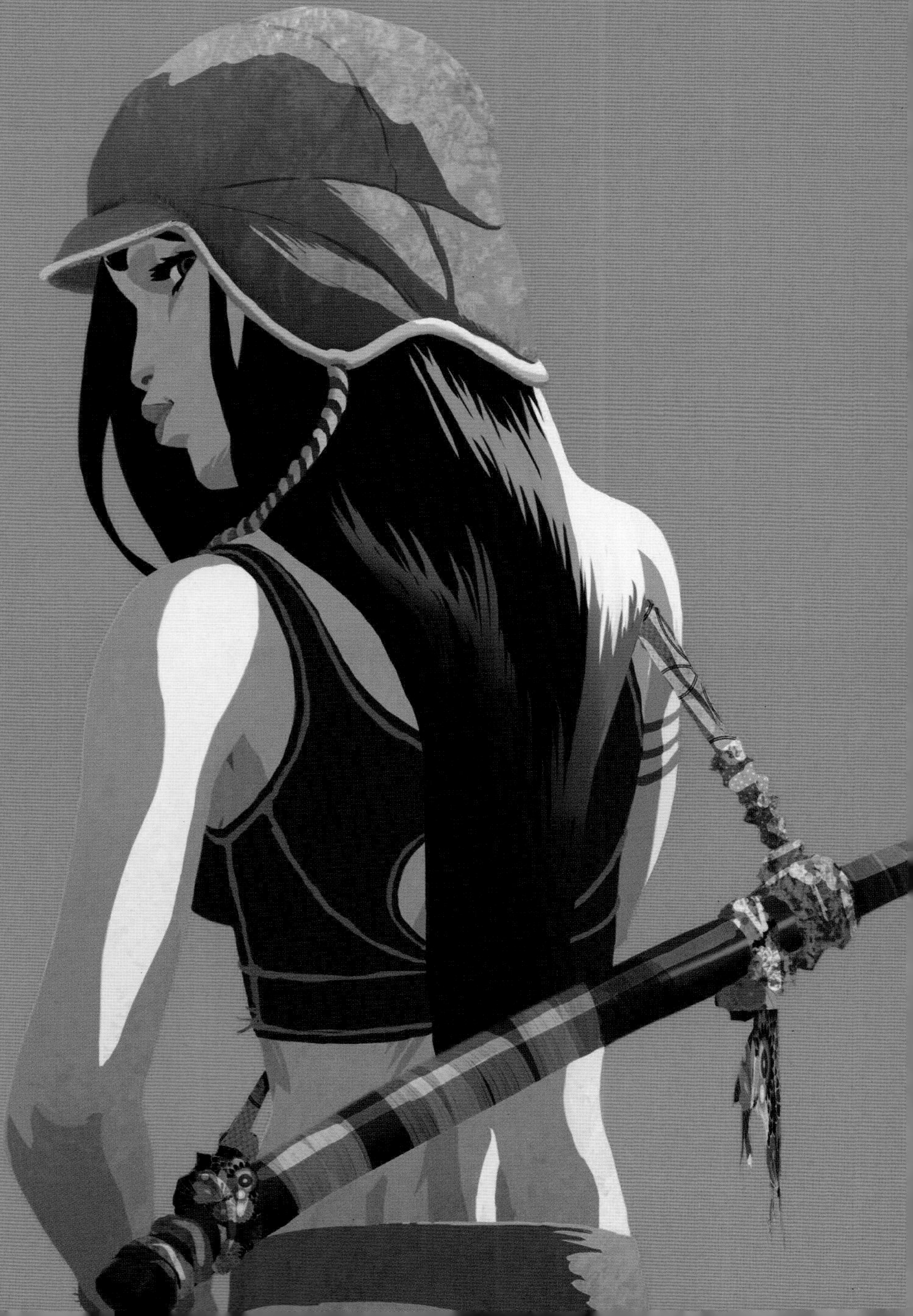

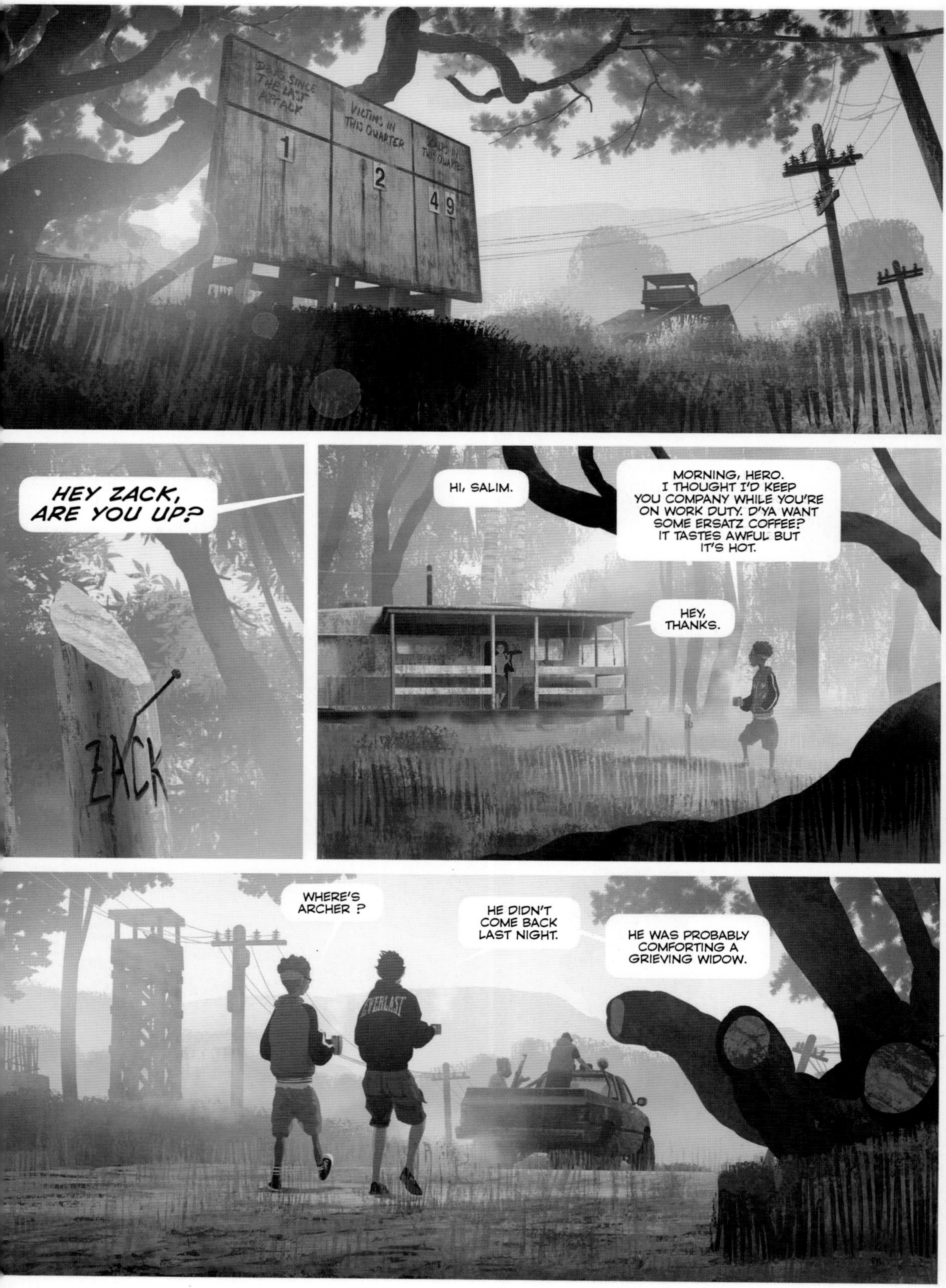
THE LAST ATTACK
VICTIMS IN THIS QUARTER
1
2
49
HEY ZACK, ARE YOU UP?
ZACK
HI, SALIM.
MORNING, HERO. I THOUGHT I'D KEEP YOU COMPANY WHILE YOU'RE ON WORK DUTY. D'YA WANT SOME ERSATZ COFFEE? IT TASTES AWFUL BUT IT'S HOT.
HEY, THANKS.
WHERE'S ARCHER ?
HE DIDN'T COME BACK LAST NIGHT.
HE WAS PROBABLY COMFORTING A GRIEVING WIDOW.
EVERLAST

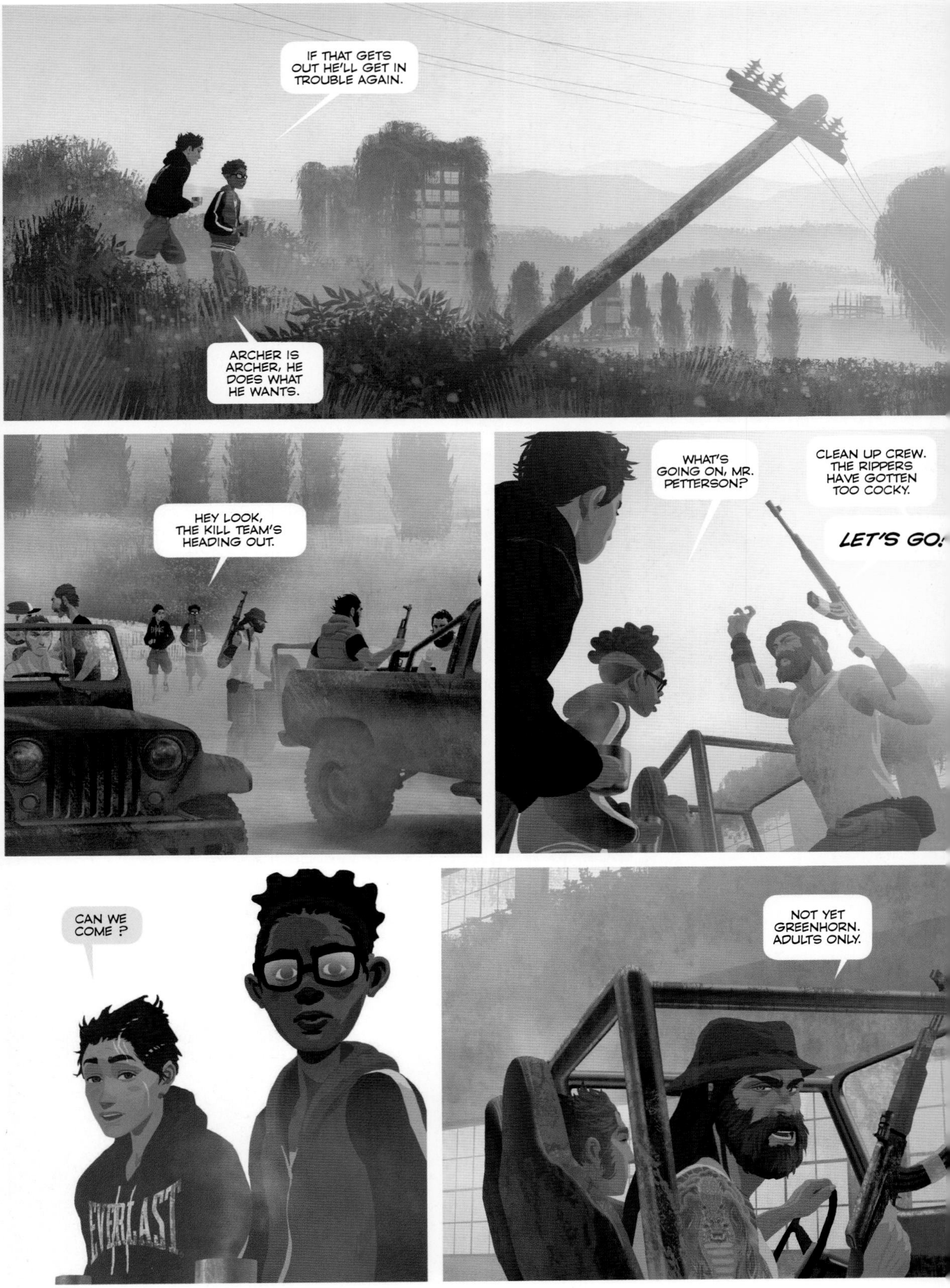
IF THAT GETS OUT HE'LL GET IN TROUBLE AGAIN.
ARCHER IS ARCHER, HE DOES WHAT HE WANTS.
HEY LOOK, THE KILL TEAM'S HEADING OUT.
WHAT'S GOING ON, MR. PETTERSON?
CLEAN UP CREW. THE RIPPERS HAVE GOTTEN TOO COCKY.
LET'S GO!
CAN WE COME ?
EVERLAST
NOT YET GREENHORN. ADULTS ONLY.

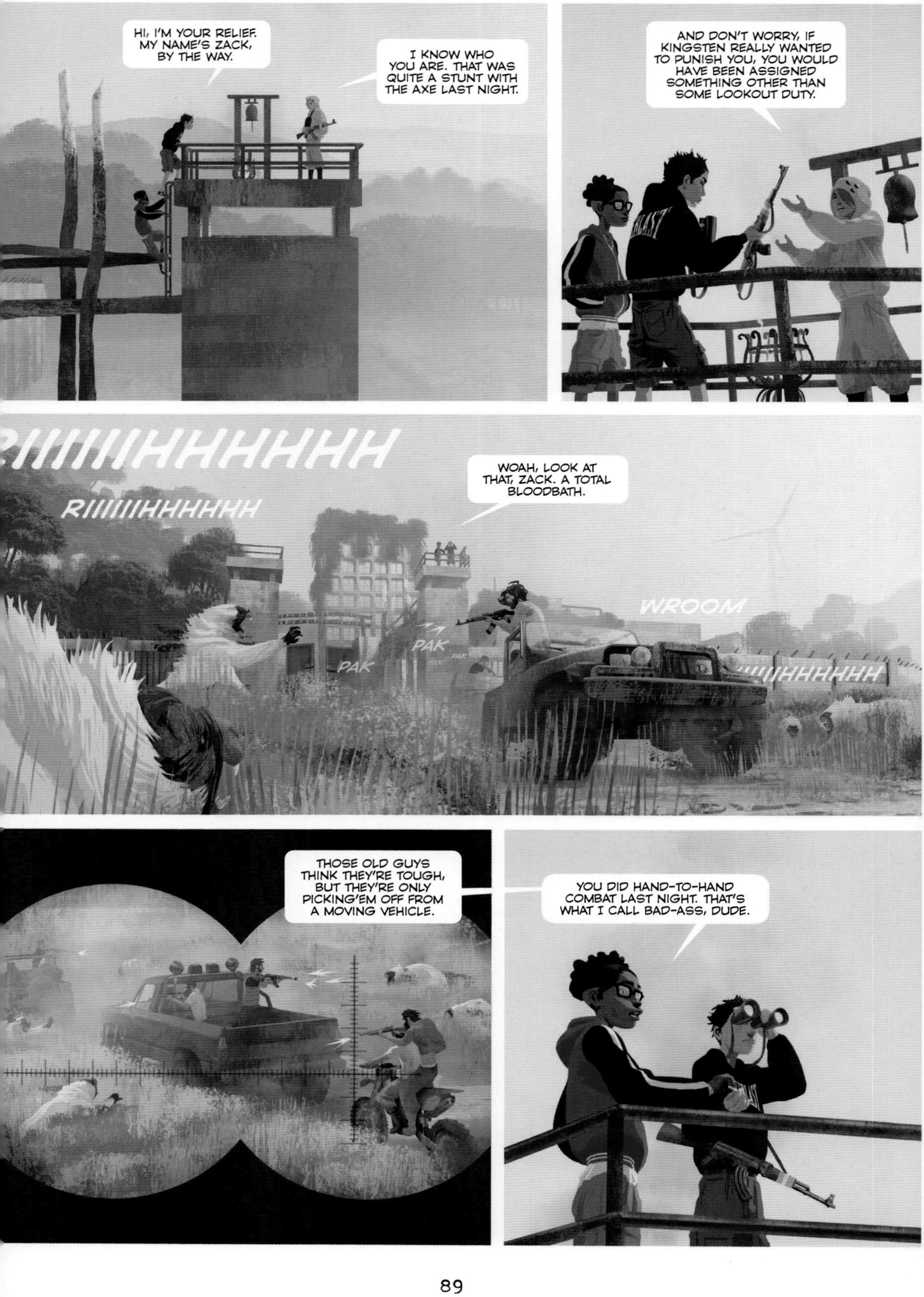
HI, I'M YOUR RELIEF. MY NAME'S ZACK, BY THE WAY.
I KNOW WHO YOU ARE. THAT WAS QUITE A STUNT WITH THE AXE LAST NIGHT.
AND DON'T WORRY, IF KINGSTEN REALLY WANTED TO PUNISH YOU, YOU WOULD HAVE BEEN ASSIGNED SOMETHING OTHER THAN SOME LOOKOUT DUTY.
RIIIIIHHHHHH
RIIIIIHHHHHH
WOAH, LOOK AT THAT, ZACK. A TOTAL BLOODBATH.
WROOM
PAK
PAK
IIIIIHHHHHH
THOSE OLD GUYS THINK THEY'RE TOUGH, BUT THEY'RE ONLY PICKING'EM OFF FROM A MOVING VEHICLE.
YOU DID HAND-TO-HAND COMBAT LAST NIGHT. THAT'S WHAT I CALL BAD-ASS, DUDE.

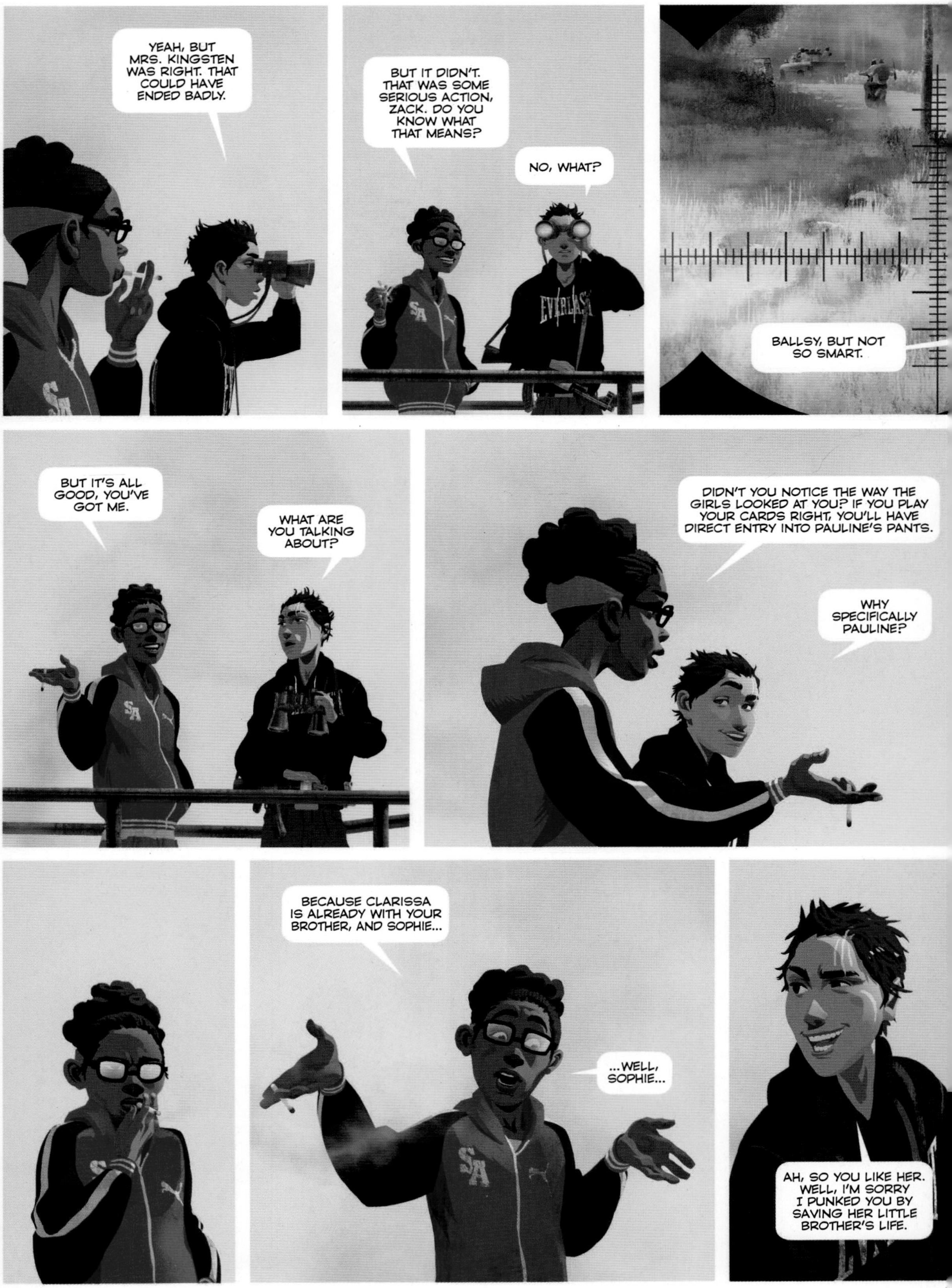
YEAH, BUT MRS. KINGSTEN WAS RIGHT. THAT COULD HAVE ENDED BADLY.
BUT IT DIDN'T. THAT WAS SOME SERIOUS ACTION, ZACK. DO YOU KNOW WHAT THAT MEANS?
NO, WHAT?
EVERLAST
BALLSY, BUT NOT SO SMART.
BUT IT'S ALL GOOD, YOU'VE GOT ME.
WHAT ARE YOU TALKING ABOUT?
DIDN'T YOU NOTICE THE WAY THE GIRLS LOOKED AT YOU? IF YOU PLAY YOUR CARDS RIGHT, YOU'LL HAVE DIRECT ENTRY INTO PAULINE'S PANTS.
WHY SPECIFICALLY PAULINE?
BECAUSE CLARISSA IS ALREADY WITH YOUR BROTHER, AND SOPHIE...
...WELL, SOPHIE...
AH, SO YOU LIKE HER. WELL, I'M SORRY I PUNKED YOU BY SAVING HER LITTLE BROTHER'S LIFE.

YEAH, DUDE, YOU TOTALLY STOLE THE LIMELIGHT. I'M NOT THE GO-GETTER. I HAVE TO RELY ON MY CHARM AND EXOTIC NATURE.

I THINK SOPHIE LIKES ME, BUT I'M WORRIED SHE SEES ME AS JUST A FRIEND. I'M WAITING FOR THE RIGHT OPPORTUNITY.

DON'T WAIT TOO LONG, YOU COULD BE DEAD TOMORROW.

OR SOPHIE.

HEY, COULD YOU COVER ME FOR A WHILE? I HAVE TO GO CLEAR SOMETHING UP.

WEEEH

WEEH

TDTDTD TDTDTDTD

TDTDTDTDTDTDTDTDTDTDTDTDTD

91

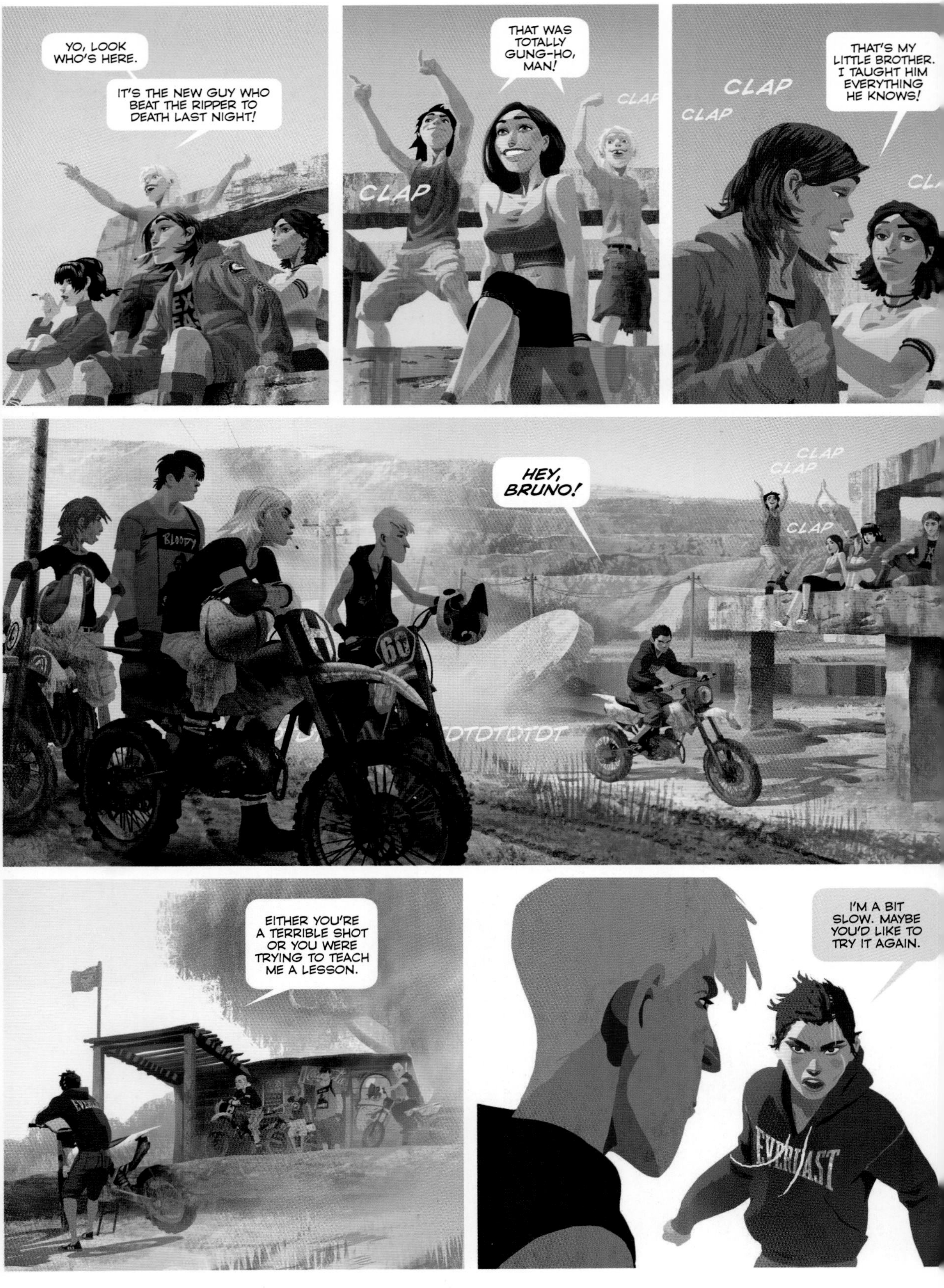
YO, LOOK WHO'S HERE.
IT'S THE NEW GUY WHO BEAT THE RIPPER TO DEATH LAST NIGHT!
THAT WAS TOTALLY GUNG-HO, MAN!
CLAP
CLAP
CLAP
CLAP
THAT'S MY LITTLE BROTHER. I TAUGHT HIM EVERYTHING HE KNOWS!
HEY, BRUNO!
CLAP
CLAP
CLAP
EITHER YOU'RE A TERRIBLE SHOT OR YOU WERE TRYING TO TEACH ME A LESSON.
I'M A BIT SLOW. MAYBE YOU'D LIKE TO TRY IT AGAIN.

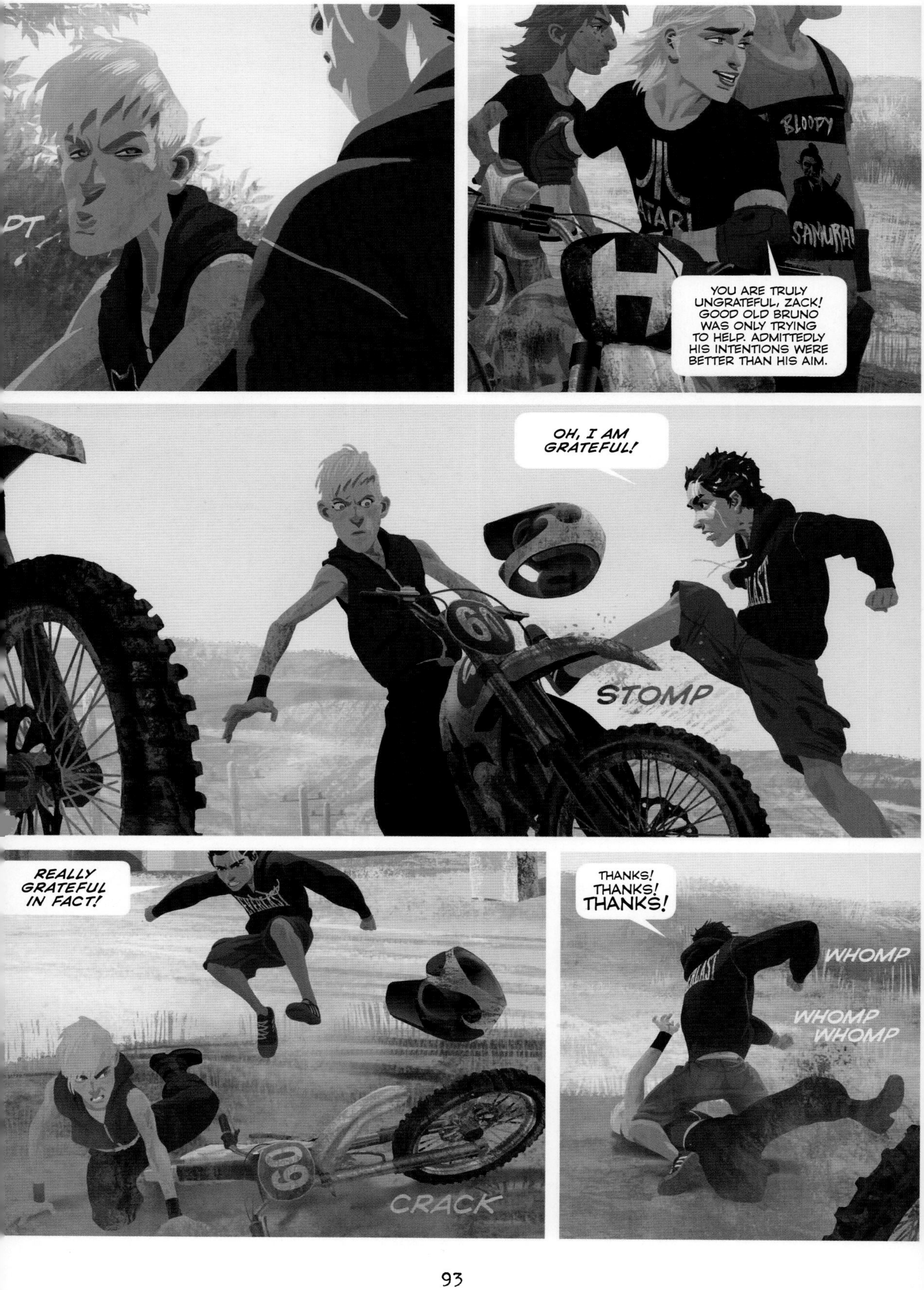
YOU ARE TRULY UNGRATEFUL, ZACK! GOOD OLD BRUNO WAS ONLY TRYING TO HELP. ADMITTEDLY HIS INTENTIONS WERE BETTER THAN HIS AIM.
OH, I AM GRATEFUL!
STOMP
REALLY GRATEFUL IN FACT!
CRACK
THANKS! THANKS! THANKS!
WHOMP
WHOMP WHOMP

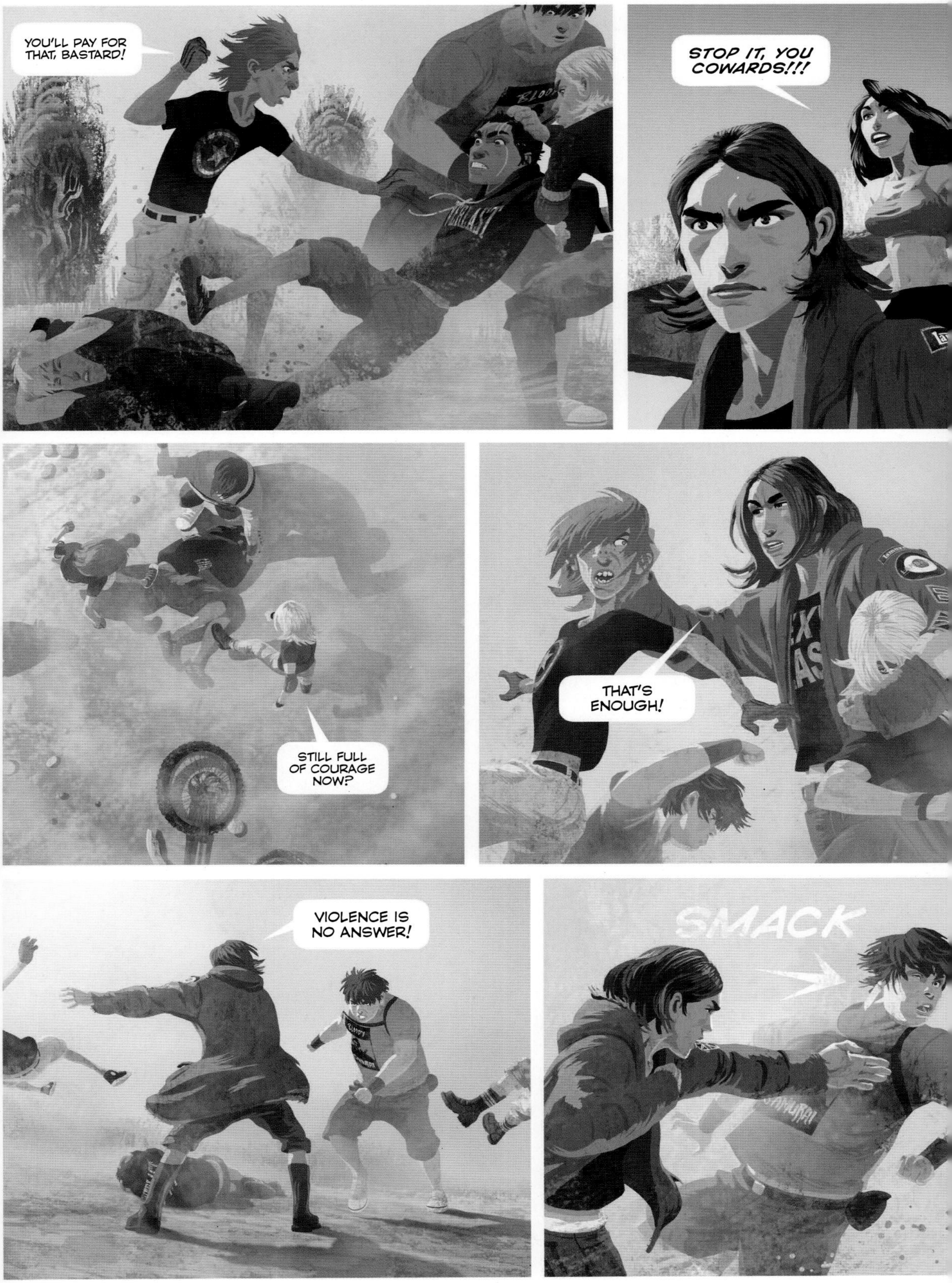
YOU'LL PAY FOR THAT, BASTARD!
STOP IT, YOU COWARDS!!!
STILL FULL OF COURAGE NOW?
THAT'S ENOUGH!
VIOLENCE IS NO ANSWER!
SMACK

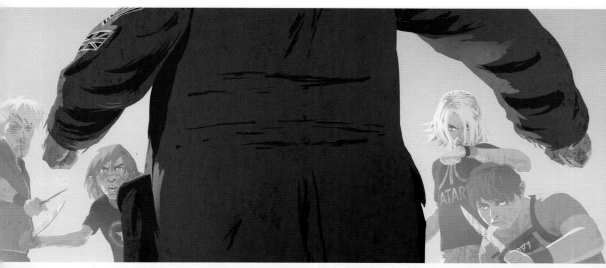

ZACK, ARE YOU OK?

NOW EASY BOYS.

THIS STARTED OUT A BIT ROUGH , BUT WE CAN STILL ALL BE FRIENDS.

YOU HAVE A CHOICE NOW IN WHAT YOU SWALLOW.

LEAD OR TENNESSEE WHISKY.

GOOD OLD ARCHER HAS PLENTY OF BOTH.

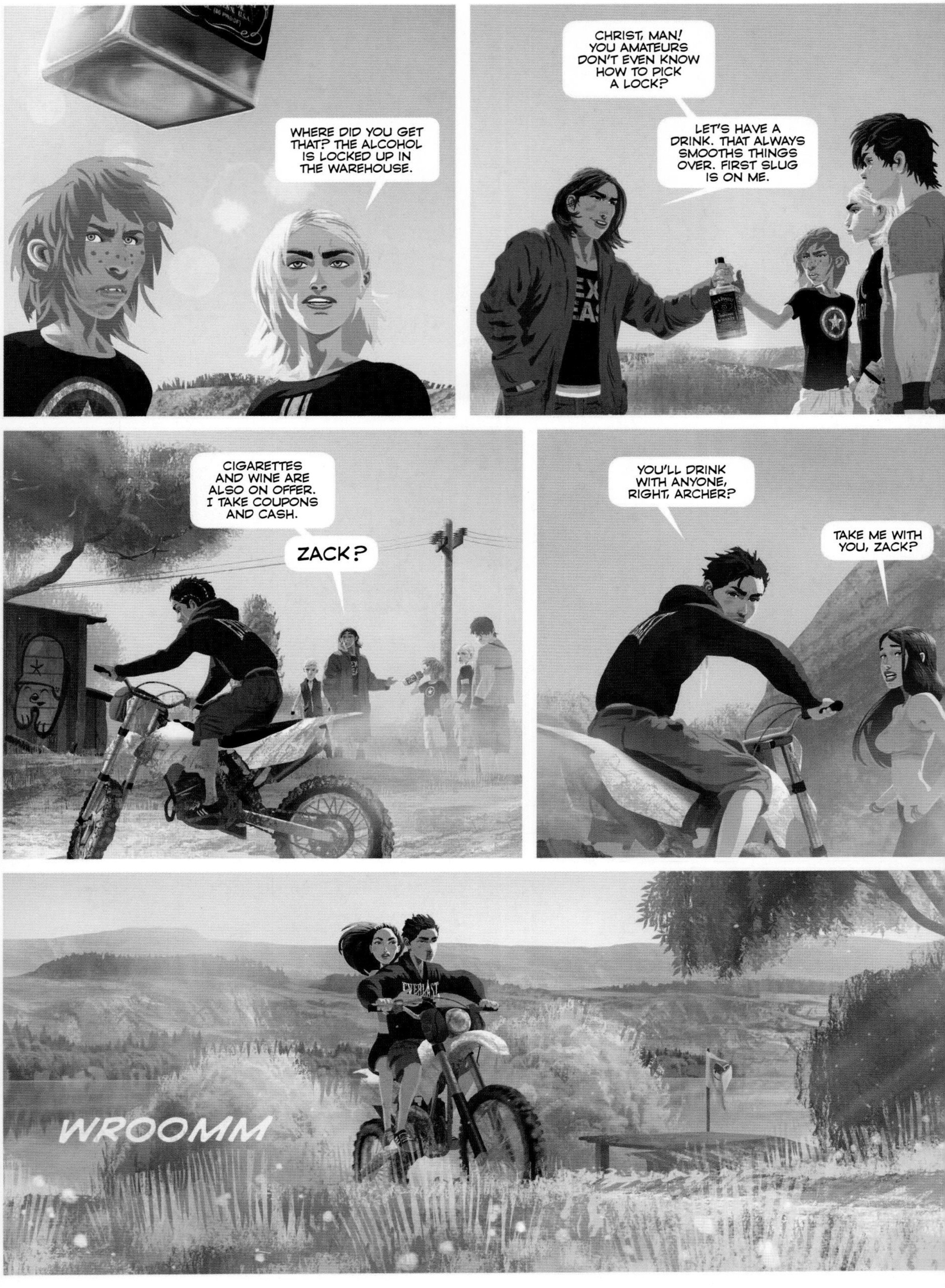

WHERE DID YOU GET THAT? THE ALCOHOL IS LOCKED UP IN THE WAREHOUSE.
CHRIST, MAN! YOU AMATEURS DON'T EVEN KNOW HOW TO PICK A LOCK?
LET'S HAVE A DRINK. THAT ALWAYS SMOOTHS THINGS OVER. FIRST SLUG IS ON ME.
CIGARETTES AND WINE ARE ALSO ON OFFER. I TAKE COUPONS AND CASH.
ZACK?
YOU'LL DRINK WITH ANYONE, RIGHT, ARCHER?
TAKE ME WITH YOU, ZACK?
WROOMM

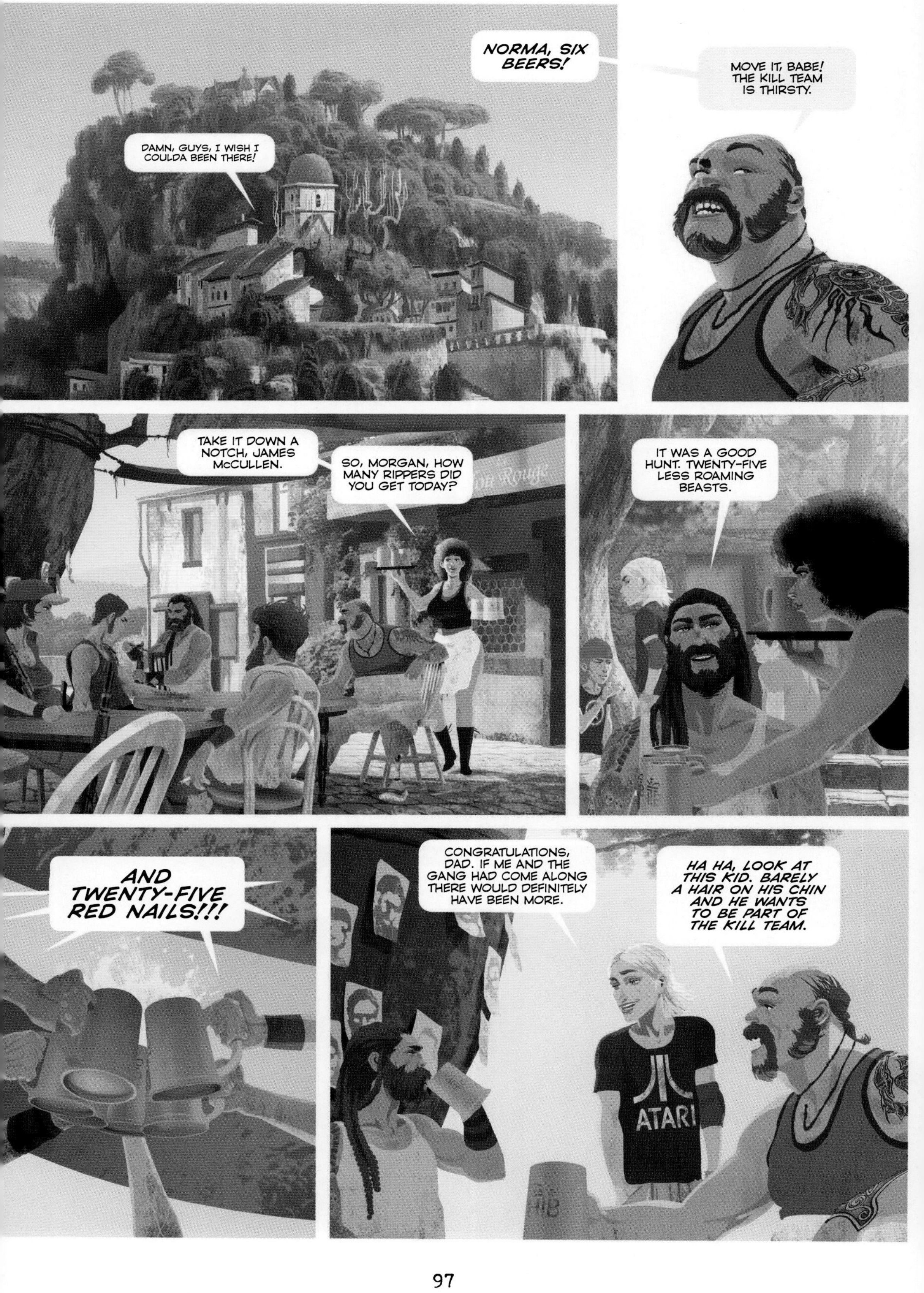
DAMN, GUYS, I WISH I COULDA BEEN THERE!
NORMA, SIX BEERS!
MOVE IT, BABE! THE KILL TEAM IS THIRSTY.
TAKE IT DOWN A NOTCH, JAMES McCULLEN.
SO, MORGAN, HOW MANY RIPPERS DID YOU GET TODAY?
IT WAS A GOOD HUNT. TWENTY-FIVE LESS ROAMING BEASTS.
AND TWENTY-FIVE RED NAILS!!!
CONGRATULATIONS, DAD. IF ME AND THE GANG HAD COME ALONG THERE WOULD DEFINITELY HAVE BEEN MORE.
HA HA, LOOK AT THIS KID. BARELY A HAIR ON HIS CHIN AND HE WANTS TO BE PART OF THE KILL TEAM.
ATARI

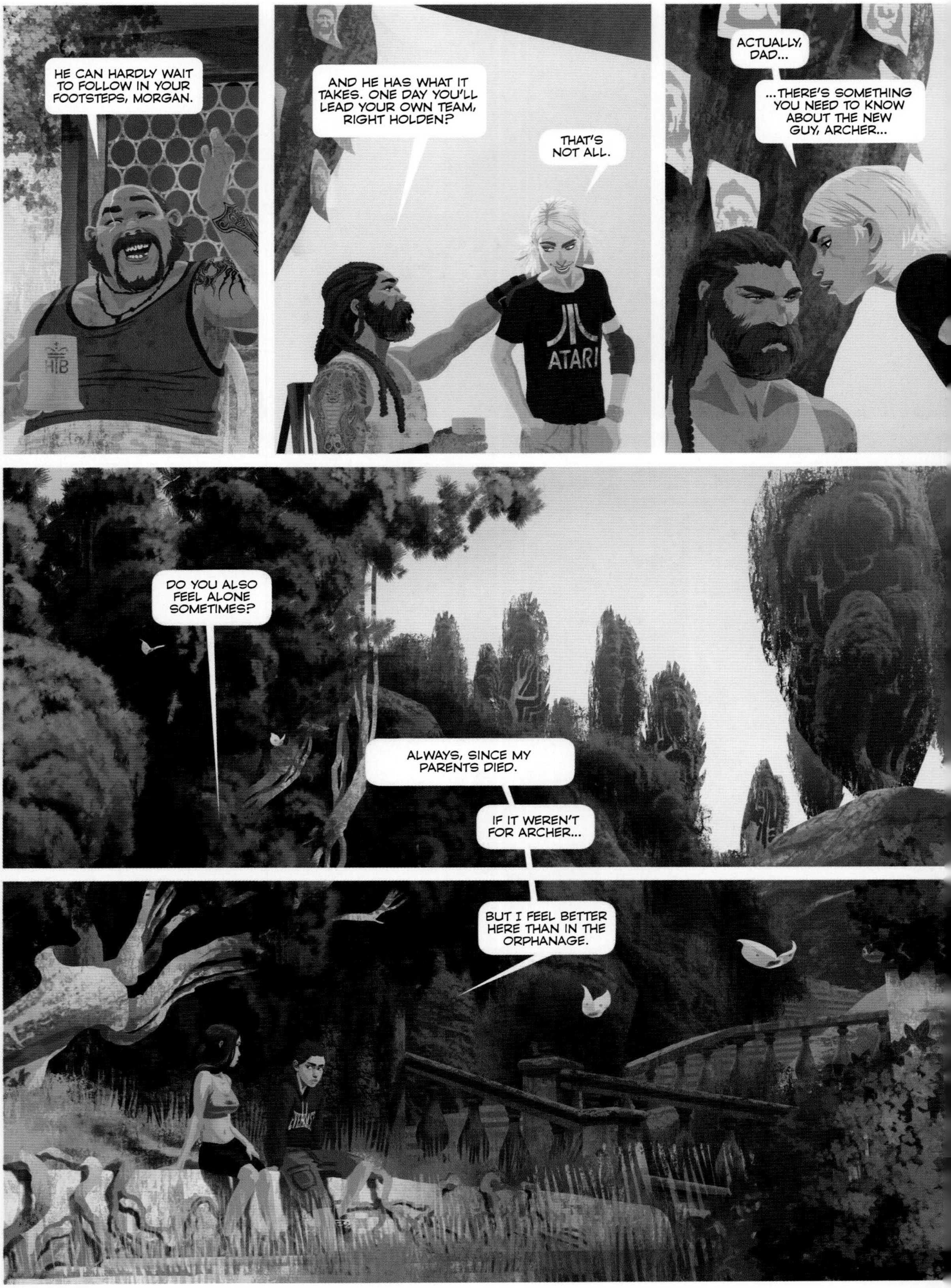
HE CAN HARDLY WAIT TO FOLLOW IN YOUR FOOTSTEPS, MORGAN.
HIB
AND HE HAS WHAT IT TAKES. ONE DAY YOU'LL LEAD YOUR OWN TEAM, RIGHT HOLDEN?
THAT'S NOT ALL.
ATARI
ACTUALLY, DAD...
...THERE'S SOMETHING YOU NEED TO KNOW ABOUT THE NEW GUY, ARCHER...
DO YOU ALSO FEEL ALONE SOMETIMES?
ALWAYS, SINCE MY PARENTS DIED.
IF IT WEREN'T FOR ARCHER...
BUT I FEEL BETTER HERE THAN IN THE ORPHANAGE.

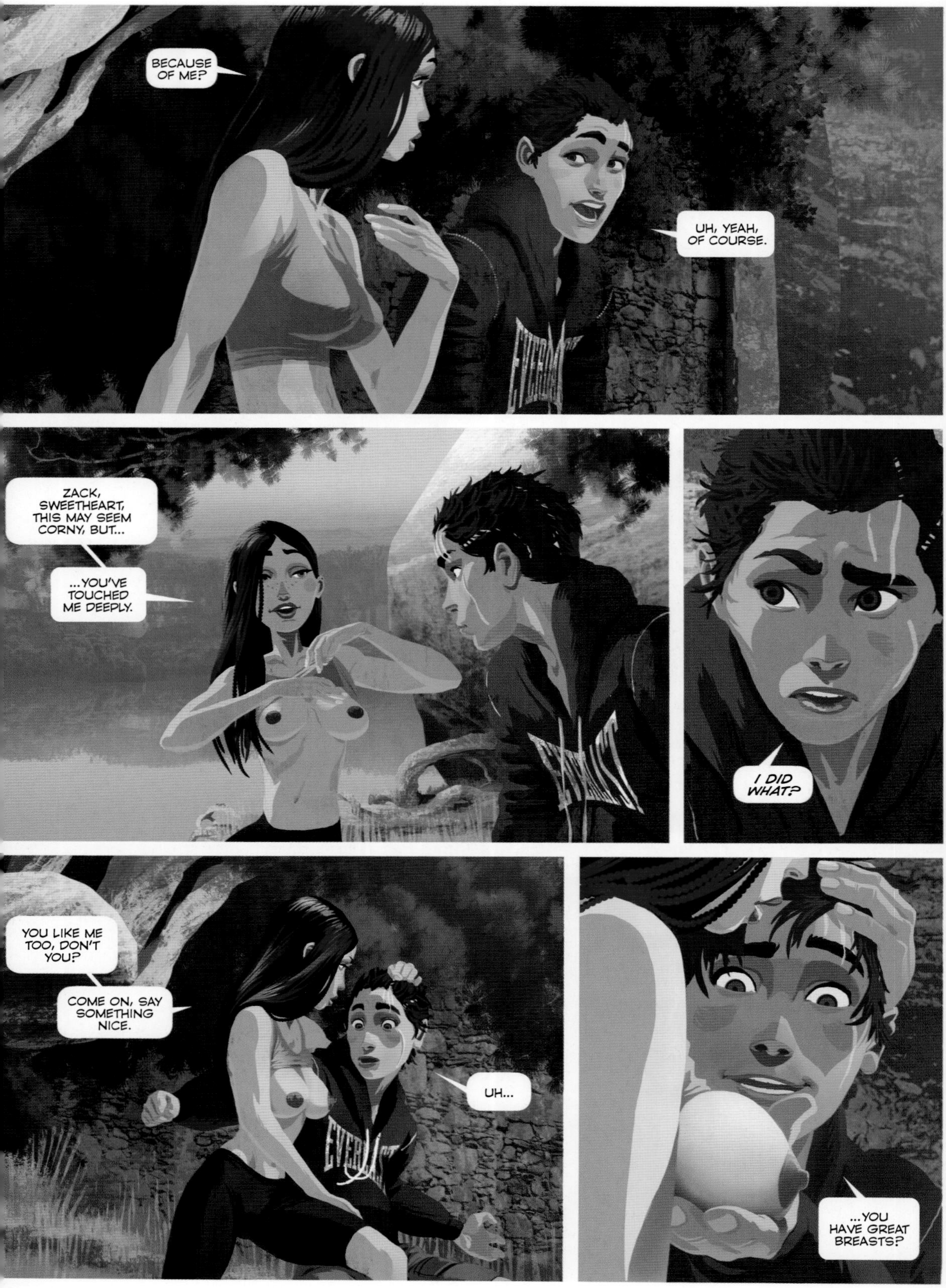
BECAUSE OF ME?
UH, YEAH, OF COURSE.
ZACK, SWEETHEART, THIS MAY SEEM CORNY, BUT...
...YOU'VE TOUCHED ME DEEPLY.
I DID WHAT?
YOU LIKE ME TOO, DON'T YOU?
COME ON, SAY SOMETHING NICE.
UH...
...YOU HAVE GREAT BREASTS?

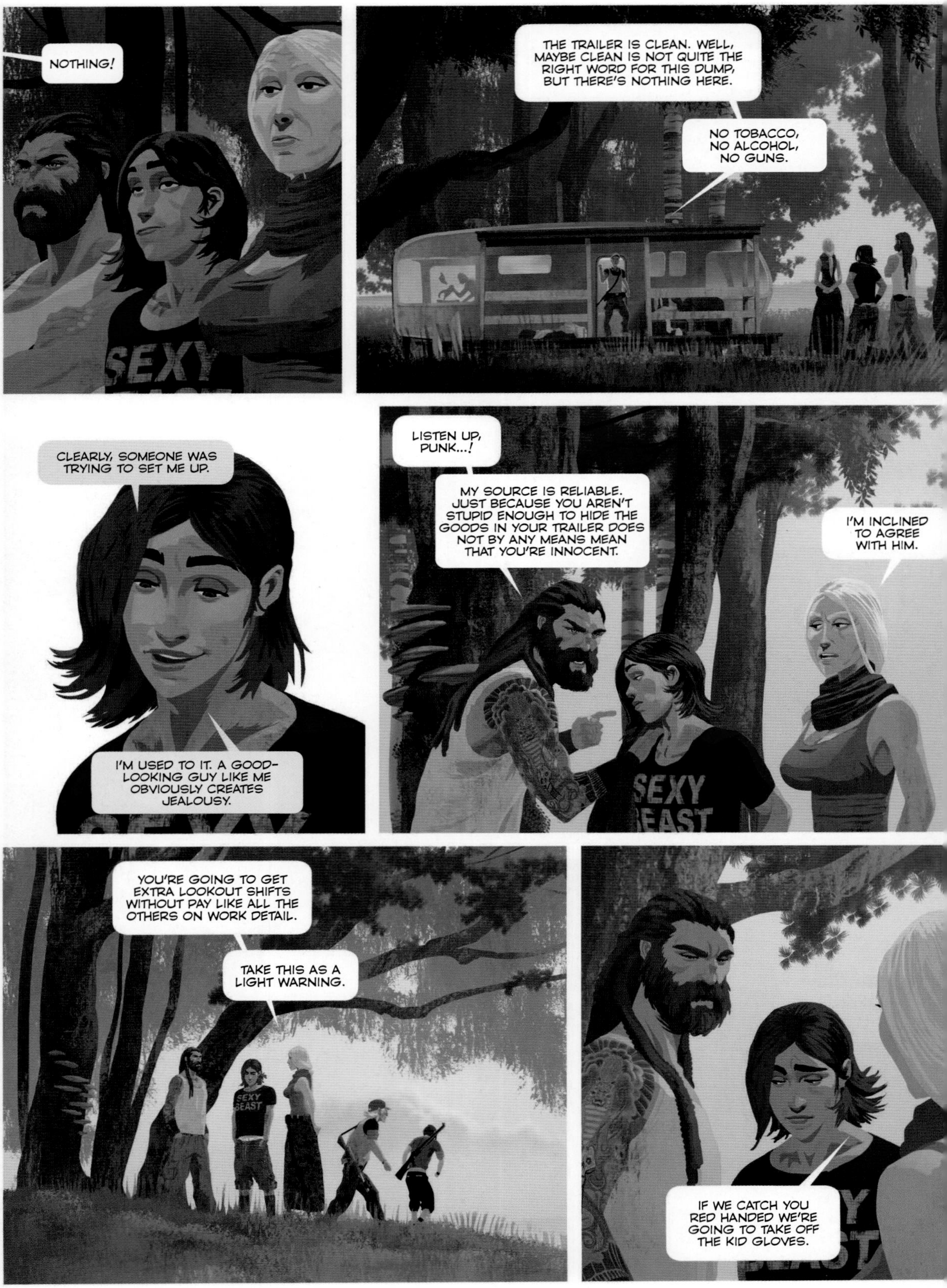
NOTHING!
THE TRAILER IS CLEAN. WELL, MAYBE CLEAN IS NOT QUITE THE RIGHT WORD FOR THIS DUMP, BUT THERE'S NOTHING HERE.
NO TOBACCO, NO ALCOHOL, NO GUNS.
SEXY
CLEARLY, SOMEONE WAS TRYING TO SET ME UP.
I'M USED TO IT. A GOOD-LOOKING GUY LIKE ME OBVIOUSLY CREATES JEALOUSY.
LISTEN UP, PUNK...!
MY SOURCE IS RELIABLE. JUST BECAUSE YOU AREN'T STUPID ENOUGH TO HIDE THE GOODS IN YOUR TRAILER DOES NOT BY ANY MEANS MEAN THAT YOU'RE INNOCENT.
I'M INCLINED TO AGREE WITH HIM.
SEXY
YOU'RE GOING TO GET EXTRA LOOKOUT SHIFTS WITHOUT PAY LIKE ALL THE OTHERS ON WORK DETAIL.
TAKE THIS AS A LIGHT WARNING.
SEXY BEAST
IF WE CATCH YOU RED HANDED WE'RE GOING TO TAKE OFF THE KID GLOVES.

SPLASH

AAAH, THAT FEELS GOOD!!!

SPLASH

HHH... HHH...

HEADSHOT!

HEADSHOT!

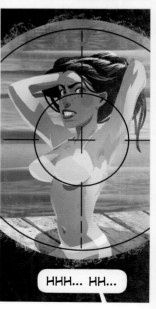

HHH... HH...

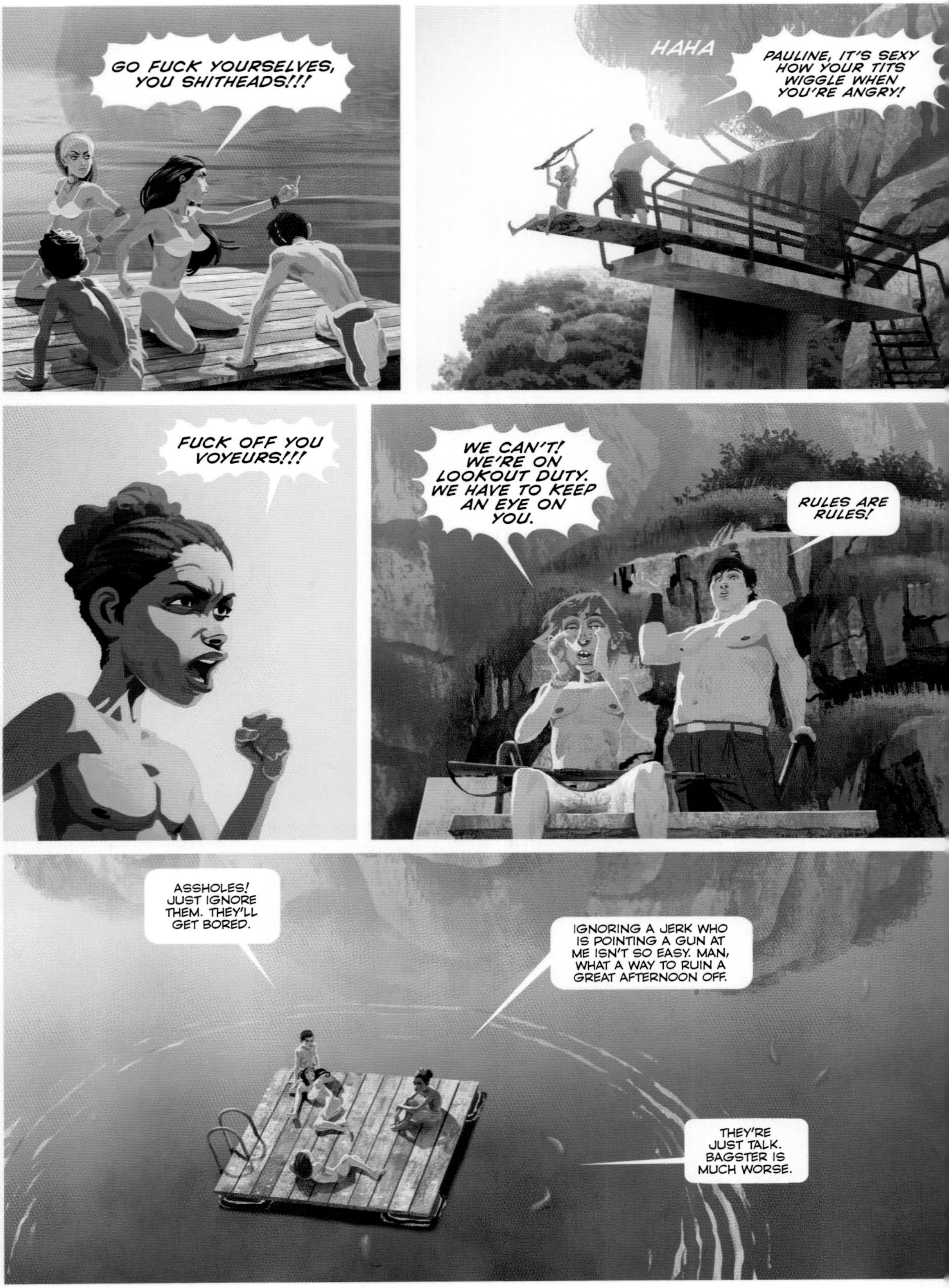
GO FUCK YOURSELVES, YOU SHITHEADS!!!
HAHA
PAULINE, IT'S SEXY HOW YOUR TITS WIGGLE WHEN YOU'RE ANGRY!
FUCK OFF YOU VOYEURS!!!
WE CAN'T! WE'RE ON LOOKOUT DUTY. WE HAVE TO KEEP AN EYE ON YOU.
RULES ARE RULES!
ASSHOLES! JUST IGNORE THEM. THEY'LL GET BORED.
IGNORING A JERK WHO IS POINTING A GUN AT ME ISN'T SO EASY. MAN, WHAT A WAY TO RUIN A GREAT AFTERNOON OFF.
THEY'RE JUST TALK. BAGSTER IS MUCH WORSE.

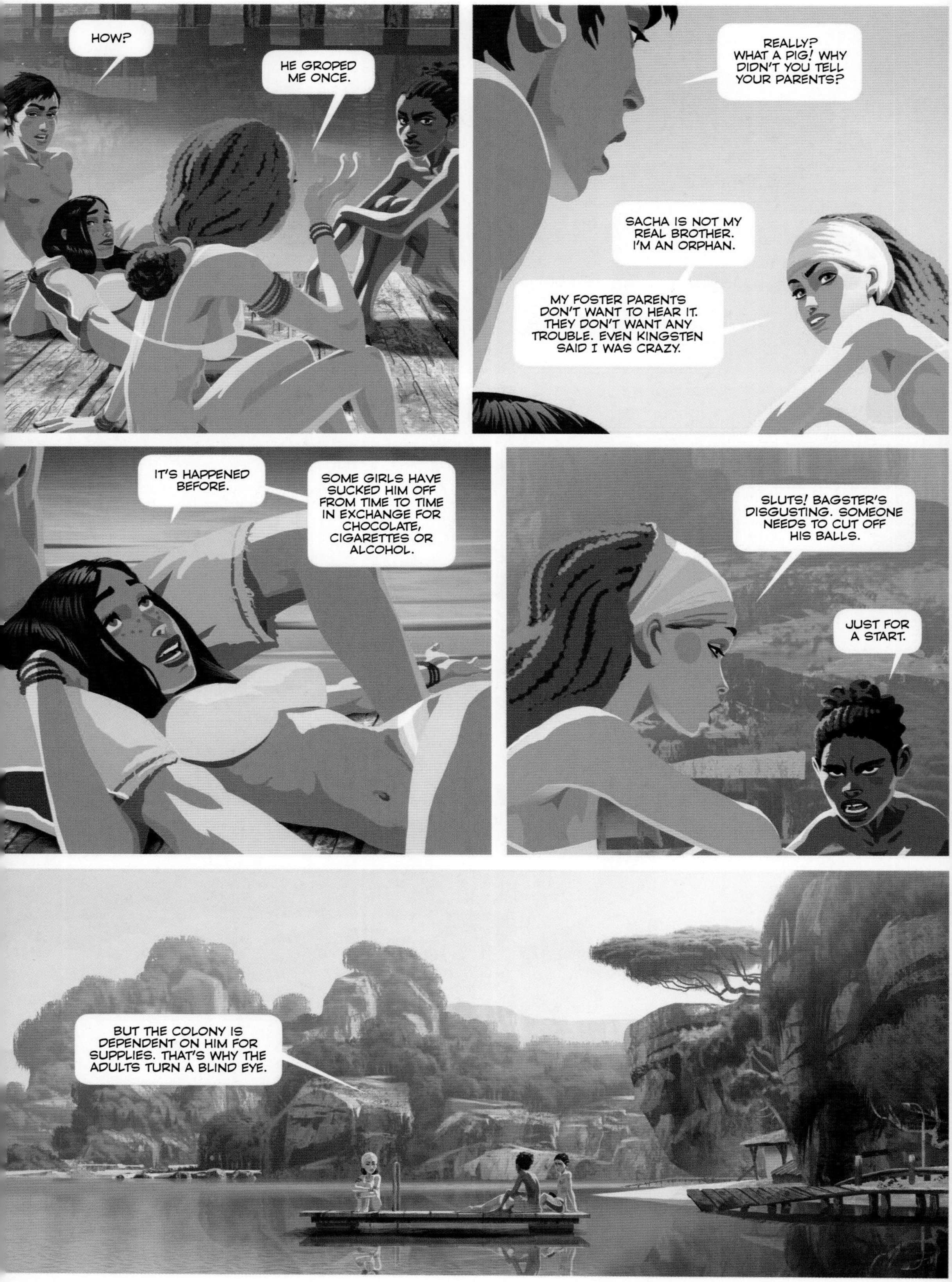
HOW?
HE GROPED ME ONCE.
REALLY? WHAT A PIG! WHY DIDN'T YOU TELL YOUR PARENTS?
SACHA IS NOT MY REAL BROTHER. I'M AN ORPHAN.
MY FOSTER PARENTS DON'T WANT TO HEAR IT. THEY DON'T WANT ANY TROUBLE. EVEN KINGSTEN SAID I WAS CRAZY.
IT'S HAPPENED BEFORE.
SOME GIRLS HAVE SUCKED HIM OFF FROM TIME TO TIME IN EXCHANGE FOR CHOCOLATE, CIGARETTES OR ALCOHOL.
SLUTS! BAGSTER'S DISGUSTING. SOMEONE NEEDS TO CUT OFF HIS BALLS.
JUST FOR A START.
BUT THE COLONY IS DEPENDENT ON HIM FOR SUPPLIES. THAT'S WHY THE ADULTS TURN A BLIND EYE.

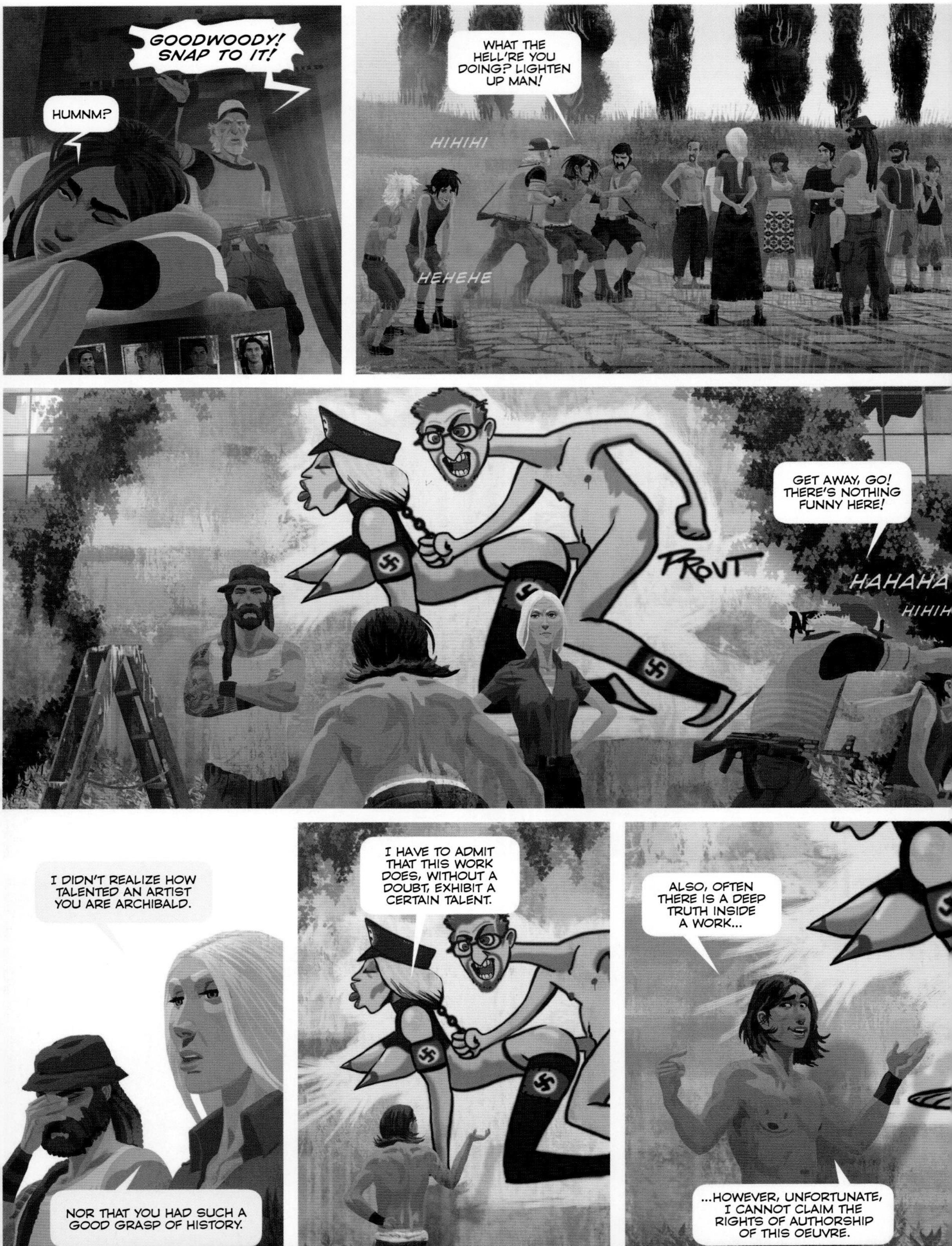
GOODWOODY! SNAP TO IT!
HUMNM?
WHAT THE HELL'RE YOU DOING? LIGHTEN UP MAN!
HIHIHI
HEHEHE
GET AWAY, GO! THERE'S NOTHING FUNNY HERE!
PROUT
HAHAHA
I DIDN'T REALIZE HOW TALENTED AN ARTIST YOU ARE ARCHIBALD.
NOR THAT YOU HAD SUCH A GOOD GRASP OF HISTORY.
I HAVE TO ADMIT THAT THIS WORK DOES, WITHOUT A DOUBT, EXHIBIT A CERTAIN TALENT.
ALSO, OFTEN THERE IS A DEEP TRUTH INSIDE A WORK...
...HOWEVER, UNFORTUNATE, I CANNOT CLAIM THE RIGHTS OF AUTHORSHIP OF THIS OEUVRE.

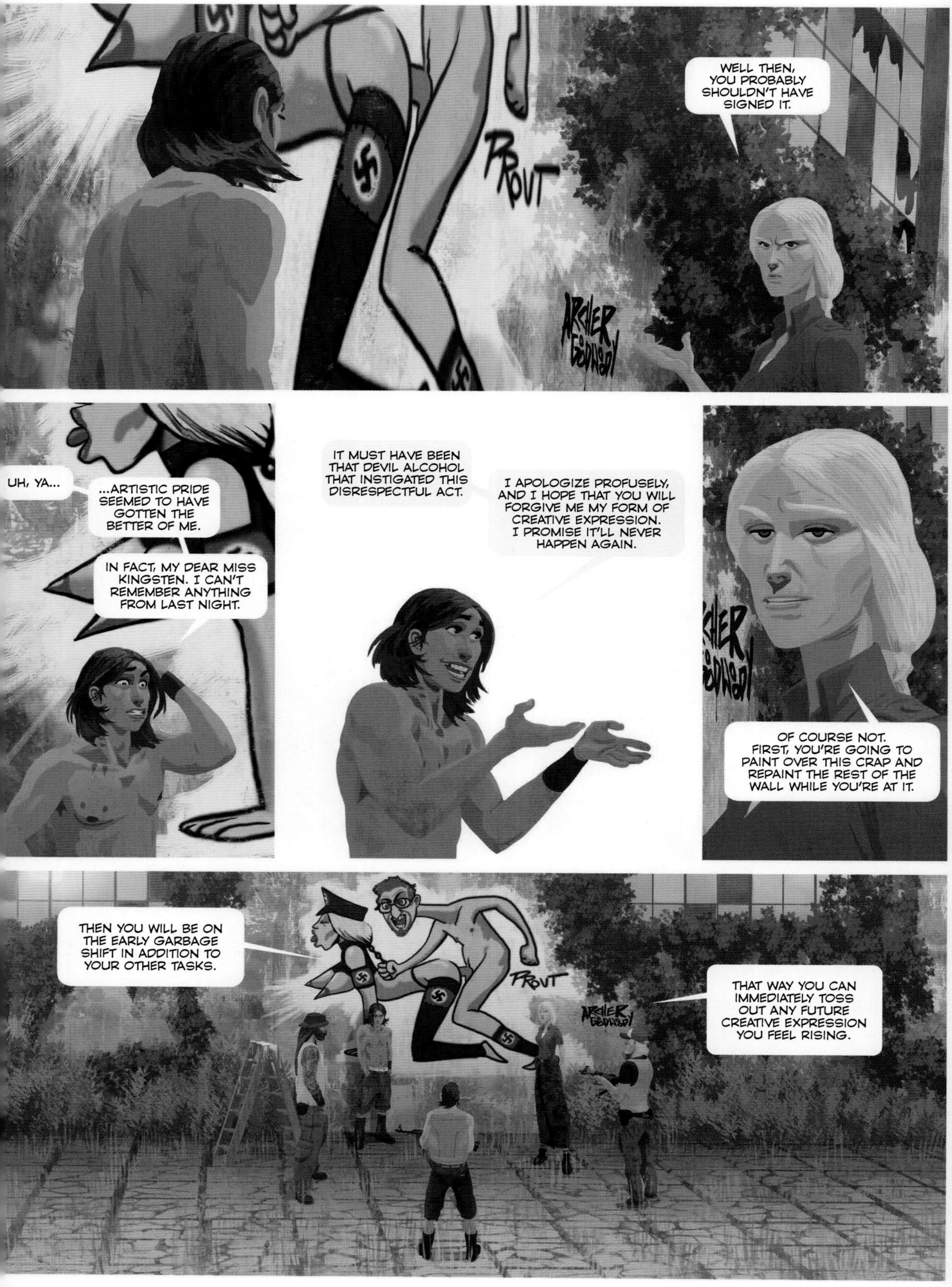
PROUT
WELL THEN, YOU PROBABLY SHOULDN'T HAVE SIGNED IT.
ARCHER GODWOOD
UH, YA...
...ARTISTIC PRIDE SEEMED TO HAVE GOTTEN THE BETTER OF ME.
IN FACT, MY DEAR MISS KINGSTEN. I CAN'T REMEMBER ANYTHING FROM LAST NIGHT.
IT MUST HAVE BEEN THAT DEVIL ALCOHOL THAT INSTIGATED THIS DISRESPECTFUL ACT.
I APOLOGIZE PROFUSELY, AND I HOPE THAT YOU WILL FORGIVE ME MY FORM OF CREATIVE EXPRESSION. I PROMISE IT'LL NEVER HAPPEN AGAIN.
OF COURSE NOT. FIRST, YOU'RE GOING TO PAINT OVER THIS CRAP AND REPAINT THE REST OF THE WALL WHILE YOU'RE AT IT.
THEN YOU WILL BE ON THE EARLY GARBAGE SHIFT IN ADDITION TO YOUR OTHER TASKS.
PROUT
THAT WAY YOU CAN IMMEDIATELY TOSS OUT ANY FUTURE CREATIVE EXPRESSION YOU FEEL RISING.

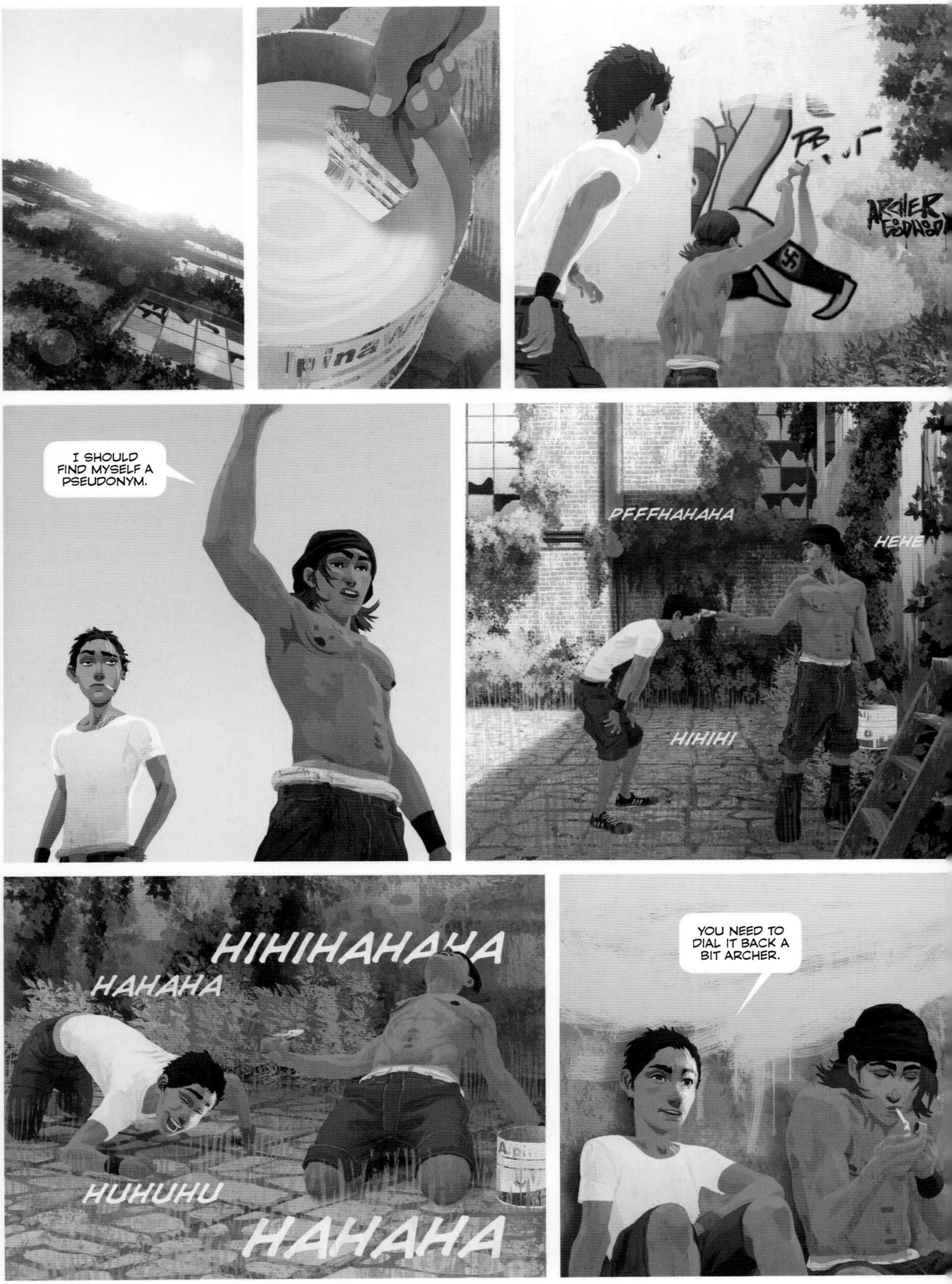

ARCHER
I SHOULD FIND MYSELF A PSEUDONYM.
PFFFHAHAHA
HEHE
HIHIHI
HIHIHAHAHA
HAHAHA
HUHUHU
HAHAHA
YOU NEED TO DIAL IT BACK A BIT ARCHER.

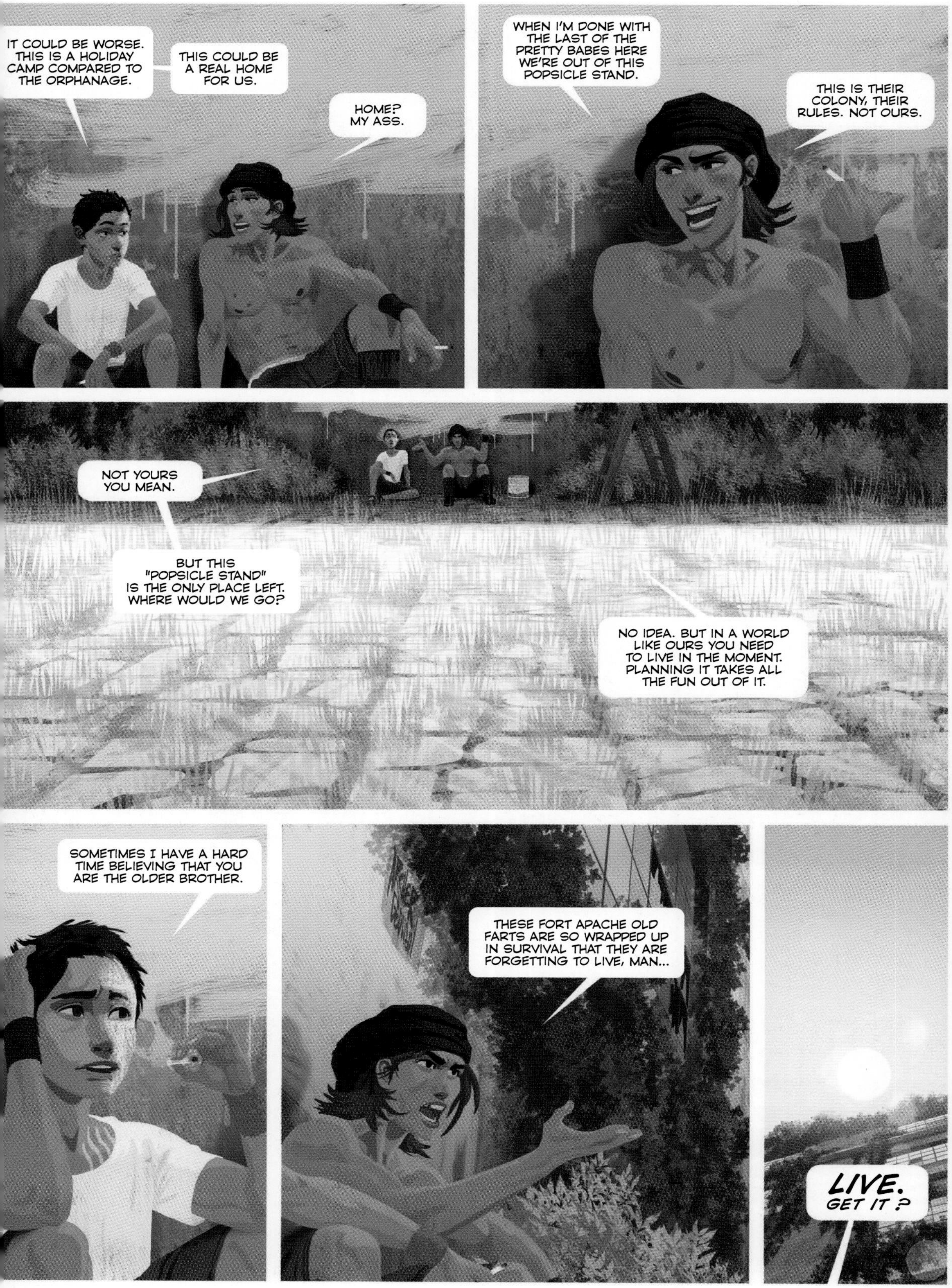

IT COULD BE WORSE. THIS IS A HOLIDAY CAMP COMPARED TO THE ORPHANAGE.
THIS COULD BE A REAL HOME FOR US.
HOME? MY ASS.
WHEN I'M DONE WITH THE LAST OF THE PRETTY BABES HERE WE'RE OUT OF THIS POPSICLE STAND.
THIS IS THEIR COLONY, THEIR RULES. NOT OURS.
NOT YOURS YOU MEAN.
BUT THIS "POPSICLE STAND" IS THE ONLY PLACE LEFT. WHERE WOULD WE GO?
NO IDEA. BUT IN A WORLD LIKE OURS YOU NEED TO LIVE IN THE MOMENT. PLANNING IT TAKES ALL THE FUN OUT OF IT.
SOMETIMES I HAVE A HARD TIME BELIEVING THAT YOU ARE THE OLDER BROTHER.
THESE FORT APACHE OLD FARTS ARE SO WRAPPED UP IN SURVIVAL THAT THEY ARE FORGETTING TO LIVE, MAN...
LIVE.
GET IT ?

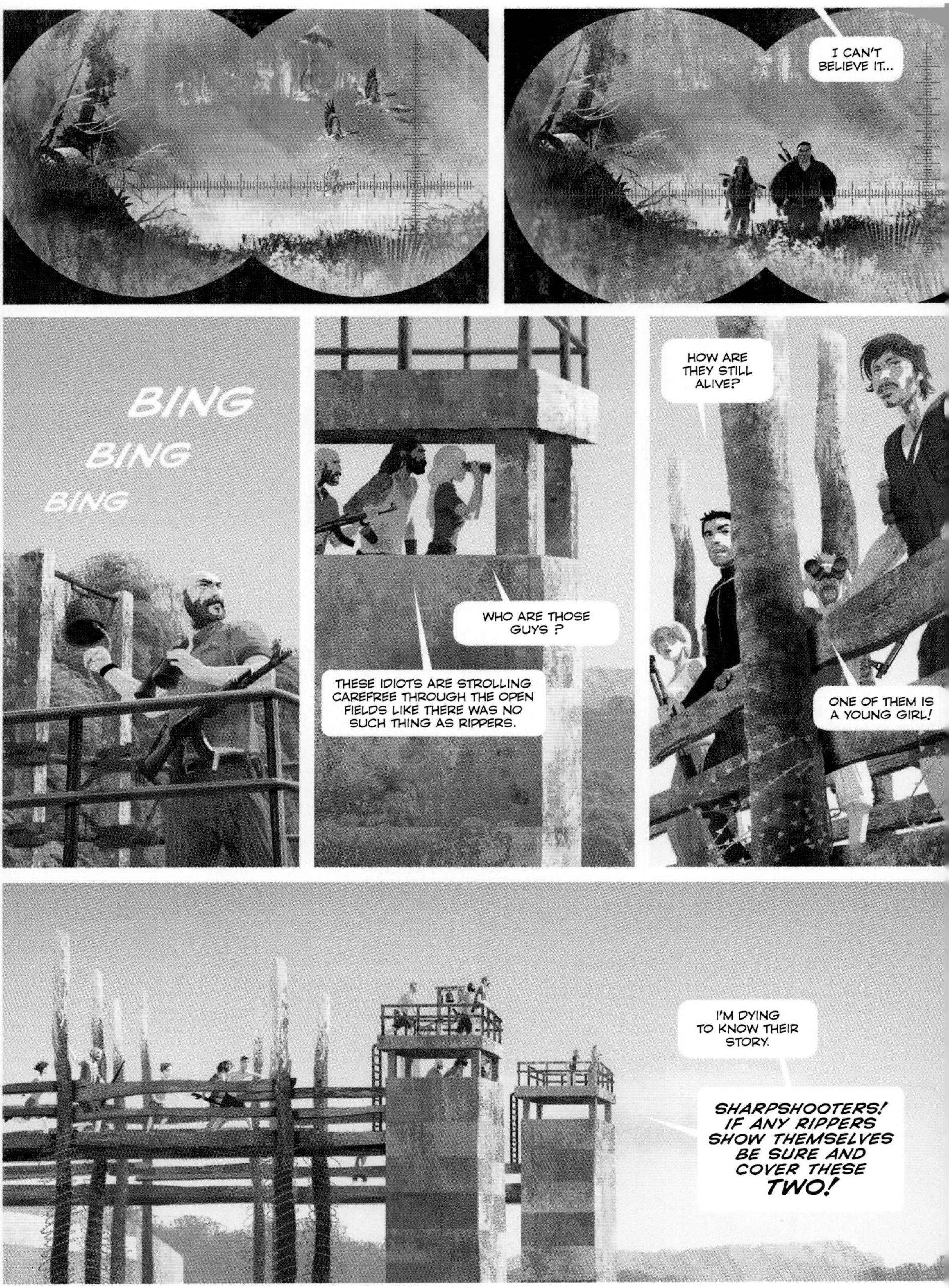

I CAN'T BELIEVE IT...
BING
BING
BING
WHO ARE THOSE GUYS ?
THESE IDIOTS ARE STROLLING CAREFREE THROUGH THE OPEN FIELDS LIKE THERE WAS NO SUCH THING AS RIPPERS.
HOW ARE THEY STILL ALIVE?
ONE OF THEM IS A YOUNG GIRL!
I'M DYING TO KNOW THEIR STORY.
SHARPSHOOTERS! IF ANY RIPPERS SHOW THEMSELVES BE SURE AND COVER THESE TWO!

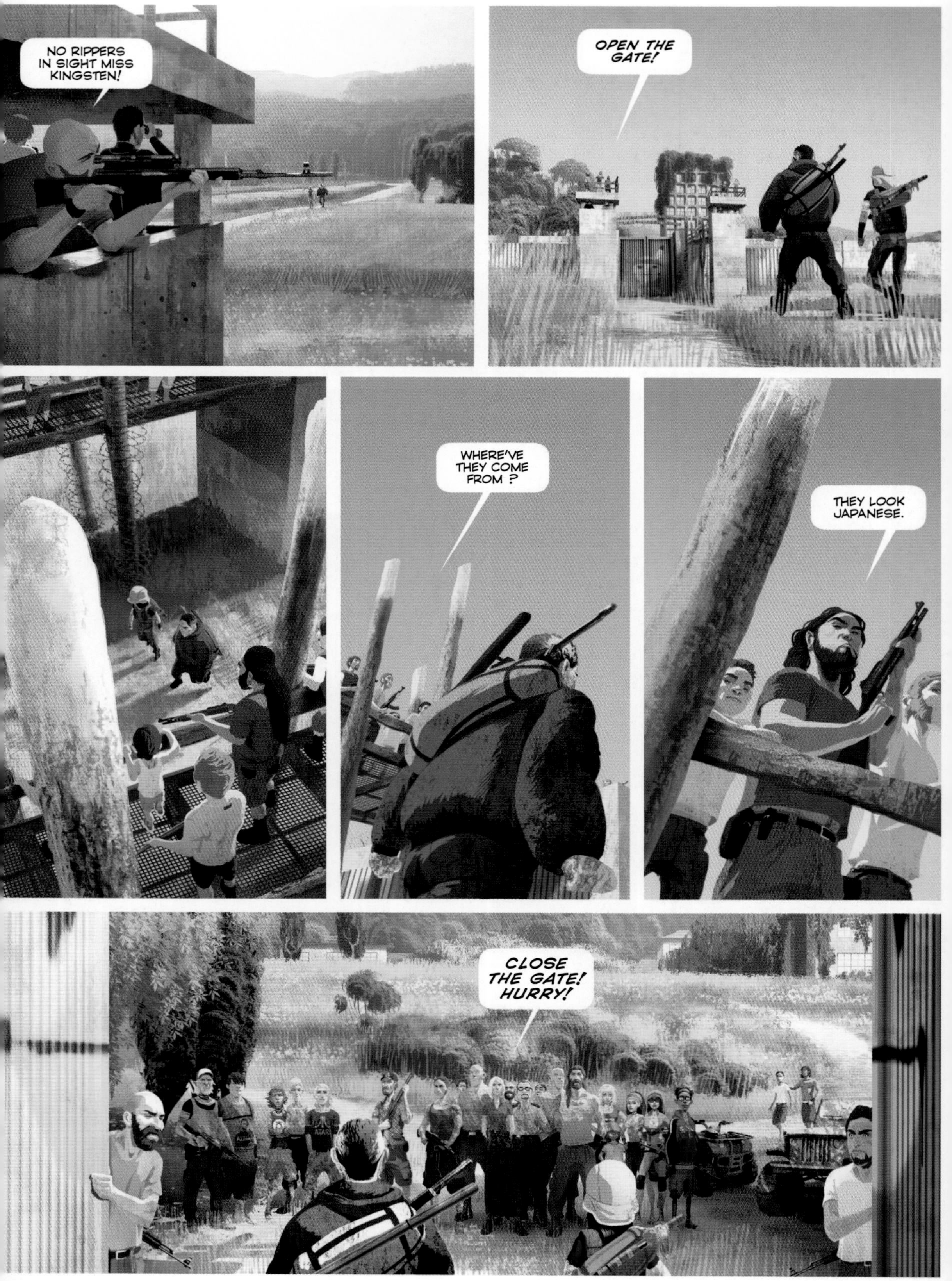
NO RIPPERS IN SIGHT MISS KINGSTEN!
OPEN THE GATE!
WHERE'VE THEY COME FROM ?
THEY LOOK JAPANESE.
CLOSE THE GATE! HURRY!

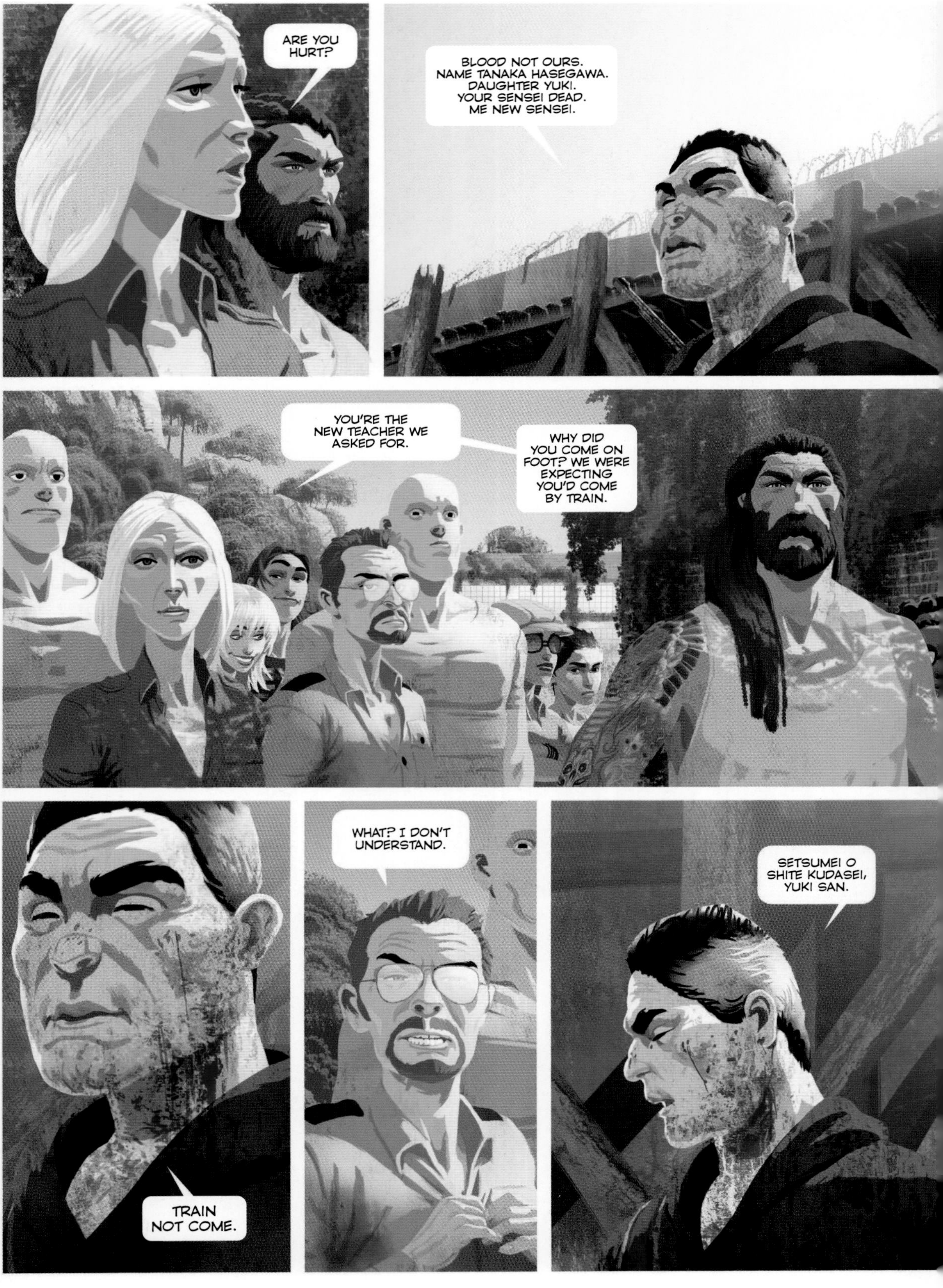
ARE YOU HURT?
BLOOD NOT OURS. NAME TANAKA HASEGAWA. DAUGHTER YUKI. YOUR SENSEI DEAD. ME NEW SENSEI.
YOU'RE THE NEW TEACHER WE ASKED FOR.
WHY DID YOU COME ON FOOT? WE WERE EXPECTING YOU'D COME BY TRAIN.
TRAIN NOT COME.
WHAT? I DON'T UNDERSTAND.
SETSUMEI O SHITE KUDASEI, YUKI SAN.

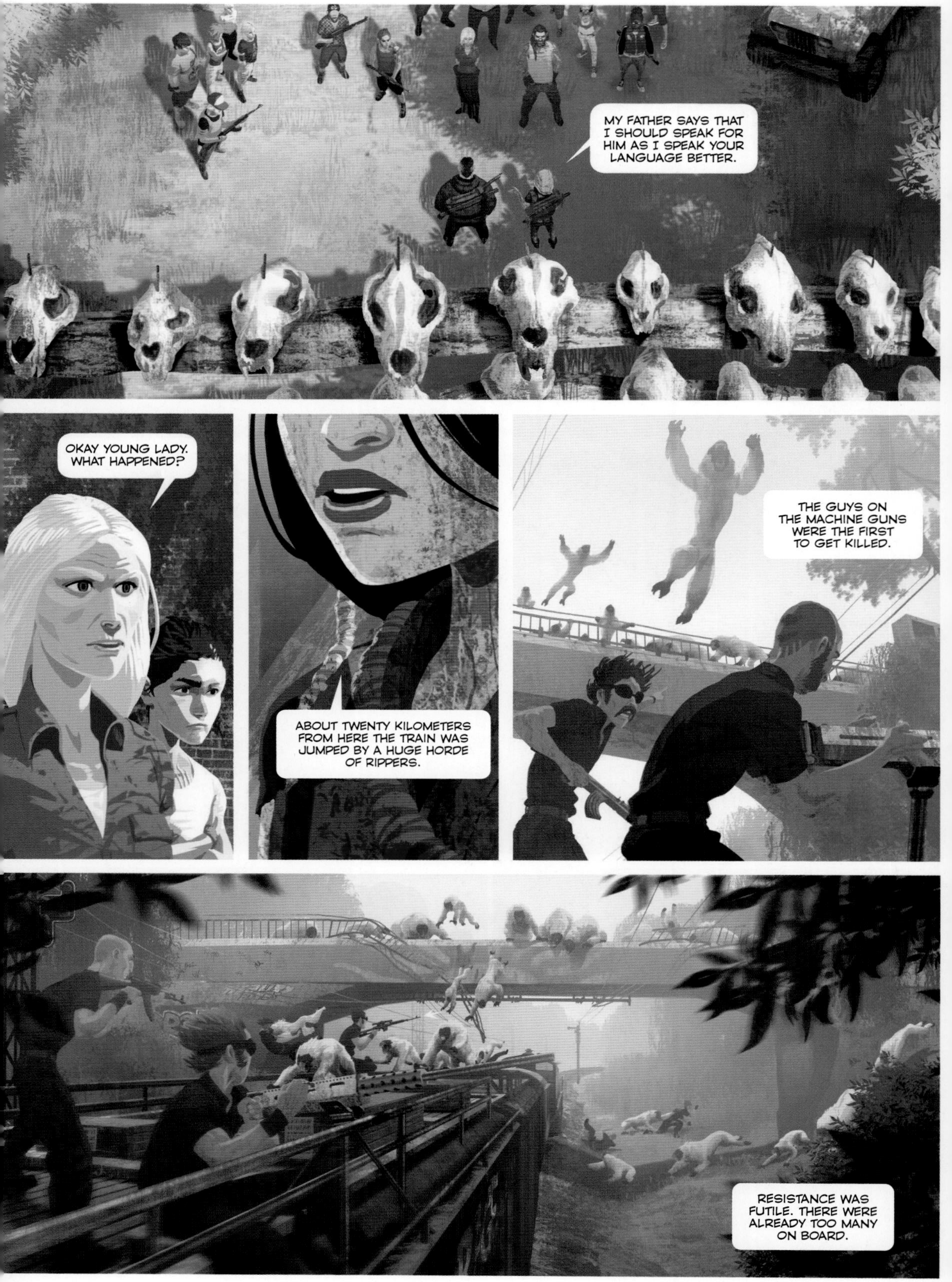
MY FATHER SAYS THAT I SHOULD SPEAK FOR HIM AS I SPEAK YOUR LANGUAGE BETTER.
OKAY YOUNG LADY. WHAT HAPPENED?
ABOUT TWENTY KILOMETERS FROM HERE THE TRAIN WAS JUMPED BY A HUGE HORDE OF RIPPERS.
THE GUYS ON THE MACHINE GUNS WERE THE FIRST TO GET KILLED.
RESISTANCE WAS FUTILE. THERE WERE ALREADY TOO MANY ON BOARD.

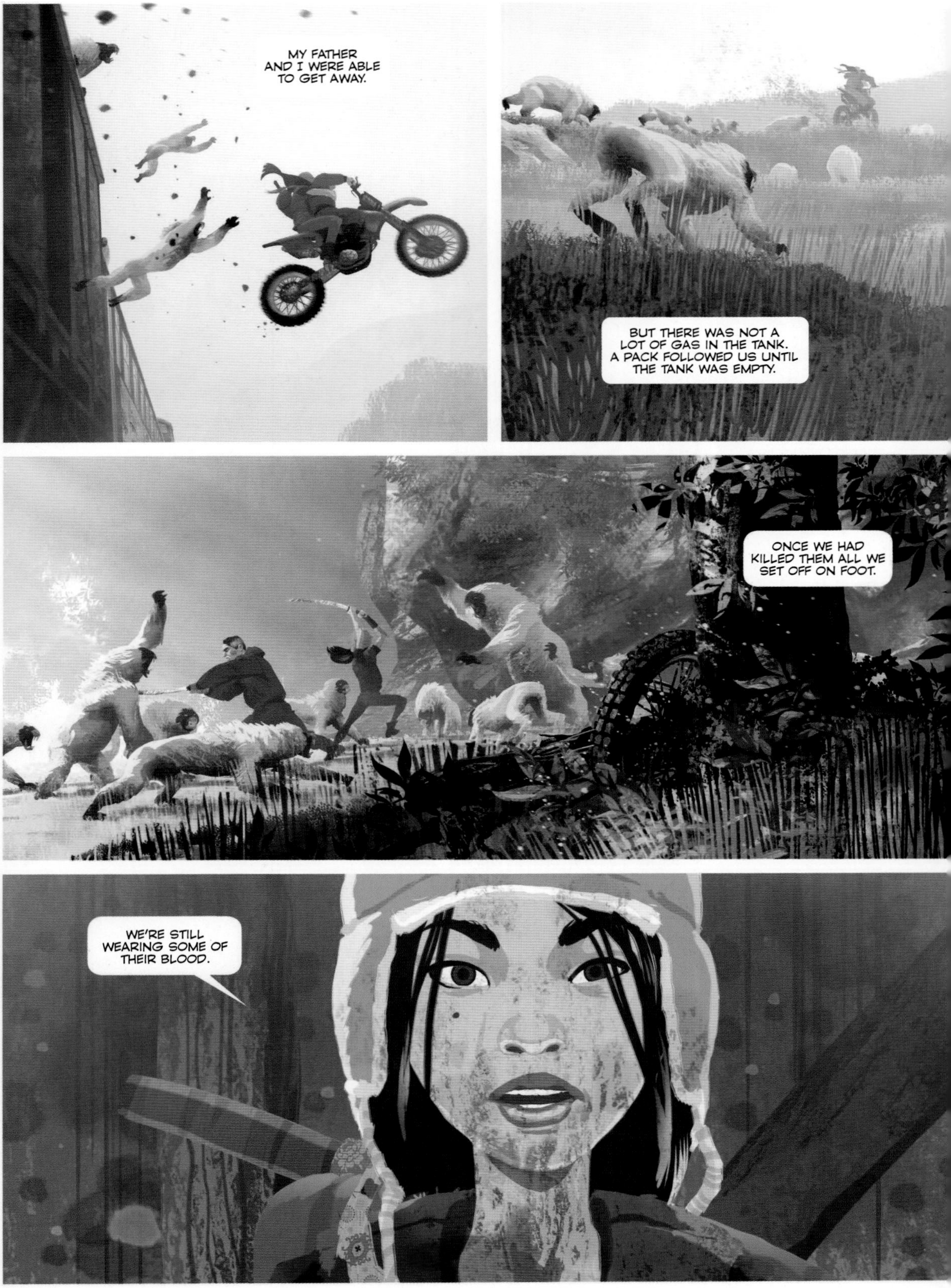
MY FATHER AND I WERE ABLE TO GET AWAY.
BUT THERE WAS NOT A LOT OF GAS IN THE TANK. A PACK FOLLOWED US UNTIL THE TANK WAS EMPTY.
ONCE WE HAD KILLED THEM ALL WE SET OFF ON FOOT.
WE'RE STILL WEARING SOME OF THEIR BLOOD.

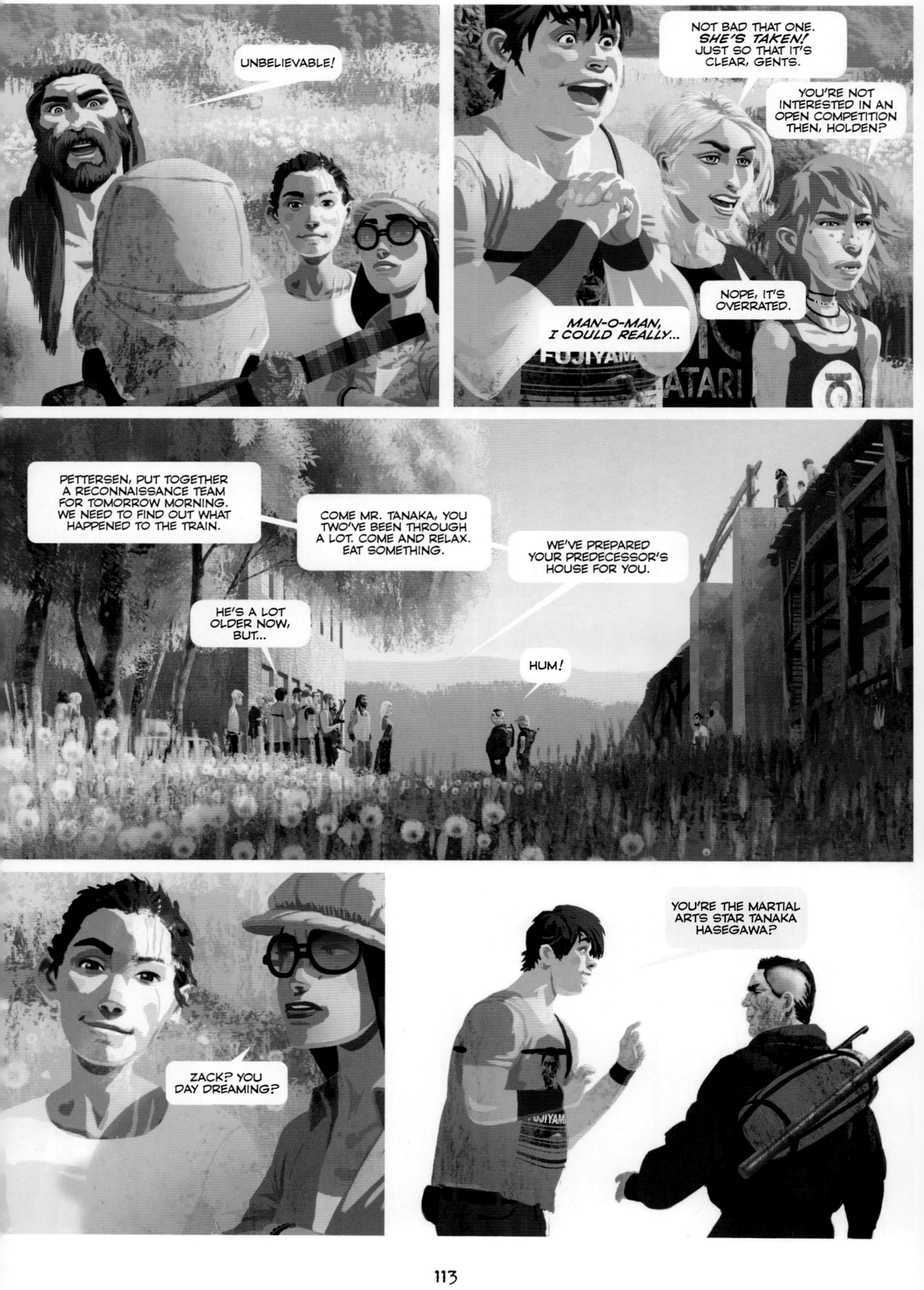
UNBELIEVABLE!
NOT BAD THAT ONE. *SHE'S TAKEN!* JUST SO THAT IT'S CLEAR, GENTS.
YOU'RE NOT INTERESTED IN AN OPEN COMPETITION THEN, HOLDEN?
MAN-O-MAN, I COULD REALLY...
NOPE, IT'S OVERRATED.
FUJIYAMA
ATARI
PETTERSEN, PUT TOGETHER A RECONNAISSANCE TEAM FOR TOMORROW MORNING. WE NEED TO FIND OUT WHAT HAPPENED TO THE TRAIN.
COME MR. TANAKA, YOU TWO'VE BEEN THROUGH A LOT. COME AND RELAX. EAT SOMETHING.
WE'VE PREPARED YOUR PREDECESSOR'S HOUSE FOR YOU.
HE'S A LOT OLDER NOW, BUT...
HUM!
ZACK? YOU DAY DREAMING?
YOU'RE THE MARTIAL ARTS STAR TANAKA HASEGAWA?

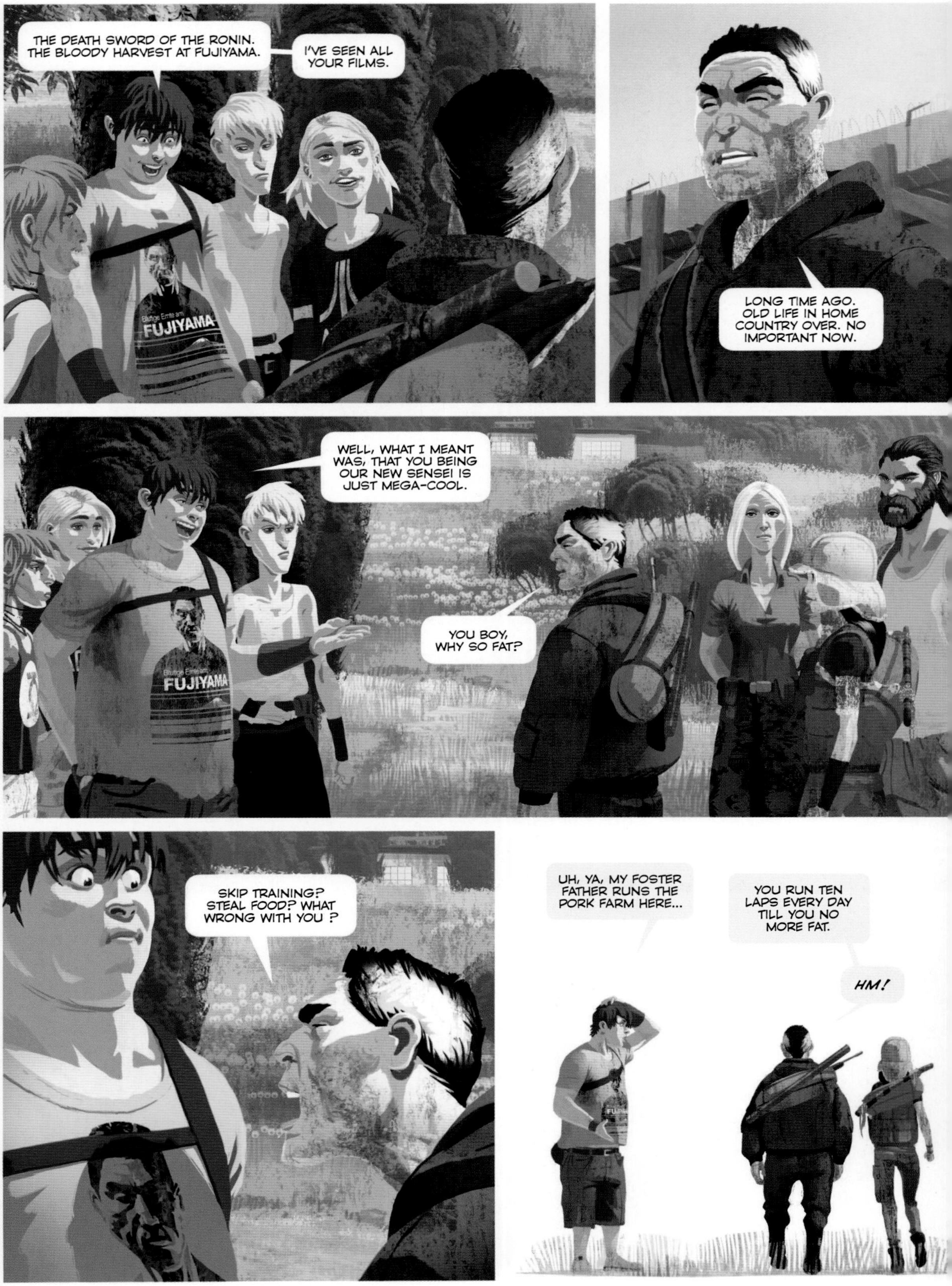
THE DEATH SWORD OF THE RONIN. THE BLOODY HARVEST AT FUJIYAMA.
I'VE SEEN ALL YOUR FILMS.
LONG TIME AGO. OLD LIFE IN HOME COUNTRY OVER. NO IMPORTANT NOW.
WELL, WHAT I MEANT WAS, THAT YOU BEING OUR NEW SENSEI IS JUST MEGA-COOL.
YOU BOY, WHY SO FAT?
SKIP TRAINING? STEAL FOOD? WHAT WRONG WITH YOU ?
UH, YA, MY FOSTER FATHER RUNS THE PORK FARM HERE...
YOU RUN TEN LAPS EVERY DAY TILL YOU NO MORE FAT.
HM!

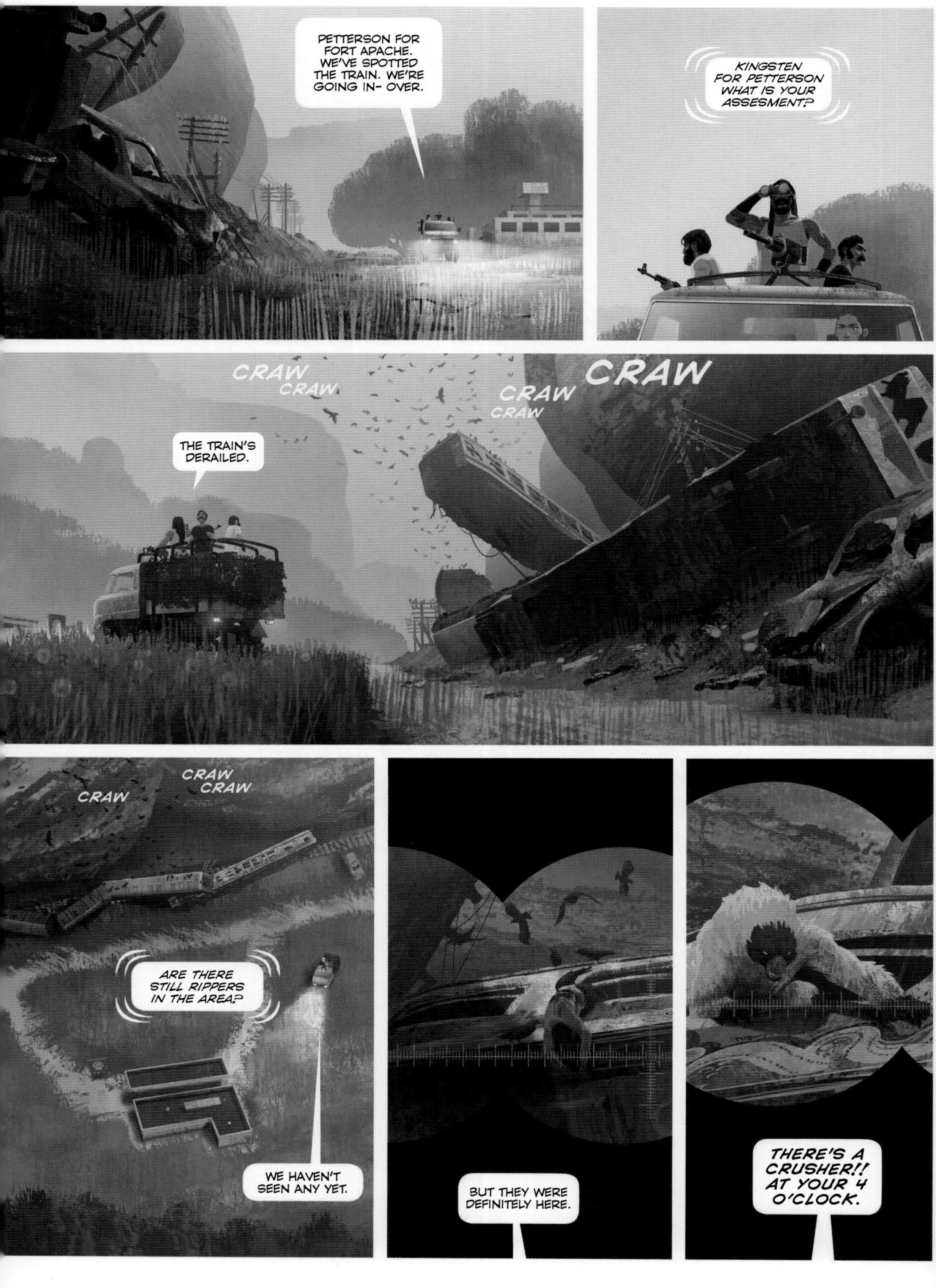
PETTERSON FOR FORT APACHE. WE'VE SPOTTED THE TRAIN. WE'RE GOING IN- OVER.
KINGSTEN FOR PETTERSON WHAT IS YOUR ASSESMENT?
CRAW CRAW
THE TRAIN'S DERAILED.
CRAW CRAW
CRAW
CRAW
CRAW CRAW
ARE THERE STILL RIPPERS IN THE AREA?
WE HAVEN'T SEEN ANY YET.
BUT THEY WERE DEFINITELY HERE.
THERE'S A CRUSHER!! AT YOUR 4 O'CLOCK.

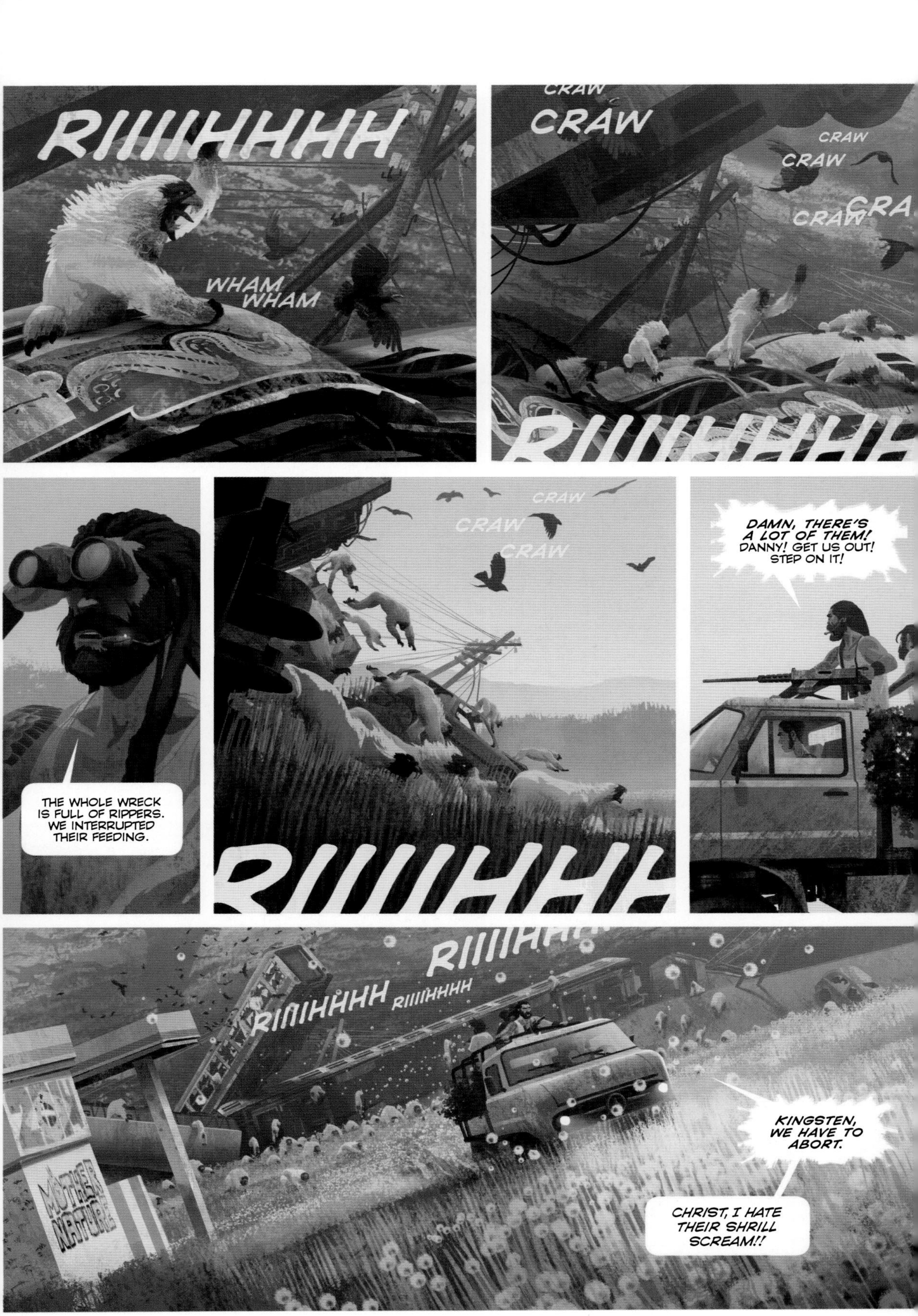
RIIIIHHHH
WHAM WHAM
CRAW
CRAW
CRAW
CRAW
CRAW
CRA
RIIIIHHHHH
THE WHOLE WRECK IS FULL OF RIPPERS. WE INTERRUPTED THEIR FEEDING.
CRAW
CRAW
CRAW
RIIIIHHHH
DAMN, THERE'S A LOT OF THEM! DANNY! GET US OUT! STEP ON IT!
RIIIIHHHH
RIIIIHHHH RIIIIHHHH
RIIIIHHHH
MOTHER NATURE
KINGSTEN, WE HAVE TO ABORT.
CHRIST, I HATE THEIR SHRILL SCREAM!!

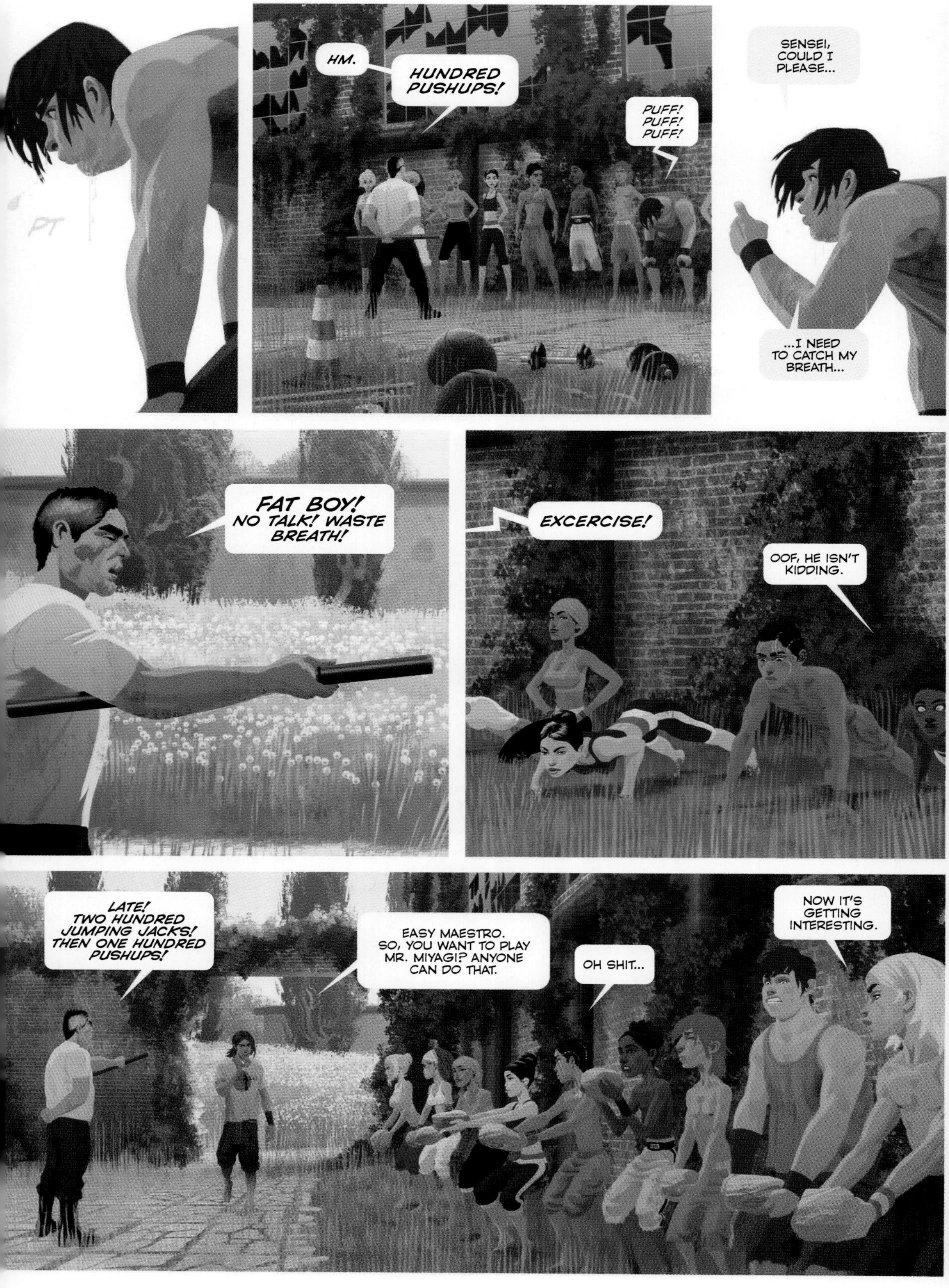
PT
HM.
HUNDRED PUSHUPS!
PUFF! PUFF! PUFF!
SENSEI, COULD I PLEASE...
...I NEED TO CATCH MY BREATH...
FAT BOY! NO TALK! WASTE BREATH!
EXCERCISE!
OOF, HE ISN'T KIDDING.
LATE! TWO HUNDRED JUMPING JACKS! THEN ONE HUNDRED PUSHUPS!
EASY MAESTRO. SO, YOU WANT TO PLAY MR. MIYAGI? ANYONE CAN DO THAT.
OH SHIT...
NOW IT'S GETTING INTERESTING.

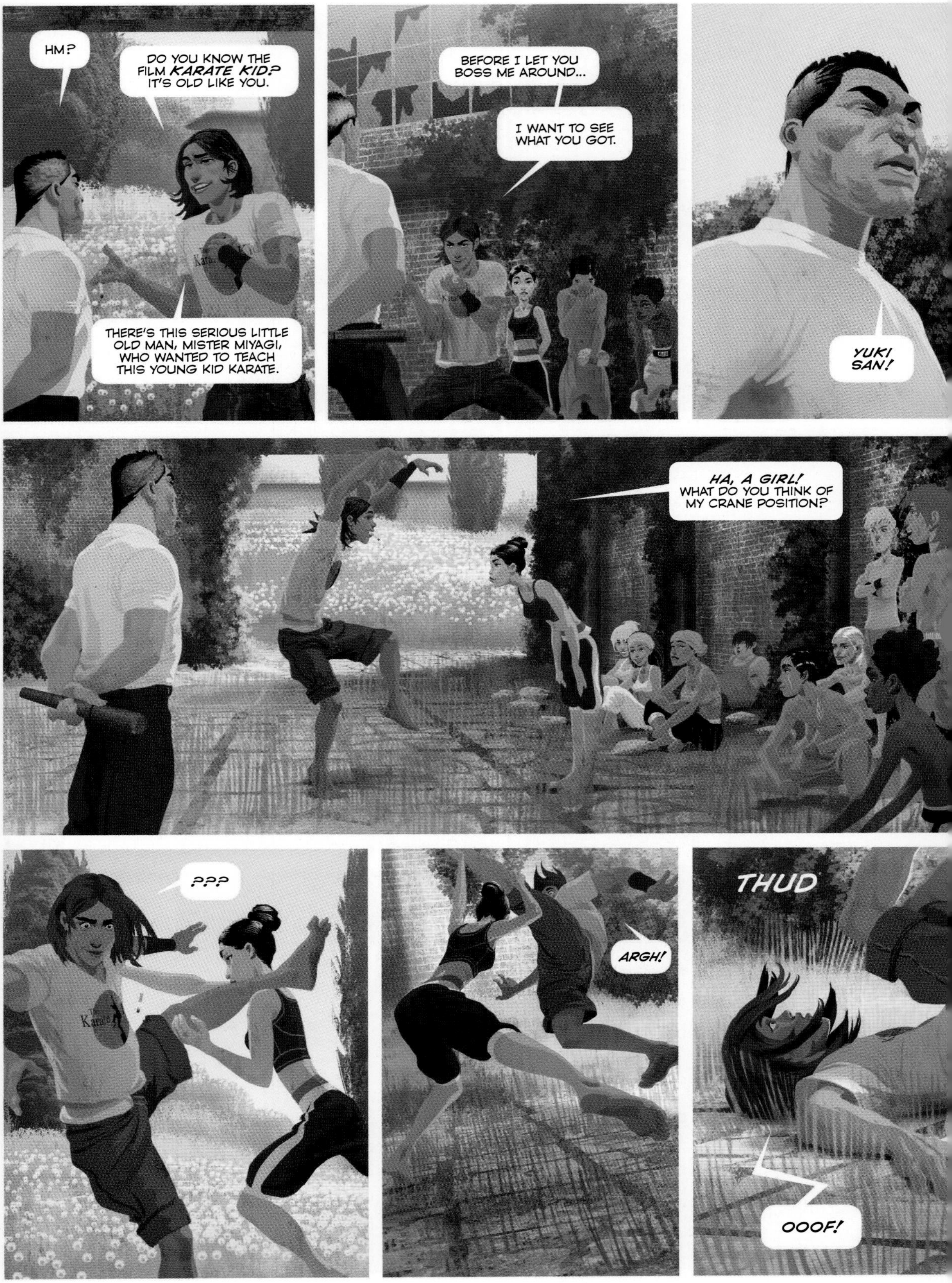
HM?
DO YOU KNOW THE FILM KARATE KID? IT'S OLD LIKE YOU.
THERE'S THIS SERIOUS LITTLE OLD MAN, MISTER MIYAGI, WHO WANTED TO TEACH THIS YOUNG KID KARATE.
BEFORE I LET YOU BOSS ME AROUND...
I WANT TO SEE WHAT YOU GOT.
YUKI SAN!
HA, A GIRL! WHAT DO YOU THINK OF MY CRANE POSITION?
???
ARGH!
THUD
OOOF!

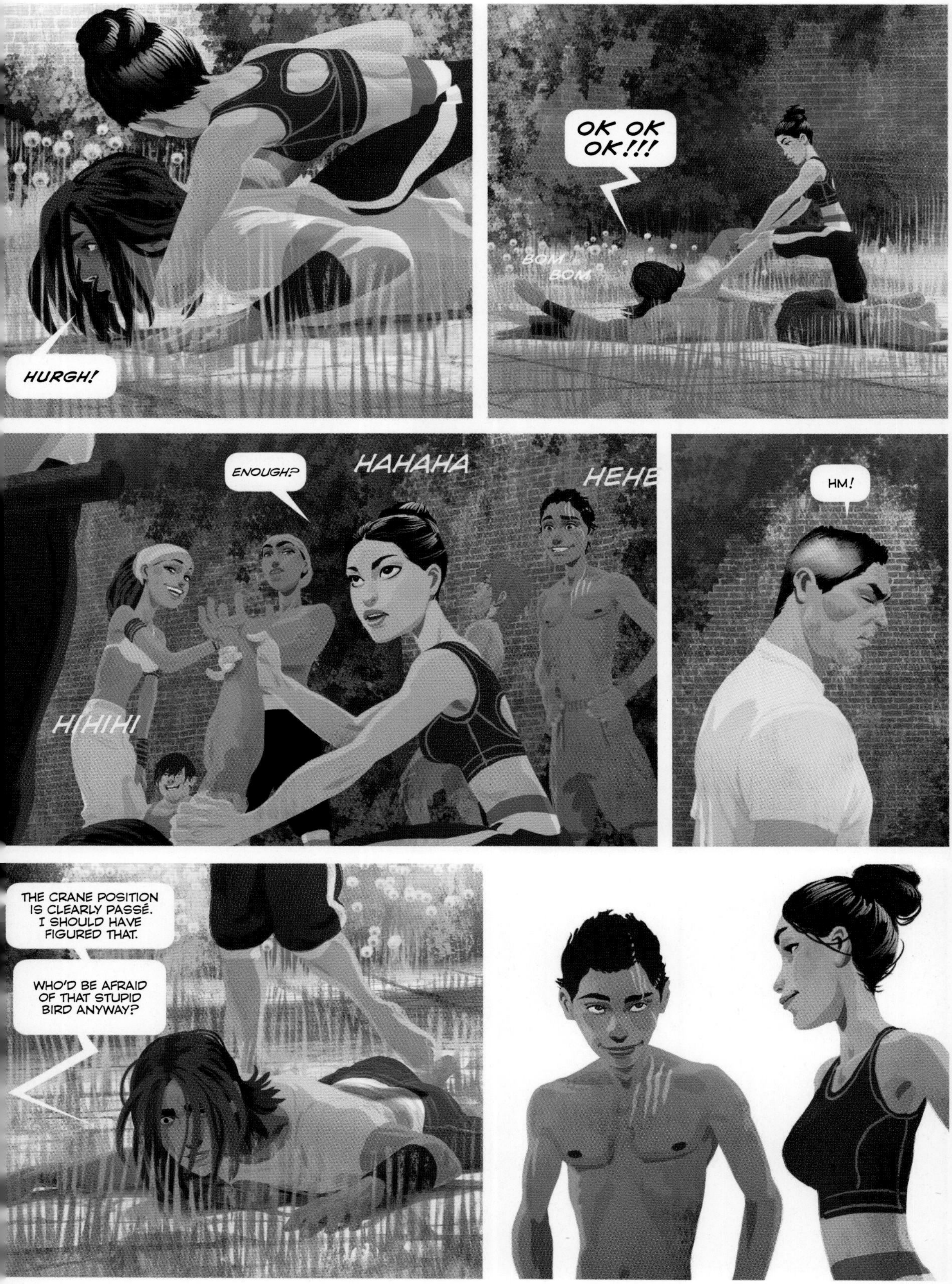
HURGH!
OK OK OK!!!
BOM BOM
ENOUGH?
HAHAHA
HEHE
HIHIHI
HM!
THE CRANE POSITION IS CLEARLY PASSÉ. I SHOULD HAVE FIGURED THAT.
WHO'D BE AFRAID OF THAT STUPID BIRD ANYWAY?

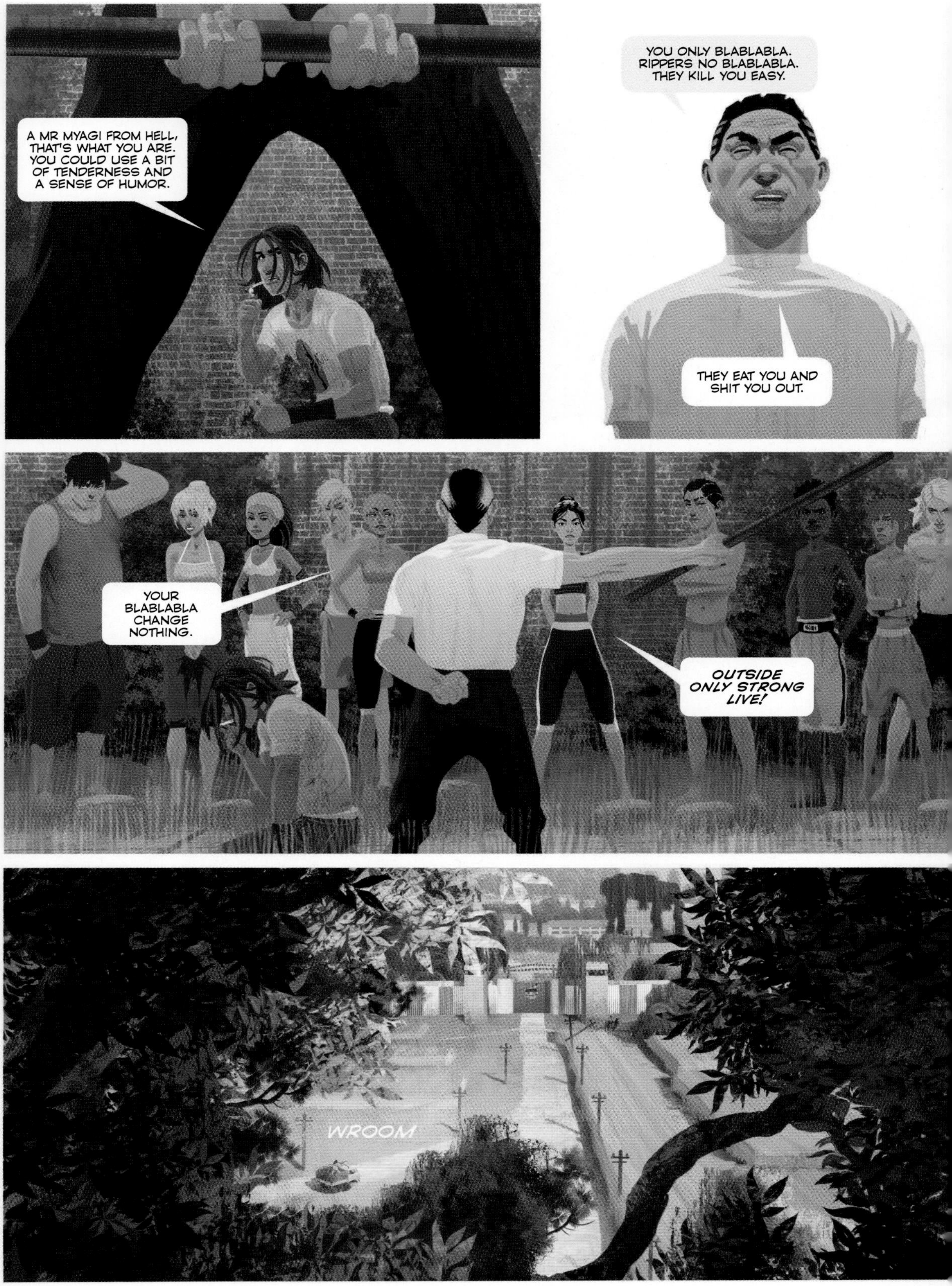
A MR MYAGI FROM HELL, THAT'S WHAT YOU ARE. YOU COULD USE A BIT OF TENDERNESS AND A SENSE OF HUMOR.
YOU ONLY BLABLABLA. RIPPERS NO BLABLABLA. THEY KILL YOU EASY.
THEY EAT YOU AND SHIT YOU OUT.
YOUR BLABLABLA CHANGE NOTHING.
OUTSIDE ONLY STRONG LIVE!
WROOM

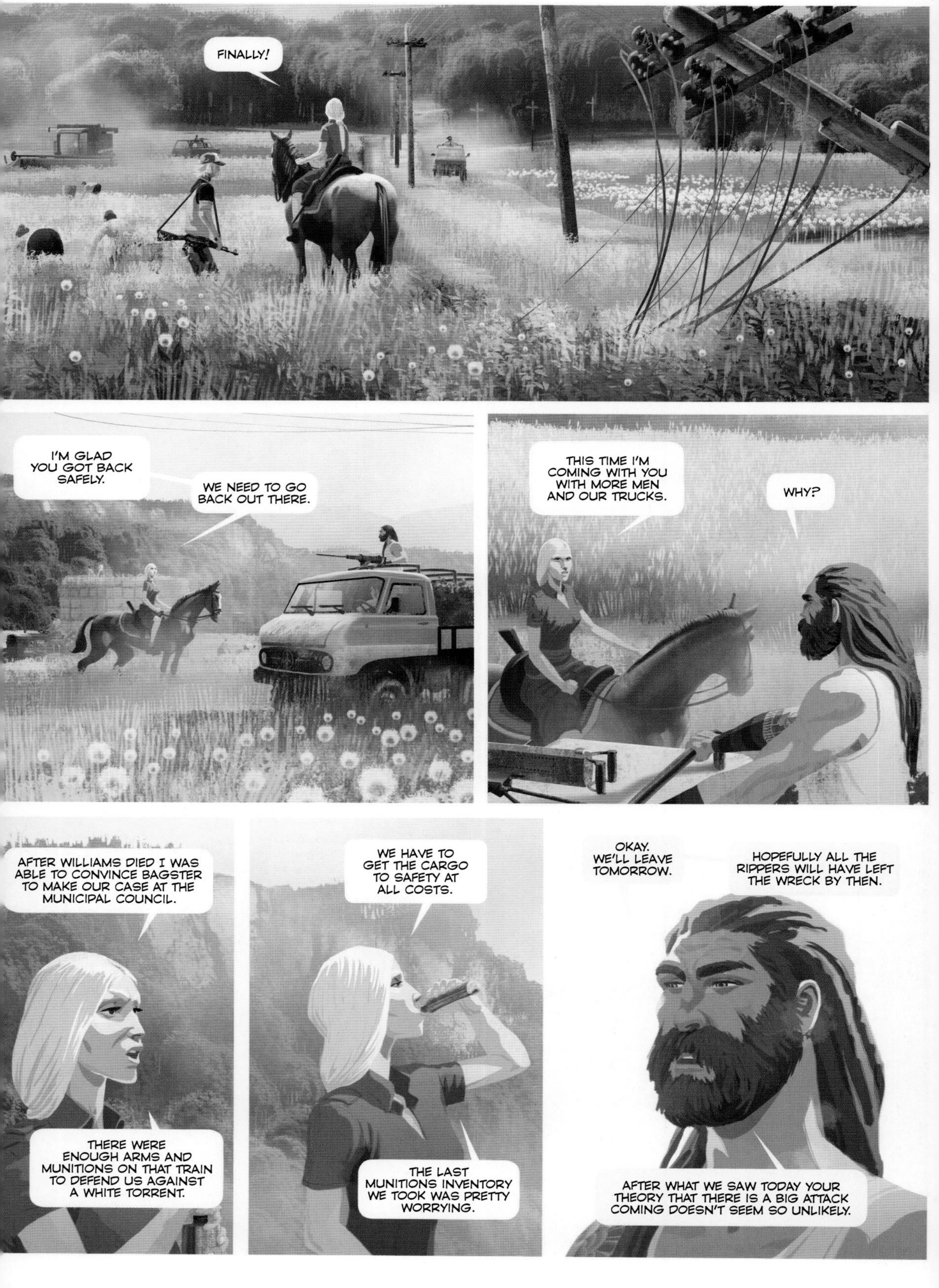
FINALLY!
I'M GLAD YOU GOT BACK SAFELY.
WE NEED TO GO BACK OUT THERE.
THIS TIME I'M COMING WITH YOU WITH MORE MEN AND OUR TRUCKS.
WHY?
AFTER WILLIAMS DIED I WAS ABLE TO CONVINCE BAGSTER TO MAKE OUR CASE AT THE MUNICIPAL COUNCIL.
THERE WERE ENOUGH ARMS AND MUNITIONS ON THAT TRAIN TO DEFEND US AGAINST A WHITE TORRENT.
WE HAVE TO GET THE CARGO TO SAFETY AT ALL COSTS.
THE LAST MUNITIONS INVENTORY WE TOOK WAS PRETTY WORRYING.
OKAY. WE'LL LEAVE TOMORROW.
HOPEFULLY ALL THE RIPPERS WILL HAVE LEFT THE WRECK BY THEN.
AFTER WHAT WE SAW TODAY YOUR THEORY THAT THERE IS A BIG ATTACK COMING DOESN'T SEEM SO UNLIKELY.

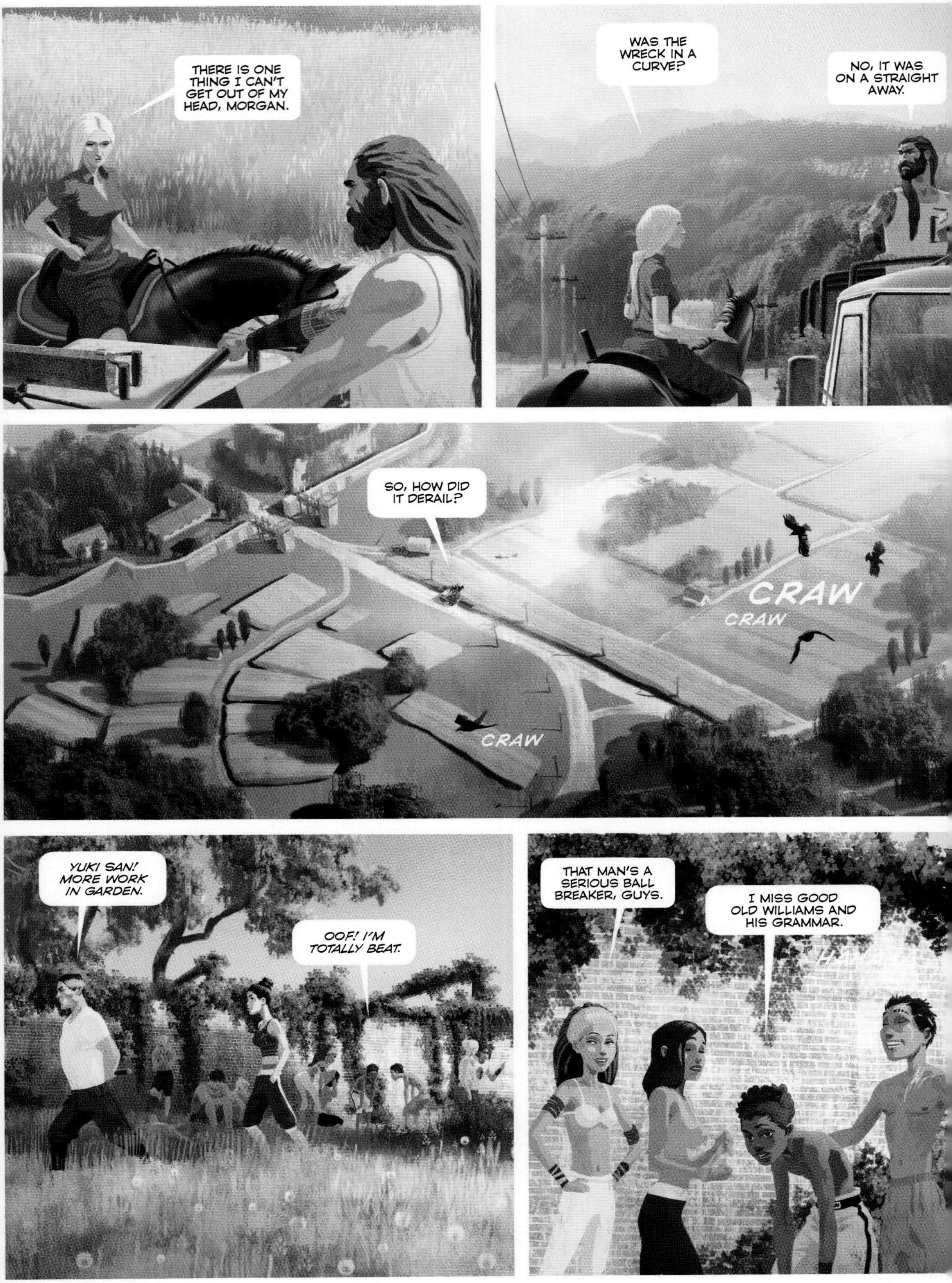
THERE IS ONE THING I CAN'T GET OUT OF MY HEAD, MORGAN.
WAS THE WRECK IN A CURVE?
NO, IT WAS ON A STRAIGHT AWAY.
SO, HOW DID IT DERAIL?
CRAW
CRAW
CRAW
YUKI SAN! MORE WORK IN GARDEN.
OOF! I'M TOTALLY BEAT.
THAT MAN'S A SERIOUS BALL BREAKER, GUYS.
I MISS GOOD OLD WILLIAMS AND HIS GRAMMAR.

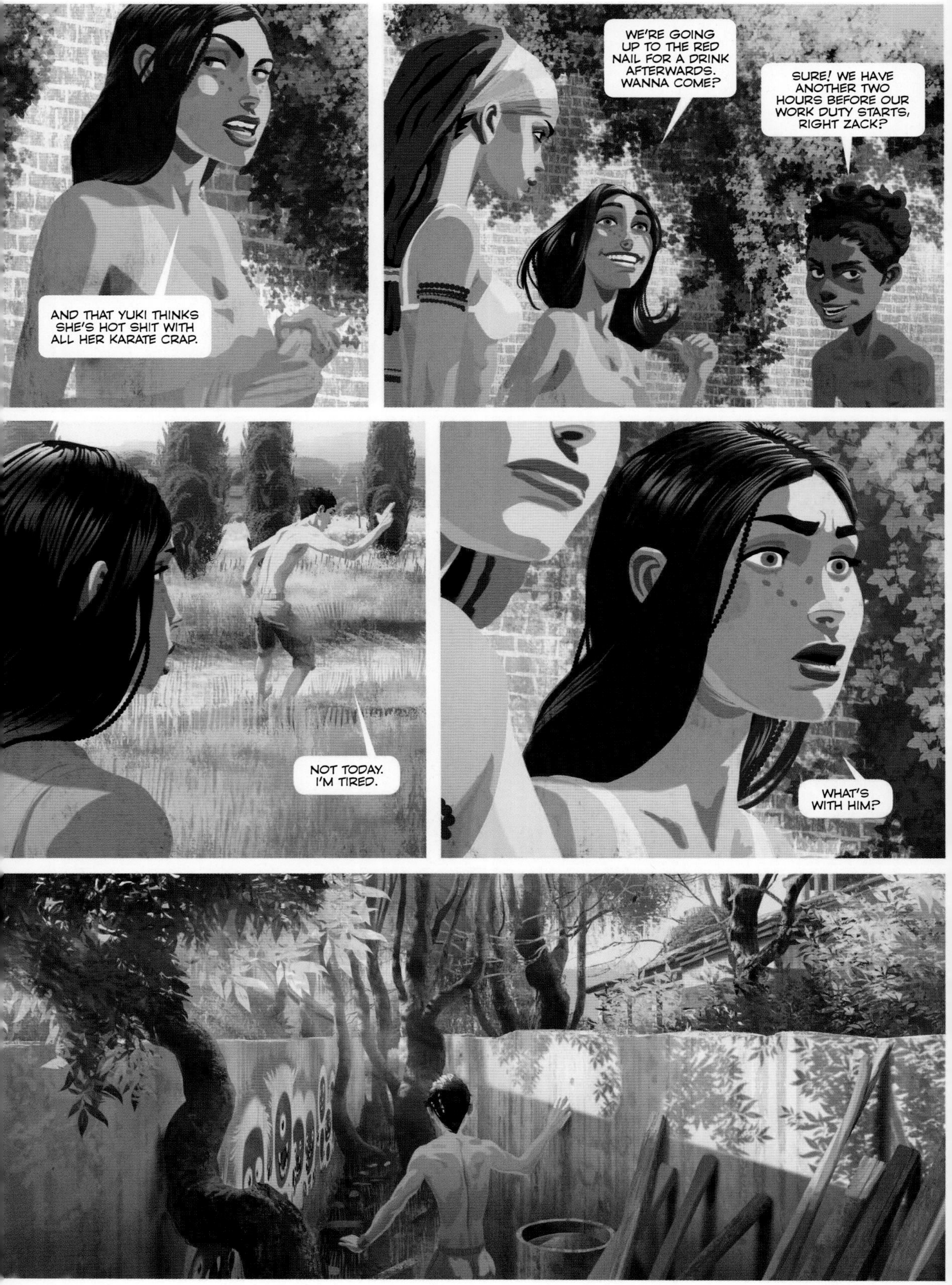
AND THAT YUKI THINKS SHE'S HOT SHIT WITH ALL HER KARATE CRAP.
WE'RE GOING UP TO THE RED NAIL FOR A DRINK AFTERWARDS. WANNA COME?
SURE! WE HAVE ANOTHER TWO HOURS BEFORE OUR WORK DUTY STARTS, RIGHT ZACK?
NOT TODAY. I'M TIRED.
WHAT'S WITH HIM?

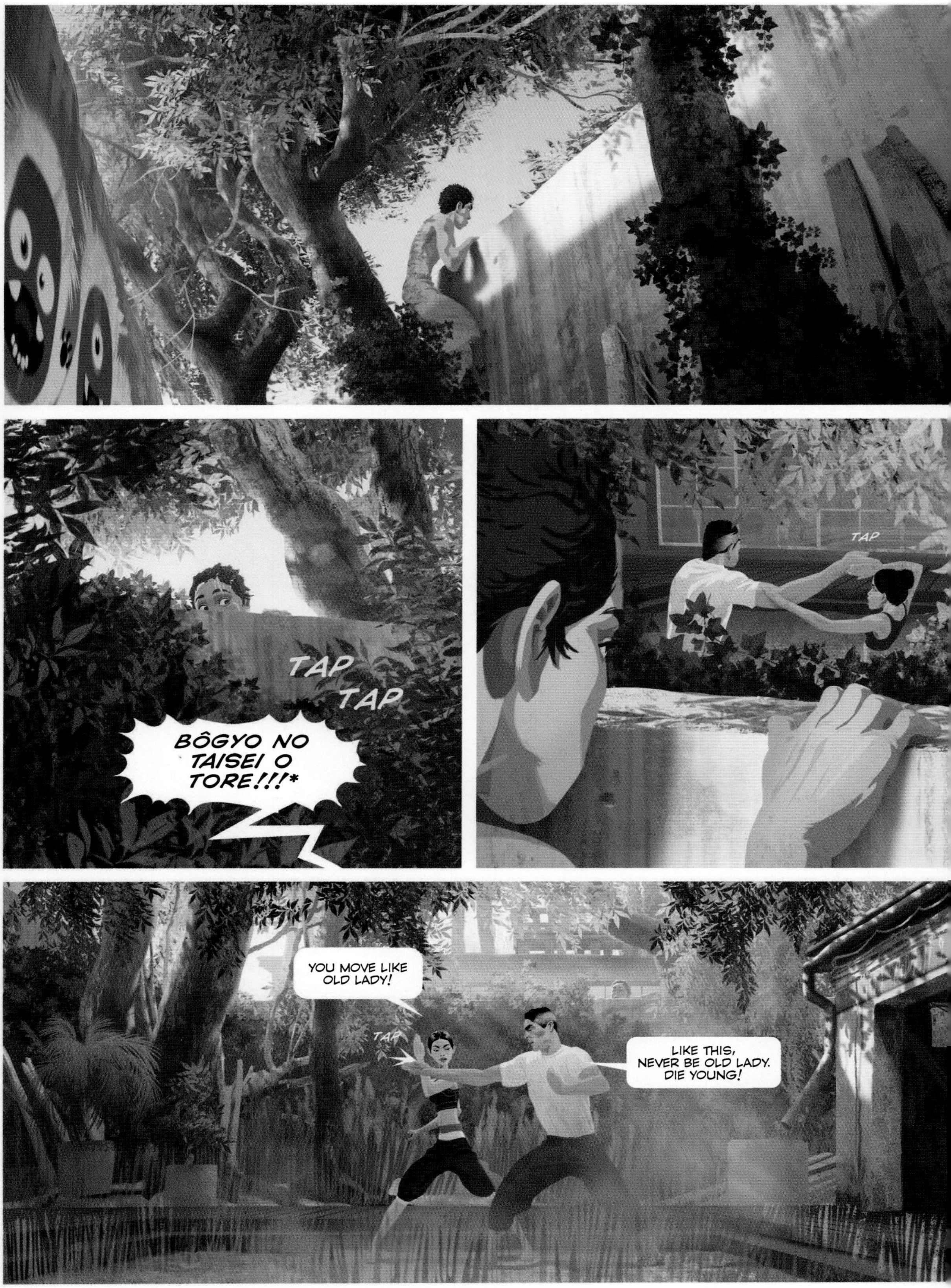
TAP
TAP
BÔGYO NO TAISEI O TORE!!!*
TAP
YOU MOVE LIKE OLD LADY!
TAP
LIKE THIS, NEVER BE OLD LADY. DIE YOUNG!

*BLOCK FROM ABOVE !!!

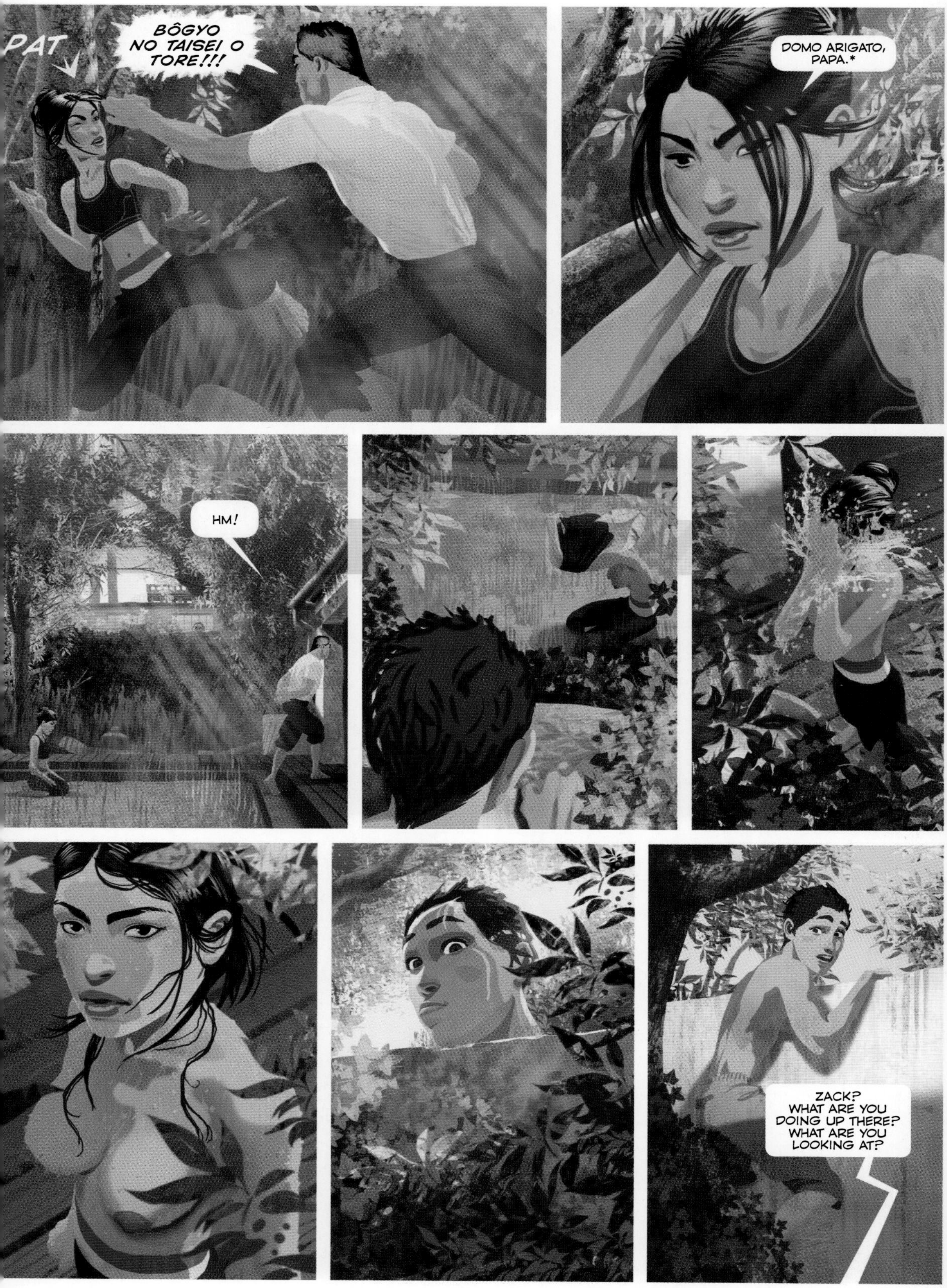
PAT
BÔGYO NO TAISEI O TORE!!!
DOMO ARIGATO, PAPA.*
HM!
ZACK? WHAT ARE YOU DOING UP THERE? WHAT ARE YOU LOOKING AT?

*THANK YOU, FATHER.

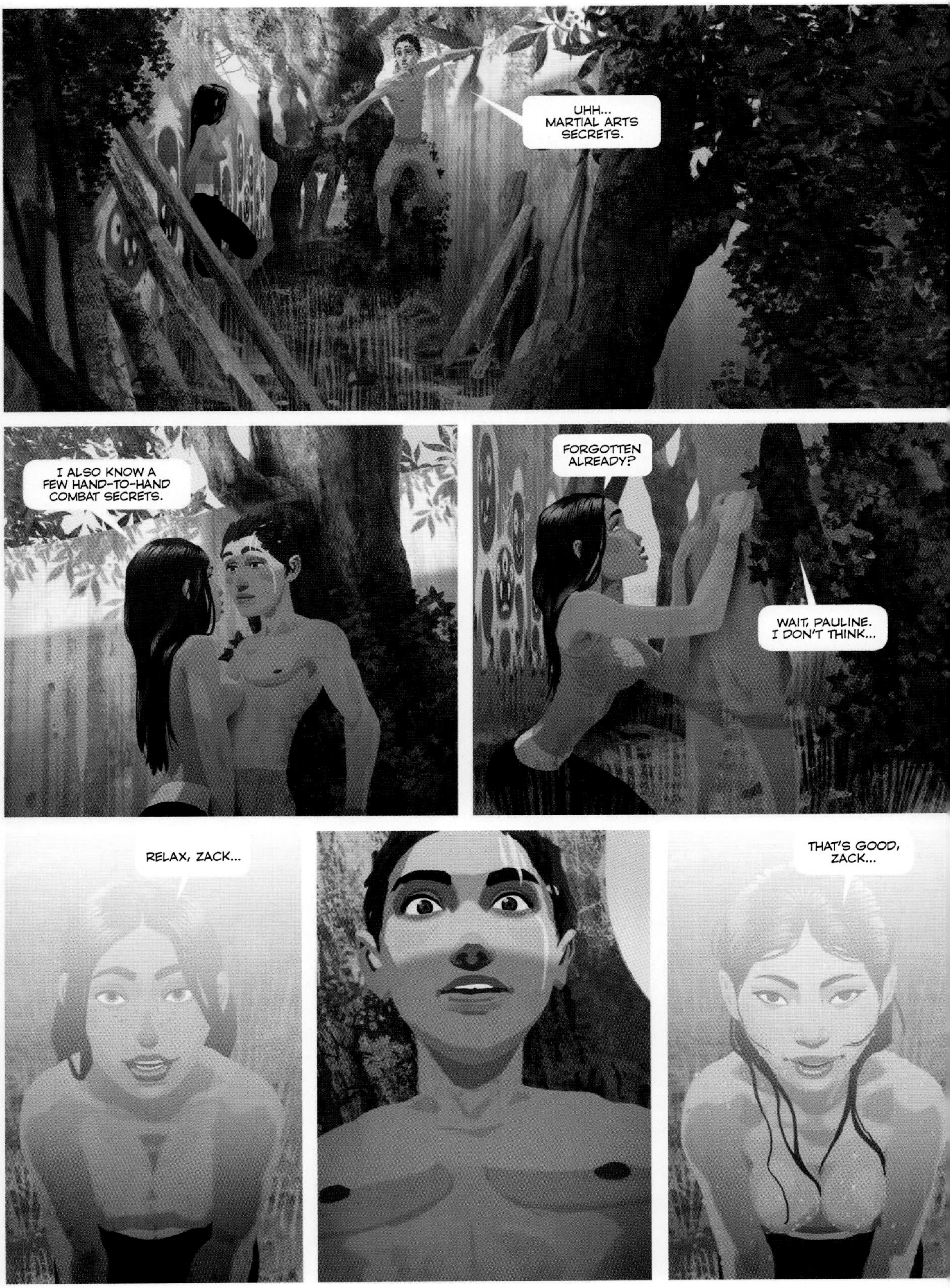
UHH... MARTIAL ARTS SECRETS.
I ALSO KNOW A FEW HAND-TO-HAND COMBAT SECRETS.
FORGOTTEN ALREADY?
WAIT, PAULINE. I DON'T THINK...
RELAX, ZACK...
THAT'S GOOD, ZACK...

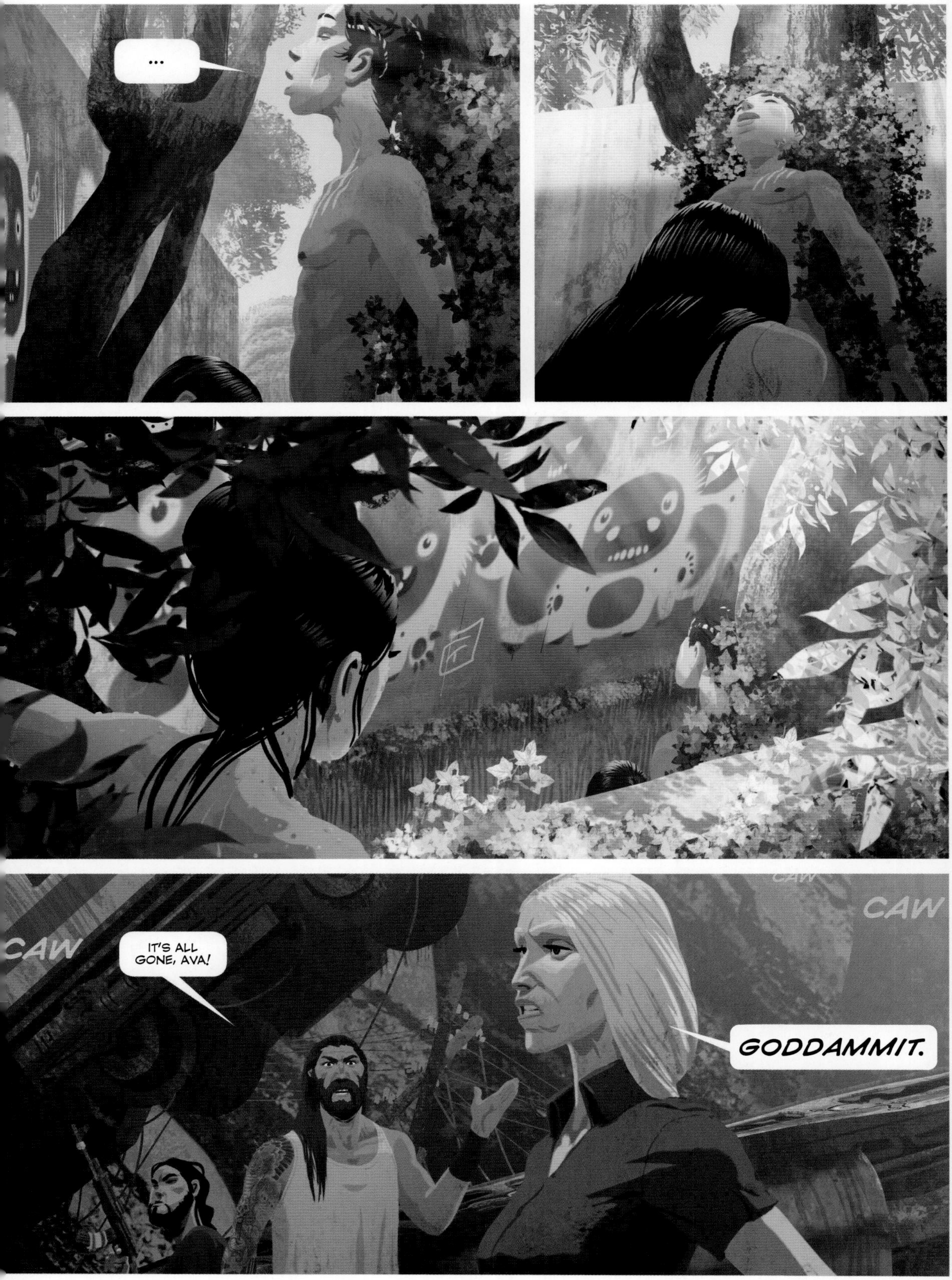
...
CAW
CAW
CAW
IT'S ALL GONE, AVA!
GODDAMMIT.

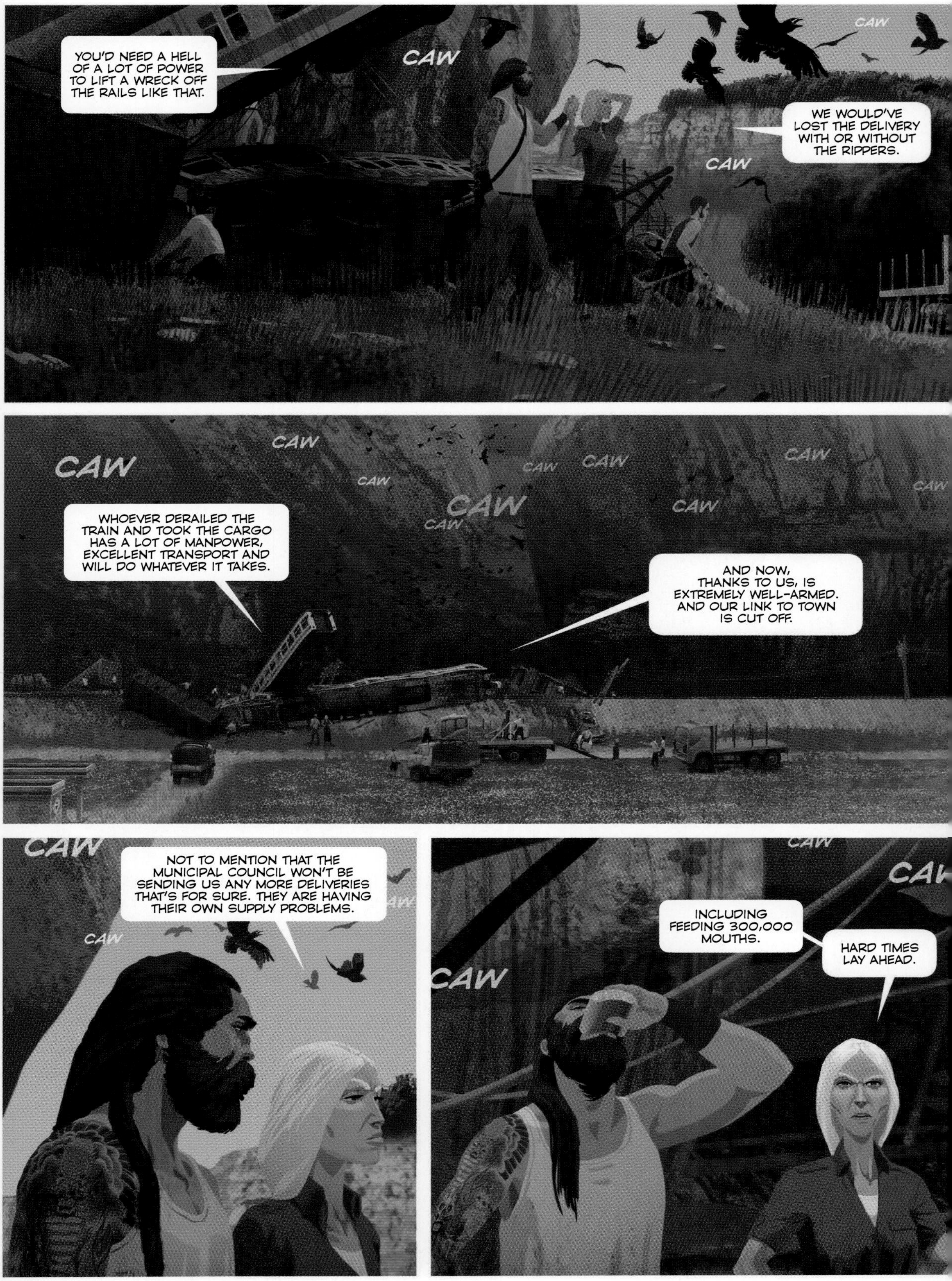

YOU'D NEED A HELL OF A LOT OF POWER TO LIFT A WRECK OFF THE RAILS LIKE THAT.
CAW
CAW
WE WOULD'VE LOST THE DELIVERY WITH OR WITHOUT THE RIPPERS.
CAW
CAW
CAW
CAW
CAW
CAW
CAW
CAW
CAW
CAW
CAW
WHOEVER DERAILED THE TRAIN AND TOOK THE CARGO HAS A LOT OF MANPOWER, EXCELLENT TRANSPORT AND WILL DO WHATEVER IT TAKES.
AND NOW, THANKS TO US, IS EXTREMELY WELL-ARMED. AND OUR LINK TO TOWN IS CUT OFF.
CAW
NOT TO MENTION THAT THE MUNICIPAL COUNCIL WON'T BE SENDING US ANY MORE DELIVERIES THAT'S FOR SURE. THEY ARE HAVING THEIR OWN SUPPLY PROBLEMS.
CAW
CAW
CAW
INCLUDING FEEDING 300,000 MOUTHS.
HARD TIMES LAY AHEAD.

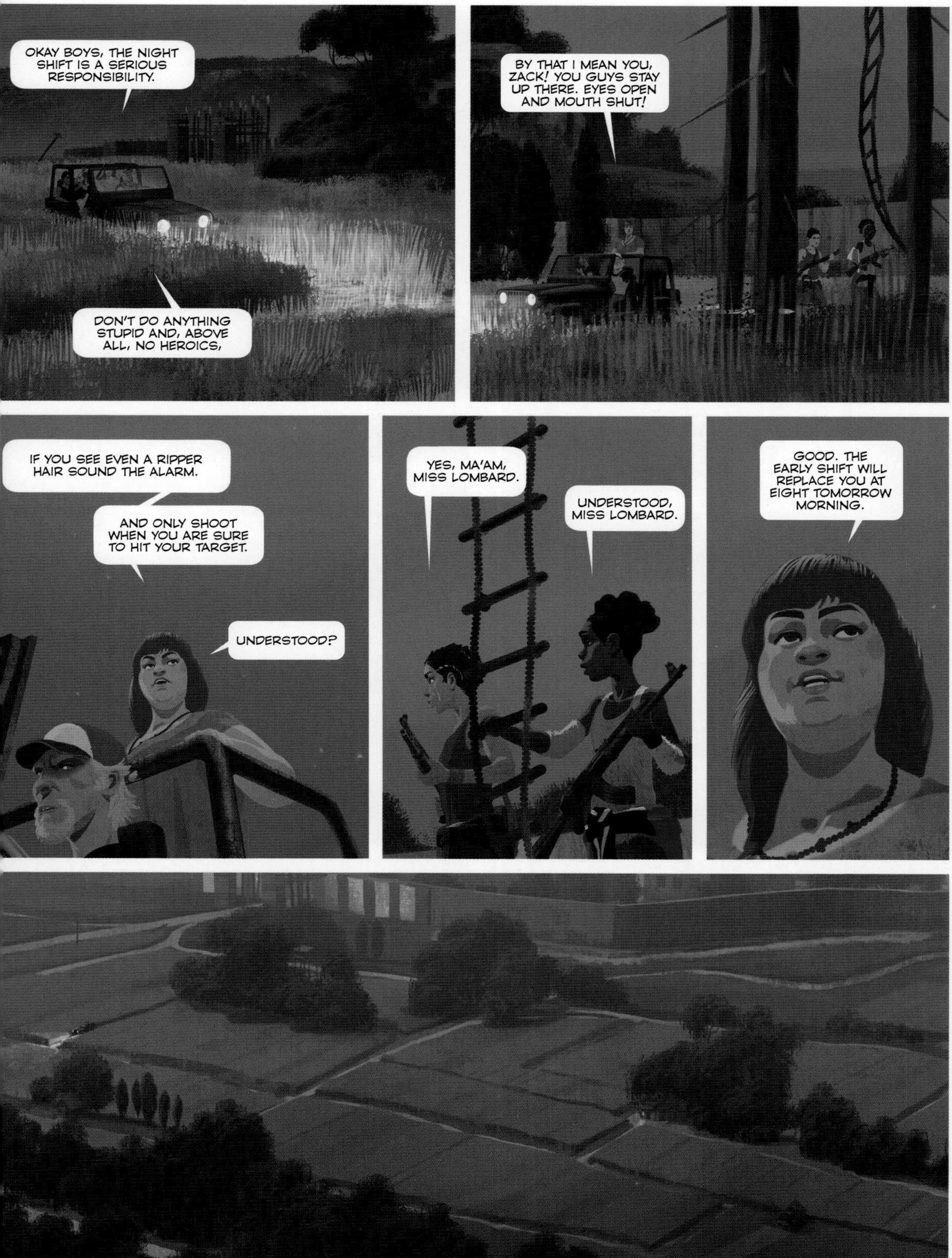
OKAY BOYS, THE NIGHT SHIFT IS A SERIOUS RESPONSIBILITY.
DON'T DO ANYTHING STUPID AND, ABOVE ALL, NO HEROICS,
BY THAT I MEAN YOU, ZACK! YOU GUYS STAY UP THERE. EYES OPEN AND MOUTH SHUT!
IF YOU SEE EVEN A RIPPER HAIR SOUND THE ALARM.
AND ONLY SHOOT WHEN YOU ARE SURE TO HIT YOUR TARGET.
UNDERSTOOD?
YES, MA'AM, MISS LOMBARD.
UNDERSTOOD, MISS LOMBARD.
GOOD. THE EARLY SHIFT WILL REPLACE YOU AT EIGHT TOMORROW MORNING.

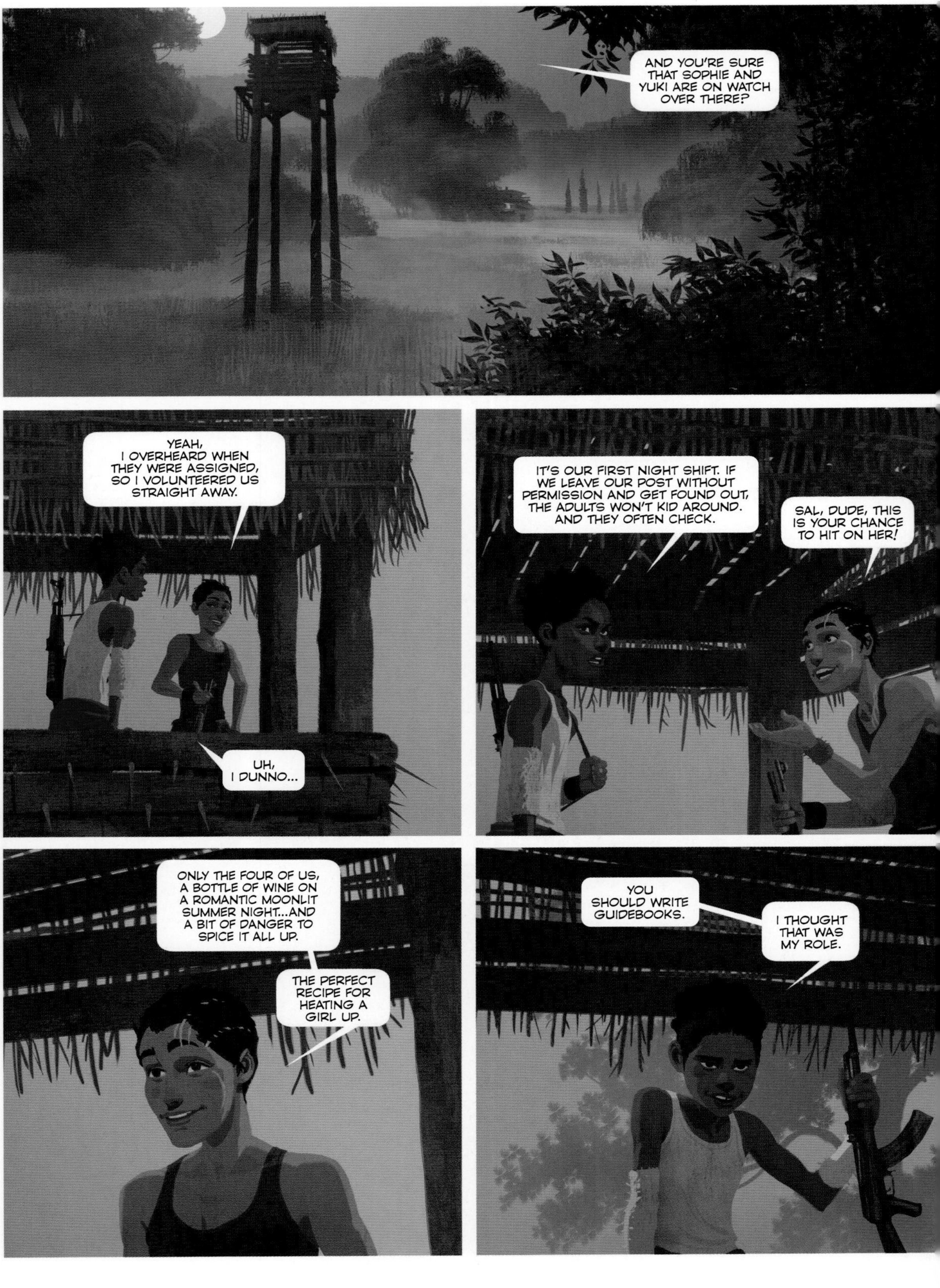
AND YOU'RE SURE THAT SOPHIE AND YUKI ARE ON WATCH OVER THERE?
YEAH, I OVERHEARD WHEN THEY WERE ASSIGNED, SO I VOLUNTEERED US STRAIGHT AWAY.
UH, I DUNNO...
IT'S OUR FIRST NIGHT SHIFT. IF WE LEAVE OUR POST WITHOUT PERMISSION AND GET FOUND OUT, THE ADULTS WON'T KID AROUND. AND THEY OFTEN CHECK.
SAL, DUDE, THIS IS YOUR CHANCE TO HIT ON HER!
ONLY THE FOUR OF US, A BOTTLE OF WINE ON A ROMANTIC MOONLIT SUMMER NIGHT...AND A BIT OF DANGER TO SPICE IT ALL UP.
THE PERFECT RECIPE FOR HEATING A GIRL UP.
YOU SHOULD WRITE GUIDEBOOKS.
I THOUGHT THAT WAS MY ROLE.

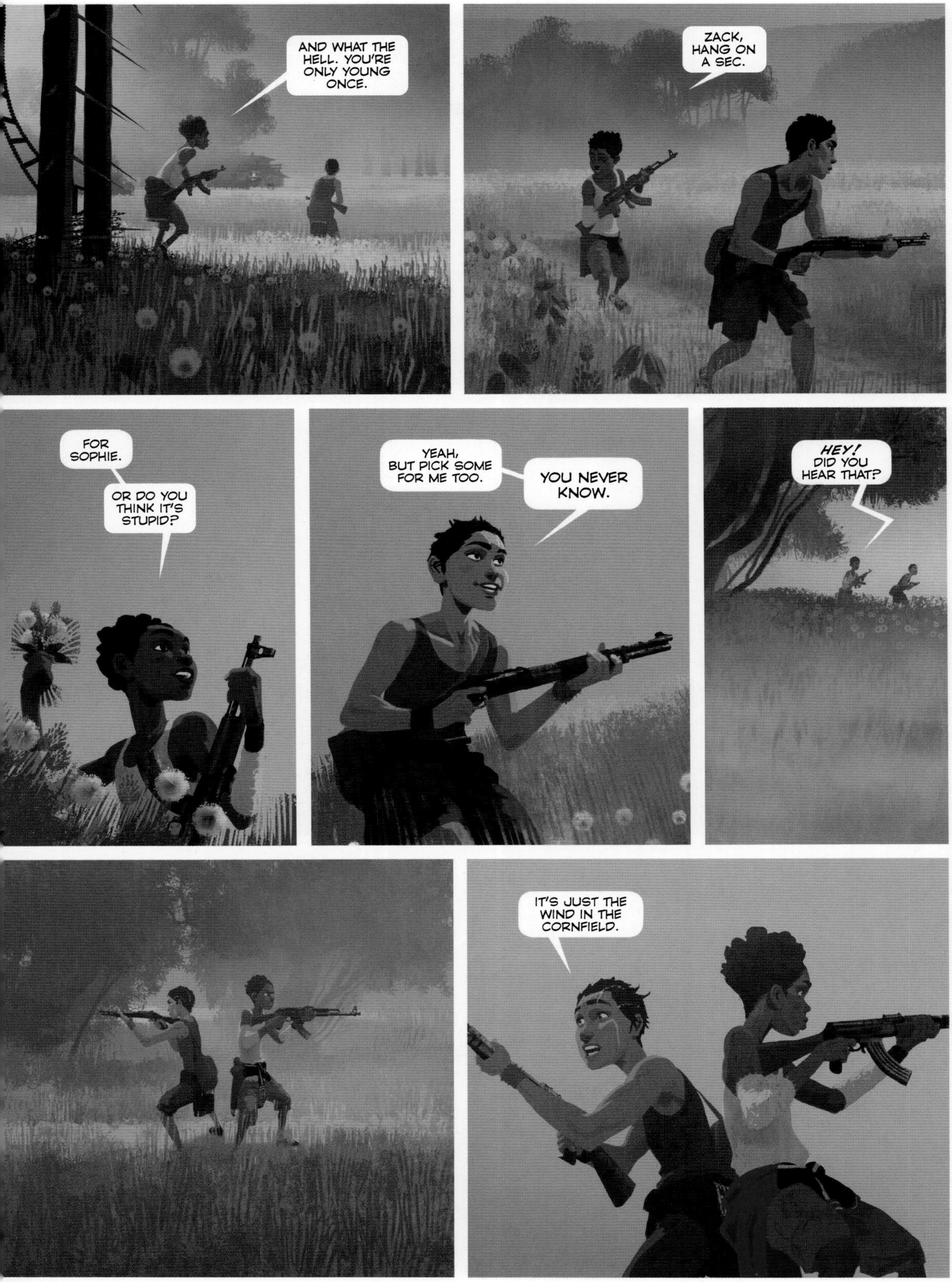
AND WHAT THE HELL. YOU'RE ONLY YOUNG ONCE.
ZACK, HANG ON A SEC.
FOR SOPHIE.
OR DO YOU THINK IT'S STUPID?
YEAH, BUT PICK SOME FOR ME TOO.
YOU NEVER KNOW.
HEY! DID YOU HEAR THAT?
IT'S JUST THE WIND IN THE CORNFIELD.

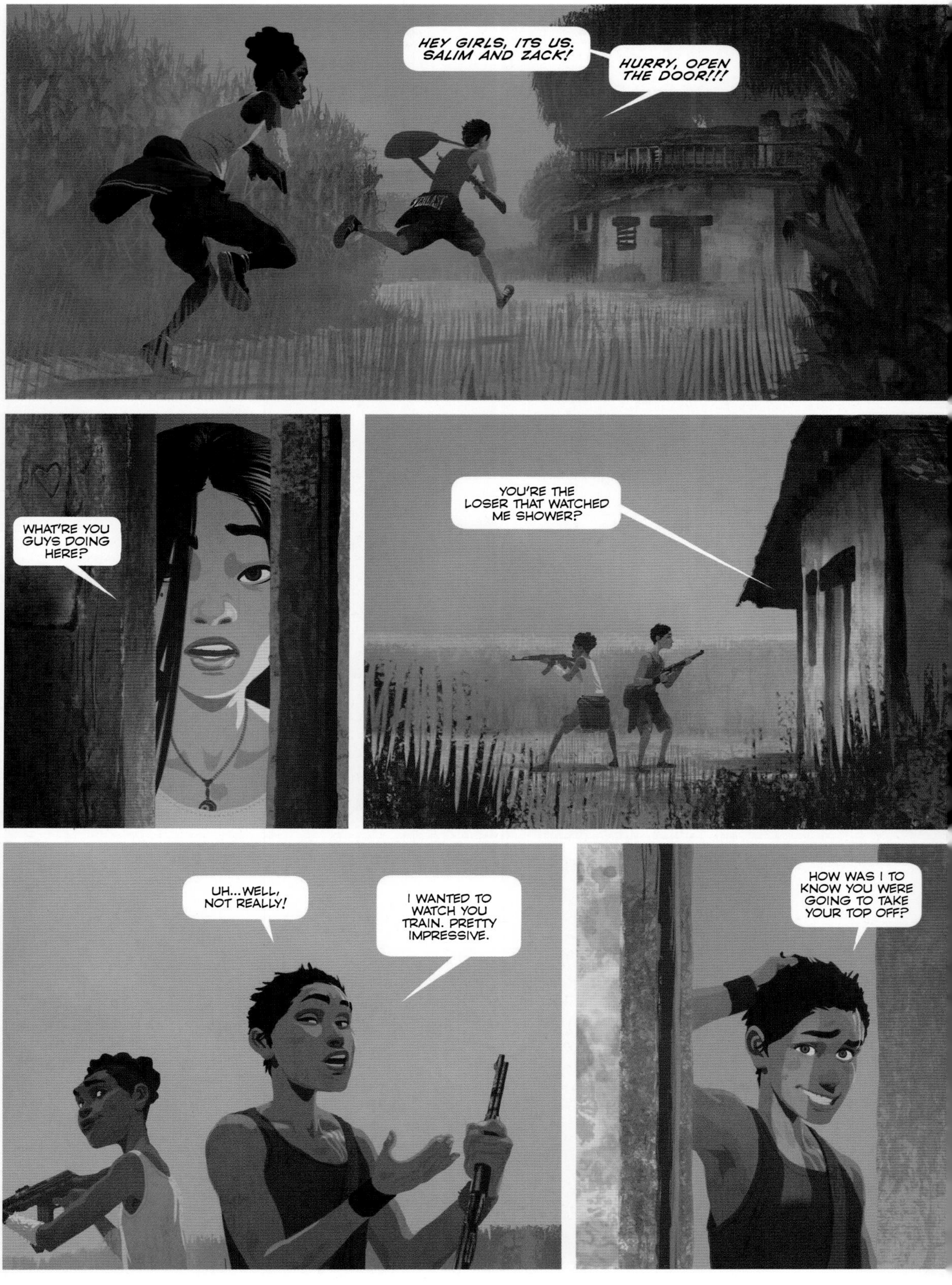
HEY GIRLS, ITS US. SALIM AND ZACK!
HURRY, OPEN THE DOOR!!!
WHAT'RE YOU GUYS DOING HERE?
YOU'RE THE LOSER THAT WATCHED ME SHOWER?
UH...WELL, NOT REALLY!
I WANTED TO WATCH YOU TRAIN. PRETTY IMPRESSIVE.
HOW WAS I TO KNOW YOU WERE GOING TO TAKE YOUR TOP OFF?

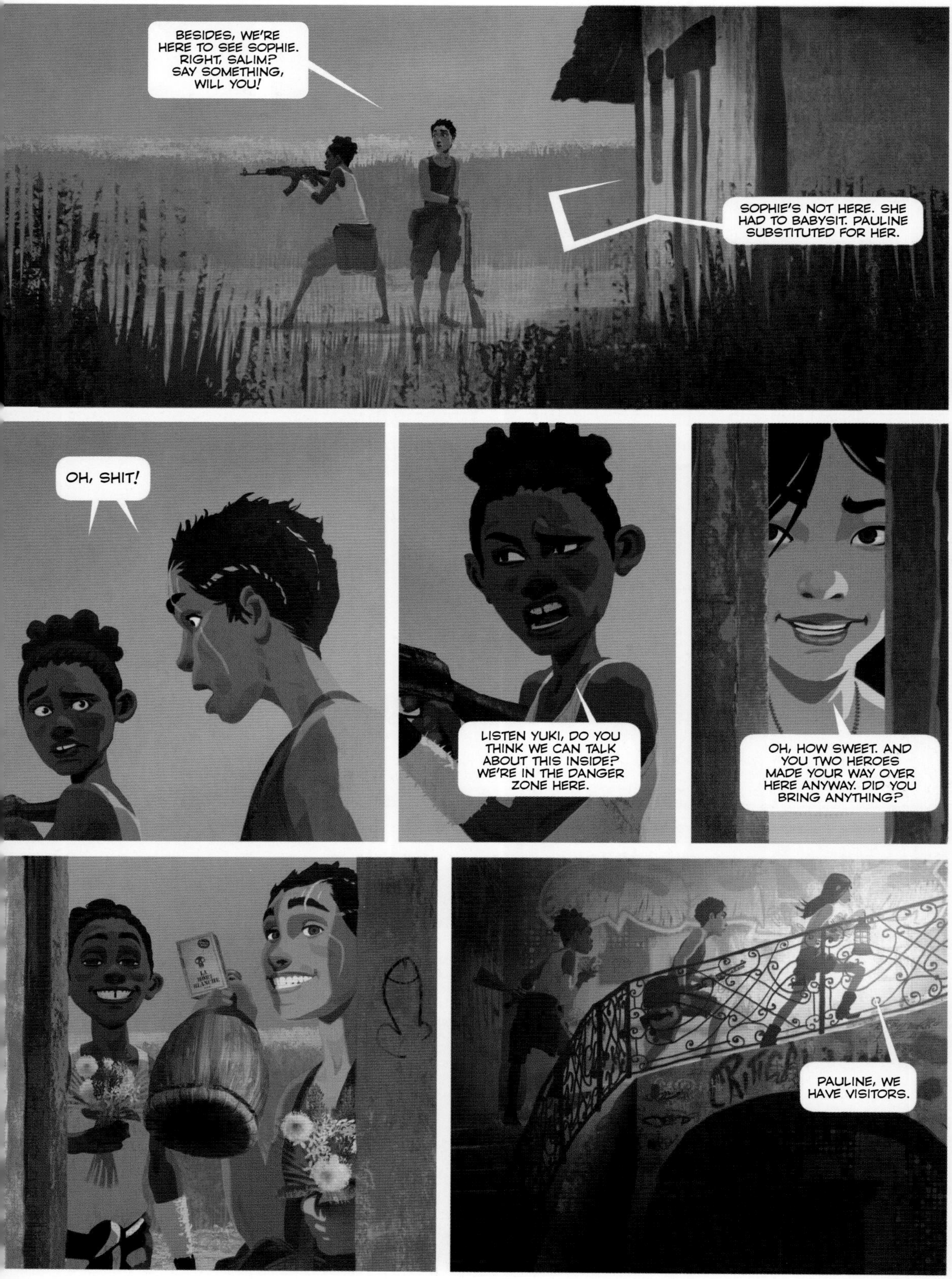
BESIDES, WE'RE HERE TO SEE SOPHIE. RIGHT, SALIM? SAY SOMETHING, WILL YOU!
SOPHIE'S NOT HERE. SHE HAD TO BABYSIT. PAULINE SUBSTITUTED FOR HER.
OH, SHIT!
LISTEN YUKI, DO YOU THINK WE CAN TALK ABOUT THIS INSIDE? WE'RE IN THE DANGER ZONE HERE.
OH, HOW SWEET. AND YOU TWO HEROES MADE YOUR WAY OVER HERE ANYWAY. DID YOU BRING ANYTHING?
PAULINE, WE HAVE VISITORS.

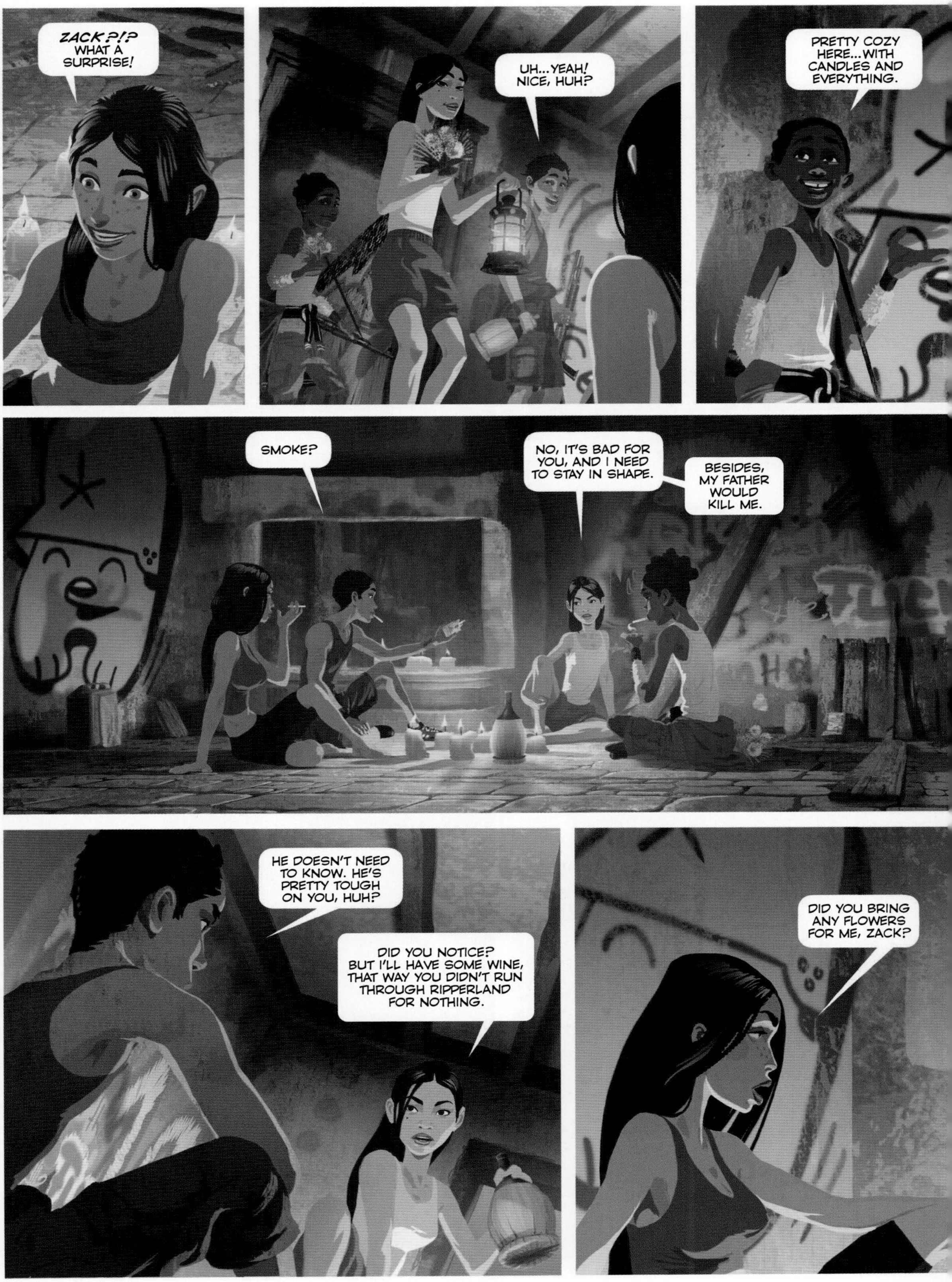
ZACK?!? WHAT A SURPRISE!
UH...YEAH! NICE, HUH?
PRETTY COZY HERE...WITH CANDLES AND EVERYTHING.
SMOKE?
NO, IT'S BAD FOR YOU, AND I NEED TO STAY IN SHAPE.
BESIDES, MY FATHER WOULD KILL ME.
HE DOESN'T NEED TO KNOW. HE'S PRETTY TOUGH ON YOU, HUH?
DID YOU NOTICE? BUT I'LL HAVE SOME WINE, THAT WAY YOU DIDN'T RUN THROUGH RIPPERLAND FOR NOTHING.
DID YOU BRING ANY FLOWERS FOR ME, ZACK?

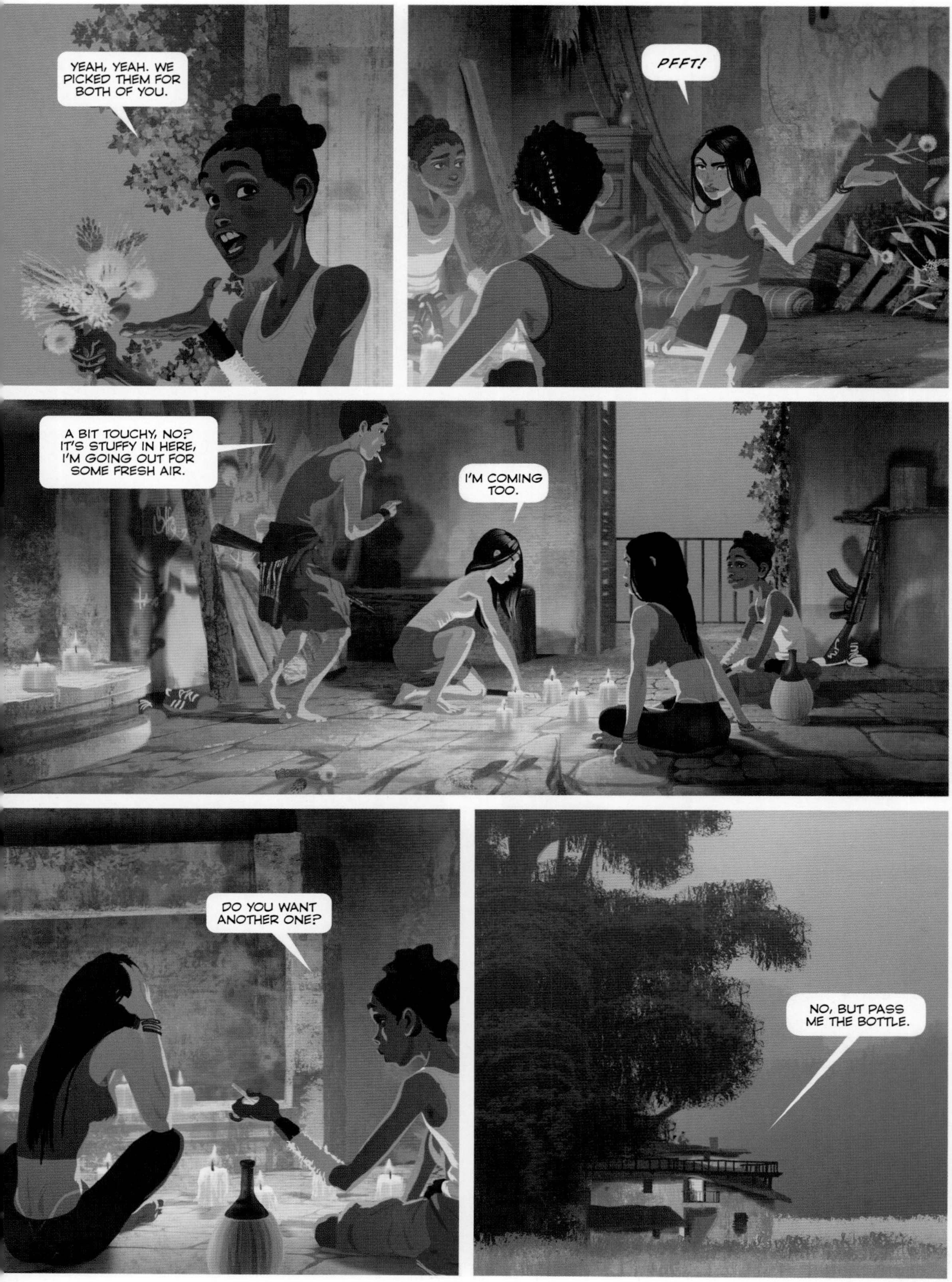
YEAH, YEAH. WE PICKED THEM FOR BOTH OF YOU.
PFFT!
A BIT TOUCHY, NO? IT'S STUFFY IN HERE, I'M GOING OUT FOR SOME FRESH AIR.
I'M COMING TOO.
DO YOU WANT ANOTHER ONE?
NO, BUT PASS ME THE BOTTLE.

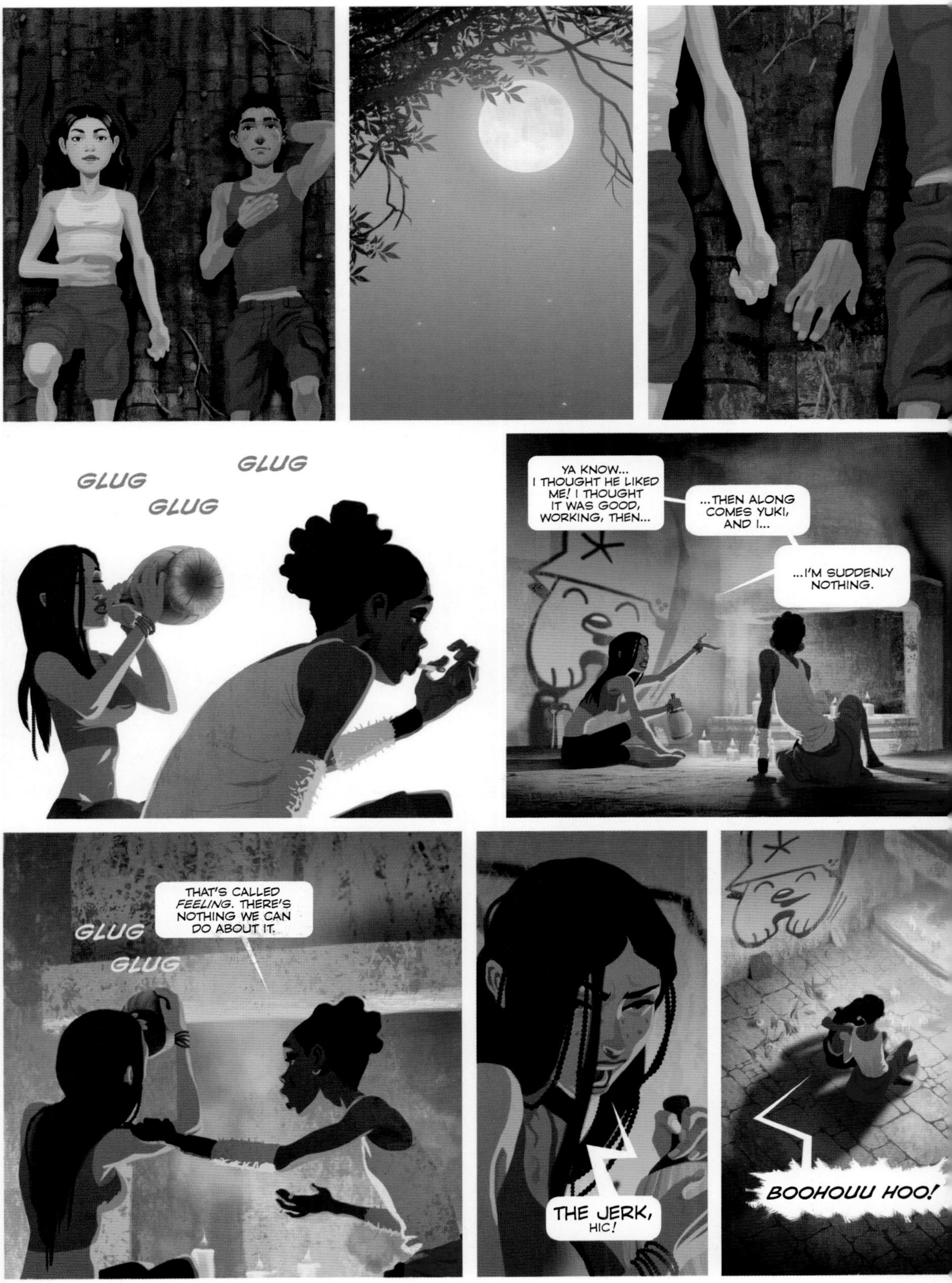
GLUG
GLUG
GLUG
YA KNOW... I THOUGHT HE LIKED ME! I THOUGHT IT WAS GOOD, WORKING, THEN...
...THEN ALONG COMES YUKI, AND I...
...I'M SUDDENLY NOTHING.
GLUG
GLUG
THAT'S CALLED *FEELING*. THERE'S NOTHING WE CAN DO ABOUT IT.
THE JERK, HIC!
BOOHOUU HOO!

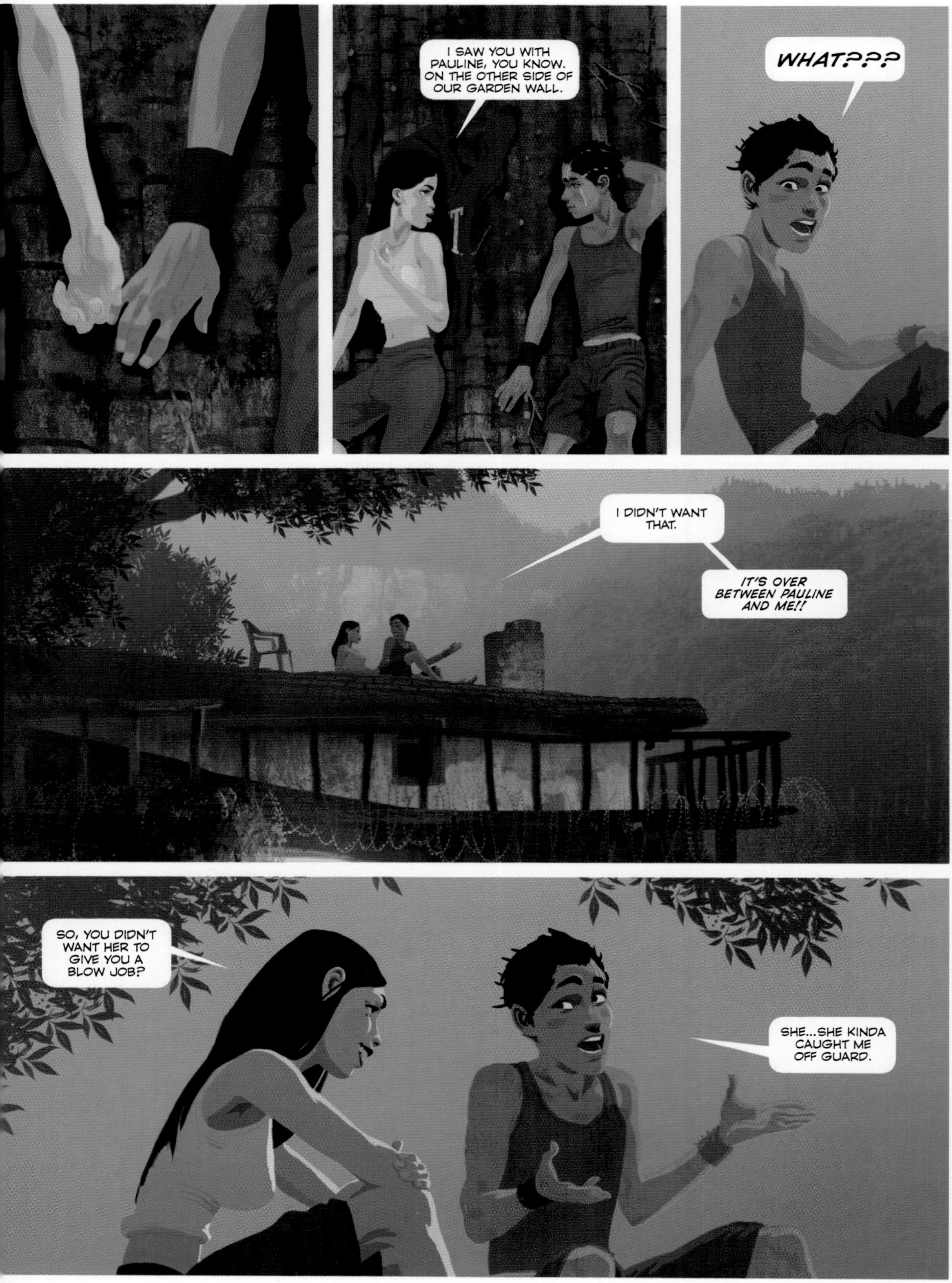
I SAW YOU WITH PAULINE, YOU KNOW. ON THE OTHER SIDE OF OUR GARDEN WALL.
WHAT???
I DIDN'T WANT THAT.
IT'S OVER BETWEEN PAULINE AND ME!!
SO, YOU DIDN'T WANT HER TO GIVE YOU A BLOW JOB?
SHE...SHE KINDA CAUGHT ME OFF GUARD.

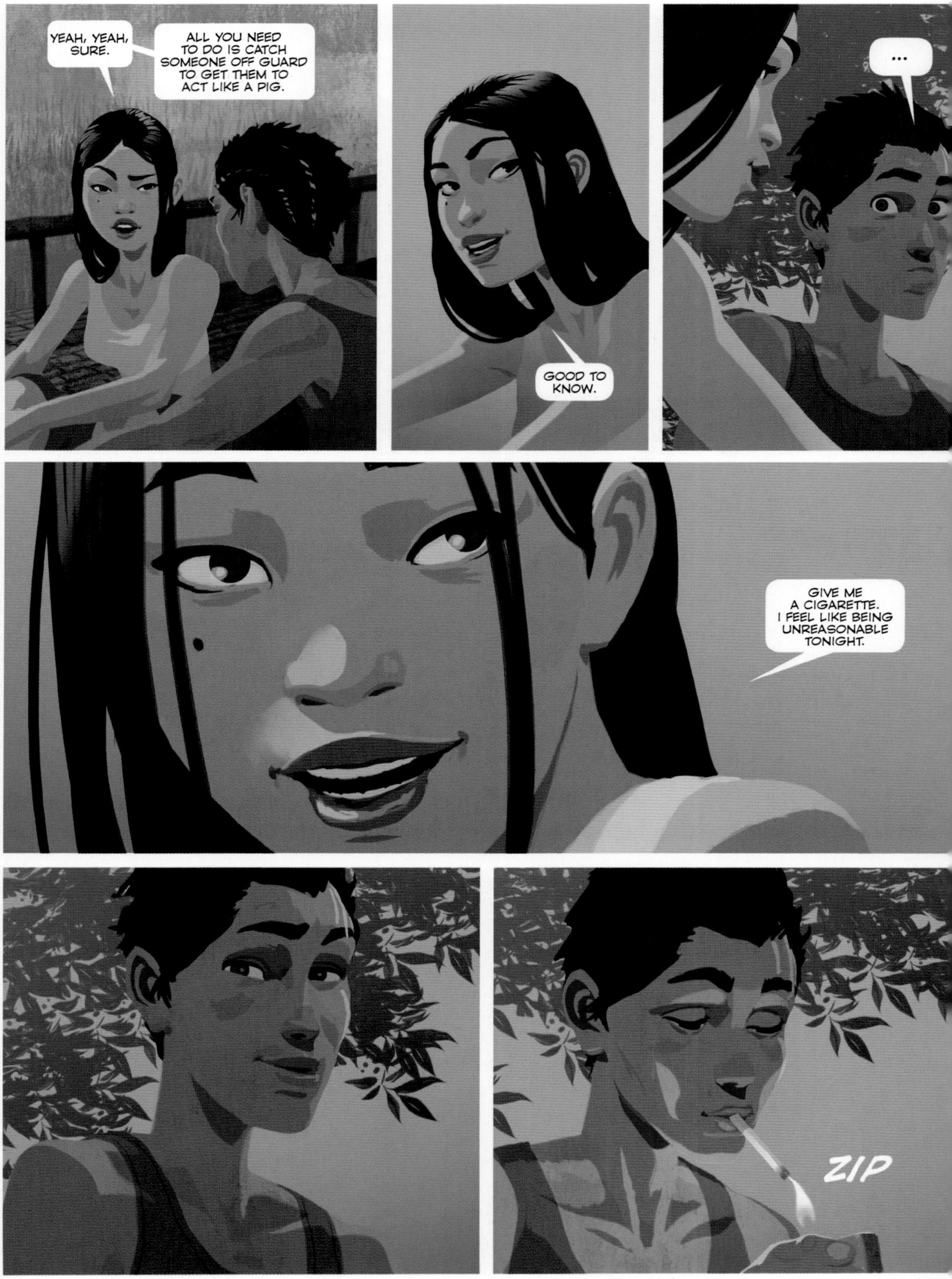
YEAH, YEAH, SURE.
ALL YOU NEED TO DO IS CATCH SOMEONE OFF GUARD TO GET THEM TO ACT LIKE A PIG.
GOOD TO KNOW.
...
GIVE ME A CIGARETTE. I FEEL LIKE BEING UNREASONABLE TONIGHT.
ZIP

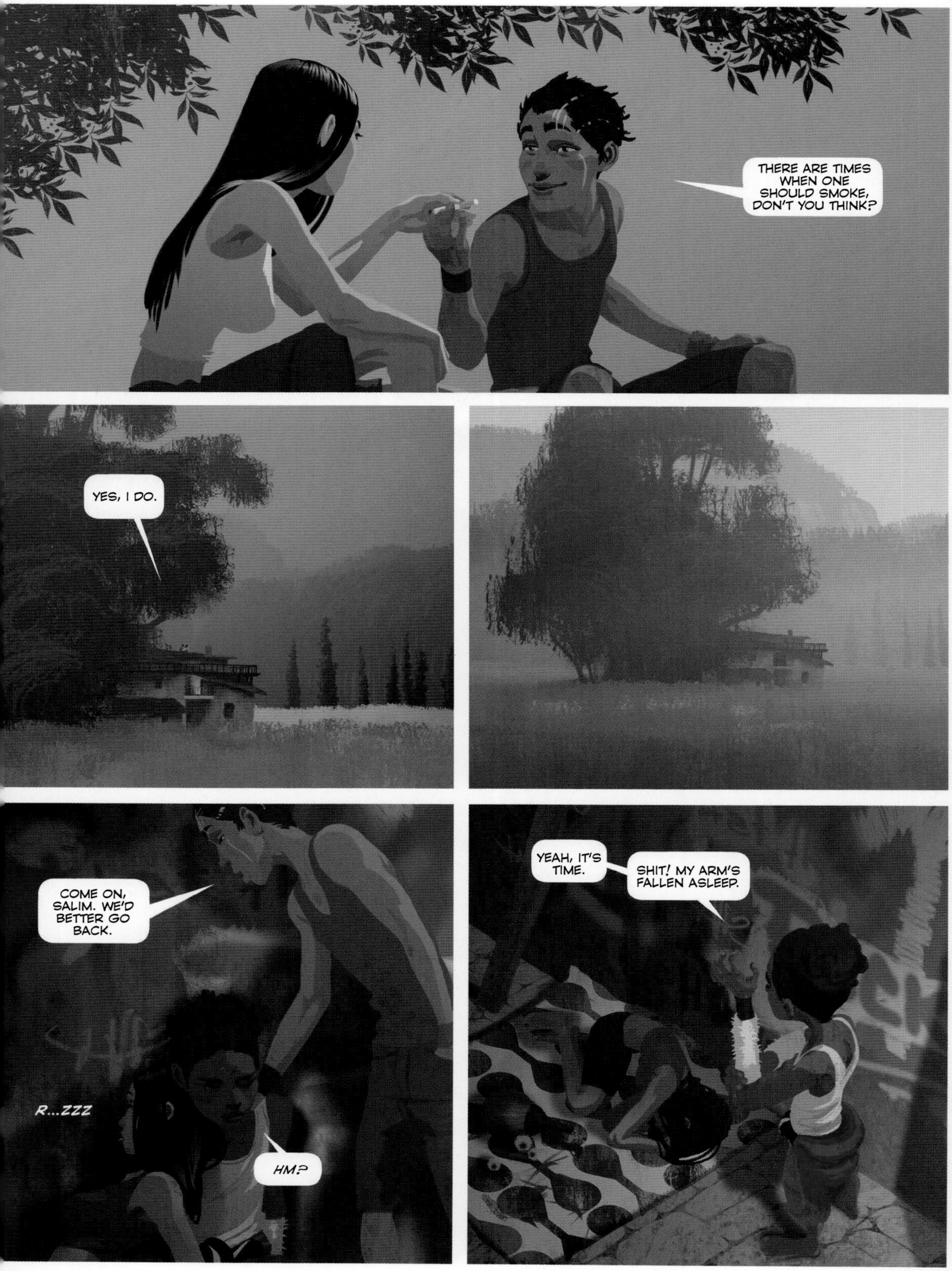
THERE ARE TIMES WHEN ONE SHOULD SMOKE, DON'T YOU THINK?
YES, I DO.
COME ON, SALIM. WE'D BETTER GO BACK.
R...ZZZ
HM?
YEAH, IT'S TIME.
SHIT! MY ARM'S FALLEN ASLEEP.

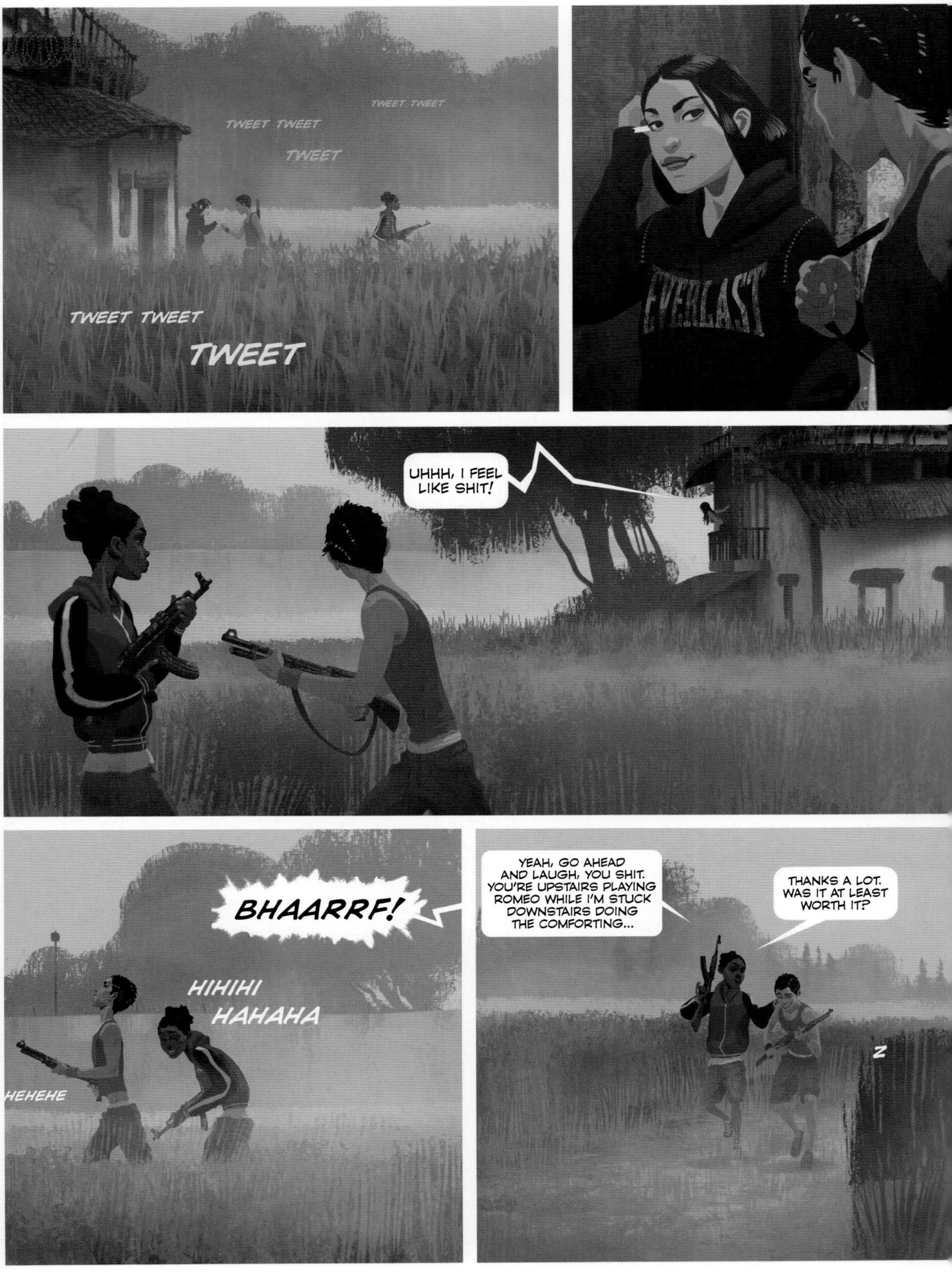
TWEET TWEET
TWEET
TWEET TWEET
TWEET TWEET
TWEET
UHHH, I FEEL LIKE SHIT!
BHAARRF!
HIHIHI
HAHAHA
HEHEHE
YEAH, GO AHEAD AND LAUGH, YOU SHIT. YOU'RE UPSTAIRS PLAYING ROMEO WHILE I'M STUCK DOWNSTAIRS DOING THE COMFORTING...
THANKS A LOT. WAS IT AT LEAST WORTH IT?
Z

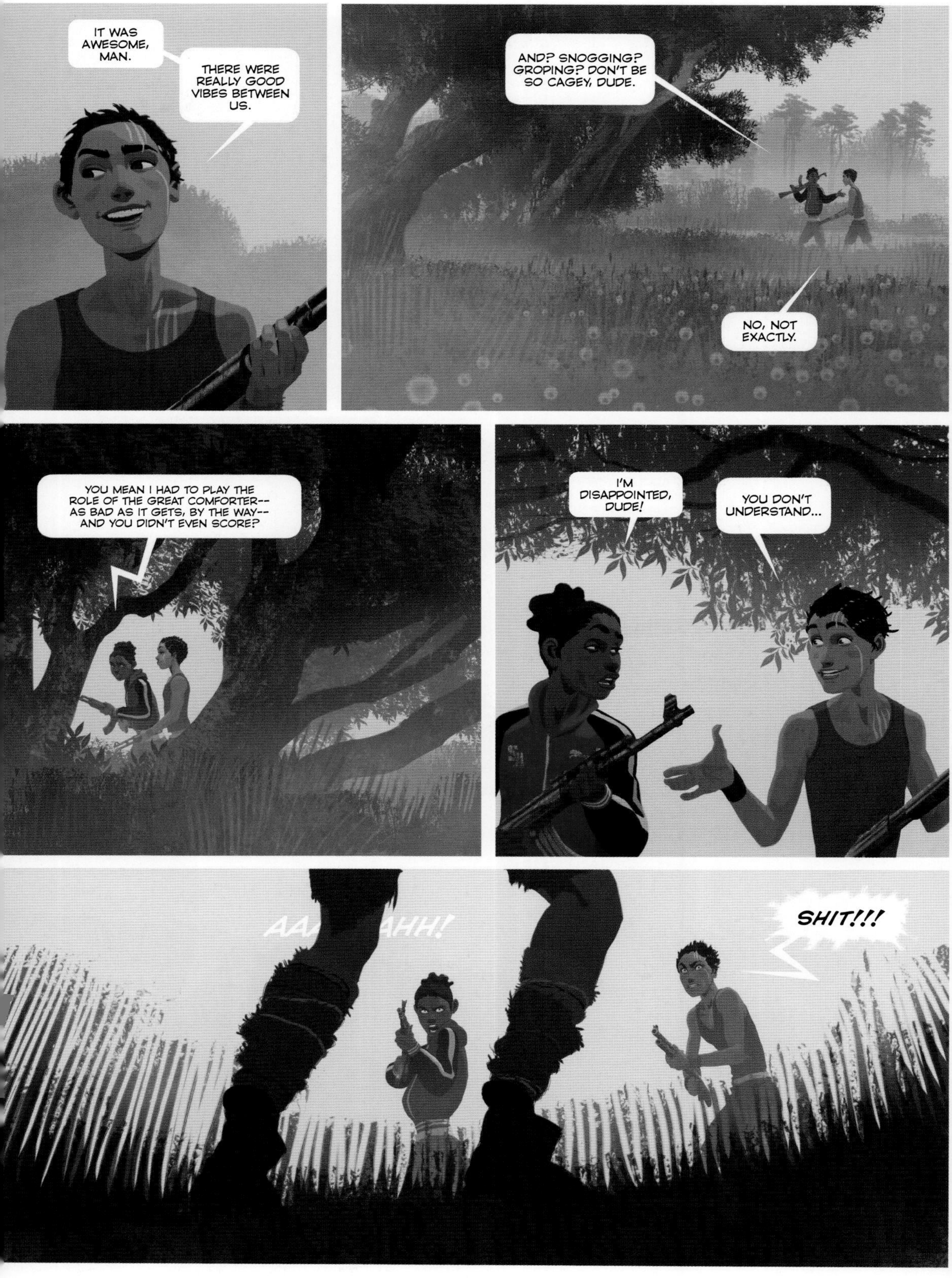
IT WAS AWESOME, MAN.
THERE WERE REALLY GOOD VIBES BETWEEN US.
AND? SNOGGING? GROPING? DON'T BE SO CAGEY, DUDE.
NO, NOT EXACTLY.
YOU MEAN I HAD TO PLAY THE ROLE OF THE GREAT COMFORTER-- AS BAD AS IT GETS, BY THE WAY-- AND YOU DIDN'T EVEN SCORE?
I'M DISAPPOINTED, DUDE!
YOU DON'T UNDERSTAND...
SHIT!!!

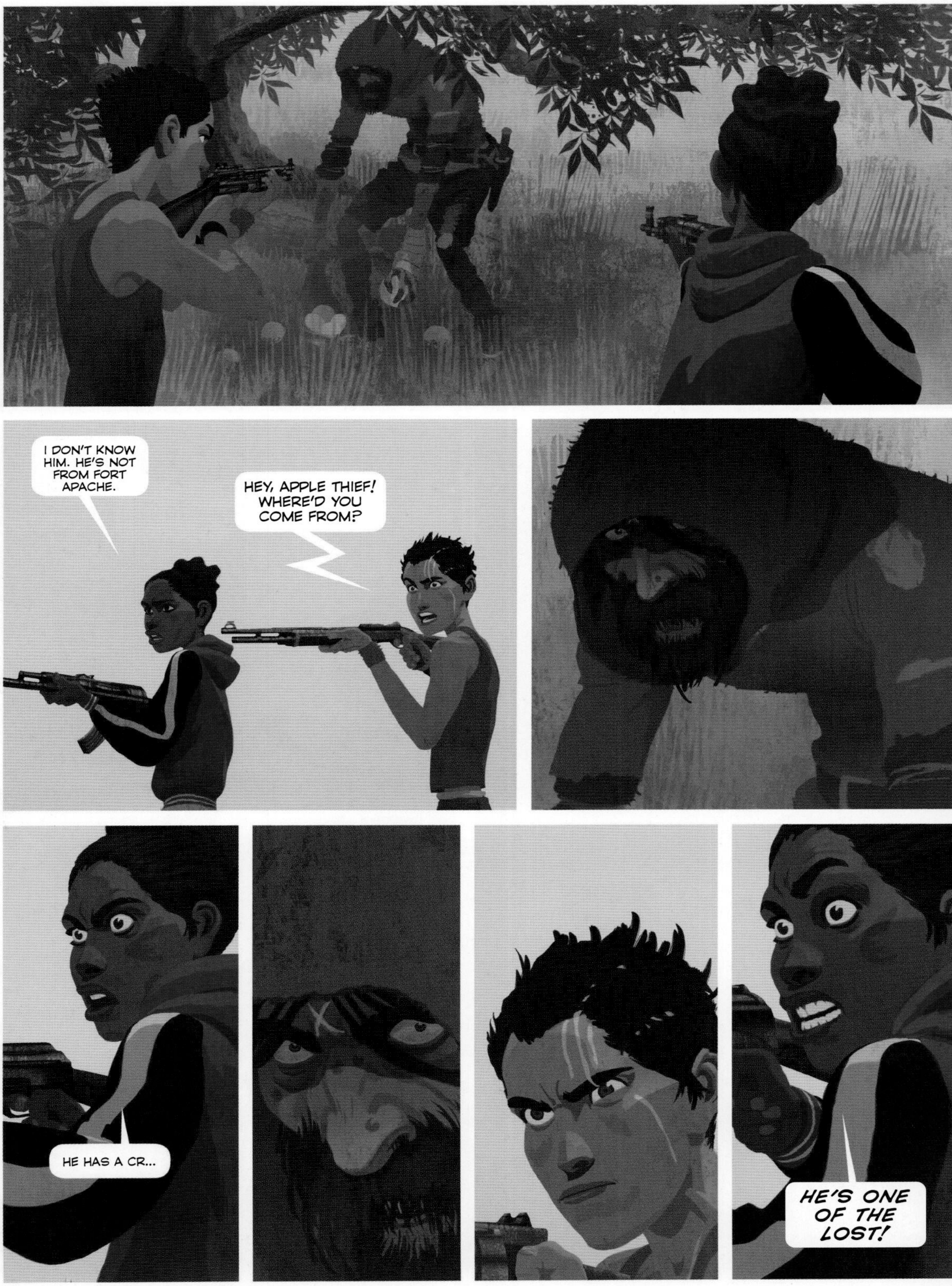
I DON'T KNOW HIM. HE'S NOT FROM FORT APACHE.
HEY, APPLE THIEF! WHERE'D YOU COME FROM?
HE HAS A CR...
HE'S ONE OF THE LOST!

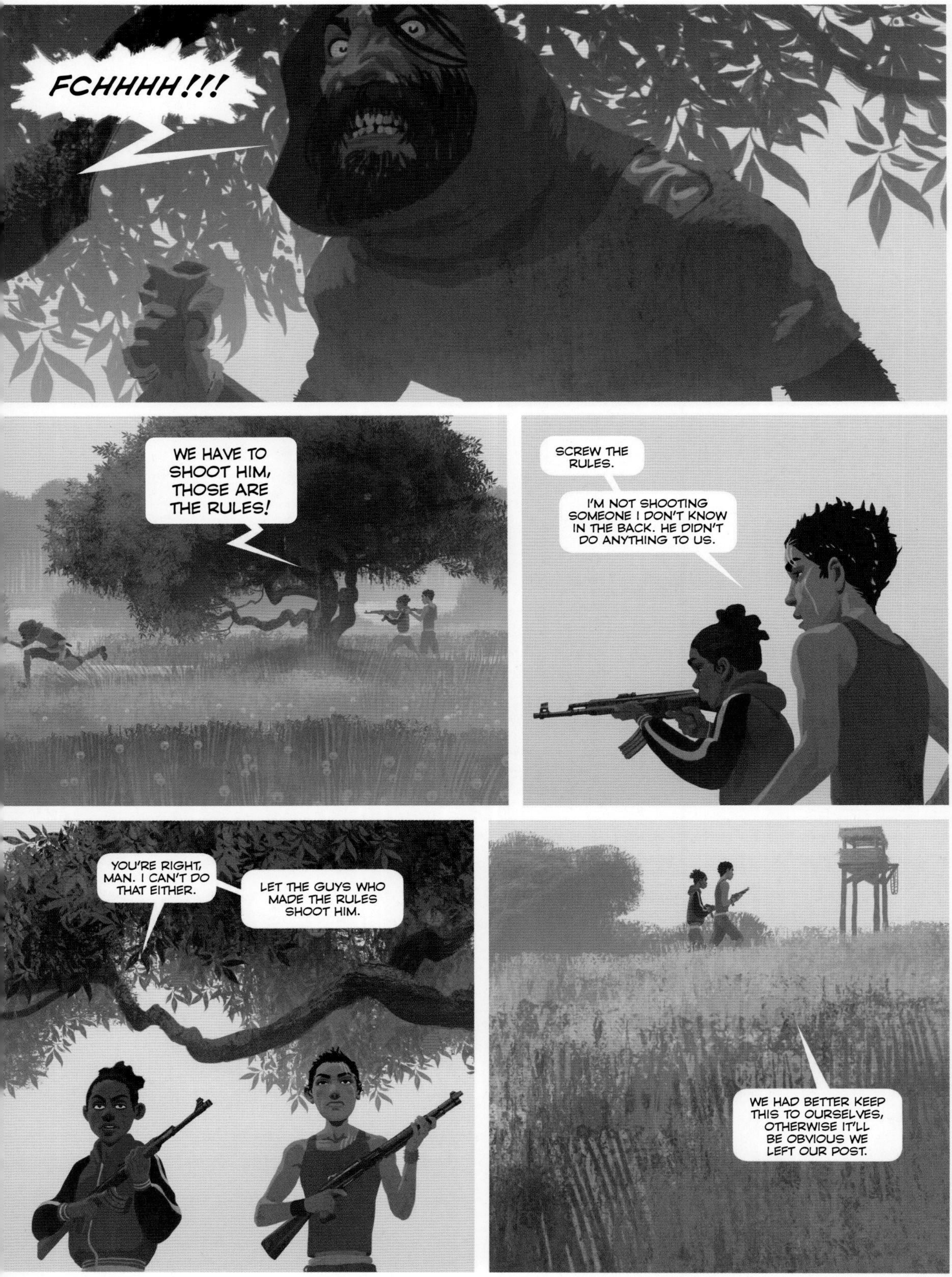
FCHHHH!!!
WE HAVE TO SHOOT HIM, THOSE ARE THE RULES!
SCREW THE RULES.
I'M NOT SHOOTING SOMEONE I DON'T KNOW IN THE BACK. HE DIDN'T DO ANYTHING TO US.
YOU'RE RIGHT, MAN. I CAN'T DO THAT EITHER.
LET THE GUYS WHO MADE THE RULES SHOOT HIM.
WE HAD BETTER KEEP THIS TO OURSELVES, OTHERWISE IT'LL BE OBVIOUS WE LEFT OUR POST.

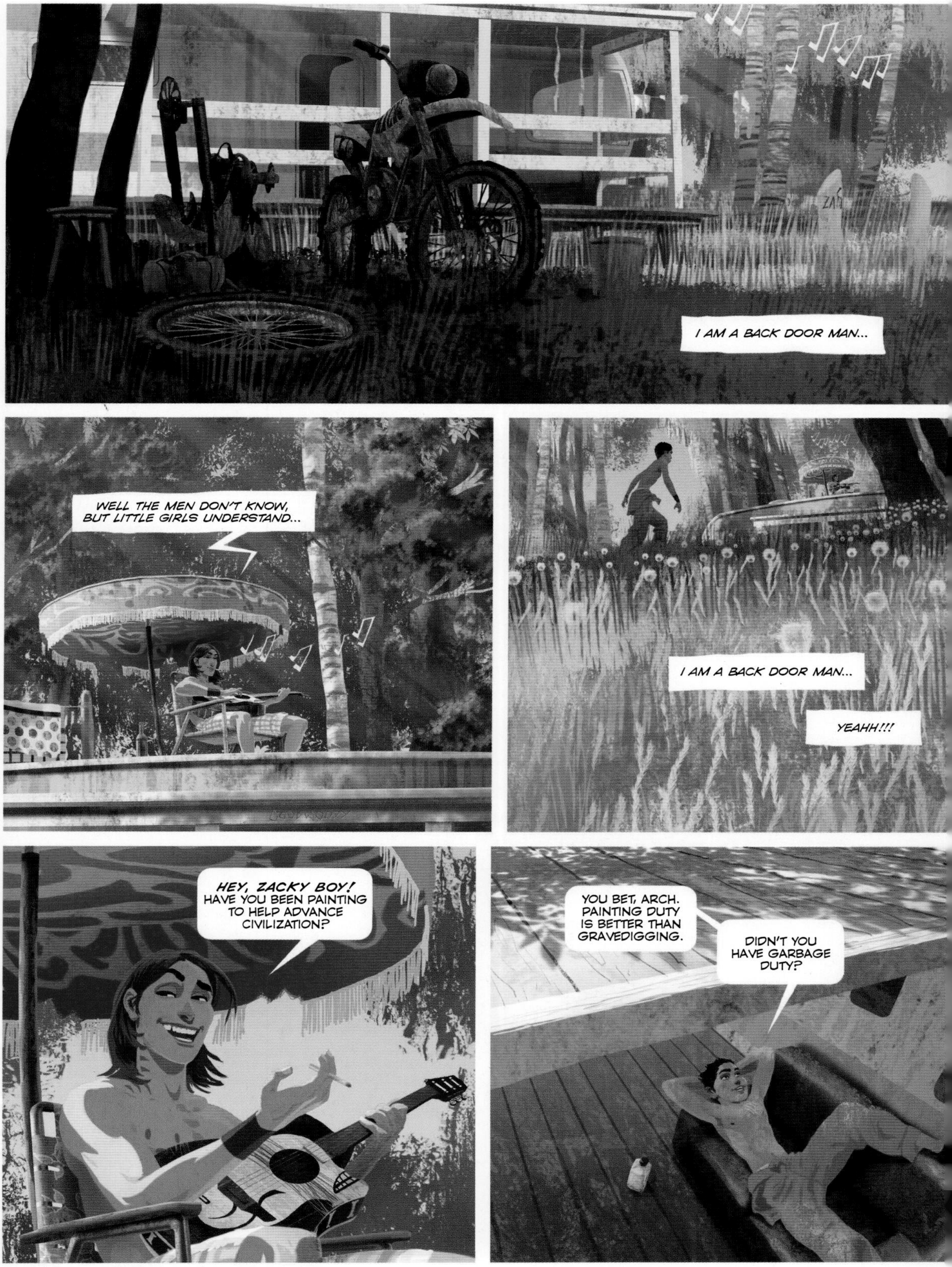
I AM A BACK DOOR MAN...
WELL THE MEN DON'T KNOW, BUT LITTLE GIRLS UNDERSTAND...
I AM A BACK DOOR MAN...
YEAHH!!!
HEY, ZACKY BOY! HAVE YOU BEEN PAINTING TO HELP ADVANCE CIVILIZATION?
YOU BET, ARCH. PAINTING DUTY IS BETTER THAN GRAVEDIGGING.
DIDN'T YOU HAVE GARBAGE DUTY?

SONGTEXT: BACK DOOR MAN BY HOWLIN' WOLF

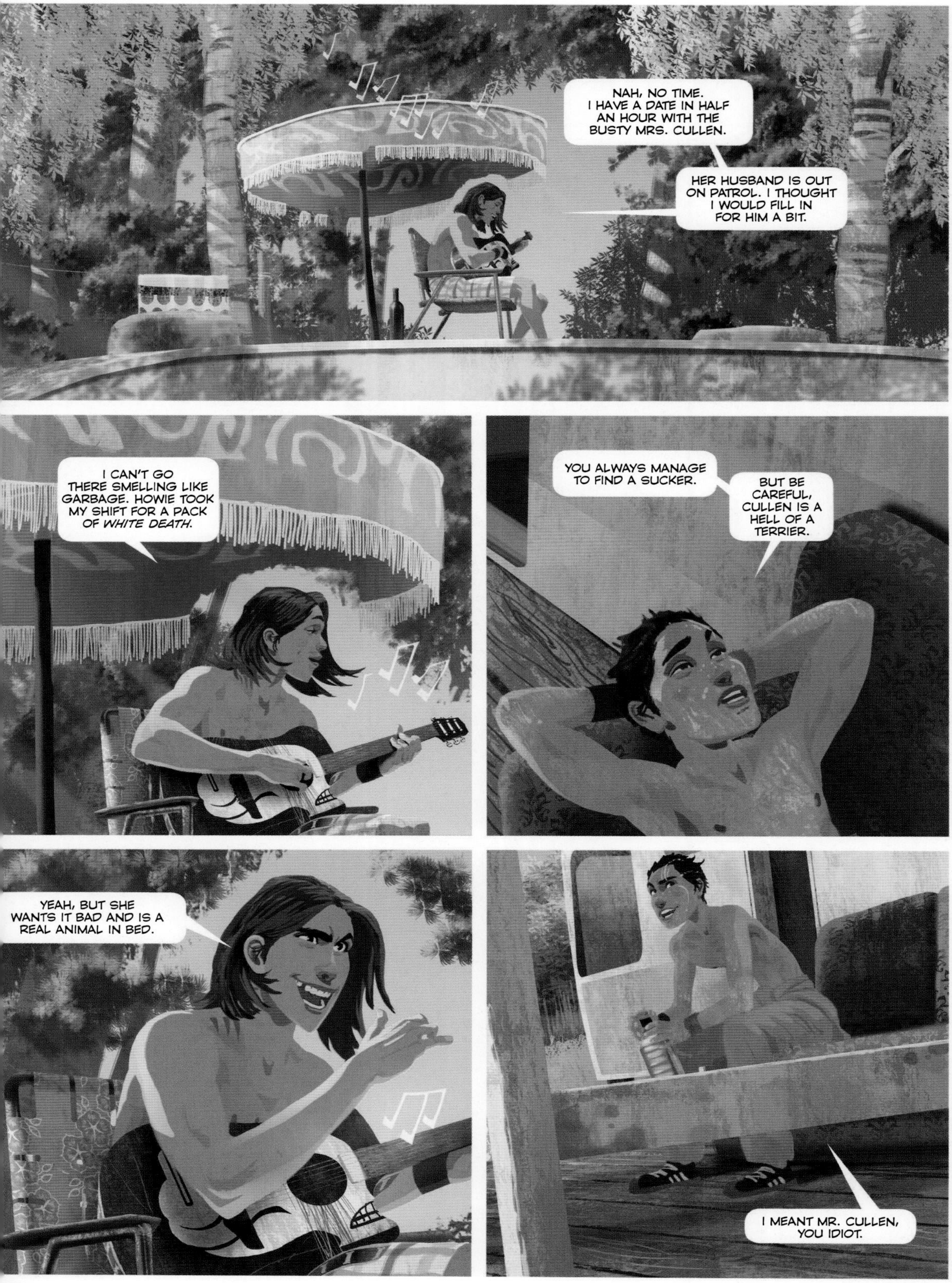
NAH, NO TIME. I HAVE A DATE IN HALF AN HOUR WITH THE BUSTY MRS. CULLEN.
HER HUSBAND IS OUT ON PATROL. I THOUGHT I WOULD FILL IN FOR HIM A BIT.
I CAN'T GO THERE SMELLING LIKE GARBAGE. HOWIE TOOK MY SHIFT FOR A PACK OF *WHITE DEATH*.
YOU ALWAYS MANAGE TO FIND A SUCKER.
BUT BE CAREFUL, CULLEN IS A HELL OF A TERRIER.
YEAH, BUT SHE WANTS IT BAD AND IS A REAL ANIMAL IN BED.
I MEANT MR. CULLEN, YOU IDIOT.

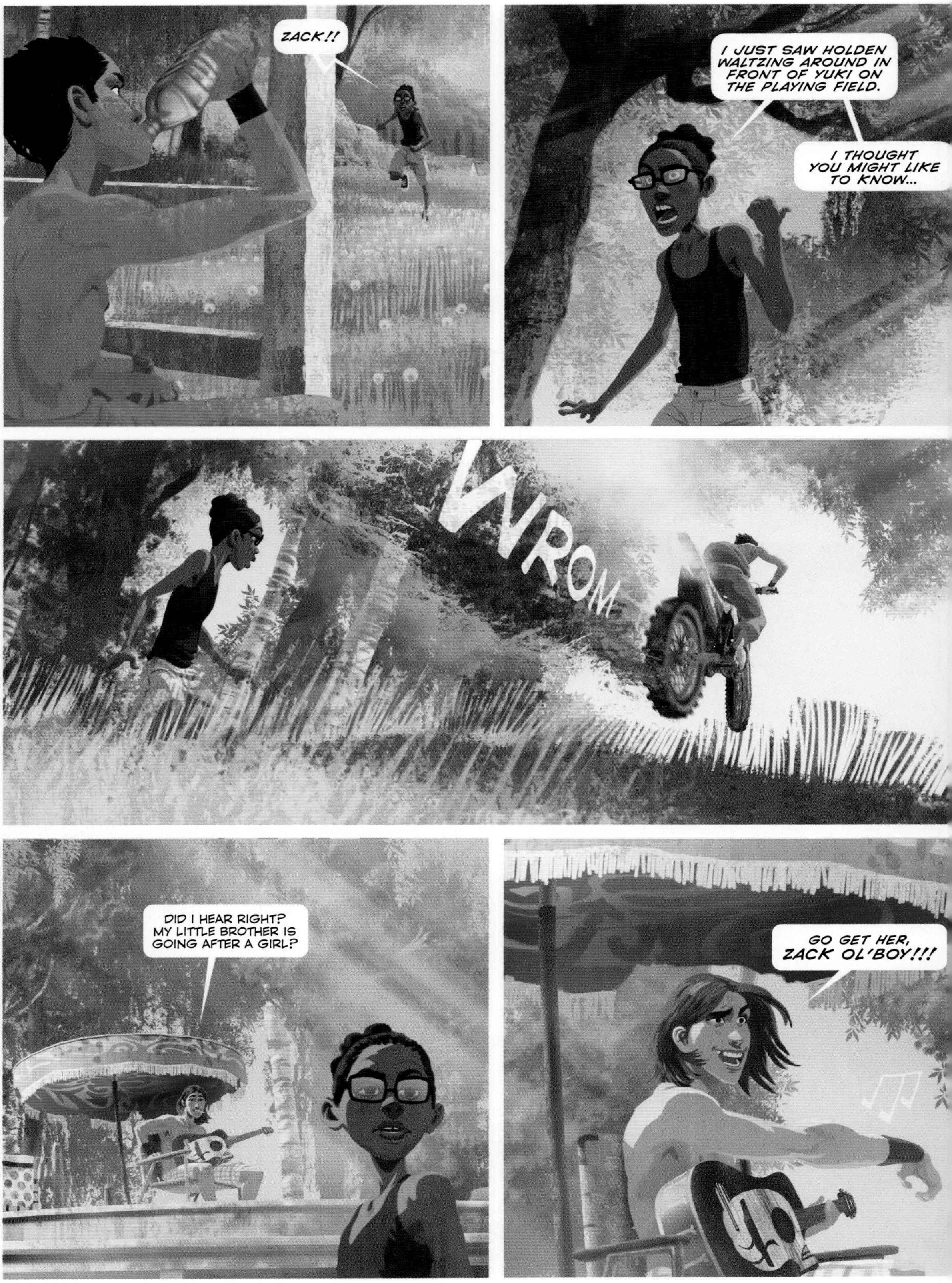
ZACK!!
I JUST SAW HOLDEN WALTZING AROUND IN FRONT OF YUKI ON THE PLAYING FIELD.
I THOUGHT YOU MIGHT LIKE TO KNOW...
WROM
DID I HEAR RIGHT? MY LITTLE BROTHER IS GOING AFTER A GIRL?
GO GET HER, ZACK OL'BOY!!!

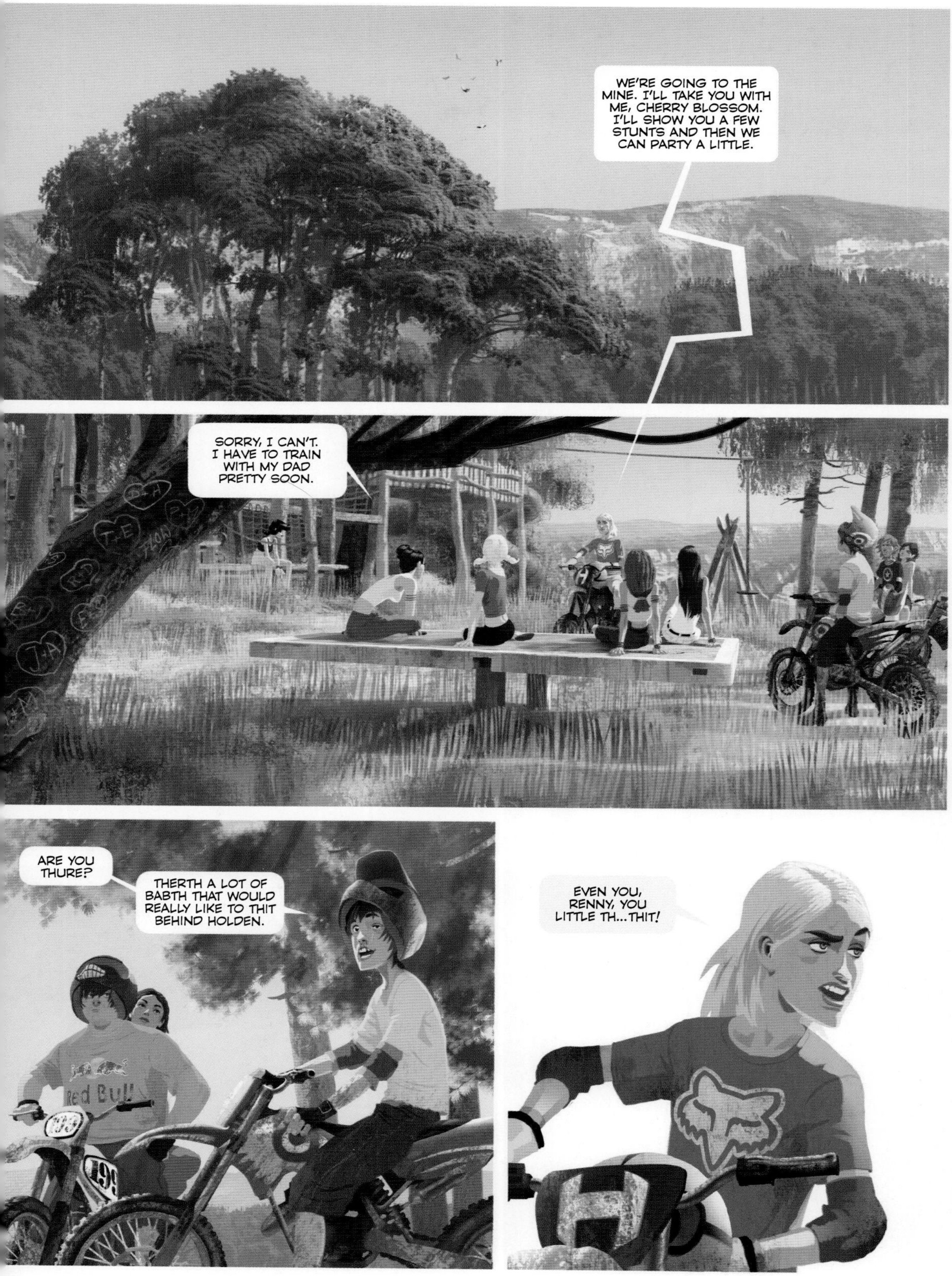
WE'RE GOING TO THE MINE. I'LL TAKE YOU WITH ME, CHERRY BLOSSOM. I'LL SHOW YOU A FEW STUNTS AND THEN WE CAN PARTY A LITTLE.
SORRY, I CAN'T. I HAVE TO TRAIN WITH MY DAD PRETTY SOON.
ARE YOU THURE?
THERTH A LOT OF BABTH THAT WOULD REALLY LIKE TO THIT BEHIND HOLDEN.
EVEN YOU, RENNY, YOU LITTLE TH...THIT!

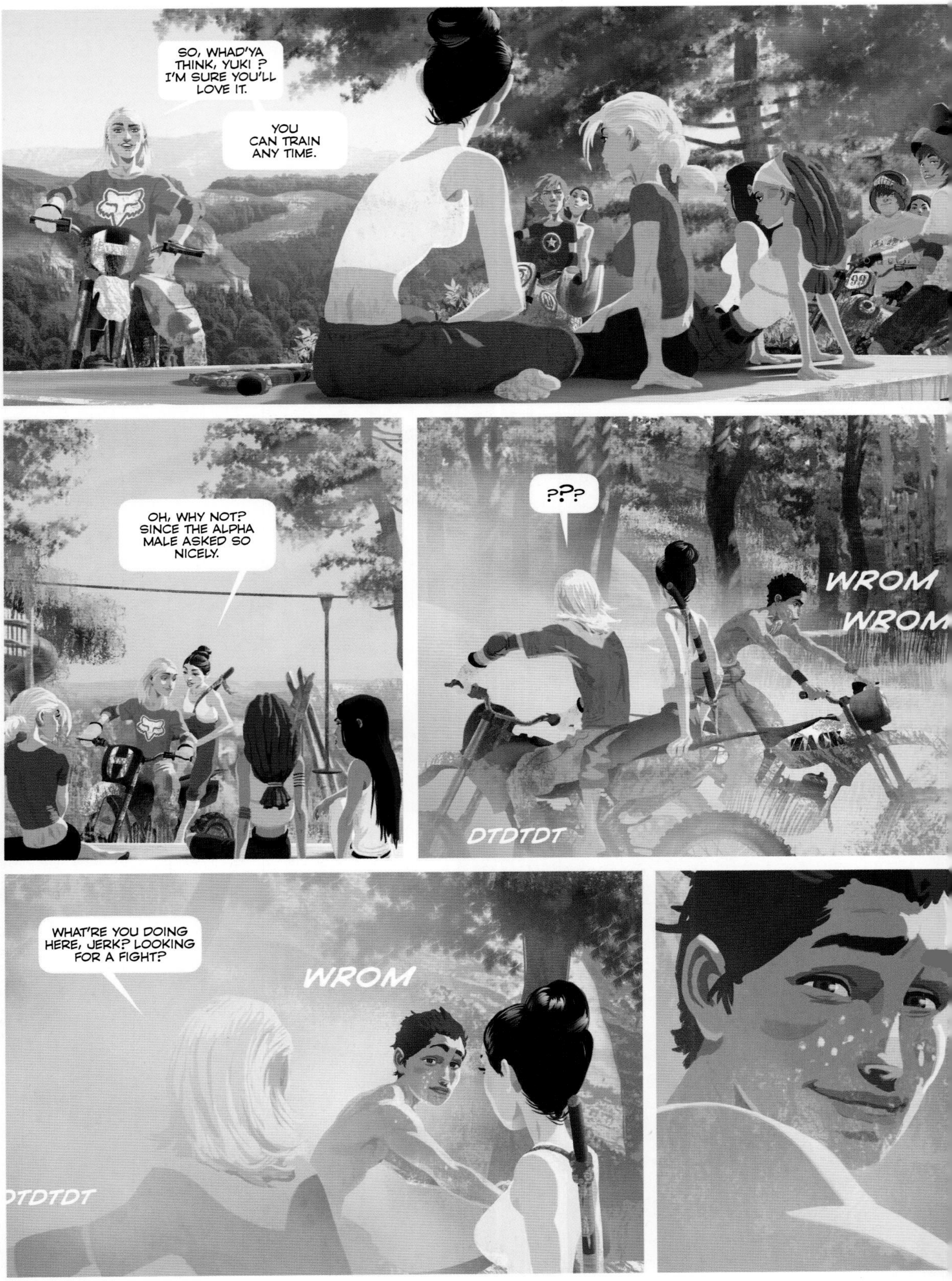
SO, WHAD'YA THINK, YUKI ? I'M SURE YOU'LL LOVE IT.
YOU CAN TRAIN ANY TIME.
OH, WHY NOT? SINCE THE ALPHA MALE ASKED SO NICELY.
???
WROM
WROM
DTDTDT
WHAT'RE YOU DOING HERE, JERK? LOOKING FOR A FIGHT?
WROM
DTDTDT

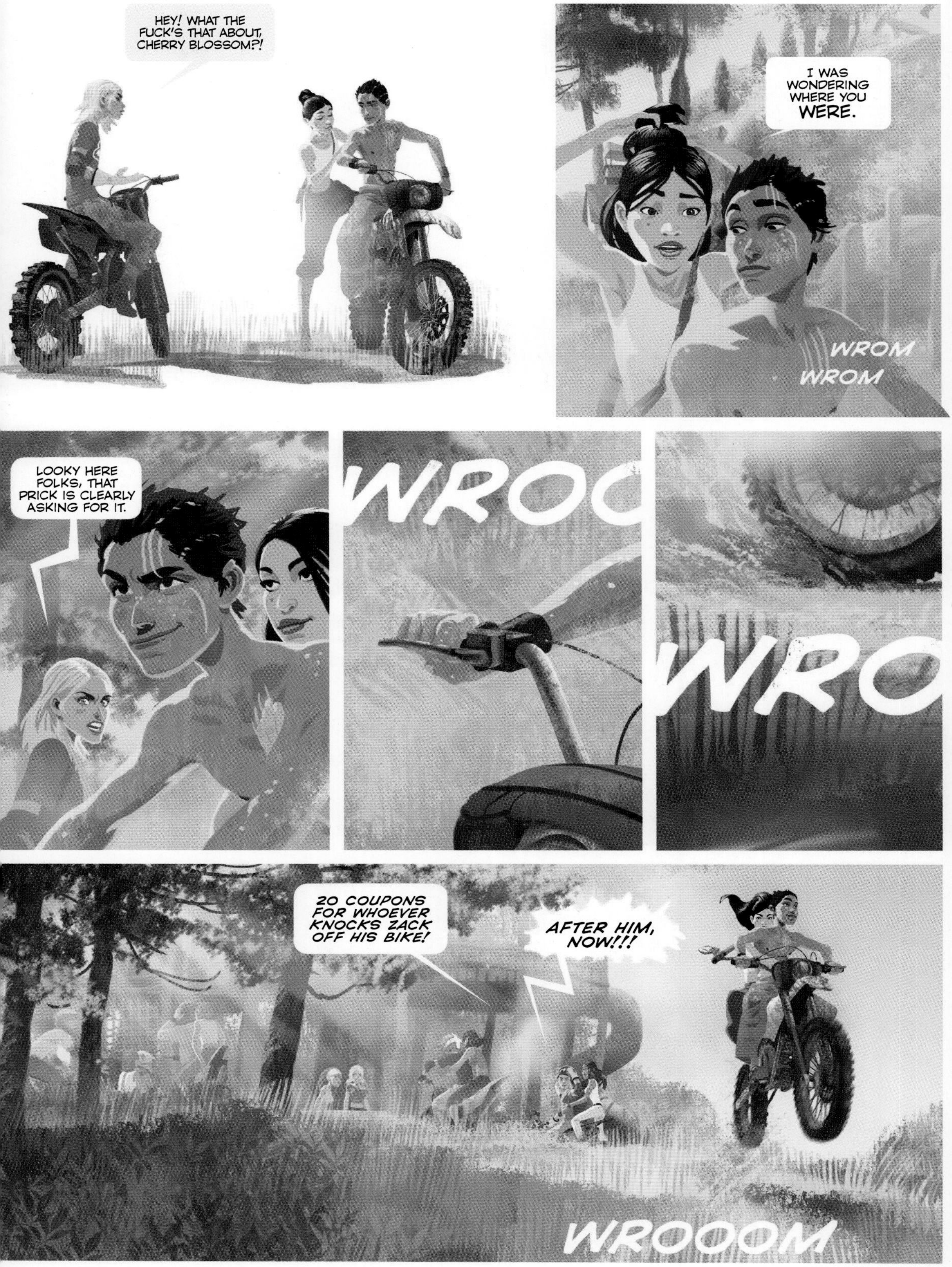
HEY! WHAT THE FUCK'S THAT ABOUT, CHERRY BLOSSOM?!
I WAS WONDERING WHERE YOU WERE.
WROM WROM
LOOKY HERE FOLKS, THAT PRICK IS CLEARLY ASKING FOR IT.
WROO
WRO
20 COUPONS FOR WHOEVER KNOCKS ZACK OFF HIS BIKE!
AFTER HIM, NOW!!!
WROOOM

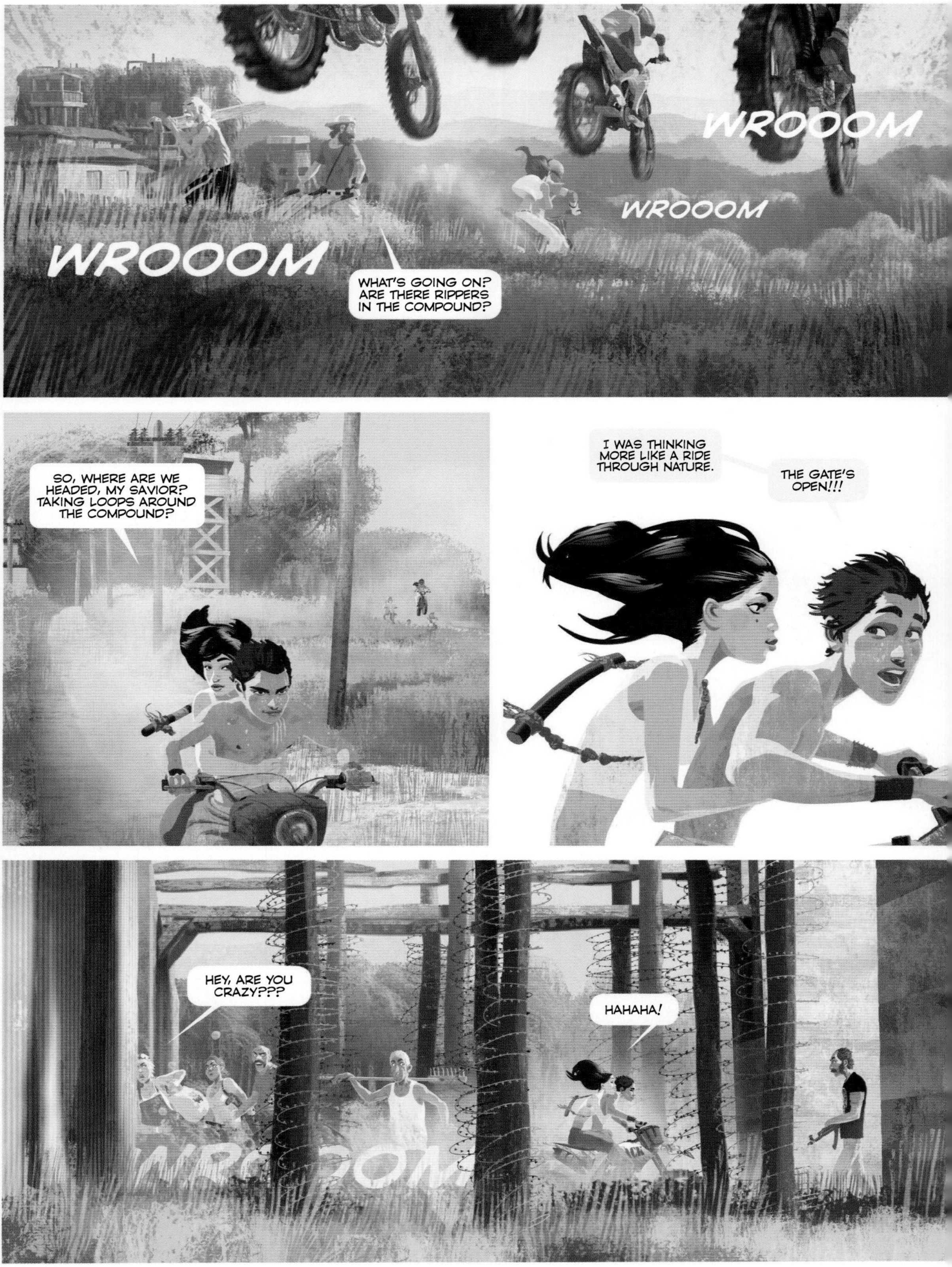
WROOOM
WROOOM
WROOOM
WHAT'S GOING ON? ARE THERE RIPPERS IN THE COMPOUND?
SO, WHERE ARE WE HEADED, MY SAVIOR? TAKING LOOPS AROUND THE COMPOUND?
I WAS THINKING MORE LIKE A RIDE THROUGH NATURE.
THE GATE'S OPEN!!!
HEY, ARE YOU CRAZY???
HAHAHA!

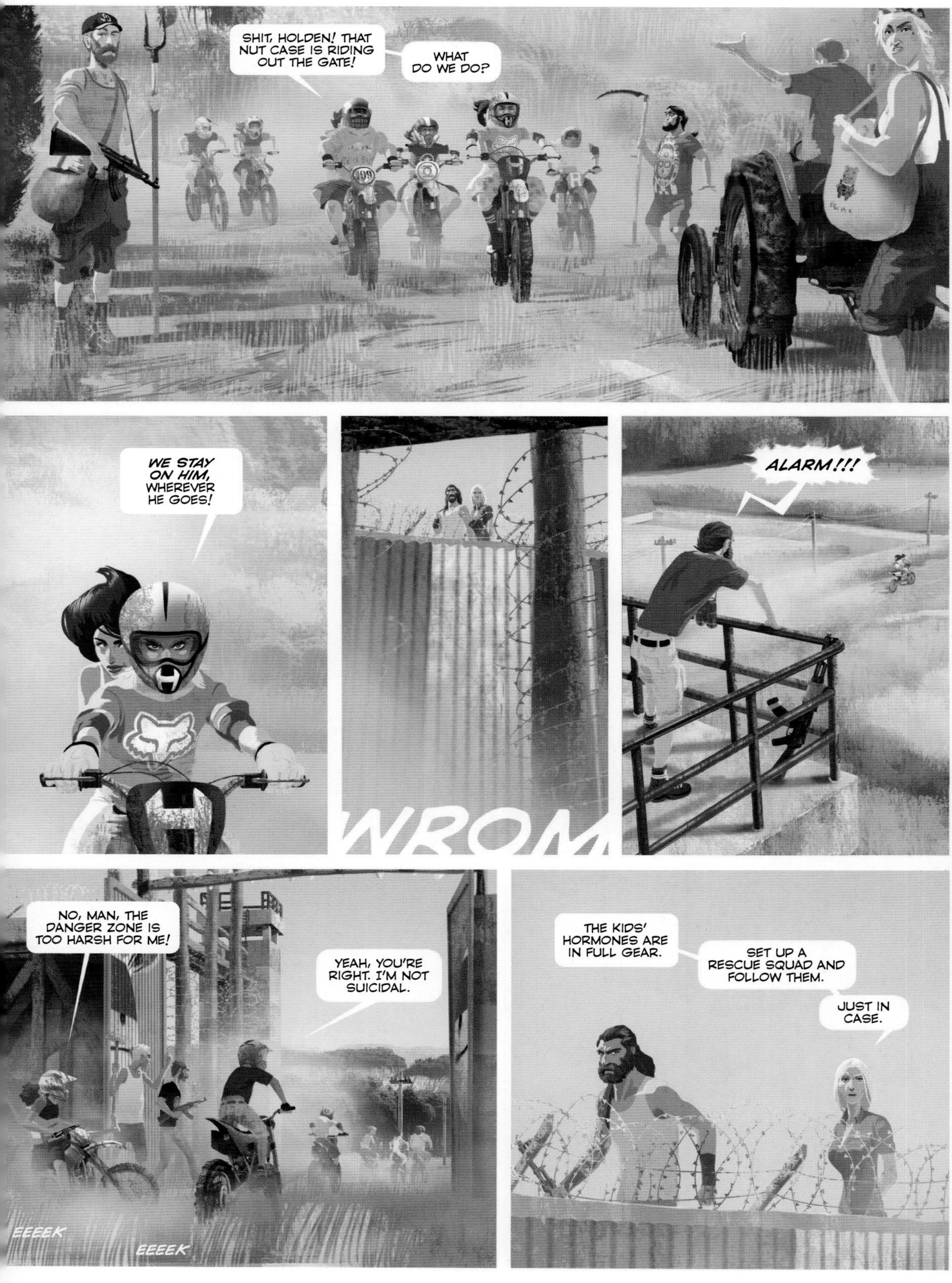

SHIT, HOLDEN! THAT NUT CASE IS RIDING OUT THE GATE!
WHAT DO WE DO?
WE STAY ON HIM, WHEREVER HE GOES!
WROM
ALARM!!!
NO, MAN, THE DANGER ZONE IS TOO HARSH FOR ME!
YEAH, YOU'RE RIGHT. I'M NOT SUICIDAL.
EEEEK
EEEEK
THE KIDS' HORMONES ARE IN FULL GEAR.
SET UP A RESCUE SQUAD AND FOLLOW THEM.
JUST IN CASE.

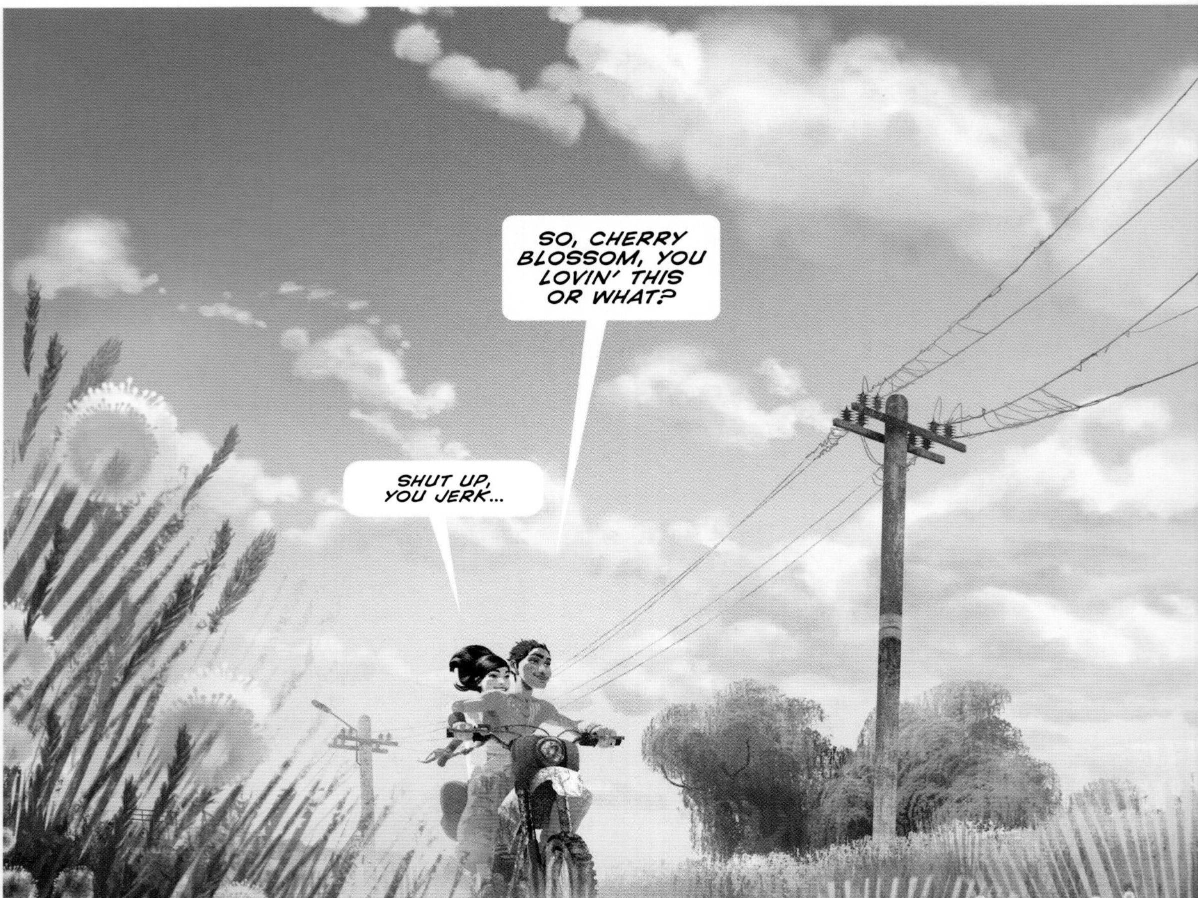
SO, CHERRY BLOSSOM, YOU LOVIN' THIS OR WHAT?
SHUT UP, YOU JERK...

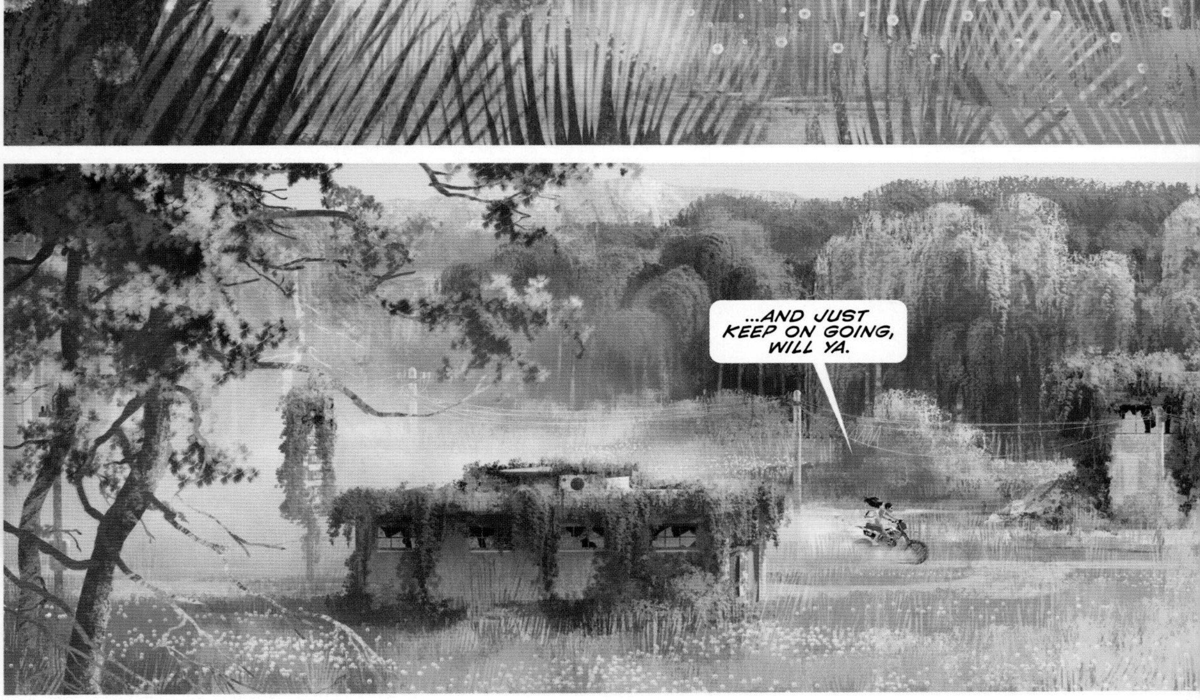
...AND JUST KEEP ON GOING, WILL YA.

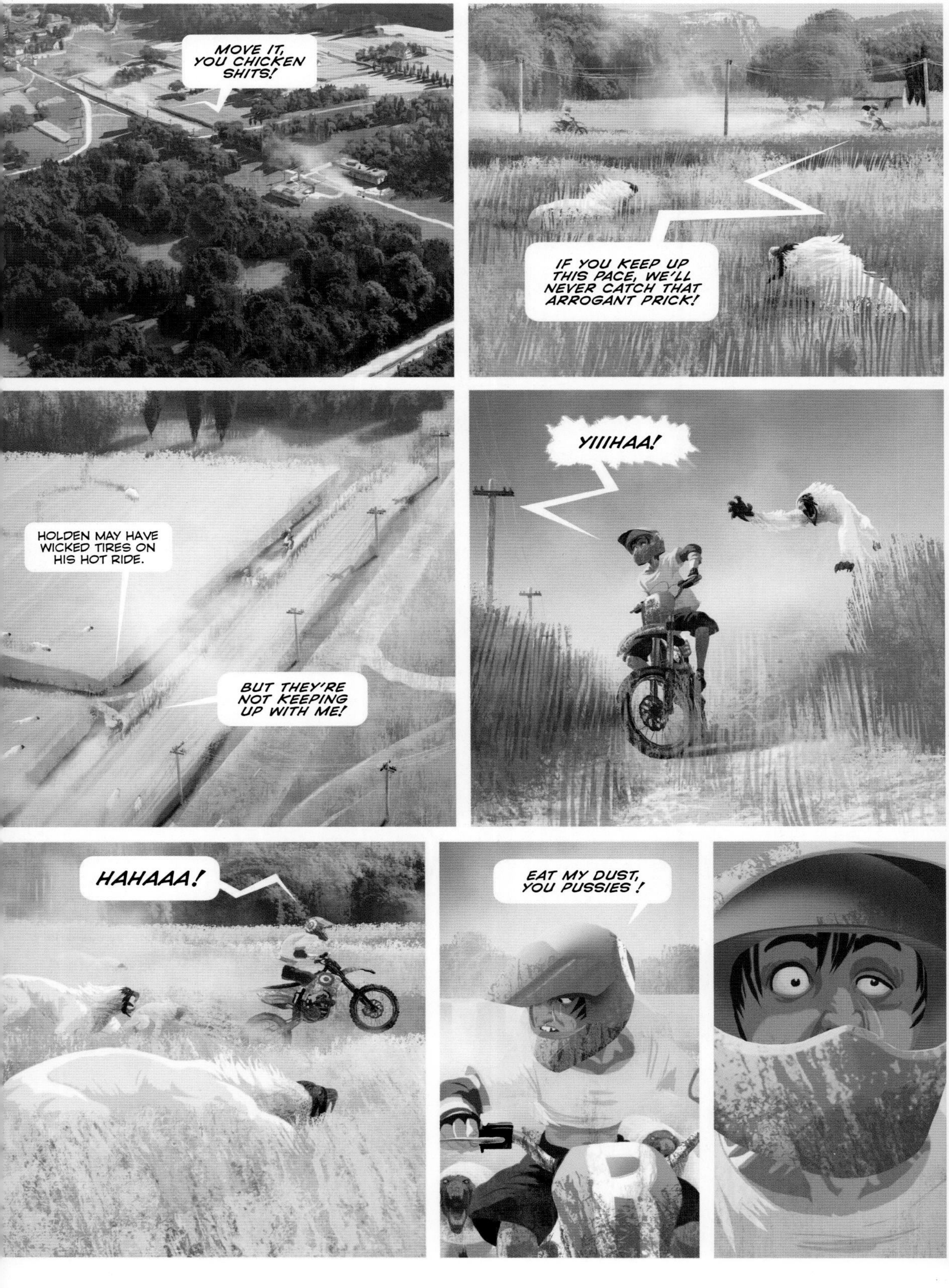
MOVE IT, YOU CHICKEN SHITS!
IF YOU KEEP UP THIS PACE, WE'LL NEVER CATCH THAT ARROGANT PRICK!
HOLDEN MAY HAVE WICKED TIRES ON HIS HOT RIDE.
BUT THEY'RE NOT KEEPING UP WITH ME!
YIIIHAA!
HAHAAA!
EAT MY DUST, YOU PUSSIES !

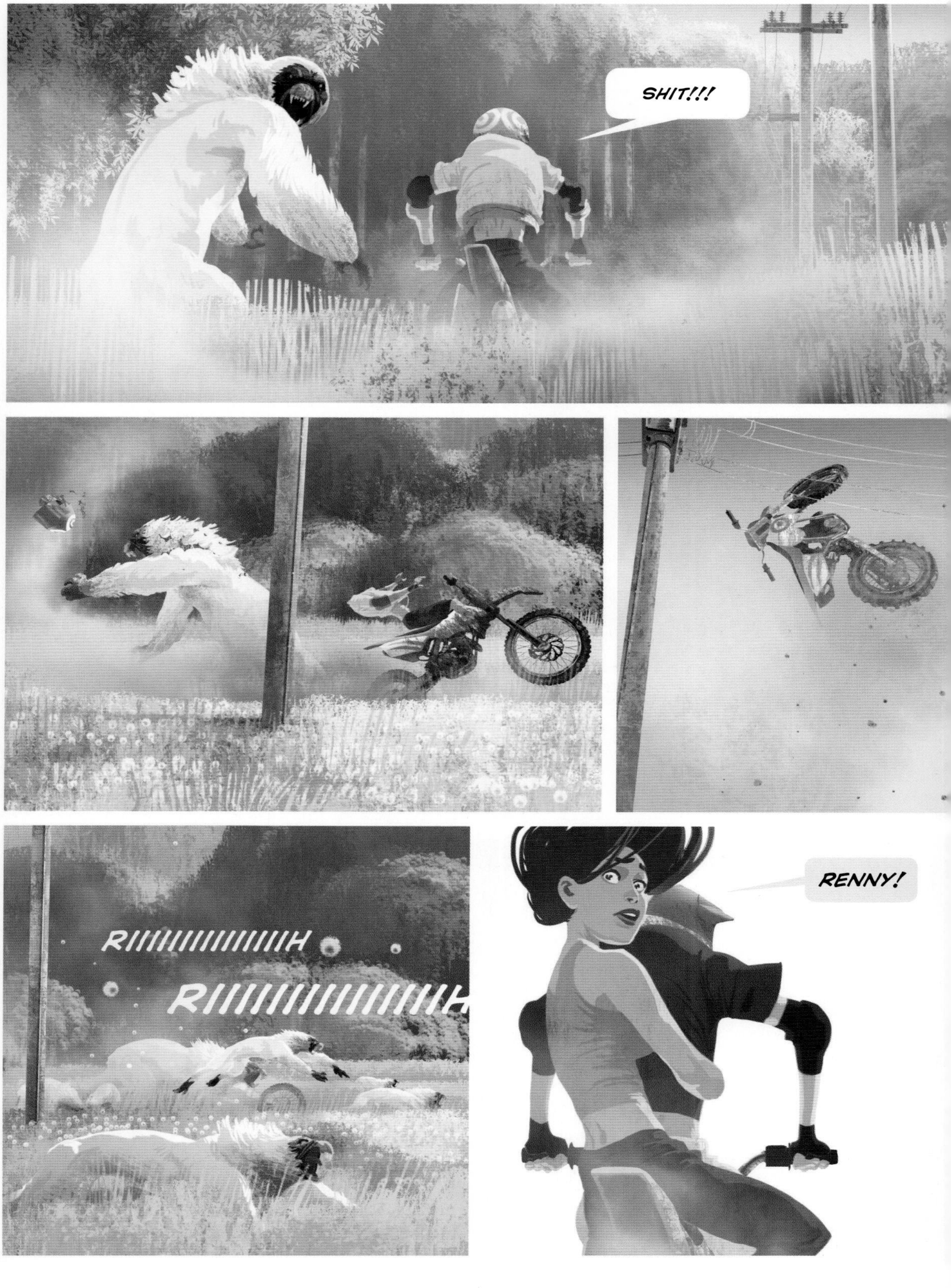
SHIT!!!
RIIIIIIIIIIIIIIH
RIIIIIIIIIIIIIIIH
RENNY!

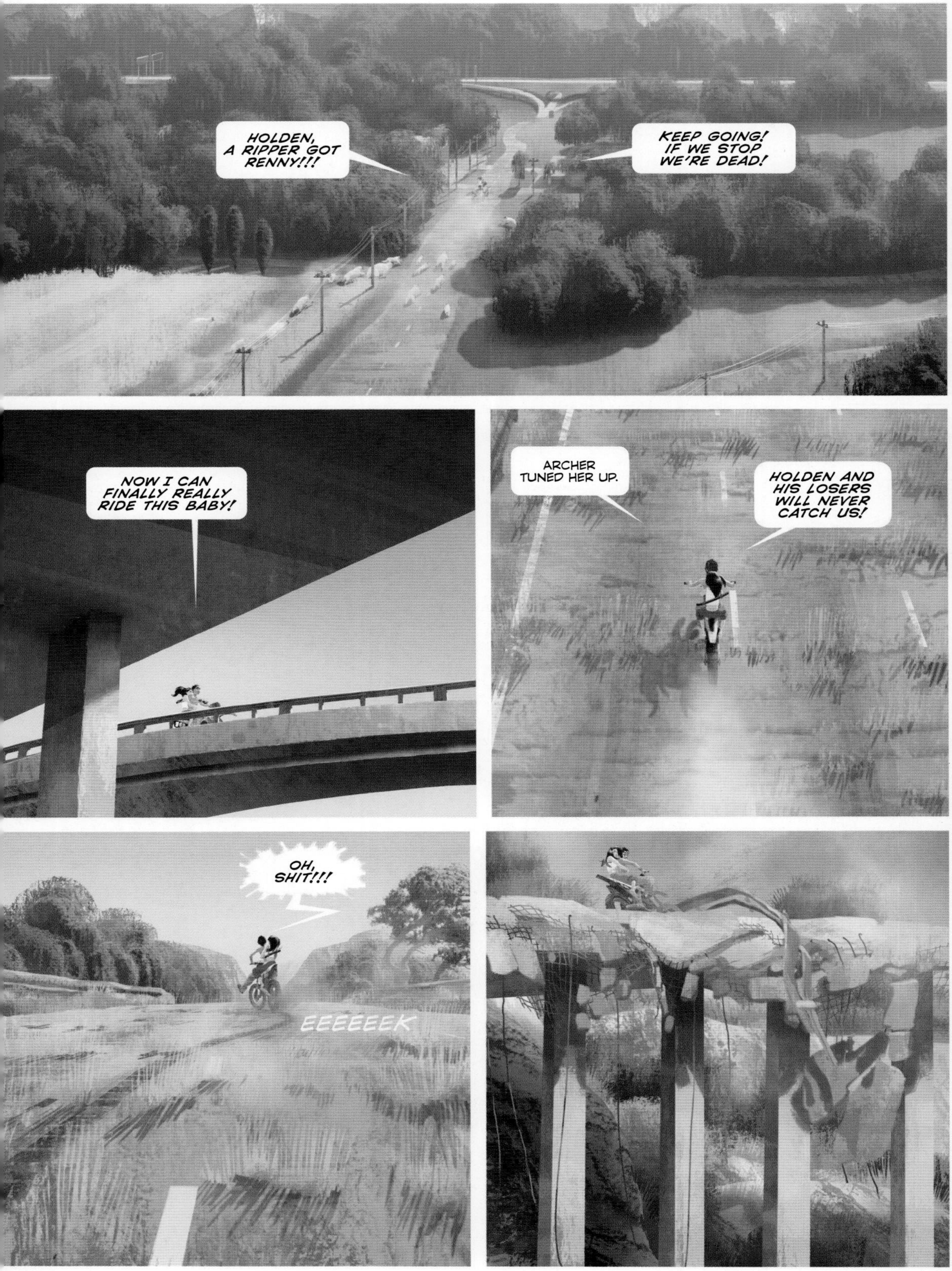
HOLDEN, A RIPPER GOT RENNY!!!
KEEP GOING! IF WE STOP WE'RE DEAD!
NOW I CAN FINALLY REALLY RIDE THIS BABY!
ARCHER TUNED HER UP.
HOLDEN AND HIS LOSERS WILL NEVER CATCH US!
OH, SHIT!!!
EEEEEEK

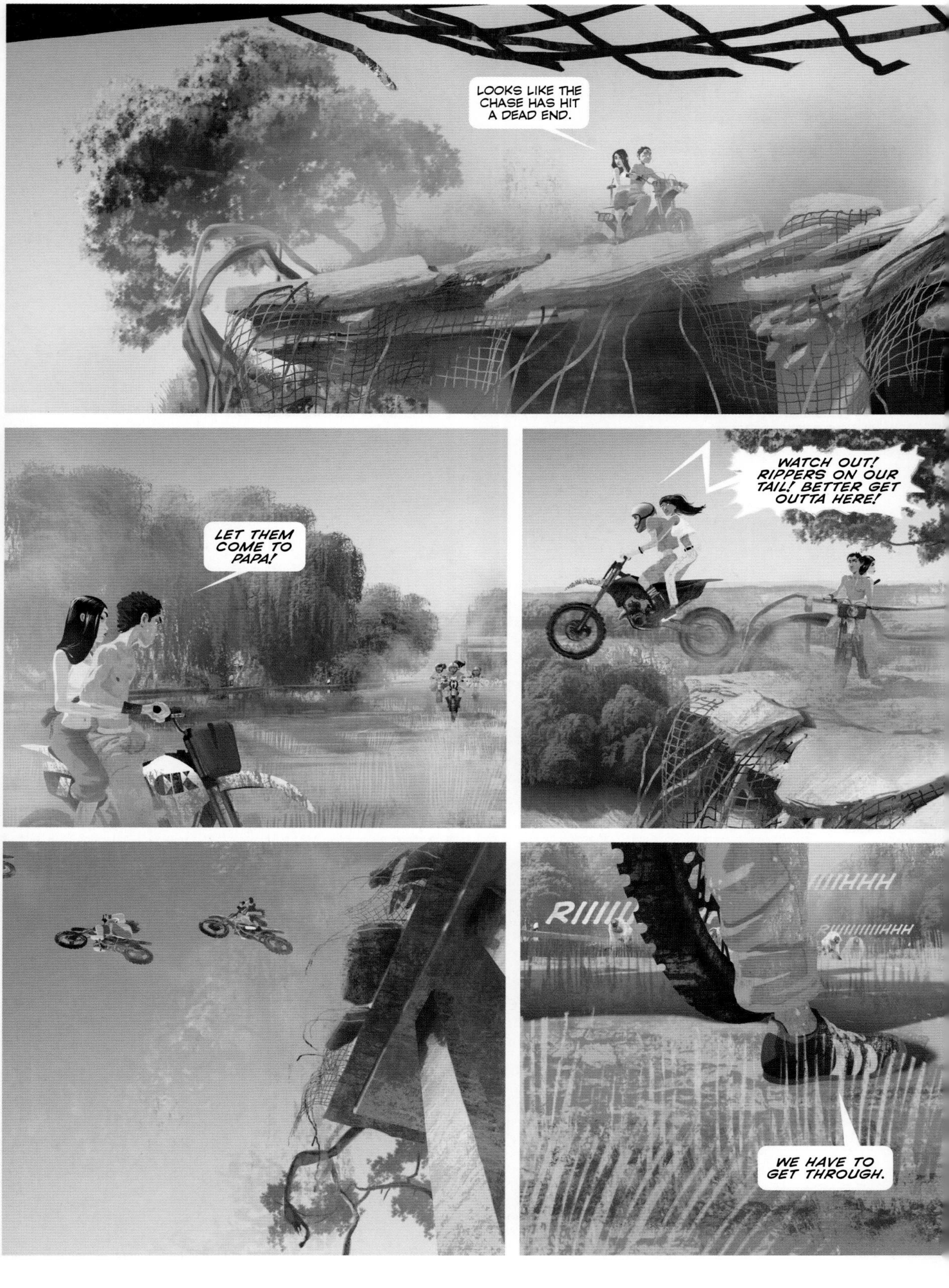
LOOKS LIKE THE CHASE HAS HIT A DEAD END.
LET THEM COME TO PAPA!
WATCH OUT! RIPPERS ON OUR TAIL! BETTER GET OUTTA HERE!
RIIIII
IIIIIHHH
RIIIIIIIIIHHH
WE HAVE TO GET THROUGH.

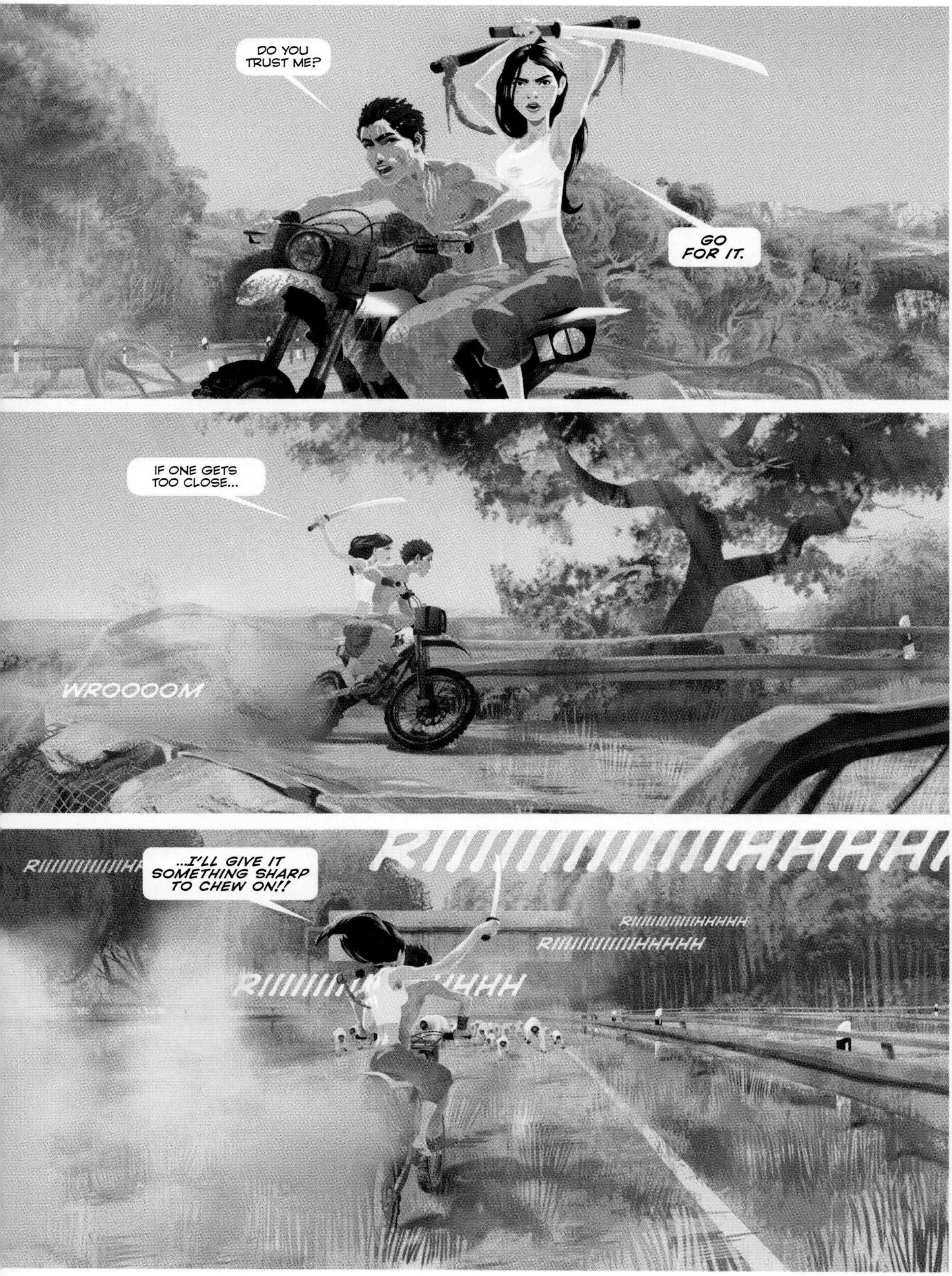
DO YOU TRUST ME?
GO FOR IT.
IF ONE GETS TOO CLOSE...
WROOOOM
RIIIIIIIIIIIIIH
...I'LL GIVE IT SOMETHING SHARP TO CHEW ON!!
RIIIIIIIIIIIIIAAAAAA
RIIIIIIIIIIIIHHHHH
RIIIIIIIIIIIIHHHHHH
RIIIIIII
HHHH

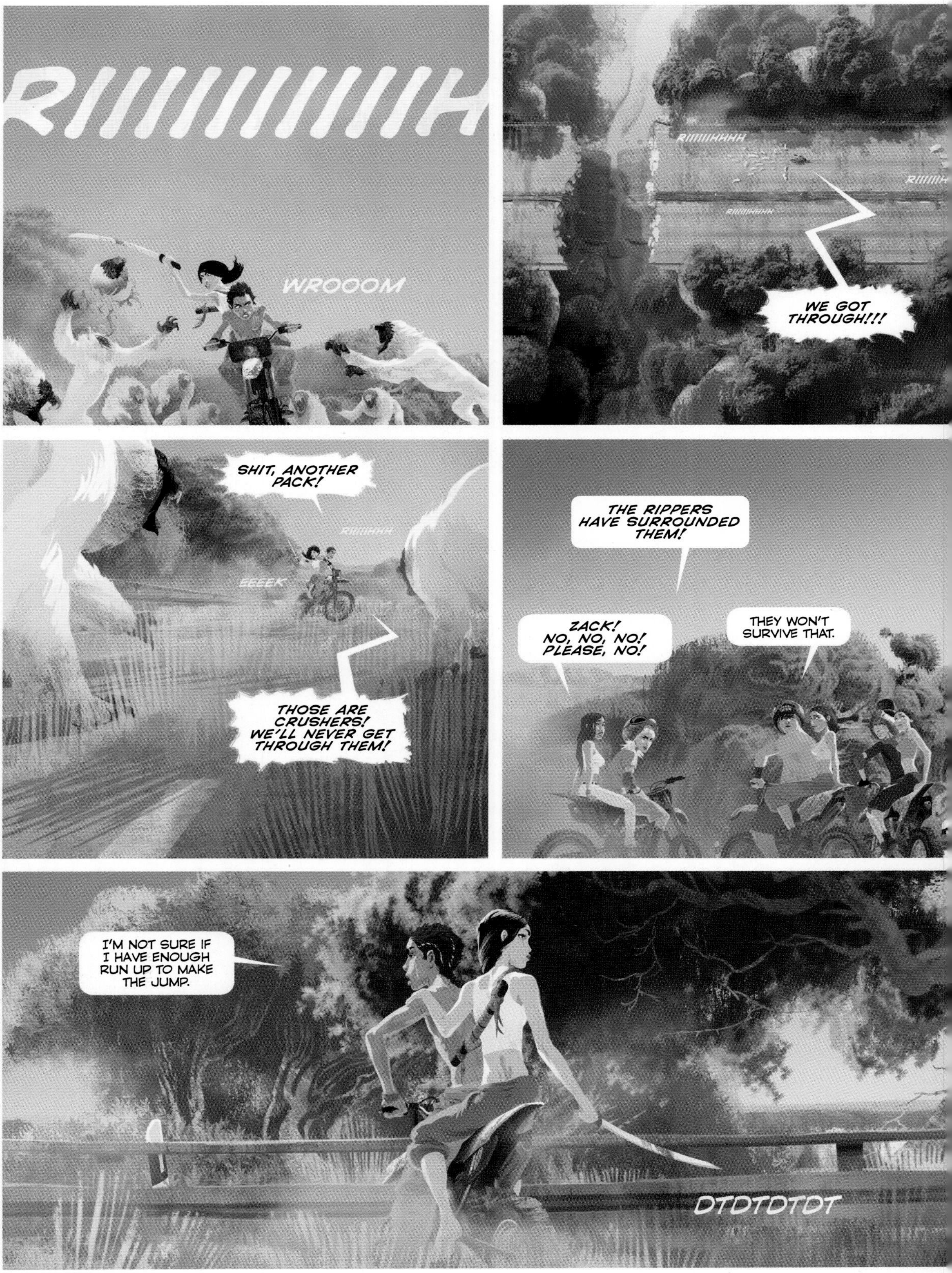
RIIIIIIIIIH
WROOOM
RIIIIIHHHH
RIIIIIH
RIIIIIHHHH
WE GOT THROUGH!!!
SHIT, ANOTHER PACK!
RIIIIIHHH
EEEEK
THOSE ARE CRUSHERS! WE'LL NEVER GET THROUGH THEM!
THE RIPPERS HAVE SURROUNDED THEM!
ZACK! NO, NO, NO! PLEASE, NO!
THEY WON'T SURVIVE THAT.
I'M NOT SURE IF I HAVE ENOUGH RUN UP TO MAKE THE JUMP.
DTDTDTDT

GIVE IT ALL YOU GOT, COWBOY. IF WE MAKE IT IN ONE PIECE THERE'S A KISS ON THE OTHER SIDE FOR YOU.

NOT ENOUGH.

TONGUES.

HANG ON TIGHT!

RIIIIIHHH

WRROOOOM

RIIIIIIHH

RIIIIIHHH

RIIIIHHHH

RIIIIIHHH

159

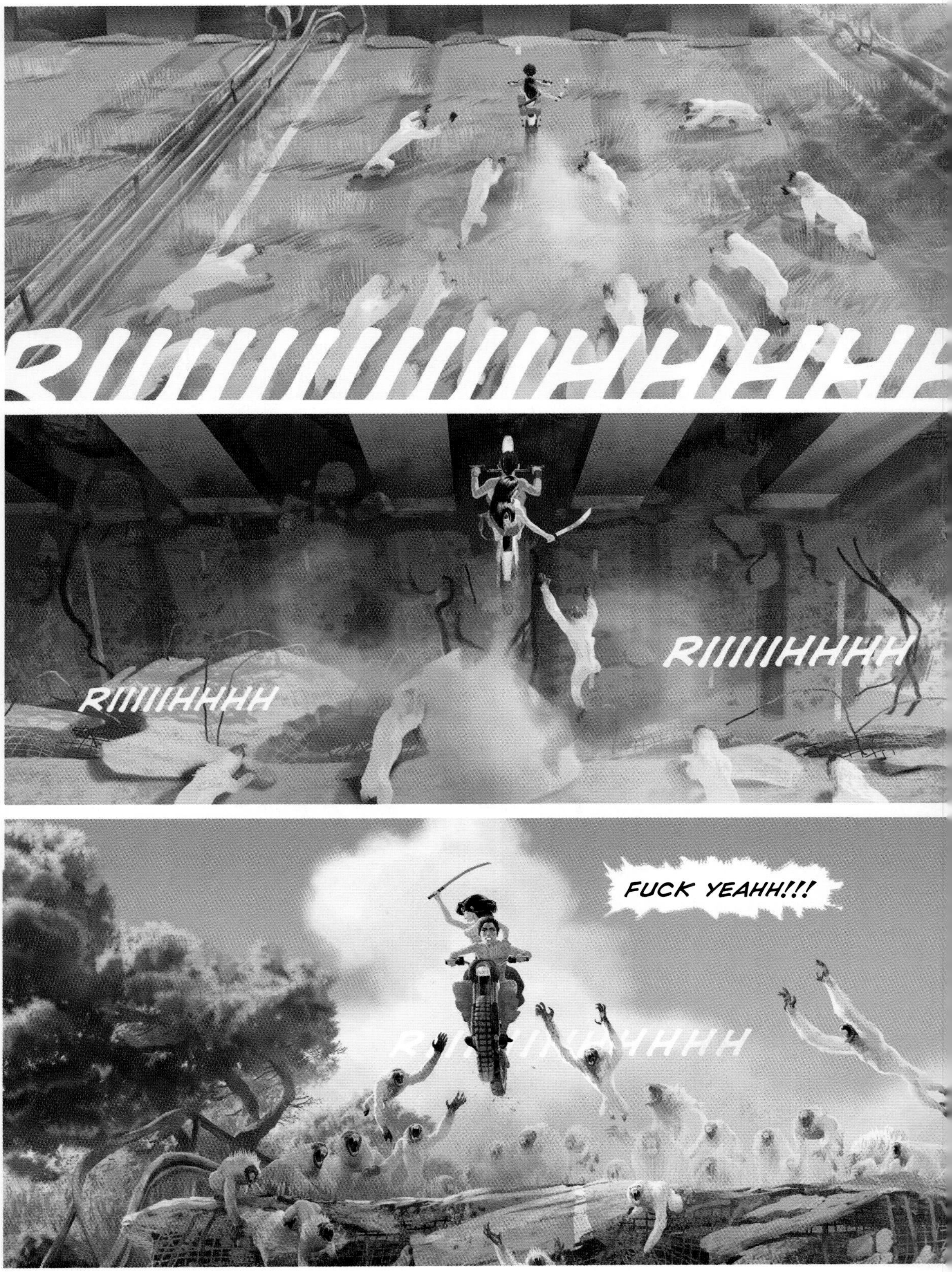
RIIIIIIIIIHHHHH
RIIIIHHHH
RIIIIIHHHH
FUCK YEAHH!!!

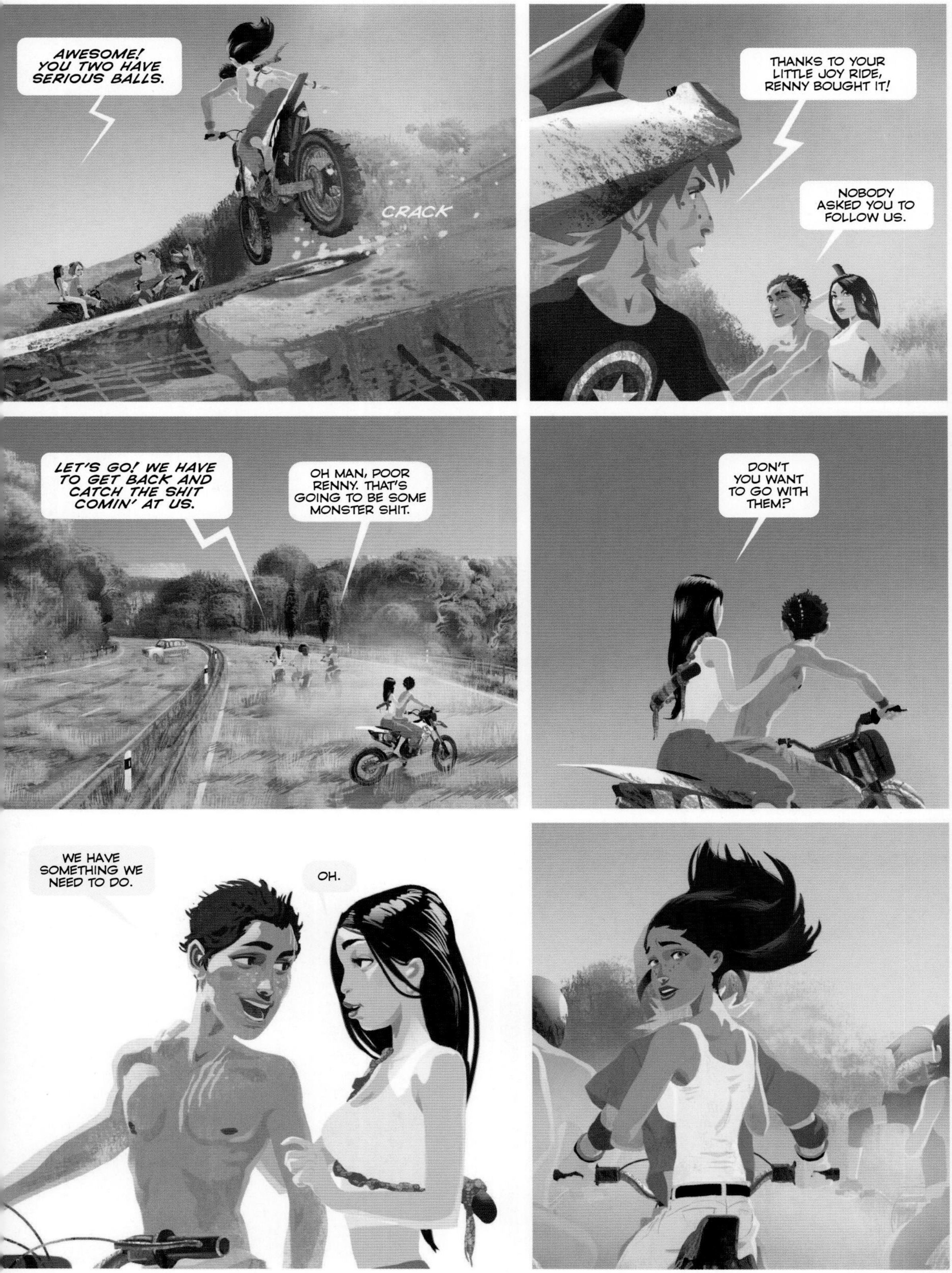
AWESOME! YOU TWO HAVE SERIOUS BALLS.
CRACK
THANKS TO YOUR LITTLE JOY RIDE, RENNY BOUGHT IT!
NOBODY ASKED YOU TO FOLLOW US.
LET'S GO! WE HAVE TO GET BACK AND CATCH THE SHIT COMIN' AT US.
OH MAN, POOR RENNY. THAT'S GOING TO BE SOME MONSTER SHIT.
DON'T YOU WANT TO GO WITH THEM?
WE HAVE SOMETHING WE NEED TO DO.
OH.

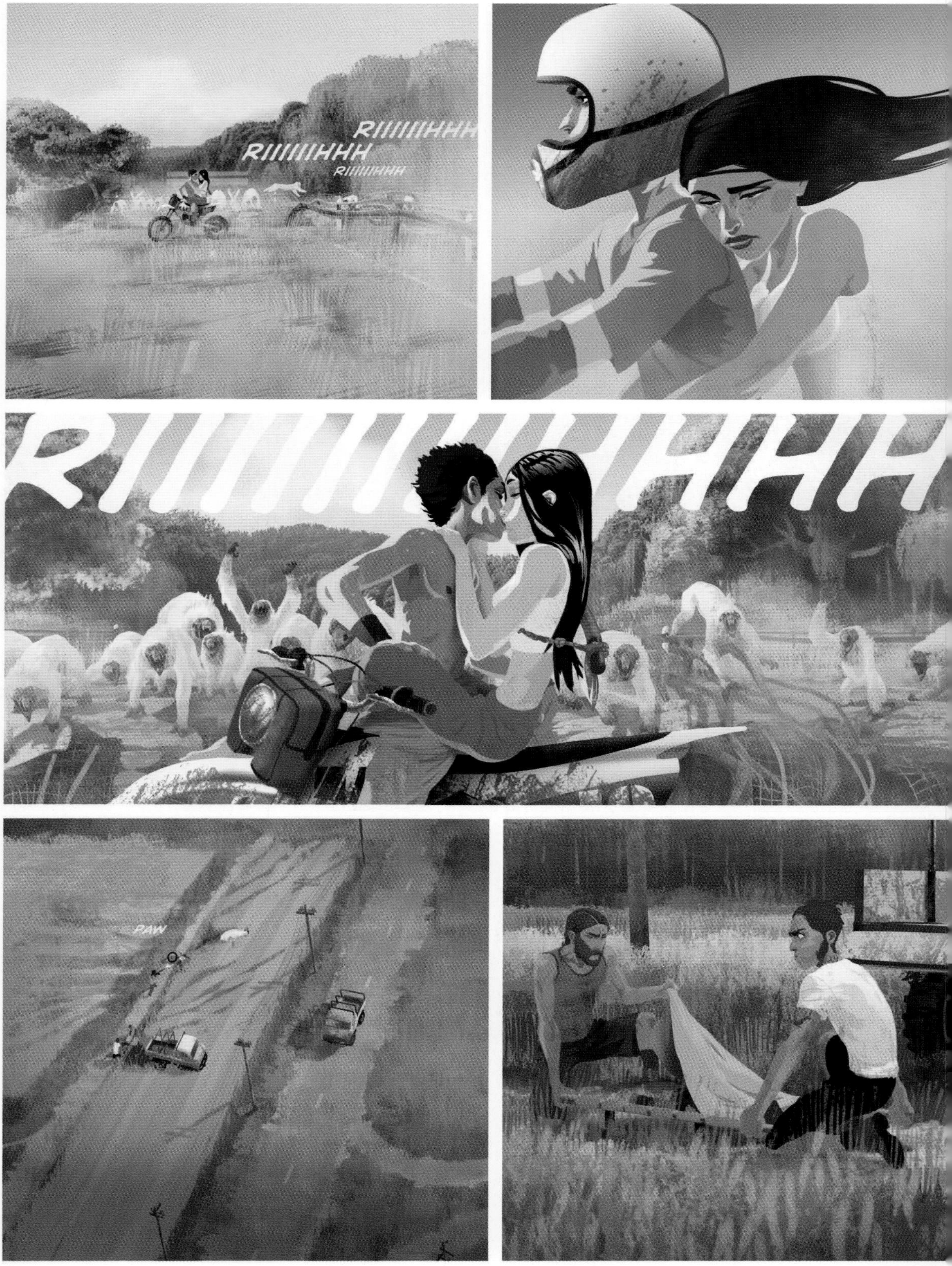
RIIIIIIHHH
RIIIIIIHHH
RIIIIIIHHH
RIIIIIIHHHH
PAW

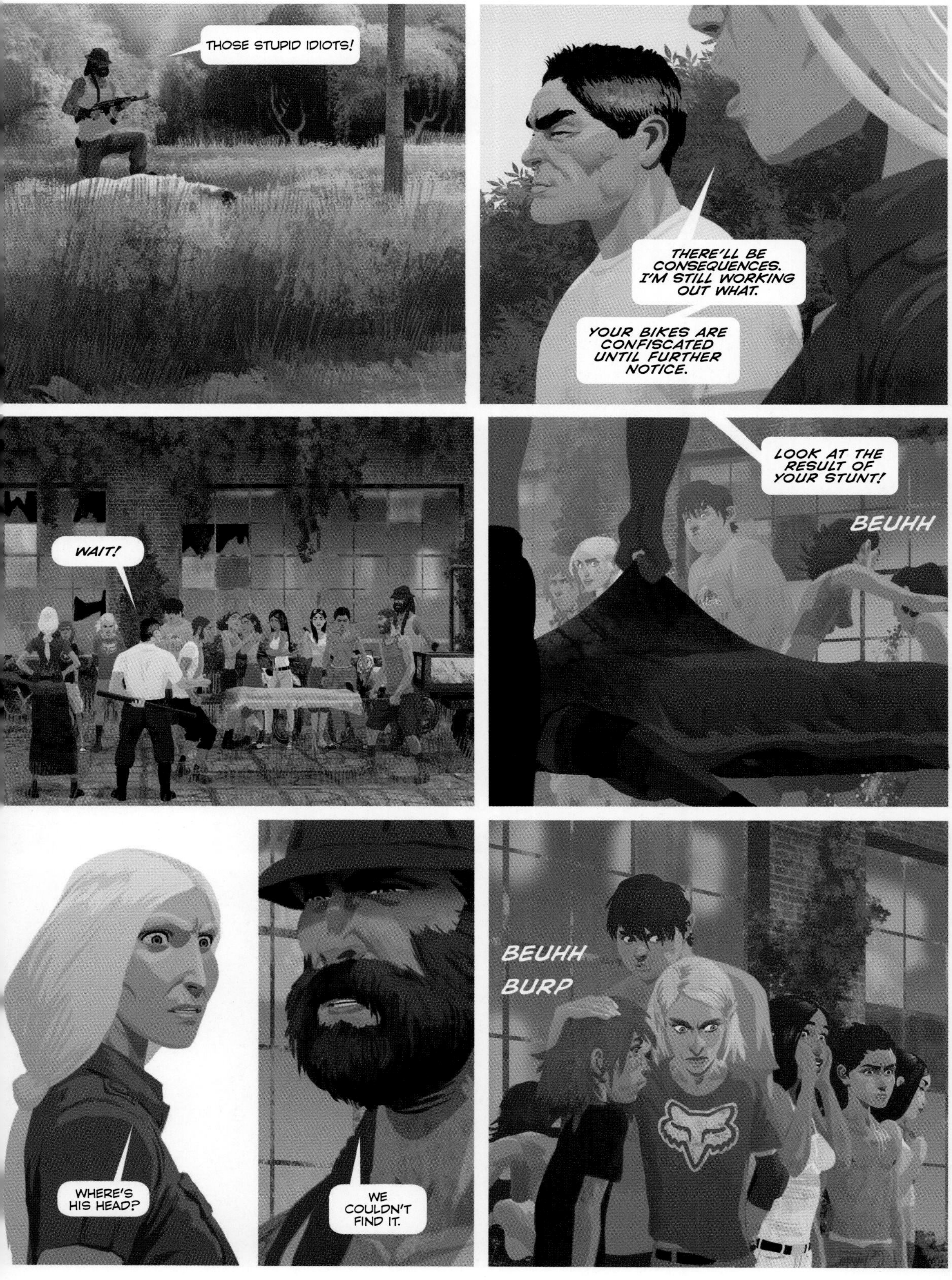
THOSE STUPID IDIOTS!
THERE'LL BE CONSEQUENCES. I'M STILL WORKING OUT WHAT.
YOUR BIKES ARE CONFISCATED UNTIL FURTHER NOTICE.
WAIT!
LOOK AT THE RESULT OF YOUR STUNT!
BEUHH
WHERE'S HIS HEAD?
WE COULDN'T FIND IT.
BEUHH
BURP

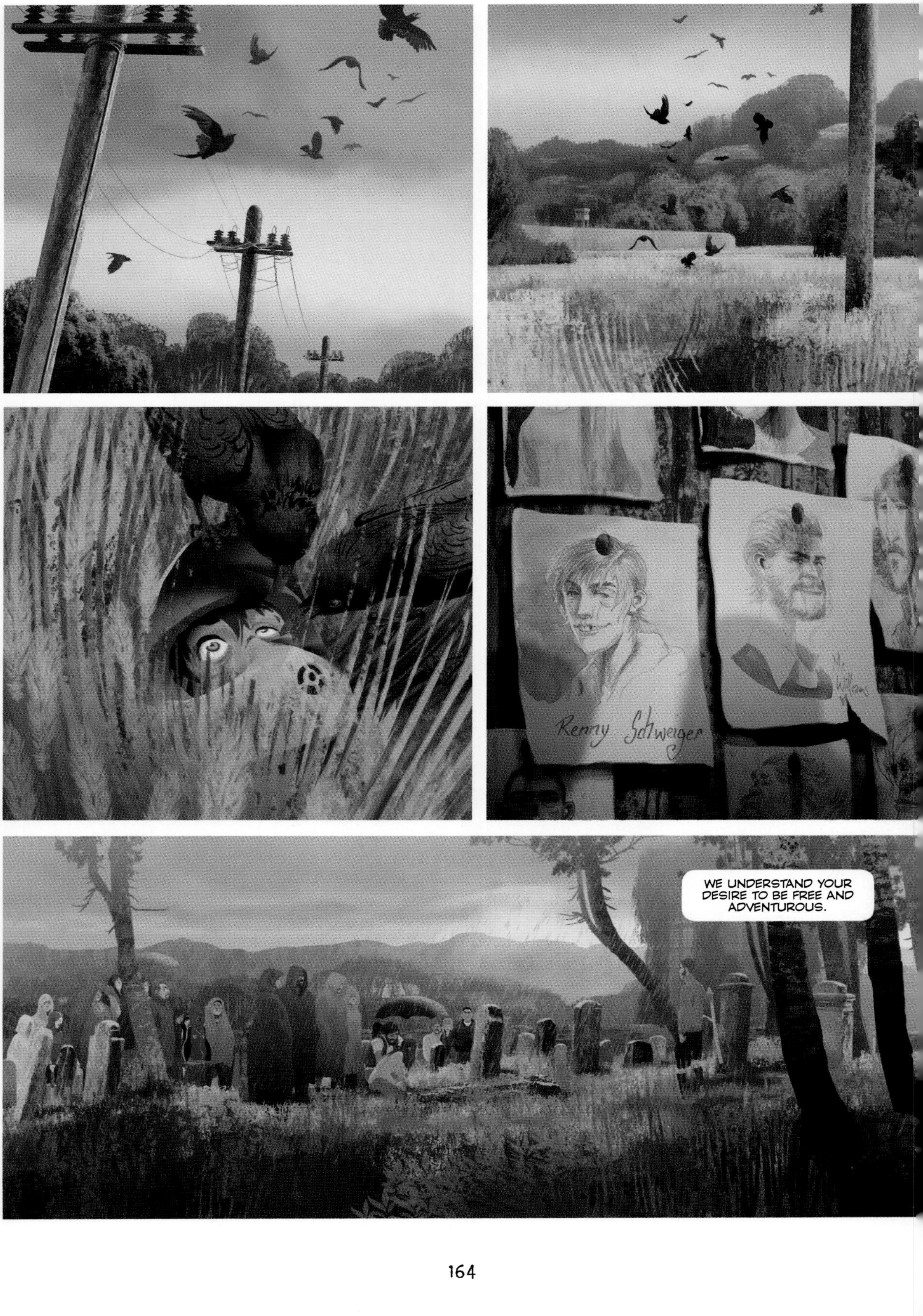
Renny Schweiger
Mr. Williams
WE UNDERSTAND YOUR DESIRE TO BE FREE AND ADVENTUROUS.

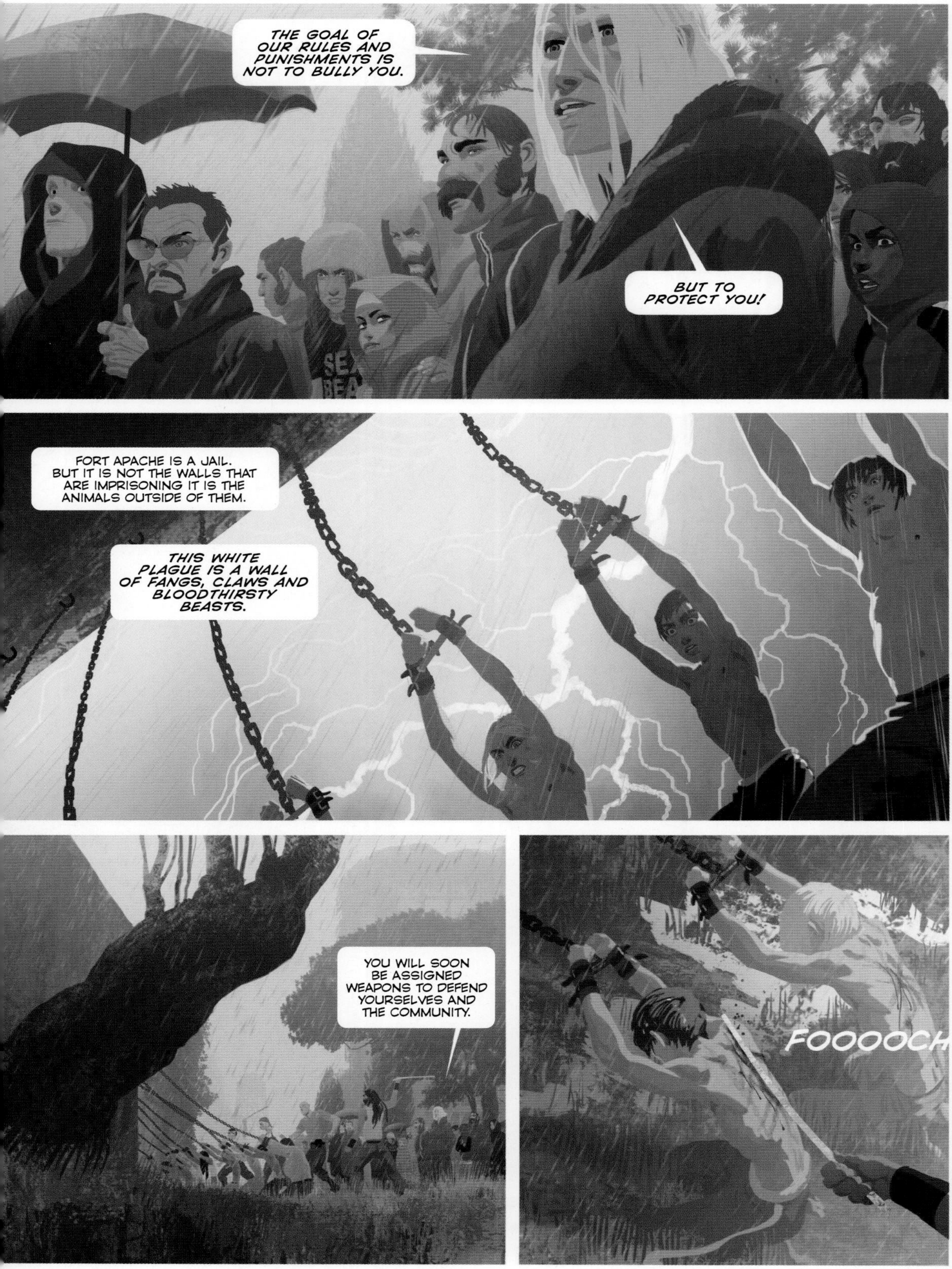
THE GOAL OF OUR RULES AND PUNISHMENTS IS NOT TO BULLY YOU.
BUT TO PROTECT YOU!
FORT APACHE IS A JAIL. BUT IT IS NOT THE WALLS THAT ARE IMPRISONING IT IS THE ANIMALS OUTSIDE OF THEM.
THIS WHITE PLAGUE IS A WALL OF FANGS, CLAWS AND BLOODTHIRSTY BEASTS.
YOU WILL SOON BE ASSIGNED WEAPONS TO DEFEND YOURSELVES AND THE COMMUNITY.
FOOOOCH

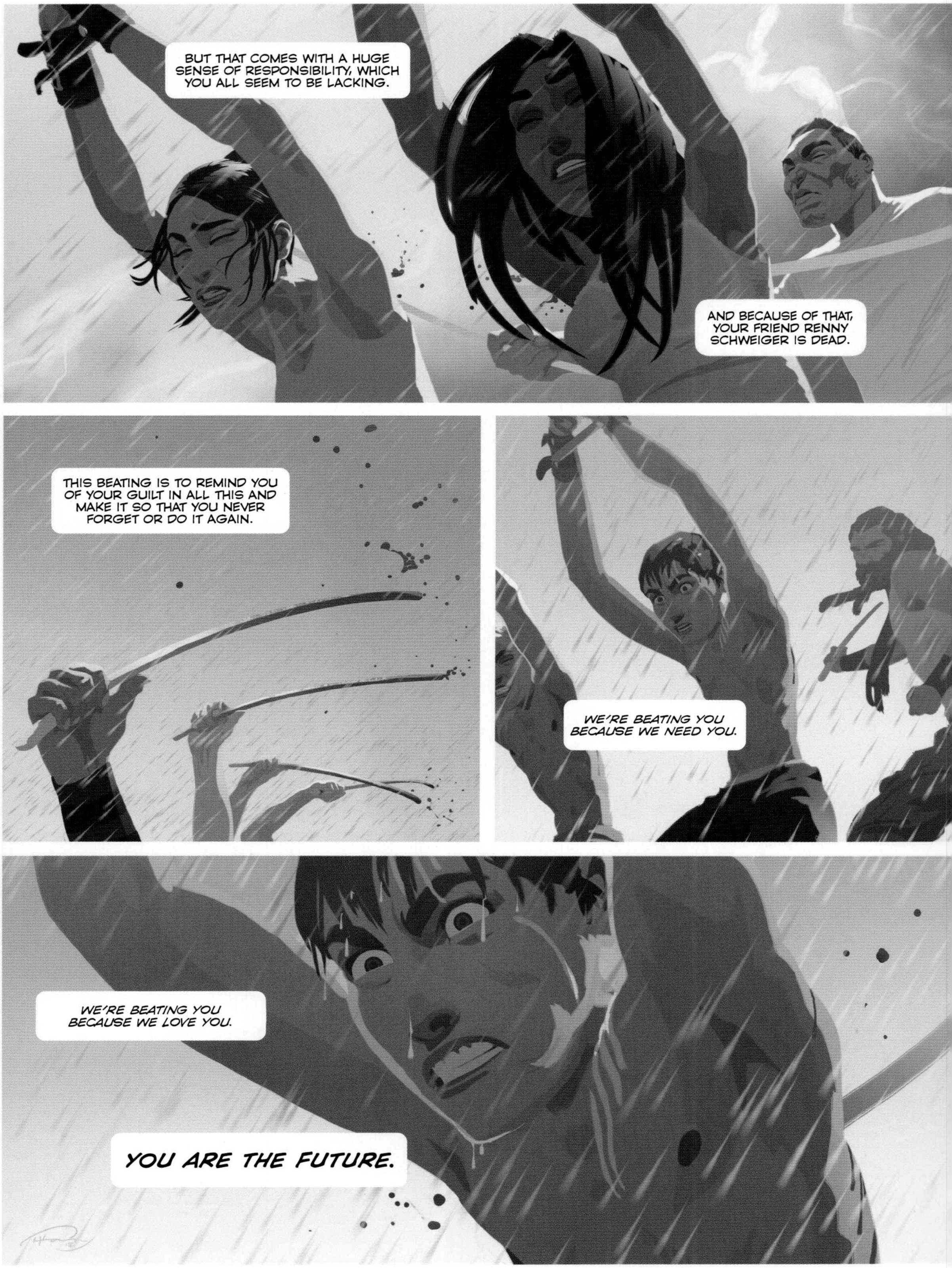
BUT THAT COMES WITH A HUGE SENSE OF RESPONSIBILITY, WHICH YOU ALL SEEM TO BE LACKING.
AND BECAUSE OF THAT, YOUR FRIEND RENNY SCHWEIGER IS DEAD.
THIS BEATING IS TO REMIND YOU OF YOUR GUILT IN ALL THIS AND MAKE IT SO THAT YOU NEVER FORGET OR DO IT AGAIN.
WE'RE BEATING YOU BECAUSE WE NEED YOU.
WE'RE BEATING YOU BECAUSE WE LOVE YOU.
YOU ARE THE FUTURE.

END OF VOLUME 1

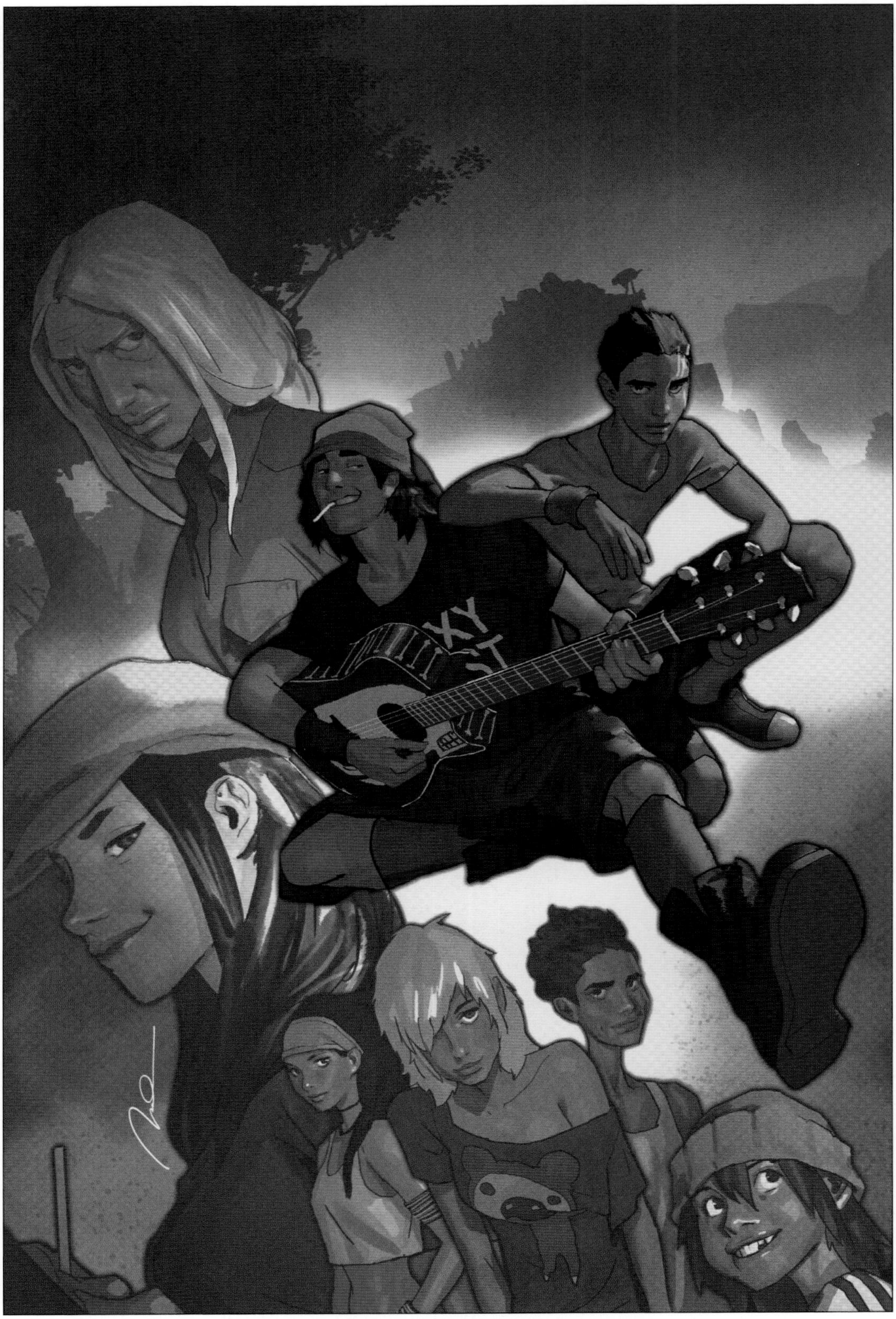

ISSUE 1 MAIN COVER
BY GERALD PAREL

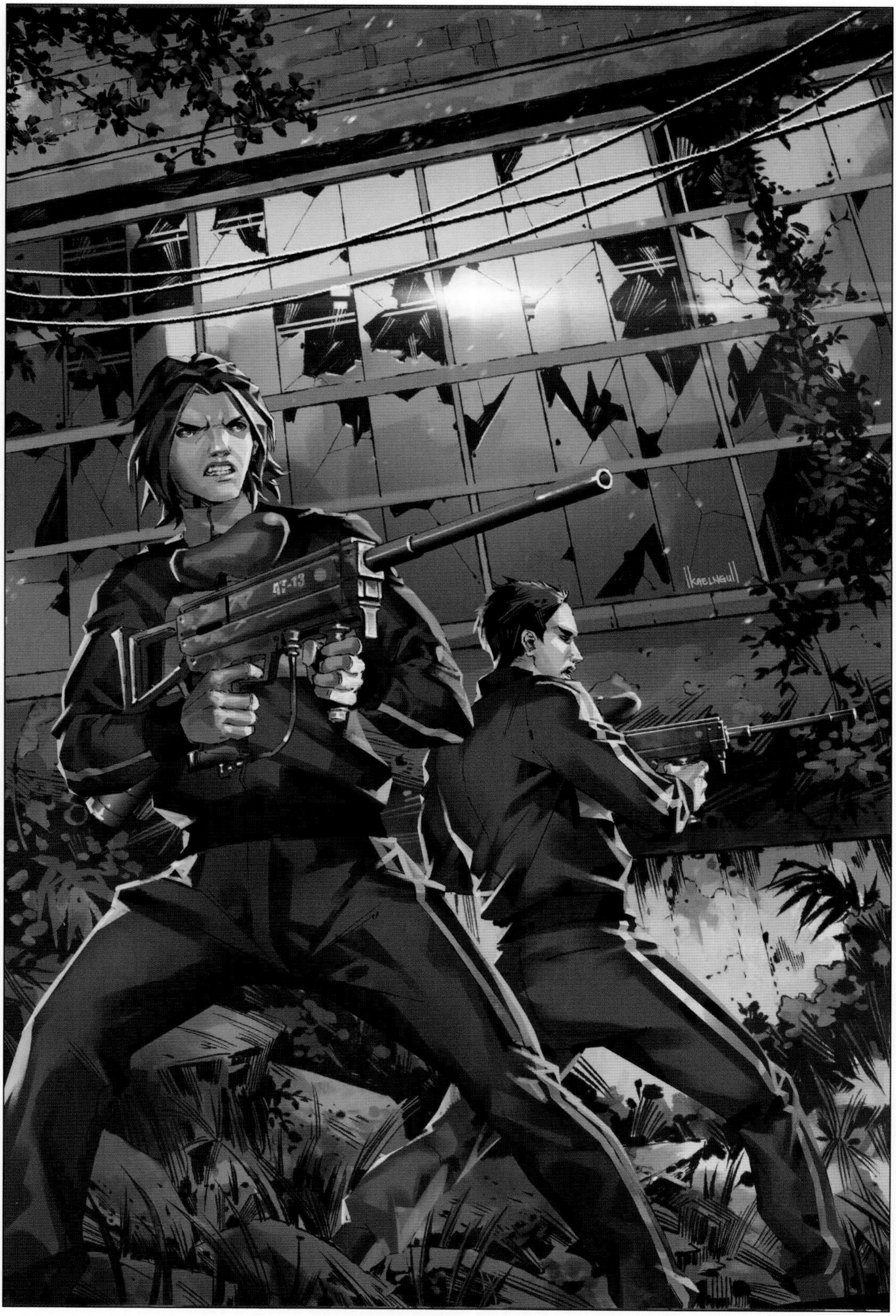
AT-13
KAELNGU

ISSUE 2 MAIN COVER
BY KAEL NGU

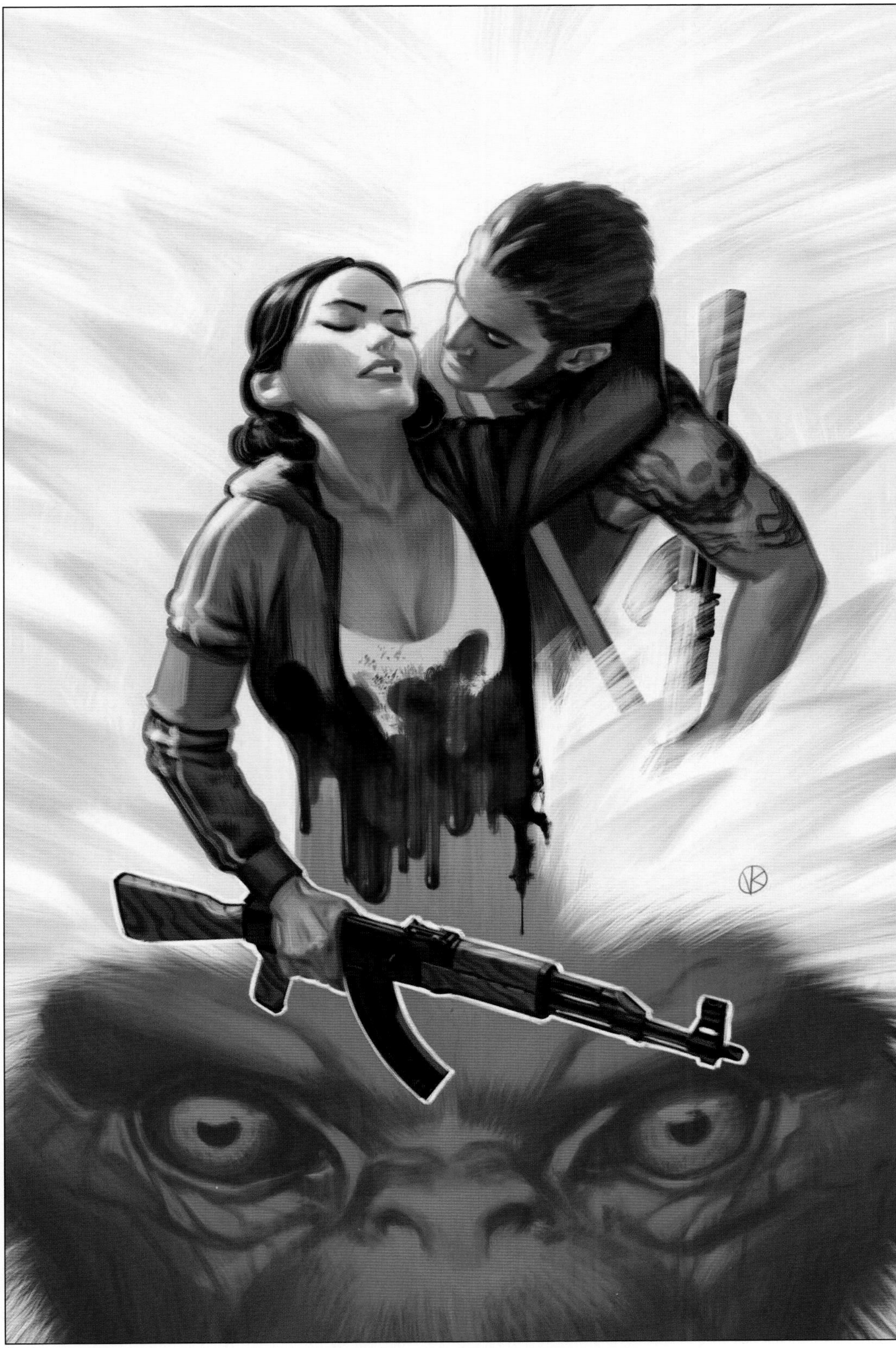
VK

ISSUE 3 MAIN COVER
BY VIKTOR KALVACHEV

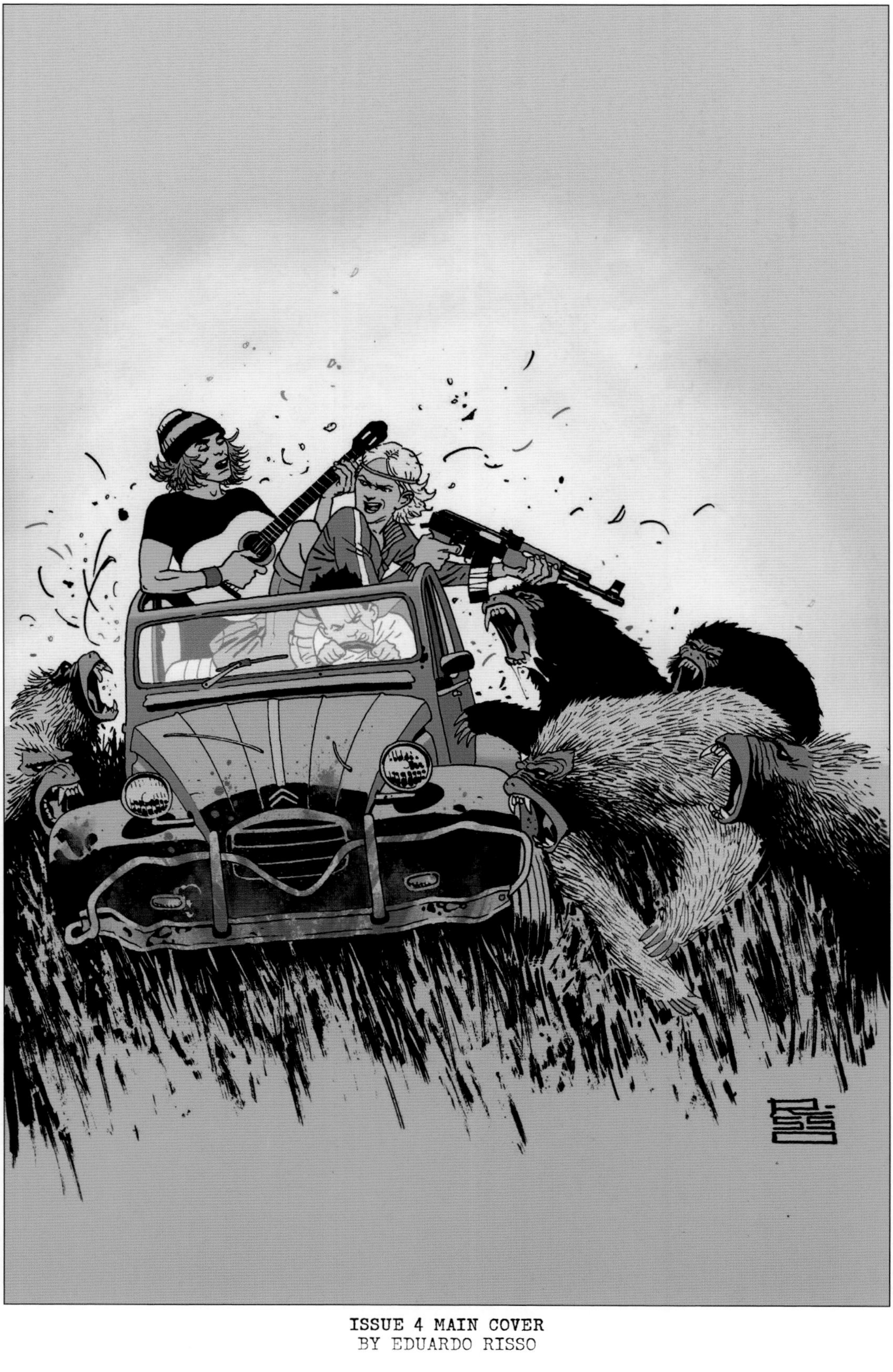

ISSUE 4 MAIN COVER
BY EDUARDO RISSO

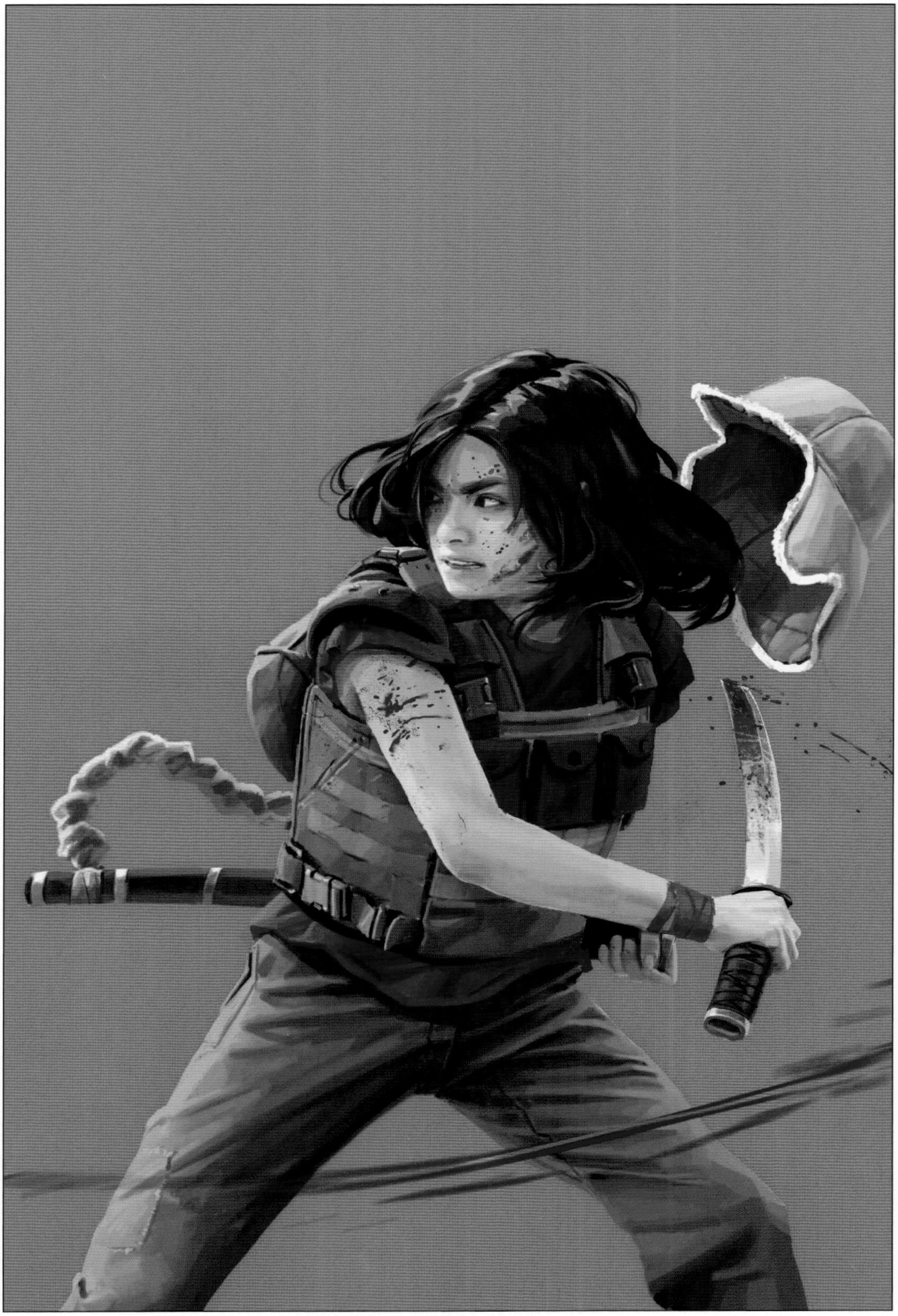

ISSUE 5 MAIN COVER
BY DANIEL CLARKE

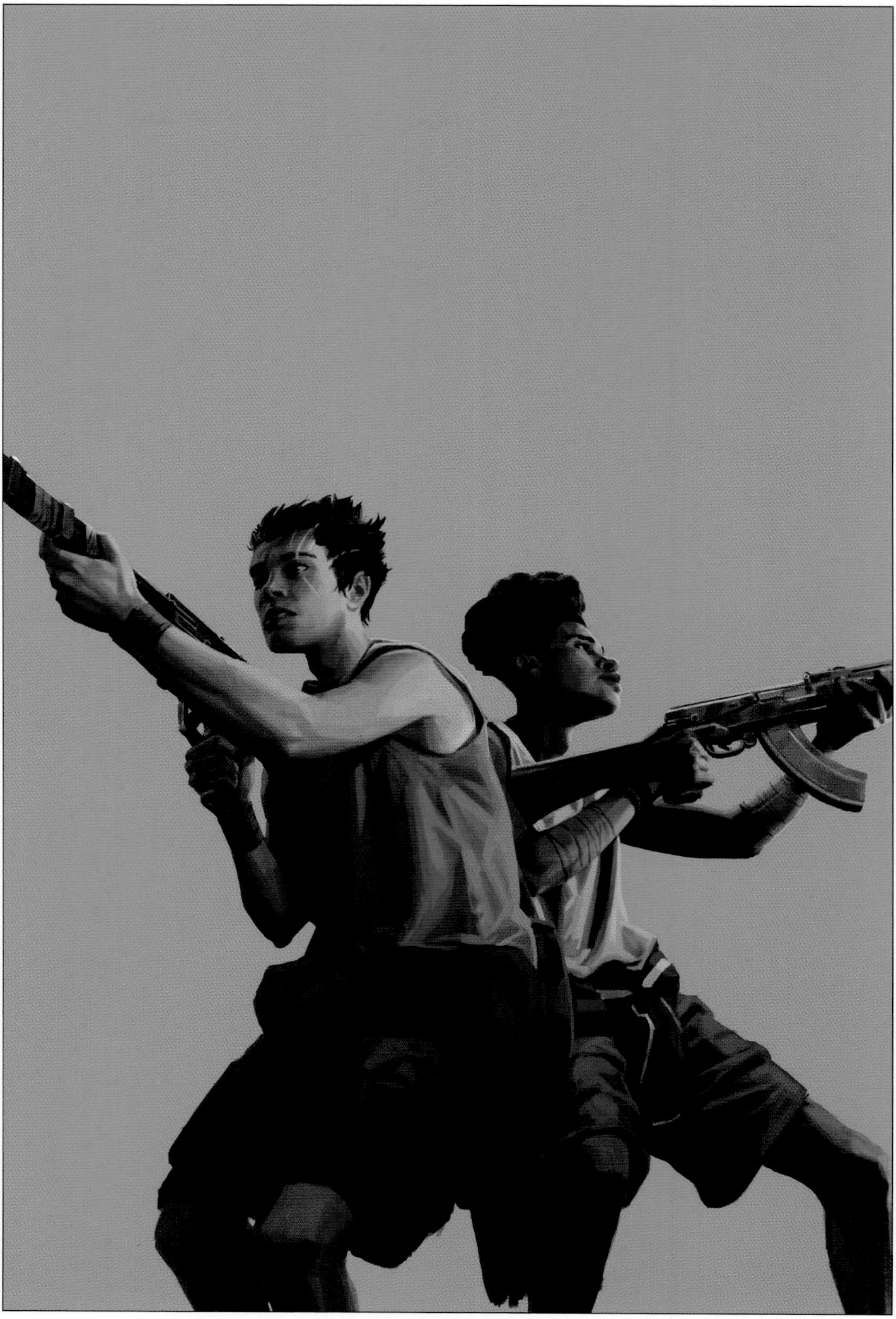

ISSUE 6 MAIN COVER
BY DANIEL CLARKE

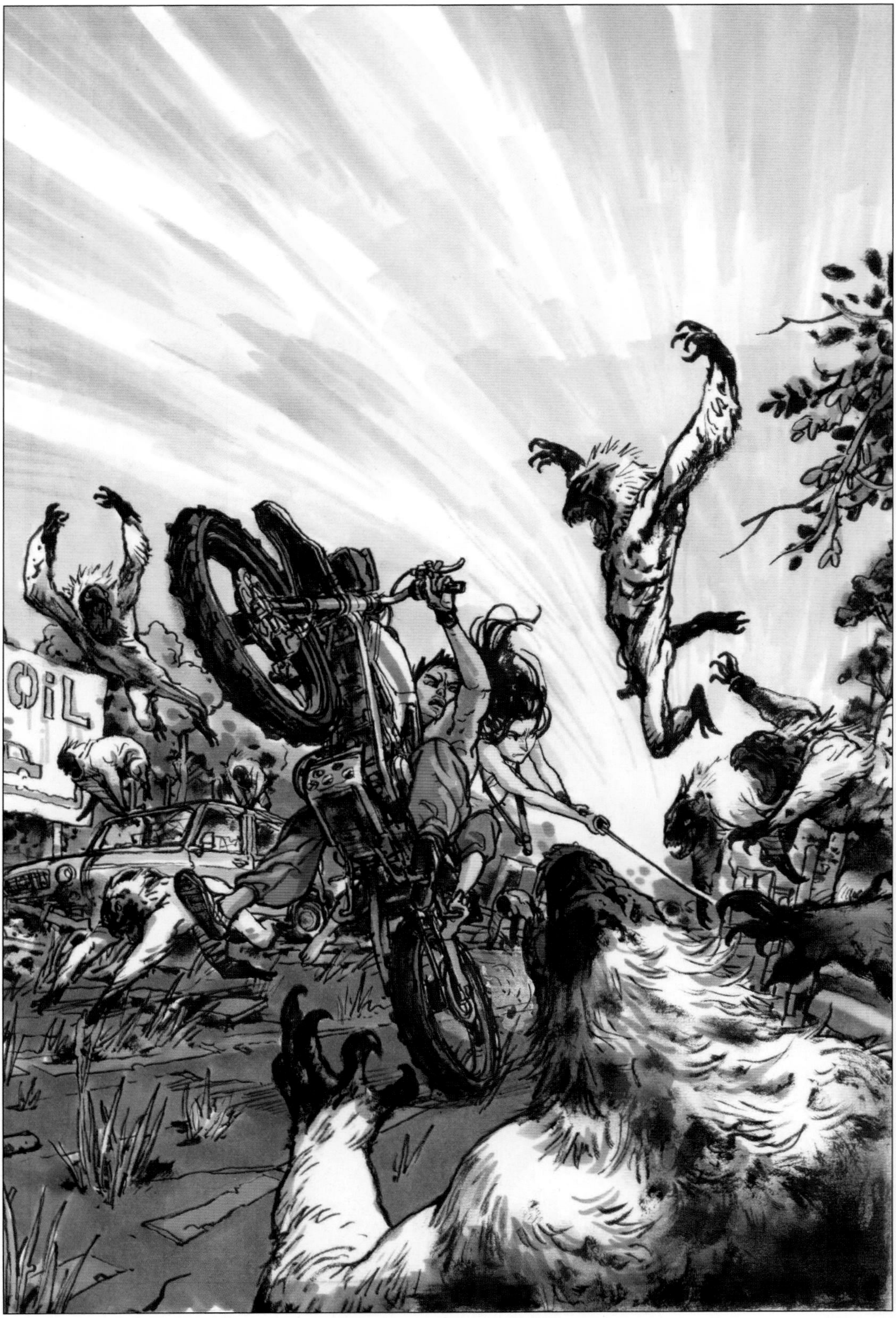
OIL

ISSUE 7 MAIN COVER
BY KIM JUNG GI

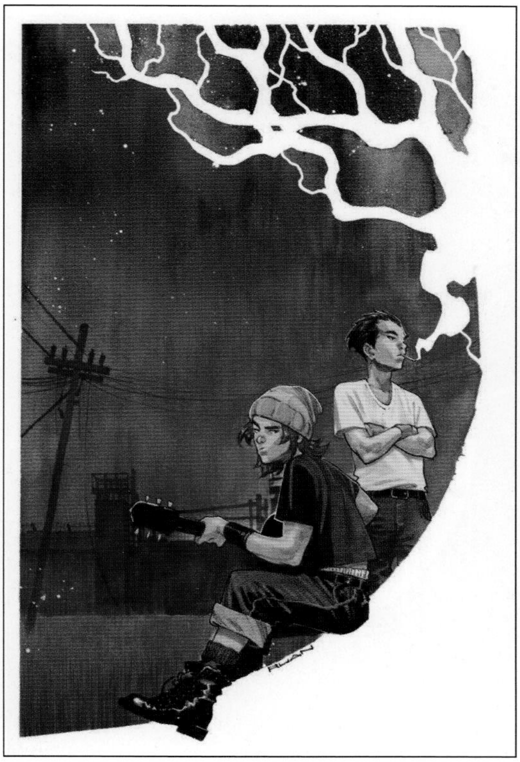

ISSUE 1 VARIANT
BY DIKE RUAN

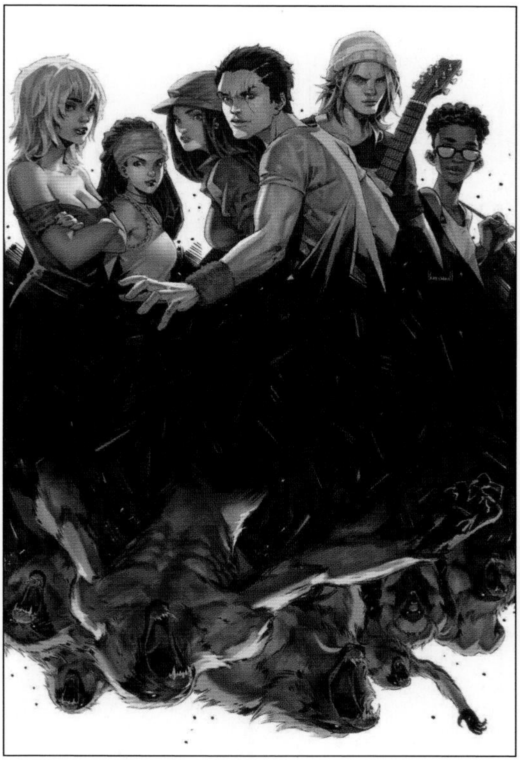

ISSUE 1 WALKING DEAD PARODY VARIANT
BY KAEL NGU

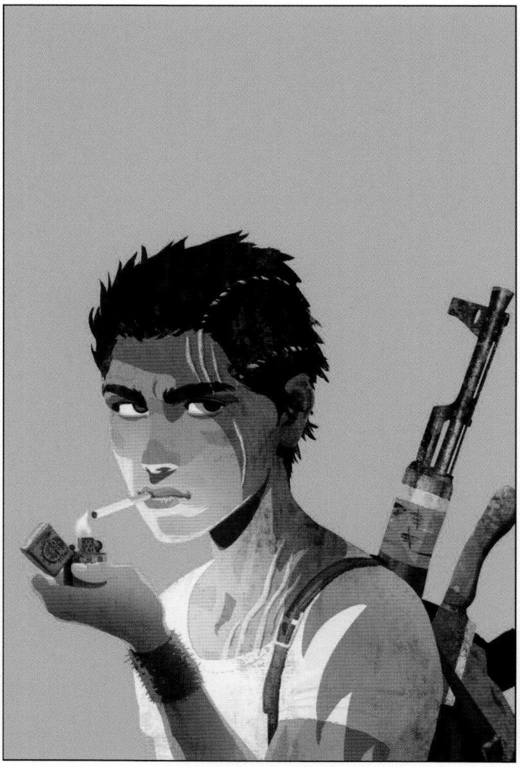

ISSUE 1 VARIANT
THOMAS VON KUMMANT

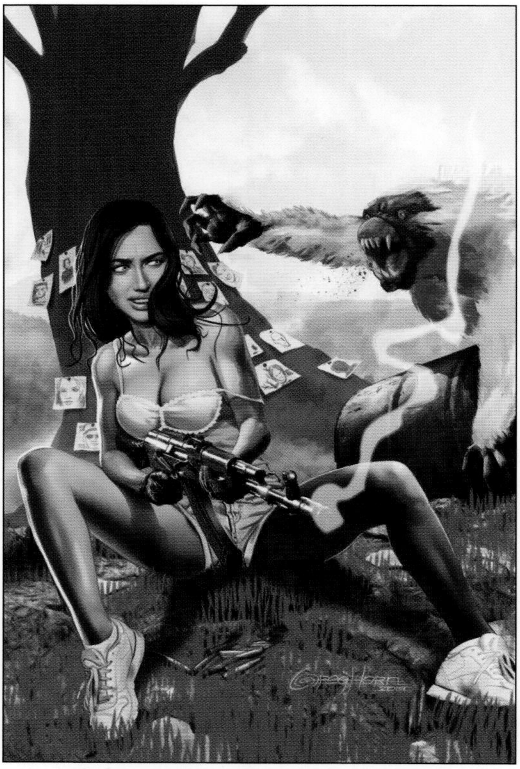

ISSUE 1 COMIC KINGDOM OF CANADA
EXCLUSIVE VARIANT
BY GREG HORN

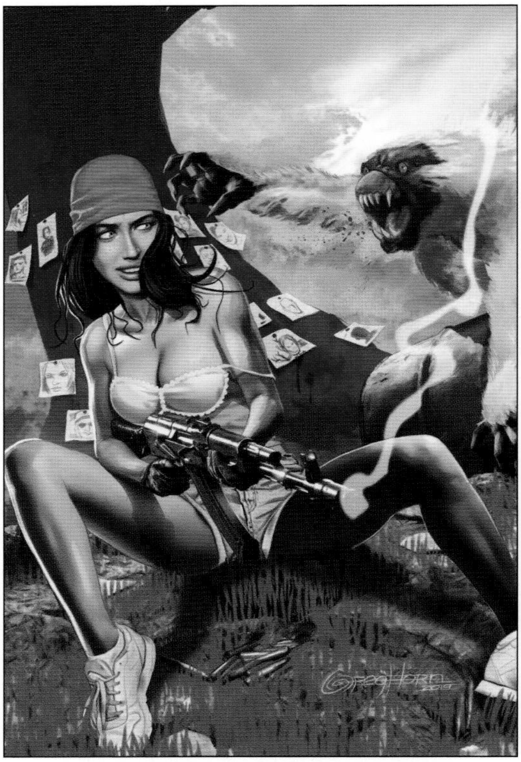

ISSUE 1 COMIC KINGDOM OF CANADA
EXCLUSIVE VARIANT
BY GREG HORN

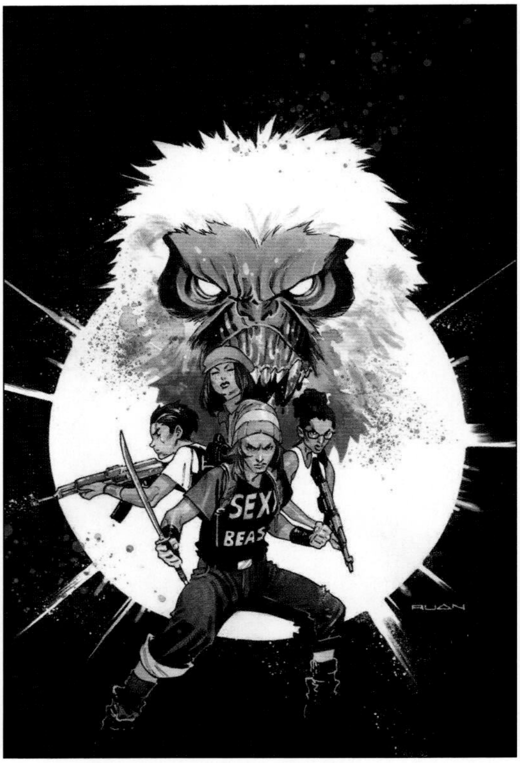
RUAN

ISSUE 2 STAR WARS #1 PARODY VARIANT
BY DIKE RUAN

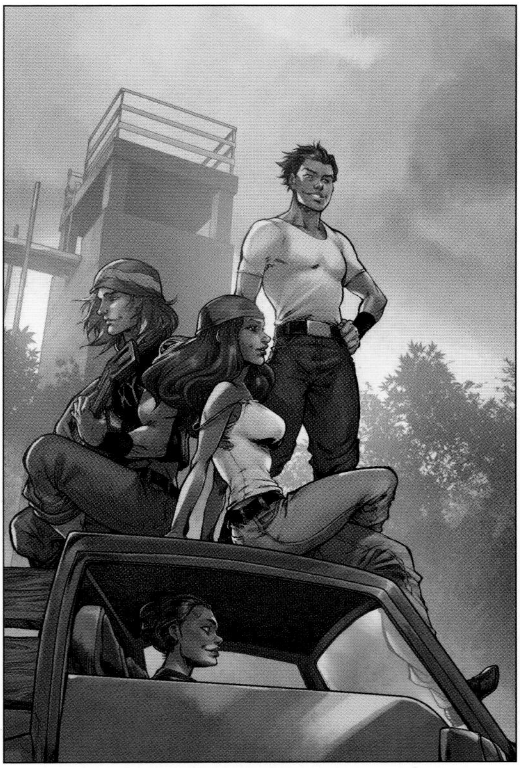

ISSUE 2 VARIANT
BY MATEO GUERRERO

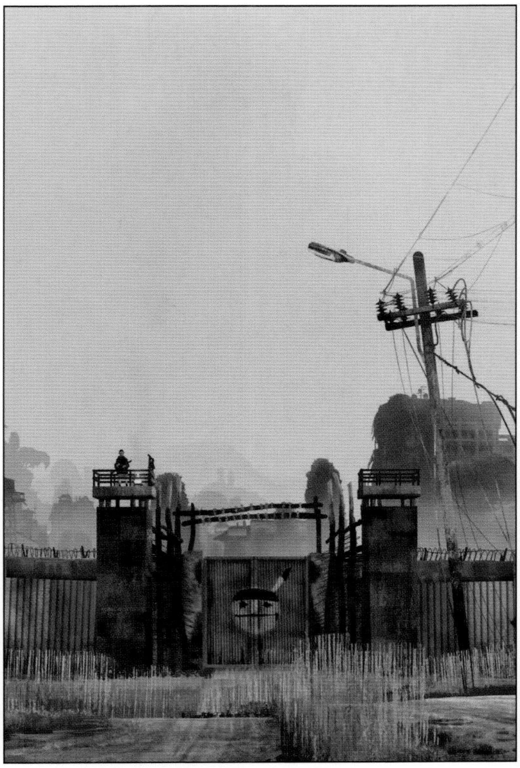

ISSUE 2 VARIANT
BY THOMAS VON KUMMANT

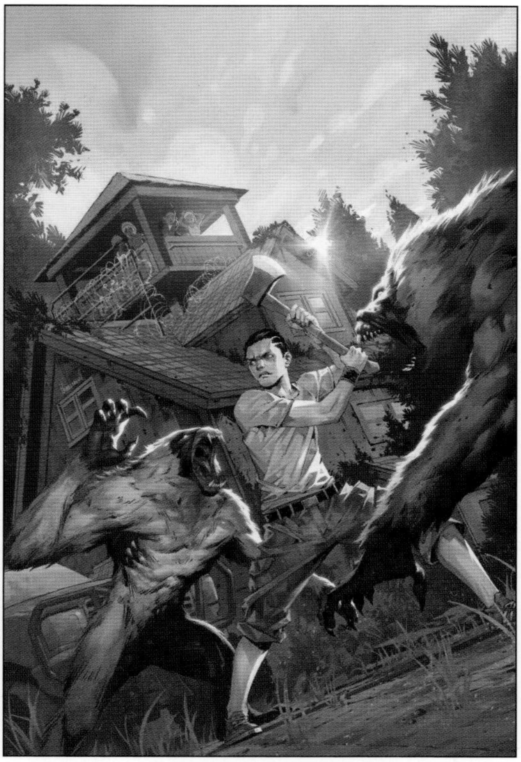

ISSUE 3 VARIANT
BY KAEL NGU

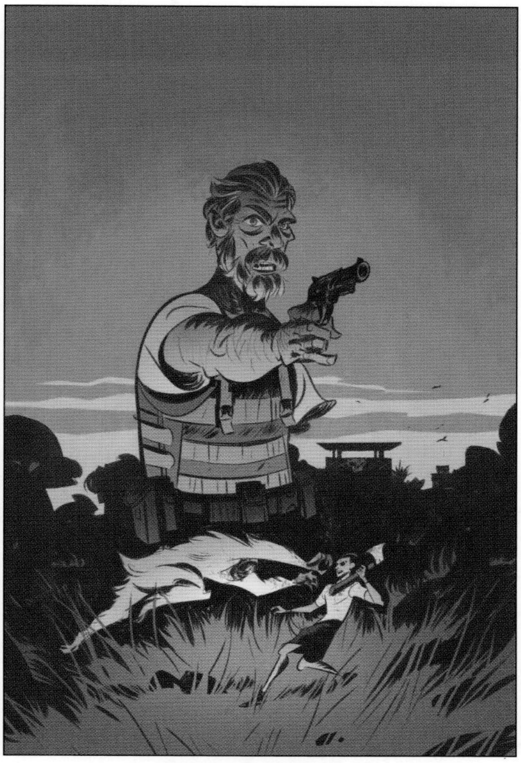

ISSUE 3 VARIANT
BY PETER NGUYEN

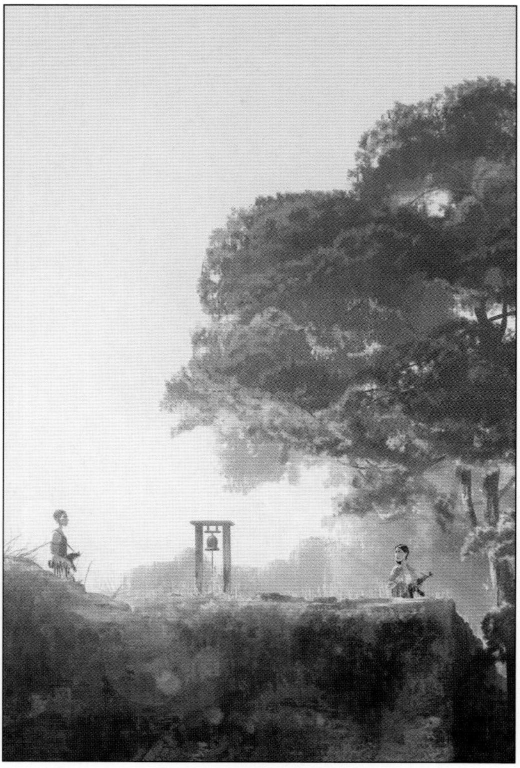

ISSUE 3 VARIANT
BY THOMAS VON KUMMANT

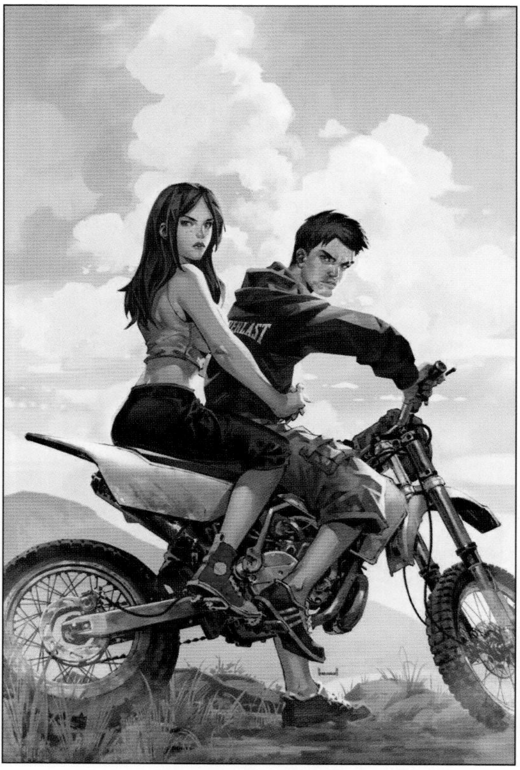

ISSUE 4 VARIANT
BY KAEL NGU

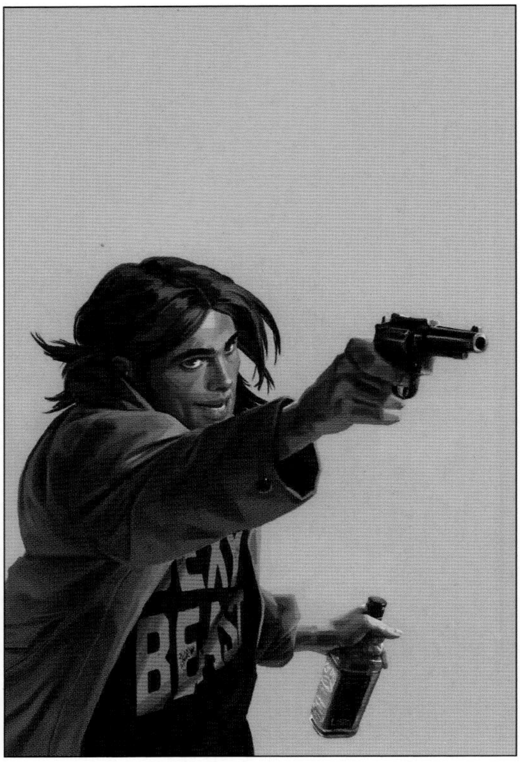

ISSUE 4 VARIANT
BY DANIEL CLARKE

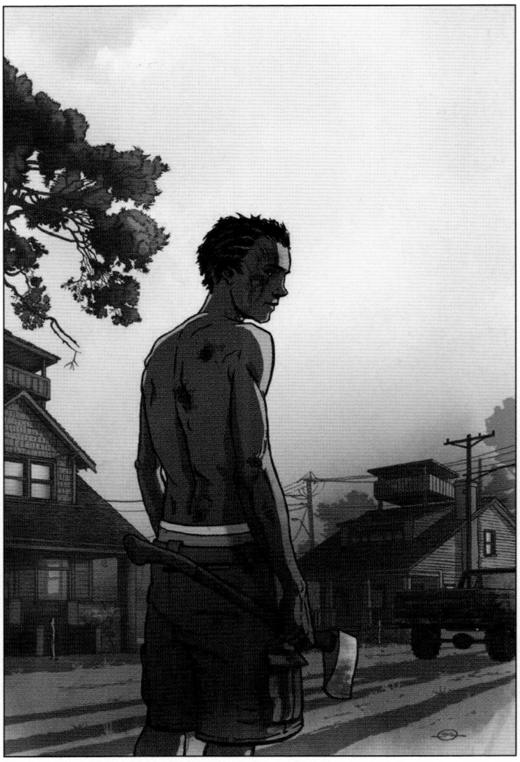

ISSUE 4 VARIANT
BY BENJAMIN VON ECKARTSBERG

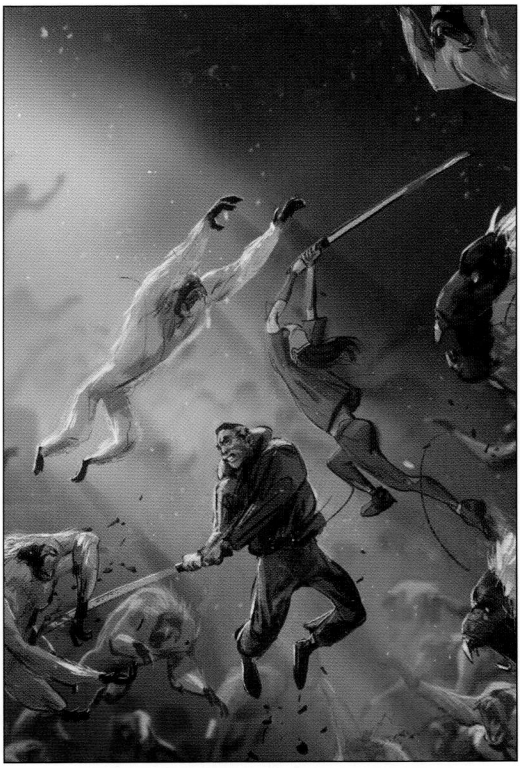

ISSUE 5 VARIANT
BY ELIZA IVANOVA

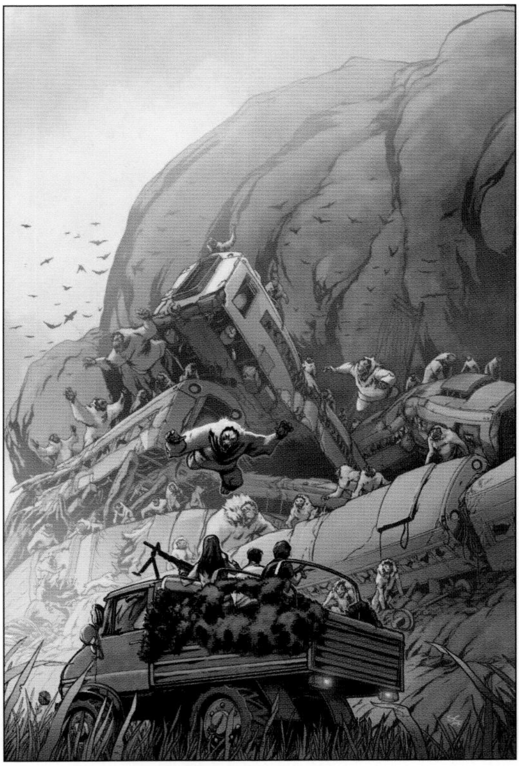

ISSUE 5 VARIANT
BY STEVEN CUMMINGS

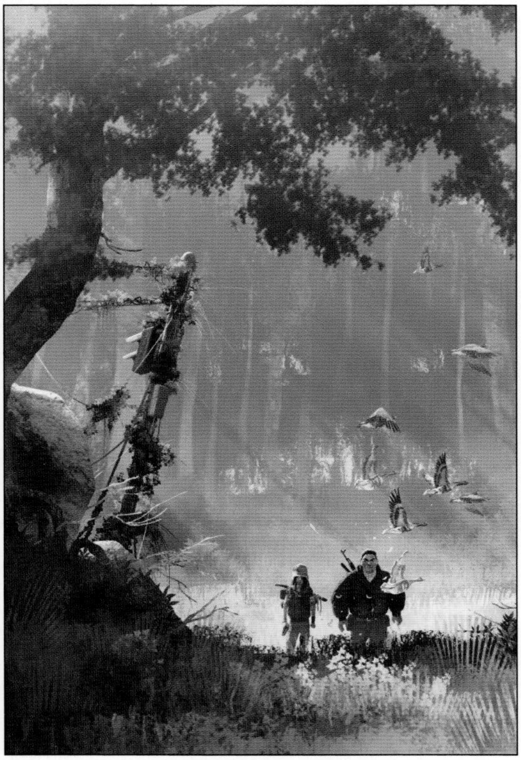

ISSUE 5 VARIANT
BY THOMAS VON KUMMANT

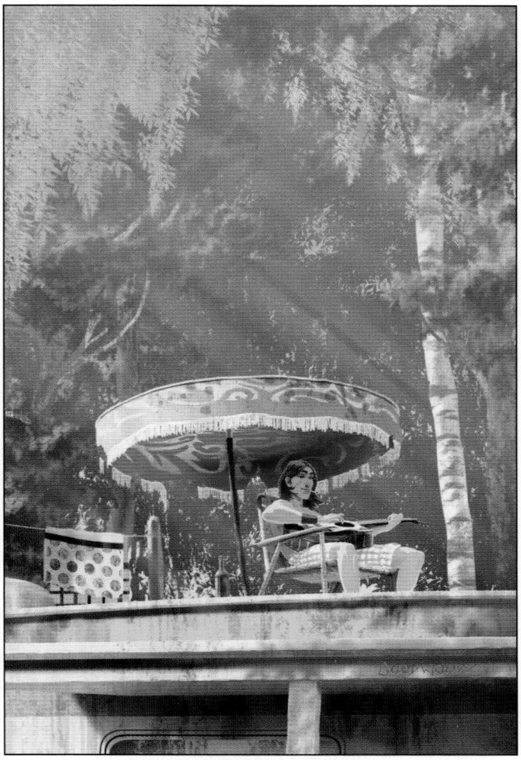

ISSUE 6 ARCHER FAKE CIGARETTE AD VARIANT
BY THOMAS VON KUMMANT

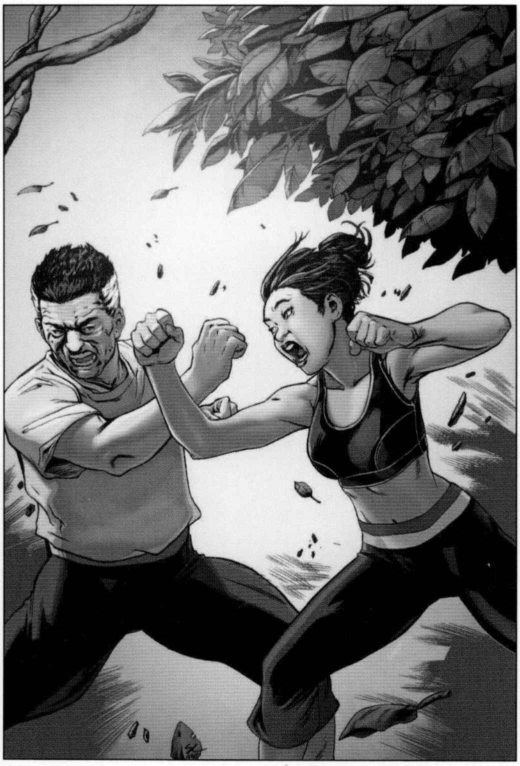

ISSUE 6 VARIANT
BY STEVEN CUMMINGS

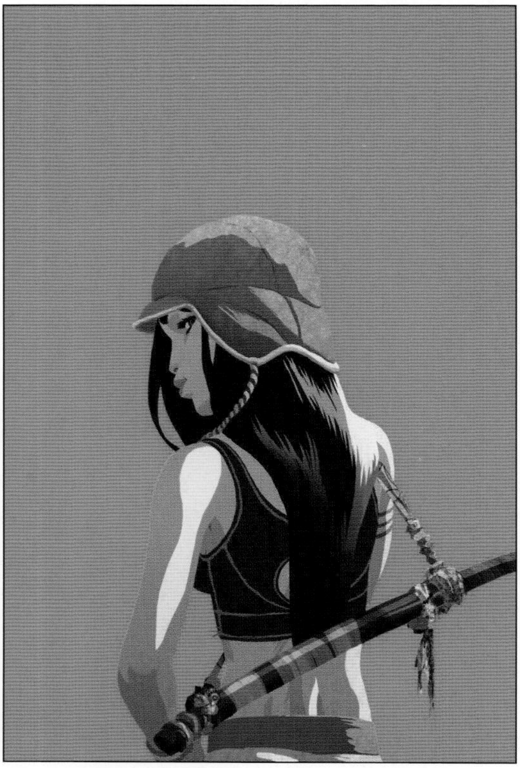

ISSUE 6 YUKI PINK VARIANT
BY THOMAS VON KUMMANT

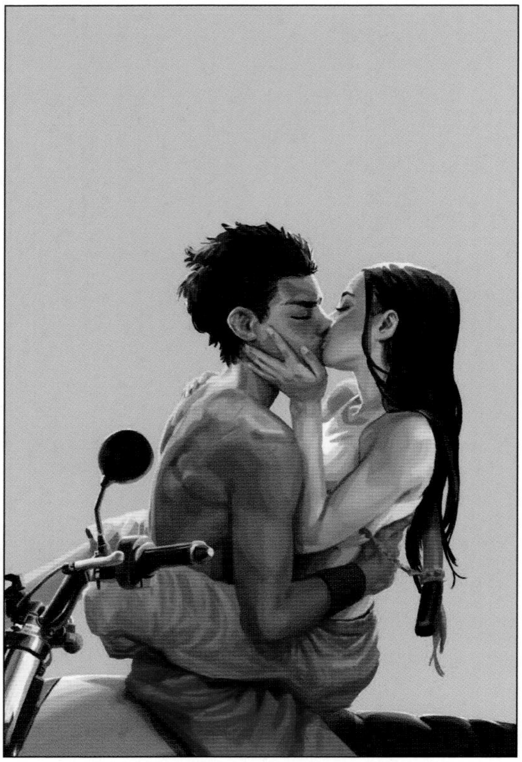

ISSUE 7 VARIANT
BY DANIEL CLARKE

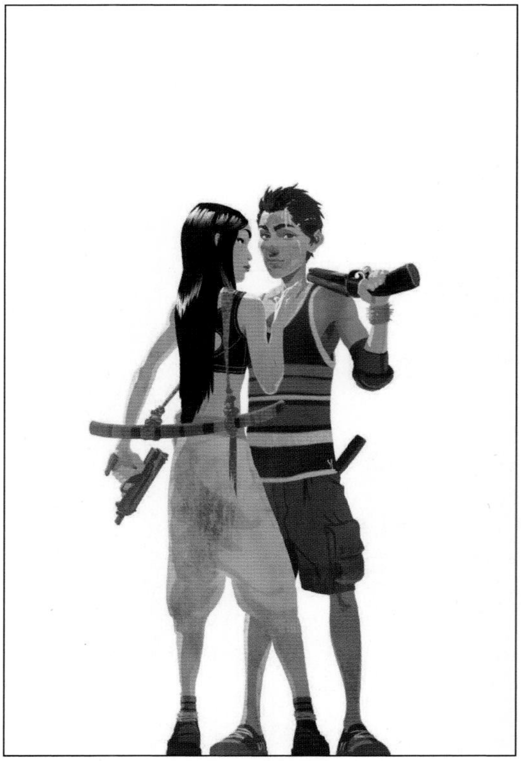

ISSUE 7 ZACK AND YUKI VARIANT
BY THOMAS VON KUMMANT

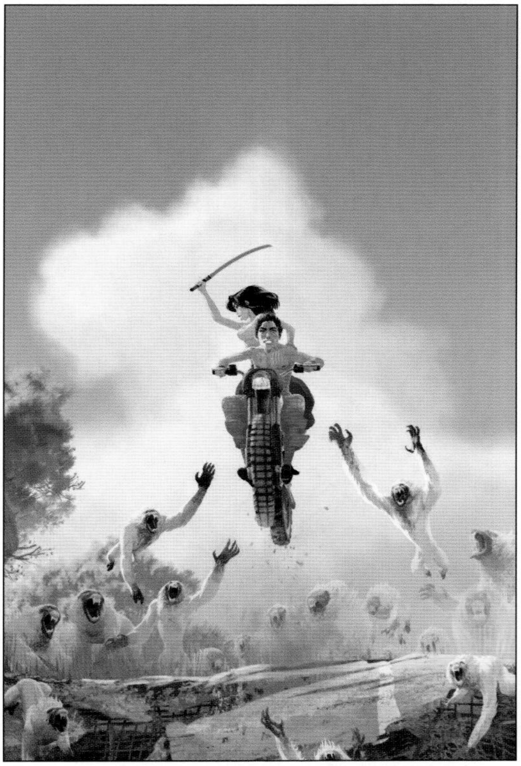

ISSUE 7 ESCAPING THE WHITE PLAGUE VARIANT
BY THOMAS VON KUMMANT

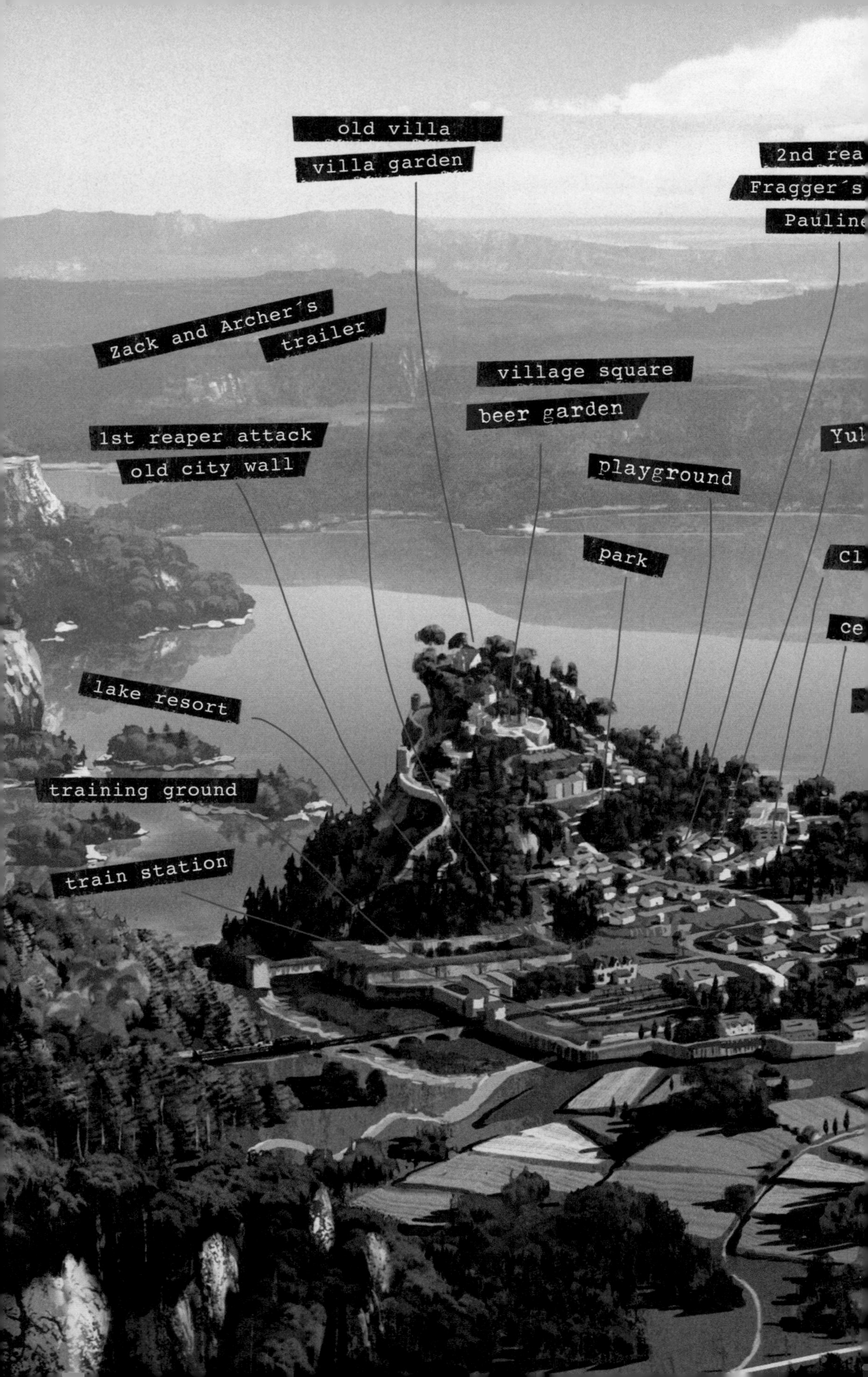
old villa
villa garden
2nd rea
Fragger´s
Pauline
Zack and Archer´s
trailer
village square
beer garden
1st reaper attack
old city wall
playground
Yul
park
Cl
ce
lake resort
training ground
train station